NOB
CRIMES

SELECTED AND INTRODUCED BY MARIE SMITH

Carroll & Graf Publishers, Inc.
New York

First published in Great Britain by Xanadu Publications Limited 1992. First published in the United States of America by Carroll & Graf Publishers, Inc. 1992, by arrangement with Xanadu Publications Limited.

Carroll & Graf Publishers Inc.,
260 Fifth Avenue,
New York, NY 10001.

Library of Congress Cataloging-in-Publication Data is available.

ISBN 1-88184-914-6

Manufactured in Great Britain.

Contents

Introduction

It's a wonder that no-one has thought of using the Nobel Prize as the theme for a murder mystery, for it would seem to furnish all the right elements. To begin with, it is a prize worth having: not only is it the most prestigious of all awards, but it gains the recipient quite a large sum of money—always a good motive. Secondly, it can be awarded only to *living* people, so that if one's rival on the shortlist were suddenly to die of a rare or unidentifiable disease, let us say, which should not be too difficult to arrange with top biochemists in the running ... well, the possibilities are endless. Finally, the Nobel Committee has in the past (I'm sure it's different now) often seemed to be a hotbed of personal and political intrigue, with must infighting and bitterness, and the prizes sometimes being awarded to wildly unlikely figures: people that no-one has ever heard of, even *after* they won the prize. Giosuè Caducci, anybody?

Nobel Crimes isn't that mystery—I offer the idea freely to anyone who might care to take it up—but a selection of short stories by some of the writers that have won the Nobel Prize for Literature; it is the first of a projected series of such collections each with a different theme, and this one concentrates on stories of crime, mystery and detection—for no better reasons that than I thought it might make an interesting and unusual book, offering mystery devotees something outside the usual range of anthology-fodder and more mainstream readers a diversion from *their* customary fare. It would also, I thought, be instructive to discover how such distinguished writers tackle the subject of crime, mystery and murder. These are, after all, serious matters.

It proved to be an interesting task, and the first job was obviously to check through the list of prize-winners. As I suggested earlier, there are some surprising names on it. I dutifully researched them all, usually to find that the more obscure figures on the whole deserve their obscurity (I except from this sweeping generalization the various poets and playrights among the prize-winners who, apart from T.S. Eliot among the poets and George Bernard Shaw among the playrights, seemingly had nothing to offer a collection like this one so remained on the whole unresearched), and it was vexing to see so many superb writers *nearly* winning the Nobel prize but being pipped at the post, often for the most bizarre reasons. The very first prize should by rights have gone to Tolstoi, for instance, and the author of *Crime and Punishment* would surely have found a place in these pages, but one of the eighteen judges raised objections to some of his beliefs and the prize went not to Tolstoi, nor to Zola (another nominee for that first award), but to Sully-Prudhomme for his *Stanzas and Poems.* Quite.

Other non-winners include Thomas Hardy, Joesph Conrad, August Strindberg (drank too much, and believed in black magic), Marcel Proust (beaten by Carl F.G. Spitteler), James Joyce ("James Joyce? Who is he?" asked Dr. Sven Hedin, one of the Swedish judges), Maxim Gorki, Sigmund Freud, H.G. Wells and W. Somerset Maugham (both ousted in 1944 by Johannes V. Jensen), Gunter Grass, Jorgoi Luis Borges... The list goes on and on, and one begins to wonder just why the Nobel Prize remains *the* prize when the judges have so often got it so spectacularly wrong. Nonetheless, the Nobel retains its mysterious *cachet*, and having decided on my plan for the book it was pointless to regret what might have been and to speculate on the stories that could have been included had things been otherwise. In any case, it is fun trying to solve puzzles, and if they have no limitations they are not very good puzzles at all.

So in putting together the pieces of this particular puzzle it was a joy to re-read—or in some cases to discover for the fist time—the stories of those excellent writers who did, sometimes against all the odds, win the Nobel Prize for Literature, and a fine bunch they are. Some of the stories pretty well chose themselves. 'The Gentleman from San Francisco' is such a classic that it had to be included, even though purists might wonder where the crime element is (OK, let's call it a suspense story), and the same considerations apply to Hemingway's 'The Killers', William Faulkner's 'Smoke', (Borges' favourite, though others by Faulkner are almost as good), and, in a different vein, T.S. Eliot's *McCavity*. Other stories may be ranked as discoveries—they were new to me, anyway—and among the ones that particularly please me are Heinrich Boll's 'In the Darkness', one of the most chilling stories I have ever read, the Marquez tale (I should have known his work better, but shamingly didn't), and the one by the most recent winner of the Nobel Prize before this book goes to press, Nadine Gordimer.

The stories I finally selected could scarcely be more different from one another in style, treatment, attitude and any other aspect one might care to name, and I believe that this makes for varied and stimulating reading. I rather dislike 'theme' anthologies, finding that if I have just read a story about a murderous dentist, let's say, the very last thing I want to do is to read eleven or twelve more stories about murderous dentists. To build a collection around the idea of the Nobel Prize might seem curious, but it its really no more than an excuse to assemble a group of very good stories indeed. I hope that you agree, and that Alfred Nobel—who, let us not forget, built his fortune on the invention of dynamite—would have approved.

—MARIE SMITH

Sources and Acknowledgements

'In the Darkness' by Heinrich Böll, translated by Leila Vennewitz, from *The Stories of Heinrich Böll* (London: Secker and Warburg Ltd, 1986), copyright © by Leila Vennewitz and the Estate of Heinrich Böll, reprinted by permission of the publishers.

'Ransom' by Pearl Buck copyright © 1938 by Hearst Magazines, Inc., renewed 1965 by P.S.S. Reprinted by permission of Harold Ober Associates, Inc.

'The Gentleman from San Francisco' by Ivan Bunin, translated by David Richards, from *The Gentleman from San Franscisco and Other Stories* (Angel Books), translation copyright © by David Richards, reprinted by permission of the publishers.

'The Guest' by Albert Camus, translated by Justin O'Brien, from *The Collected Fiction of Albert Camus* (London: Hamish Hamilton, 1962), copyright © 1957, 1958 by Alfred A. Knopf, Inc., reprinted by permission of the publishers.

'McCavity the Mystery Cat' by T.S. Eliot, from *Old Possum's Book of Practical Cats* (London: Faber, 1956), copyright © 1956 by the Estate of T.S. Eliot, reprinted by permission of the publishers.

'Smoke' by William Faulkner, from *Knight's Gambit*, copyright © 1932, renewed 1960 by the Estate of William Faulkner, reprinted by permission of Random House, Inc.

'The Moment the Gun Went Off' by Nadine Gordime, from *Jump and Other Stories* (London: Bloomsbury, 1991), copyright © 1991 by Felix Licensing BV, reprinted by permission of the publishers.

'The Killers' by Ernest Hemingway, from *Men Without Women* (New York: Scribners, 1927), copyright © 1927 by the Estate of Ernest Hemingway, reprinted by permission of the author's agents.

'The Post-Mortem Murder' by Sinclair Lewis, copyright © 1920 by Sinclair Lewis, copyright renewed, reprinted by permission of Curtis Brown Ltd.

'The Woman Who Came At Six O'Clock' by Gabriel Garcia Marquez, from *Innocent Erendira* (London: Cape, 1979), English translation copyright © 1978 by Harper and Row Publishers, Inc., New York, reprinted by permission of the publishers.

'All Passion Spent' by Luigi Pirandello, translated by Frederick May, from *Pirandello Short Stories* (OUP, 1975), translation copyright © 1965 by Oxford University Press, reprinted by permission of the publishers.

'The Corsican Ordeal of Miss X' by Bertrand Russell, from *Satan in the Suburbs and Other Stories* (London: Bodley Head, 1953), copyright © 1953 by the Estate of Bertrand Russell, reprinted by permission of the publishers.

'The Miraculous Revenge' by George Bernard Shaw, copyright © 1934 by the Estate of George Bernard Shaw, reprinted by permission of The Society of Authors on behalf of GBS's Estate.

'Under the Knife' by Isaac Bashevis Singer, from *Short Friday* (New York: Farrar, Straus & Giroux, 1964), copyright © 1962 by Isaac Bashevis Singer, reprinted by permission of the publishers.

'The Murder' by John Steinbeck, from *The Long Valley* (New York: Viking), copyright © 1934, renewed 1962 by the Estate of John Steinbeck, reprinted by permission of Viking Penguin, Inc.

Whilst every effort has been made to trace authors and copyright holders in a few cases this has proved impossible. The publishers would like to hear from any such parties so that any errors or omissions may be rectified.

HEINRICH BÖLL

In the Darkness

'Light the candle,' said a voice.

There was no sound, only that exasperating, aimless rustle of someone trying to get to sleep.

'Light the candle, I say,' came the voice again, on a sharper note this time.

The sounds at last became distinguishable as someone moving, throwing aside the blanket, and sitting up; this was apparent from the breathing, which now came from above. The straw rustled too.

'Well?' said the voice.

'The lieutenant said we weren't to light the candle except on orders, in an emergency,' said a younger, diffident voice.

'Light the candle, I say, you little pipsqueak,' the older voice shouted back.

He sat up now too, their heads were on the same level in the dark, their breathing was parallel.

The one who had first spoken irritably followed the movements of the other, who had tucked the candle away somewhere in his pack. His breathing relaxed when he eventually heard the sound of the matchbox.

The match flared up and there was light: a sparse yellow light.

Their eyes met. Invariably, as soon as there was enough light, their eyes met. Yet they knew one another so well, much too well. They almost hated each other, so familar was each to each; they knew one another's very smell, the smell of every pore, so to speak, but still their eyes met, those of the older man and the younger. The younger one was pale and slight with a nondescript face, and the older one was pale and slight and unshaven with a nondescript face.

'Now, listen,' said the older man, calmer now, 'when are you ever going to learn that you don't do everything the lieutenants tell you?'

'He'll . . .' the younger one tried to begin.

'He won't do a thing,' said the older one, in a sharper tone again and lighting a cigarette from the candle. 'He'll keep his trap shut, and if he doesn't, and I don't happen to be around, then tell him to wait till I get back, it was me who lit the candle, understand? Do you understand?'

'Yessir.'

'To hell with that Yessir crap, just Yes when your're talking to me. And undo your belt,' he was shouting again now, 'take that damm crappy belt off when you go to sleep.'

The younger man looked at him nervously and took off his belt, placing it beside him in the straw.

'Roll your coat up into a pillow. That's right. OK . . . and now go to sleep, I'll wake you when it's time for you to die. . . .'

The younger man rolled onto his side and tried to sleep. All that was visible was the young brown hair, matted and untidy, a very thin neck, and the empty shoulders of his uniform tunic. The candle flickered gently, letting its meager light swing back and forth in the dark dugout like a great yellow butterfly uncertain where to settle.

The older man stayed as he was, knees drawn up, puffing out cigarette smoke at the ground in front of him. The ground was dark brown, here and there white blade marks showed where the spade had cut through a root or, a little closer to the surface, a tuber. The roof consisted of a few planks with a groundsheet thrown over them, and in the spaces between the planks, the groundsheet sagged a little because the earth lying on top of it was heavy, heavy and wet. Outside, it was raining. The soft swish of steadily falling water sounded indescribably persistent, and the older man, still staring fixedly at the ground, now noticed a thin trickle of water oozing into the dugout under the roof. The tiny stream backed up slightly on encountering some loose earth, then flowed on past the obstacle until it reached the next one, which was the man's feet, and the ever-growing tide flowed all around the man's feet until his black boots lay in the water just like a peninsula. The man spat his cigarette butt into the puddle and lit another from the candle. In doing so he took the candle down from the edge of the dugout and placed it beside him on an ammunition case. The half where the younger man was lying was almost in darkness, reached now by the swaying light in brief spasms only, and these gradually subsided.

'Go to sleep, damm you,' said the older man. 'D'you hear? Go to sleep!'

'Yessir...yes,' came the faint voice, obviously wider awake than before, when it had been dark.

'Hold on,' said the older man, less harshly again. 'A couple more cigarettes and then I'll put it out, and least we'll drown in the dark.'

He went on smoking, sometimes turning his head to the left, where the boy was lying, but he spat the second butt into the steadily growing puddle, lit the third, and still he could tell from the breathing beside him that the kid couldn't sleep.

He then took the spade, thrust it into the soft earth, and made a little mud wall behind the blanket forming the entrance. Behind this wall he heaped up a second layer of earth. With a spadeful of earth he covered the puddle at his feet. Outside, there was no sound save the gentle swish of the rain; little by little, the earth lying on top of the groundsheet had evidently become saturated, for water was now beginning to drip from above too.

'Oh shit,' muttered the older man. 'Are you asleep?'

'No.'

The man spat the third cigarette butt over the mud wall and blew out the candle. He pulled up his blanket again, worked his feet into a comfortable position, and lay back with a sigh. It was quite silent and quite dark, and again the only sound was that aimless rustle of someone trying to get to sleep, and the swish of the rain, very gentle.

'Willi's been wounded,' the boy's voice said suddenly,

after a few minutes' silence. The voice was more awake than ever, in fact not even sleepy.

'What d'you mean?' asked the man in reply.

'Just that – wounded,' came the younger voice, with something like triumph in it, pleased that it knew some important piece of news which the older voice obviously knew nothing about. 'Wounded while he was shitting.'

'You're nuts,' said the man; then he gave another sigh and went on, 'That's what I call a real break; I never heard of such luck. One day you come back from leave and the next day you get wounded while you're shitting. Is it serious?'

'No,' said the boy with a laugh, 'though actually it's not minor either. A bullet fracture, but in the arm.'

'A bullet fracture in the arm! You come back from leave and while you're shitting you get wounded, a bullet fracture in the arm! What a break. . . . How did it happen?'

'When they went for water last evening,' came the younger voice, quite animated now. 'When they went for water, they were going down the hill at the back, carrying their water cans, and Willi told Sergeant Schubert, "I've got to shit, Sergeant!" "Nothing doing," said the sergeant. But Willi couldn't hold on any longer so he just ran off, pulled down his pants, and bang! A grenade. And they actually had to pull up his pants for him. His left arm was wounded, and his right arm was holding it, so he ran off like that to get it bandaged, with his pants around his ankles. They all laughed, everyone laughed, even Sergeant Schubert laughed.' He added the last few words almost apologetically, as if to excuse his own laughter, because he was laughing now. . . .

But the older man wasn't laughing.

'Light!' he said with an oath. 'Here, give me the matches, let's have some light!' He struck a match, cursing as it flared up. 'At least I want some light, even if I don't get wounded. At least let's have some light, the least they can do is give us enough candles if they want to play war. Light! Light!' He was shouting again as he lit another cigarette.

The younger voice had sat up again and was poking around with a spoon in a greasy can held on his knees.

And there they sat, crouching side by side, without a word,

in the yellow light.

The man smoked aggressively, and the boy was already looking somewhat greasy: his childish face smeared, bread crumbs sticking to his matted hair around most of his hairline.

The boy then proceeded to scrape out the grease can with a piece of bread.

All of a sudden there was silence: the rain had stopped. Neither of them moved, they looked at each other, the man with the cigarette in his hand, the boy holding the bread in his trembling fingers. It was uncannily quiet, they took a few breaths, and then heard rain still dripping somewhere from the groundsheet.

'Hell,' said the older man. 'D'you suppose the sentry's still there? I can't hear a thing.'

The boy put the bread into his mouth and threw the can into the straw beside him.

'I don't know,' said the boy. 'They're going to let us know when it's our turn to relieve.'

The older man got up quickly. He blew out the light, jammed on his steel helmet, and thrust aside the blanket. What came through the opening was not light. Just cool damp darkness. The man pinched out his cigarette and stuck his head outside.

'Hell,' he muttered outside, 'not a thing. Hey!' he called softly. Then his dark head reappeared inside, and he asked, 'Where's the next dugout?'

The boy groped his way to his feet and stood next to the other man in the opening.

'Quiet!' said the man suddenly, in a sharp, low tone. 'Something's crawling around out there.'

They peered ahead. It was true: in the silent darkness there was a sound of someone crawling, and all of a sudden an unearthly snapping sound that made them both jump. It sounded as if someone had flung a live cat against the wall: the sound of breaking bones.

'Hell,' muttered the older man, 'there's something funny going on. Where's the sentry?'

'Over there,' said the boy, groping in the dark for the other man's hand and lifting it toward the right. 'Over there,' he repeated. 'That's where the dugout is too.'

'Wait here,' said the older man, 'and better get your rifle, just in case.'

Once again they heard that sickening snapping sound, then silence, and someone crawling.

The older man crept forward through the mud, occasionally halting and quietly listening, until after a few yards he finally heard a muffled voice; then he saw a faint gleam of light from the ground, felt around till he found the entrance, and called, 'Hey, chum!'

The voice stopped, the light went out, a blanket was pushed aside, and a man's dark head came up out of the ground.

'What's up?'

'Where's the sentry?'

'Over there – right here.'

'Where?'

'Hey there, Neuer! . . . Hey there!'

No answer: the crawling sound had stopped, all sound had stopped, there was only darkness out there, silent darkness. 'God damn it, that's queer,' said the voice of the man who had come up out of the ground. 'Hey there! . . . That's funny, he was standing right here by the dugout, only a few feet away.' He pulled himself up over the edge and stood beside the man who had called him.

'There was someone crawling around out there,' said the man who had come across from the other dugout. 'I know there was. The bastard's quiet now.'

'Better have a look,' said the man who had come up out of the ground. 'Shall we take a look?'

'Hm, there certainly ought to be a sentry here.'

'You fellows are next.'

'I know, but . . .'

'Ssh!'

Once again they could hear someone crawling out there, perhaps twenty feet away.

'God damn it,' said the man who had come up out of the ground, 'you're right.'

'Maybe someone still alive from last night, trying to crawl

away.'

'Or new ones.'

'But what about the sentry, for God's sake?'

'Shall we go?'

'OK.'

Both men instantly dropped to the ground and started to move forward, crawling through the mud. From down there, from a worm's-eye view, everything looked different. Every minutest elevation in the soil became a mountain range behind which, far off, something strange was visible: a slightly lighter darkness, the sky. Pistol in hand, they crawled on, yard by yard through the mud.

'God damn it,' whispered the man who had come up out of the ground, 'a Russki from last night.'

His companion also soon bumped into a corpse, a mute, leaden bundle. Suddenly they were silent, holding their breath: there was that cracking sound again, quite close, as if someone had been given a terrific wallop on the jaw. Then they heard someone panting.

'Hey,' called the man who had come up out of the ground, 'who's there?'

The call silenced all sound, the very air seemed to hold its breath, until a quavering voice spoke, 'It's me. . . .'

'God damn it, what the hell are you doing out there, you old asshole, driving us all nuts?' shouted the man who had come up out of the ground.

'I'm looking for something,' came the voice again.

The two men had got to their feet and now walked over to the spot where the voice was coming from the ground.

'I'm looking for a pair of shoes,' said the voice, but now they were standing next to him. Their eyes had become accustomed to the dark, and they could see corpses lying all around, ten or a dozen, lying there like logs, black and motionless, and the sentry was squatting beside one of these logs, fumbling around its feet.

'Your job's to stick to your post,' said the man who had come up out of the ground.

The other man, the one who had summoned him out of the ground, dropped like a stone and bent over the dead man's face. The man who had been squatting suddenly covered his face with his hands and began whimpering like a cowed animal.

'Oh no,' said the man who had summoned the other out of the ground, adding in an undertone, 'I guess you need teeth too, eh? Gold teeth, eh?'

'What's that?' asked the man who had come up out of the ground, while at his feet the cringing figure whimpered louder than ever.

'Oh no,' said the first man again, and the weight of the world seemed to be lying on his breast.

'Teeth?' asked the man who had come up out of the ground, whereupon he threw himself down beside the cringing figure and ripped a cloth bag from his hand.

'Oh no!' the cringing figure cried too, and every extremity of human terror was expressed in this cry.

The man who had summoned the other out of the ground turned away, for the man who had come up out of the ground had placed his pistol against the cringing figure's head, and he pressed the trigger.

'Teeth,' he muttered, as the sound of the shot died away. 'Gold teeth.'

They walked slowly back, stepping very carefully as long as they were in the area where the dead lay.

'You fellows are on now,' said the man who had come up out of the ground, before vanishing into the ground again.

'Right,' was all the other man said, and he too crawled slowly back through the mud before vanishing into the ground again.

He could tell at once that the boy was still awake; there was that aimless rustle of someone trying to get to sleep.

'Light the candle,' he said quietly.

The yellow flame leaped up again, feebly illuminating the little hole.

'What happened?' asked the boy in alarm, catching sight of the older man's face.

'The sentry's gone; you'll have to replace him.'

'Yes,' said the youngster. 'Give me the watch, will you, so I can wake the others.'

'Here.'

The older man squatted down on his straw and lit a cigarette, watching thoughtfully as the boy buckled on his belt, pulled on his coat, defused a hand grenade, and then wearily checked his machine pistol for ammunition.

'Right,' said the boy finally. 'So long, now.'

'So long,' said the man, and he blew out the candle and lay in total darkness all alone in the ground. . . .

PEARL BUCK

Ransom

The Beethoven Symphony stopped abruptly. A clear metallic voice broke across the melody of the third movement.

'Press radio news. The body of Jimmie Lane, kidnapped son of Mr. Headley Lane, has been found on the bank of the Hudson River near his home this afternoon. This ends the search of – '

'Kent, turn it off, please!' Allin exclaimed.

Kent Crothers hesitated a second. Then he turned off the radio. In the silence Allin sat biting her lower lip. 'That poor mother! All these days – not giving up hope.'

'I suppose it is better to know something definite,' he said quietly, 'even though it is the worst.'

Perhaps this would be a good time to talk with her, to warn her that she was letting this kidnapping business grow into an obsession. After all, children did grow up in the United States, even in well-to-do families like theirs. The trouble was that they were not quite rich enough and still too rich – not rich enough to hire guards for their children, but rich enough, because his father owned the paper mill, to make them known in the neighbourhood, at least.

The thing was to take it for granted that they did not belong to the millionaire class and therefore were not prize for kidnappers. They should do this for Bruce's sake. He would be starting school next autumn. Bruce would have to walk back and forth on the streets like millions of other American children. Kent wouldn't have his son driven three blocks, even by Peter the outdoor man; it would do him more harm than . . . after all, it was a democracy they lived in, and Bruce had to grow up with the crowd.

'I'll go and see that the children are covered,' Allin said. 'Betsy throws off the covers whenever she can.'

Kent knew that she simply wanted to make sure they were there. But he rose with her, lighting his pipe, thinking how to begin. They walked up the stairs together, their fingers interlaced. Softly she opened the nursery door. It was ridiculous how even he was being affected by her fears. Whenever the door opened his heart stood cold for a second, until he saw the two beds, each with a little head on the pillow.

They were there now, of course. He stood beside Bruce's bed and looked down at his son. Handsome little devil. He was sleeping so soundly that when his mother leaned over him he did not move. His black hair was a tousle; his red lips pouted. He was dark, but he had Allin's blue eyes.

They did not speak. Allin drew the cover gently over his outflung arm, and they stood a moment longer, hand in hand, gazing at the child. Then Allin looked up at Kent and smiled, and he kissed her. He put his arm about her shoulder, and they went to Betsy's bed.

Here was his secret obsession. He could say firmly that Bruce must take his chances with the other children, because a boy had to learn to be brave. But this baby – such a tiny feminine creature, his little daughter. She had Allin's auburn colouring, but by some miracle she had his dark eyes, so that when he looked into them he seemed to be looking into himself.

She was breathing now, a little unevenly, through her tiny nose.

'How's her cold?' he whispered.

'It doesn't seem worse,' Allin whispered back. 'I put stuff on her chest.'

He was always angry when anything happened to this baby. He didn't trust her nurse, Mollie too much. She was good-hearted, maybe, but easy-going.

The baby stirred and opened her eyes. She blinked, smiled,

and put up her arms to him.

'Don't pick her up darling,' Allin counselled. 'She'll only want it every time.'

So he did not take her. Instead, he put her arms down, one and then the other, playfully, under the cover.

'Go to sleep-bye, honey,' he said. And she lay, sleepily smiling. She was a good little thing.

'Come – let's put out the light,' Allin whispered. They tiptoed out and went back to the living room.

Kent sat down, puffed on his pipe, his mind full of what he wanted to say to Allin. It was essential to their life to believe that nothing could happen to their children.

'Kidnapping's like lightning,' he began abruptly. 'It happens, of course – once in a million. What you have to remember is all the rest of the children who are perfectly safe.'

She had sat down on the ottoman before the fire, but she turned to him when he said this. 'What would you do honestly, Kent if some night when we went upstairs – ?'

'Nonsense!' he broke in. 'That's what I've been trying to tell you. It's so unlikely as to be – it's these damned newspapers! When a thing happens in one part of the country, every little hamlet hears of it.'

'Jane Eliot told me there are three times as many kidnappings as ever get into the newspapers,' Allin said.

'Janes'a newspaperwoman,' Kent said. 'You mustn't let her sense of drama –'

'Still, she's been on a lot of kidnapping cases,' Allin replied. 'She was telling me about the Wyeth case – '

This was the time to speak, now when all Allin's secret anxiety was quivering in her voice. Kent took her hand and fondled it as he spoke. He must remember how deeply she felt everything, and this thing had haunted her before Bruce was born. He had not even thought of it until one night in the darkness she had asked him the same question, 'What would we do, Kent, if – ' Only then he had not known what she meant.

'If what?' he had asked.

'If our baby were ever kidnapped.'

He had answered what he had felt then and believed now to be true. 'Why worry about what will never happen?' he had said. Nevertheless, he had followed all the cases since Bruce was born.

He kissed her palm now. 'I can't bear having you afraid,' he said. 'It isn't necessary, you know, darling. We can't live under the shadow of this thing. We have to come to some rational position on it.

'That's what I want Kent. I'd be glad not to be afraid – if I knew how.'

'After all,' he went on, 'most people bring up their families without thinking about it.'

'Most mothers think of it,' she said. 'Most of the women I know have said something about it to me – some time or other – enough to make me know they think about it all the time.'

'You'd be better off not talking about it,' he said.

But she said, 'We keep wondering what we would do, Kent.'

'That's just it!' he exclaimed. 'That's why I think if we decided now what we would do – always bearing in mind that it's only the remotest possibility – '

'What *would* we do, Kent?' she asked.

He answered half playfully, 'Promise to remember it's as remote as – an airplane attack on our home?'

She nodded.

I've always thought that if one of the children were kidnapped I'd simply turn the whole thing over to the police at once.'

'What police?' she asked instantly. 'Gossipy old Mike O'Brien, who'd tell the newspapers the first thing? It's fatal to let it get into the papers, Jane says.'

'Well, the Federal police, then – the G-men.'

'How does one get in touch with them?'

He had to confess he did not know. 'I'll find out,' he promised. 'Anyway, it's the principle, darling, that we want to determine. Once we know what we'll do, we can put it out of our minds. No ransom, Allin – that I feel sure about. As long as we keep on paying ransoms, we're going to have kidnappings. Somebody has to be strong enough to take the stand. Then maybe other people will see what they ought to do.'

But she did not look convinced. When she spoke, her voice was low and full of dread. 'The thing is, Kent, if we decided not to pay ransom, we just couldn't stick to it – not really, I mean. Suppose it were Bruce – suppose he had a cold and it was winter – and he was taken out of his warm bed in his pyjamas, we'd do anything. You know we would!' She rushed on. 'We wouldn't care about other children, Kent. We would only be thinking of our own little Bruce – and no one else. How to get him back again, at whatever cost.'

'Hush, darling,' he said. 'If you're going to be like this we can't talk about it, after all.'

'No, Kent, please. I do want to talk. I want to know what we ought to do. If only I could be not afraid!' she whispered.

'Come here by me,' he said. He drew her to the couch beside him. 'First of all, you know I love the children as much as you do, don't you?' She nodded, and he went on, 'Then, darling, I'd do anything I thought would be best for our children, wouldn't I?'

'You'd do the best you knew, Kent. The question is, do any of us know what to do?'

'I do know,' he said gravely, 'that until we make the giving and taking of ransoms unlawful we shall have kidnappers. And until somebody begins it, it will never be done. That's the law of democratic government. The people have to begin action before government takes a stand.'

'What if they said not to tell the police?' she asked.

Her concreteness confounded him. It was not as if it could happen!

'It all depends,' he retorted, 'on whether you want to give in to rascals or stand on your principle.'

'But if it were our own child?' she persisted. 'Be honest, Kent. Please don't retire into principles.'

'I am trying to be honest,' he said slowly. 'I think I would stick by principle and trust somehow to think of some way – ' He looked waveringly into her unbelieving eyes. . . .

'Try to remember exactly what happened!' he was shouting

at the silly nurse. 'Where did you leave her?'

Allin was quieter than he, but Allin's voice on the telephone half an hour ago had been like a scream: 'Kent, we can't find Betsy!'

He had been in the mill directors' meeting, but he'd risen instantly. 'Sorry,' he had said sharply. 'I have to leave at once.'

'Nothing serious, Kent?' His father's white eyebrows had lifted.

'I think not,' he'd answered. He had sense enough not to say what Allin had screamed. 'I'll let you know if it is.'

He had leaped into his car and driven home like a crazy man. He'd drawn up in a spray of gravel at his own gate. Allin was there, and Mollie, the silly nurse. Mollie was sobbing.

'We was at the gate, sir, watchin' for Brucie to come home from school, like we do every day, and I put 'er down – she's heavy to carry – while I went in to get a clean hankie to wipe her little hands. She'd stooped into a puddle from the rain this morning. When I came back, she wasn't there. I ran around the shrubs, sir, lookin' – and then I screamed for the madam.'

'Kent I've combed the place,' Allin whispered.

'The gate!' he gasped.

'It was shut, and the bar across,' Mollie wailed. 'I'd sense enough to see to that before I went in.'

'How long were you gone?' he shouted at her.

'I don't know, sir,' Mollie sobbed. 'It didn't seem a minute!'

He rushed into the yard. 'Betsy, Betsy!' he cried. 'Come to Daddy! Here's Daddy!' he stooped under the big lilac bushes. 'Have you looked in the garage?' he demanded of Allin.

'Peter's been through it twice,' she answered.

'I'll see for myself,' he said. 'Go into the house, Allin. She may have got inside, somehow.'

He tore into the garage. Peter crawled out from under the small car.

'She ain't hyah, suh,' he whispered. 'Ah done looked ev'yweah.'

But Kent looked again, Peter following him like a dog. In the back of his mind was a telephone number, National 7117.

He had found out about that number the year before, after he and Allin had talked that evening. Only he wouldn't call yet. Betsy was sure to be somewhere.

The gate clicked, and he rushed out. But it was Bruce – alone.

'Why, what's the matter with you, Daddy?' Bruce asked.

Kent swallowed – no use scaring Bruce. 'Bruce, did you – you didn't see Betsy on the way home, did you?'

'No, Daddy, I didn't see anybody except Mike to help me across the square 'cause there was a notomobile.'

'Wha'dat?' Peter was pointing at something. It was a bit of white paper, held down by a stone.

As well as he knew anything, Kent knew what it was. He had read that note a dozen times in the newspaper accounts. He stooped and picked it up. There it was – the scrawled handwriting.

We been waiting this chanse. The handwriting was there, illiterate, disguised. *Fifty grand is the price. Your dads got it if you aint. Youll hear where to put it. If you tell the police we kill the kid.*

'Daddy, what's – ' Bruce began.

'Bring him indoors,' he ordered Peter.

Where was Allin? He had to – he had promised her it would not happen! The telephone number was –

'Allin!' he shouted.

He heard her running down from the attic.

'Allin!' he gasped. She was there, white and piteous with terror – and so helpless. God, they were both so helpless! He had to have help; he had to know what to do. But had not he – he *had* decided long ago what he must do, because what did he know about crooks and kidnappers? People gave the ransom and lost their children too. He had to have advice he could trust.

'I'm going to call National 7117' he blurted at her.

'No, Kent – wait!' she cried.

'I've got to,' he insisted. Before she could move, he ran to the telephone and took up the receiver. 'I want National 7117!' he shouted.

Her face went white. He held out his hand with the crumpled note. She read it and snatched at the receiver.

'No, Kent – wait. We don't know. Wait and see what they say!'

But a calm voice was already speaking at the other end of the wire: 'This is National 7117.' And Kent was shouting hoarsely, 'I want to report a kidnapping. It's our baby girl. Kent Crothers, 134 Eastwood Avenue, Greenvale, New York.'

He listened while the voice was telling him to do nothing, to wait until tomorrow, and then at a certain village inn, 50 miles away, to meet a certain man who would wear a plain grey suit and have a blue handkerchief in his pocket.

And all the time Allin was whispering, 'They'll kill her – they'll kill her, Kent.'

'They won't know,' he whispered back. 'Nobody will know.' When he put the receiver down he cried at her angrily, 'They won't tell anybody – those fellows in Washington! Besides, I've got to have help, I tell you!'

She stood staring at him with horrified eyes. 'They'll kill her,' she repeated.

He wanted to get somewhere to weep, only men could not weep. But Allin was not weeping, either. Then suddenly they flung their arms about each other, and together broke into silent terrible tears.

He was not used to waiting, but he had to wait. And he had to help Allin wait. Men were supposed to be stronger.

At first it had been a comfort to have the directions to follow. First, everybody in the house – that was easy: simply the cook Sarah, the maid Rose, and Mollie and Peter. They of course were beyond blame, except Mollie. Perhaps Mollie was more than just a fool. They all had to be told they were to say absolutely nothing.

'Get everybody together in the dining room,' Kent had told Allin. He had gone into the dining room.

'Daddy!' He saw Bruce's terrified figure in the doorway. 'What's the matter? Where's Betsy?'

'We can't find her, son,' Kent said, trying to make his voice calm. 'Of course we will, but just now nobody must know she isn't here.'

'Shall I go out in the yard?' Bruce asked. 'Maybe I could

find her.'

'No,' Kent said sharply. 'I'd rather you went upstairs to your own room. I'll be up – in a minute.'

The servants were coming in, Allin behind them.

'I'll go with Bruce,' she said.

She was so still and so controlled, but he could tell by the quiver about her lips that she was only waiting for him.

'I'll be up in a very few minutes,' he promised her. He stood until she had gone, Bruce's hand in hers. Then he turned to the four waiting figures. Mollie was still crying. He could tell by their faces that they all knew about the note.

'I see you know what has happened,' he said. Strange how all these familiar faces looked sinister to him! Peter and Sarah had been in his mother's household. They had known him for years. And Rose was Sarah's niece. But they all looked hostile, or he imagined they did. 'And I want not one word said of this to anyone in the town,' he said harshly. 'Remember, Betsy's life depends on no one outside knowing.'

He paused, setting his jaws. He would not have believed he could cry as easily as a woman, but he could.

He cleared his throat. 'Her life depends on how we behave now – in the next few hours.' Mollie's sobbing burst out into wails. He rose. 'That's all,' he said. 'We must simply wait.'

The telephone rang, and he hurried to it. There was no way of knowing how the next message would come. But it was his father's peremptory voice: 'Anything wrong over there, Kent?'

He knew now it would never do for his father to know what had happened. His father could keep nothing to himself.

'Everything is all right, Dad,' he answered. 'Allin's not feeling very well, that's all.'

'Have you had the doctor?' his father shouted.

'We will if it is necessary, Dad,' he answered and put up the receiver abruptly.

He thought of Bruce and went to find him. He was eating his supper in the nursery, and Allin was with him. She had told Mollie to stay downstairs. She could not bear to see the girl any more than he could.

But the nursery was unbearable, too. This was the time when Betsy, fresh from her bath . . .

'I'm – I'll be downstairs in the library,' he told Allin hurriedly, and she nodded.

In the library the silence was torture. They could only wait.

And all the time who knew what was happening to the child? Tomorrow, the man had said an hour ago. Wait, he had said. But what about tonight? In what sort of place would the child be sleeping?

Kent leaped to his feet. Something had to be done. He would have a look around the yard. There might be another letter.

He went out into the early autumn twilight. He had to hold himself together to keep from breaking into foolish shouts and curses. It was the agony of not being able to do anything. Then he controlled himself. The thing was to go on following a rational plan. He had come out to see if he could find anything.

He searched every inch of the yard. There was no message of any sort.

Then in the gathering darkness he saw a man at the gate. Mist' Crothers!' It was Peter's voice. 'Fo' God, Mist' Crothers, Ah don' know why they should pick on mah ole 'ooman. When Ah come home fo' suppah, she give it to me – she cain't read, so she don' know what wuz in it.'

Kent snatched a paper from Peter's shaking hand and ran to the house. In the lighted hall he read:

Get the dough ready all banknotes dont mark any or well get the other kid to. Dont try double-crossing us. You cant get away with nothing. Put it in a box by the dead oak at the mill creek. You know where. At twelve o'clock tomorrow night.

He knew where, indeed. He had fished there from the time he was a little boy. The lightning had struck that oak tree one summer when he had been only a hundred yards away, standing in the doorway of the mill during a thunderstorm. How did they know he knew?

He turned on Peter. 'Who brought this?' he demanded.

'Ah don' know, suh,' Peter stammered. 'She couldn't tell me nothin' cep'n' it wuz a white man. He chuck it at 'er and say, "Give it to yo' ole man." So she give it to me, and Ah come a-runnin'.'

Kent stared at Peter, trying to ferret into his brain. Was Peter being used by someone – bribed, perhaps, to take a part? Did he know anything?

'If I thought you knew anything about Betsy, I'd kill you myself,' he said.

'Fo' God, Ah don', Mist' Crothers – you know me, suh! Ah done gyardened for yo' since yo' and Miss Allin got mah'ied. 'Sides, whut Ah want in such devilment? Ah got all Ah want – mah house and a sal'ry. Ah don' want nuthin'.'

It was all true, of course. The thing was, you suspected everybody.

'You tell Flossie to tell no one,' he commanded Peter.

'Ah done tole 'er,' Peter replied fervently. 'Ah tole 'er Ah'd split 'er open if she told anybody 'bout dat white man.'

'Get along, then,' said Kent. 'And remember what I told you.'

'Yassuh,' Peter replied.

'Of course we'll pay the ransom!' Allin was insisting.

They were in their own room, the door open into the narrow passage, and beyond that the door into the nursery was open, too. They sat where, in the shadowy light of a night lamp, they could see Bruce's dark head on the pillow. Impossible, of course, to sleep. Sarah had sent up some cold chicken and they had eaten it in here, and later Kent had made Allin take a hot bath and get into a warm robe and lie down on the chaise lounge. He did not undress. Someone might call.

'I'll have to see what the man says tomorrow.' he answered.

Terrifying to think how he was pinning everything on that fellow tomorrow – a man whose name, even, he did not know. All he knew was he'd wear a plain grey suit and he'd have a blue handkerchief in his pocket. That was all he had to save Betsy's life. No, that wasn't true. Behind that one man were hundreds of others, alert, strong, and ready to help.

'We've got to pay it,' Allin was saying hysterically. 'What's money now?'

'Allin!' he cried. 'You don't think I'm trying to save the money, in God's name!'

'We have about twenty thousand, haven't we, in the bank?' she said hurriedly. 'Your father would have the rest, though, and we could give him the securities. It isn't as if we didn't have it.'

'Allin, you're being absurd! The thing is to know how to – '

But she flew at him fiercely. 'The thing is to save Betsy – that's all; there's nothing else – absolutely nothing. I don't care if it takes everything your father has.

'Allin, be quiet!' he shouted at her. 'Do you mean my father would begrudge anything – ?'

'You're afraid of him, Kent,' she retorted. 'Well, I'm not! If you don't go to him I will.'

They were quarrelling now, like two insane people. They were both stretched beyond normal reason.

Suddenly Allin was sobbing. 'I can't forget what you said that night,' she cried. 'All that standing on principle! Oh, Kent, she's with strangers, horrible people, crying her little heart out; perhaps they're even – hurting her, trying to make her keep quiet. Oh, Kent, Kent!'

He took her in his arms. They must not draw apart now. He must think of her.

'I'll do anything, darling,' he said. 'The first thing in the morning I'll get hold of Dad and have the money ready.'

'If they could only *know* it,' she said.

'I could put something in the paper, perhaps,' he said. 'I believe I could word something that no one else would understand.'

'Let's try Kent!'

He took a pencil and envelope from his pocket and wrote.

'How's this?' he asked. 'Fifty agreed by dead oak at twelve.'

'I can't see how it could do any harm,' she said eagerly. 'And if they see it, they'll understand we're willing to do anything.'

'I'll go around to the newspaper office and pay for this in

cash,' he said. 'Then I won't have to give names.'

'Yes, yes!' she urged him. 'It's something more than just sitting here!'

He drove through the darkness the two miles to the small town and parked in front of the ramshackle newspaper office. A red-eyed night clerk took his advertisement and read it off.

'This is a funny one,' he said. 'We get some, now and then. That'll be a dollar, Mr. – '

Kent did not answer. He put a dollar bill on the desk.

'I don't know what I've done, even so,' he groaned to himself.

He drove back quietly through the intense darkness. The storm had not yet come, and the air was strangely silent. He kept his motor at its most noiseless, expecting somehow to hear through the sleeping stillness Betsy's voice, crying.

They scarcely slept, and yet when they looked at each other the next morning the miracle was that they had slept at all. But he had made Allin go to bed at last, and then, still dressed, he had lain down on his own bed near her. It was Bruce who waked them. He stood hesitatingly between their beds. They heard his voice.

'Betsy hasn't come back yet, Mommie.'

The name waked them. And they looked at each other.

'How could we!' Allin whispered.

'It may be a long pull, dearest,' he said trying to be steady. He got up, feeling exhausted.

'Will she come back today?' Bruce asked.

'I think so, son.'

At least it was Saturday, and Bruce need not go to school today.

'I'm going to get her tonight,' Kent said after a moment.

Instantly he felt better. They must not give up hope – not by a great deal. There was too much to do: his father to see and the money to get. Secretly, he still reserved his own judgment about the ransom. If the man in grey was against it, he would tell Allin nothing – he simply would not give it. The responsibility would be his.

'You and Mommie will have to get Betsy's things ready for her tonight,' he said cheerfully. He would take a bath and get into a fresh suit. He had to have all his wits about him today, every moment – listen to everybody, and use his own judgment finally. In an emergency, one person had to act.

He paused at the sight of himself in the mirror. Would he be able to keep it from Allin if he made a mistake? Suppose they never got Betsy back. Suppose she just – disappeared. Or suppose they found her little body somewhere.

This was the way all those other parents had felt – this sickness and faintness. If he did not pay the ransom and *that* happened, would he be able *not* to tell Allin – or to tell her it was his fault? Both were impossible.

'I'll just have to go on from one thing to the next,' he decided.

The chief thing was to try to be hopeful. He dressed and went back into the bedroom. Bruce had come in to dress in their room. But Allin was still in bed, lying against the pillows, white and exhausted.

He bent over her and kissed her. 'I'll send your breakfast up,' he said. 'I'm going to see Father first. If any message comes through, I'll be there – then at the bank.'

She nodded, glanced up at him, and closed her eyes. He stood looking down into her tortured face. Every nerve in it was quivering under the set stillness.

'Can't break yet,' he said sharply. 'The crisis is ahead.'

'I know,' she whispered. Then she sat up. 'I can't lie here!' she exclaimed. 'It's like lying on a bed of swords, being tortured. I'll be down, Kent – Bruce and I.'

She flew into the bathroom. He heard the shower turned on instantly and strongly. But he could wait for no one.

'Come down with Mother, son,' he said. And he went on alone.

'If you could let me have thirty thousand today,' he said to his father, 'I can give it back as soon as I sell some stock.'

'I don't care when I get it back,' his father said irritably. 'Good God, Kent, it's not that. It's just that I – it's none of my business, of course, but thirty thousand in cold cash! I'd like to ask what on earth you've been doing, but I won't.'

Kent had made up his mind at the breakfast table that if he

could keep the thing out of the papers, he would also keep it from his father and mother. He'd turned to the personals in the morning paper. There it was, his answer to those scoundrels. Well, he wouldn't stick to it unless it were best for Betsy. Meanwhile, silence!

To Rose, bringing in the toast, he had said sharply, 'Tell everybody to come in now before your mistress comes down.'

They had filed in, subdued and drooping, looking at him with frightened eyes.

'Oh sir!' Mollie had cried hysterically.

'Please!' he had exclaimed, glancing at her. Maybe the man in grey ought to see her. But last night he had distrusted Peter. This morning Peter looked like a faithful old dog, and as incapable of evil.

'I only want to thank you for obeying me so far,' he said wearily.

'If we can keep our trouble out of the papers, perhaps we can get Betsy back. At least, it's the only hope. If you succeed in letting no one know until we know – the end, I shall give each of you a hundred dollars as a token of my gratitude.'

'Thank you, sir,' Sarah and Rose had said. Mollie only sobbed. Peter was murmuring, 'Ah don' wan' no hundred dollahs, Mist' Crothers. All Ah wan' is dat little chile back.'

How could Peter be distrusted? Kent had wrung his hand. 'That's all I want, too, Peter,' he had said fervently.

Strange how shaky and emotional he had felt!

Now under his father's penetrating eyes, he held himself calm. 'I know it sounds outrageous, Father,' he admitted, 'but I simply ask you to trust me for a few days.'

'You're not speculating, I hope. It's no time for that. The market's uncertain.'

It was, Kent thought grimly, the wildest kind of speculation – with his own child's life.

'It's not ordinary speculation, certainly,' he said. 'I can manage through the bank, Dad,' he said. 'Never mind. I'll mortgage the house.'

'Oh, nonsense!' his father retorted. He had a checkbook out and was writing. 'I'm not going to have it get around that my son had to go mortgaging his place. Here you are.'

'Thanks,' Kent said briefly.

Now for the bank . . .

Step by step the day went. It was amazing how quickly the hours passed. It was noon before he knew it, and in an hour he must start for the inn. He went home and found Allin on the front porch in the sunshine. She had a book in her hand, and Bruce was playing with his red truck out in the yard. Anyone passing would never dream there was tragedy here.

'Do you have it?' she asked him.

He touched his breast pocket. 'All ready,' he answered.

They sat through a silent meal, listening to Bruce's chatter. Allin ate nothing and he very little, but he was grateful to her for being there, for keeping the outward shape of the day usual.

'Good sport!' he said to her across the table in the midst of Bruce's conversation. She smiled faintly. 'Thank you, no more coffee,' he said to Rose. 'I must be going, Allin.'

'Yes,' she said, and added. 'I wish it were I – instead of waiting.'

'I know,' he replied, and kissed her.

Yesterday, waiting had seemed intolerable to him, too. But now that he was going towards the hour for which he had been waiting, he clung to the hopefulness of uncertainty.

He drove alone to the inn. The well-paved roads, the tended fields and comfortable farmhouses were not different from the landscape any day. He would have said, only yesterday, that it was impossible that underneath all this peace and plenty there could be men so evil as to take a child out of its home, away from its parents, for money.

There was, he pondered, driving steadily west, no other possible reason. He had no enemies; none, that is, whom he knew. There were always discontented people, of course, who hated anyone who seemed successful. There was, of course, too, the chance that his father had enemies – he was ruthless with idle workers.

'I can't blame a man if he is born a fool,' Kent had heard his father maintain stoutly, 'but I can blame even a fool for being lazy.' It might be one of these. If only it were not some perverted mind!

He drove into the yard of the inn and parked his car. His heart was thudding in his breast, but he said casually to the woman at the door, 'Have you a bar?'

'To the right,' she answered quickly. It was Saturday afternoon, and business was good. She did not even look at him as he sauntered away.

The moment he entered the door of the bar he saw the man. He stood at the end of the bar, small, inconspicuous, in a grey suit and a blue-striped shirt. He wore a solid blue tie, and in his pocket was the blue handkerchief. Kent walked slowly to his side.

'Whiskey and soda, please,' he said to the bartender. The room was full of people at tables, drinking and talking noisily. He turned to the man in grey and smiled. 'Rather unusual to find a bar like this in a village inn.'

'Yes, it is,' the little man agreed. He had a kind, brisk voice, and he was drinking a tall glass of something clear, which he finished. 'Give me another of the same,' he remarked to the bartender. 'London Washerwoman's Treat, it's called,' he explained to Kent.

It was hard to imagine that this small hatchet-faced man had any importance.

'Going my way?' Kent asked suddenly.

'If you'll give me a lift,' the little man replied.

Kent's heart subsided. The man knew him, then. He nodded. They paid for their drinks and went out to the car.

'Drive due north into a country road,' the little man said with sudden sharpness. All his dreaminess was gone. He sat beside Kent, his arms folded. 'Please tell me exactly what's happened, Mr. Crothers.'

And Kent, driving along, told him.

He was grateful for the man's coldness; for the distrust of everything and everybody. He was like a lean hound in a life and death chase. Because of his coldness, Kent could talk without fear of breaking.

'I don't know your name,' Kent said.

'Doesn't matter, said the man. 'I'm detailed for the job.'

'As I was saying,' Kent went on, 'we have no enemies – at

least, none I know.

'Fellow always has enemies,' the little man murmured.

'It hardly seems like a gangster would – ' Kent began again.

'No, gangsters don't kidnap children,' the little man told him. 'Adults, yes. But they don't monkey with kids. It's too dangerous, for one thing. 'Kidnapping children's the most dangerous job there is in crime, and the smart ones know it. It's always some little fellow does it – him and a couple of friends, maybe.'

'Why dangerous?' Kent demanded.

'Always get caught,' the little man said, shrugging. 'Always!'

There was something so reassuring about this strange sharp creature that Kent said abruptly, 'My wife wants to pay the ransom. I suppose you think that's wrong, don't you?'

'Perfectly *right*, the man said. 'Absolutely! We aren't magicians, Mr. Crothers. We got to get in touch somehow. The only two cases I ever knew where nothing was solved was where the parents wouldn't pay. So we couldn't get a clue.'

Kent set his lips. 'Children killed?'

'Who knows?' the little man said, shrugging again. 'Anyway, one of them was. And the other never came back.'

There might be comfort, then, in death, Kent thought. He had infinitely rather hold Betsy's dead body in his arms than never know . . .

'Tell me what to do and I'll do it,' he said.

The little man lighted a cigarette. 'Go on just as though you'd never told us. Go on and pay your ransom. Make a note of the numbers of the notes, of course – no matter what the letter says. How's he going to know? But pay it over – and do what he says next. You can call me up here.' He took a paper out of his coat pocket and put it in Kent's pocket. 'I maybe ought to tell you, though, we'll tap your telephone wire.

'Do anything you like,' Kent said.

'That's all I need!' the man exclaimed. 'That's our orders – to do what the parents want. You're a sensible one. Fellow I knew once walked around with a shotgun to keep off the police. Said he'd handle things himself.'

'Did he get his child back?'

'Nope – paid the ransom, too. Paying the ransom's all right – that's the way we get 'em. But he went roarin' around the neighbourhood trying to be his own law. We didn't have a chance.'

Kent thought of one more thing. 'I don't want anything spared – money or trouble. I'll pay anything, of course.'

'Oh, sure,' the man said. 'Well, I guess that'll be all. You might let me off near the inn. I'll go in and get another drink.'

He lapsed into dreaminess again, and in silence Kent drove back to the village.

'All right,' the little man said. 'So long. Good luck to you.' He leaped out and disappeared into the bar.

And Kent, driving home through the early sunset, thought how little there was to tell Allin – really nothing at all, except that he liked and trusted the man in grey. No, it was much more than that: the fellow stood for something far greater than himself – he stood for all the power of the government organized against crimes like this. That was the comfort of the thing. Behind that man was the nation's police, all for him, Kent Crothers, helping him find his child.

When he reached home, Allin was in the hall waiting.

'He really said nothing, darling.' Kent said, kissing her, 'except you were right about the ransom. We have to pay that. Still, he was extraordinary. Somehow I feel – if she's still alive, we'll get her back. He's that sort of fellow.' He did not let her break, though he felt her trembling against him. He said very practically, 'We must check these banknotes, Allin.'

And then, when they were checking them upstairs in their bedroom with doors locked, he kept insisting that what they were doing was right.

At a quarter to 12 he was bumping down the rutted road to the forks. He knew every turn the road made, having travelled it on foot from the time he was a little boy. But that boy out on holiday had nothing to do with himself as he was tonight, an anxious harried man.

He drew up beneath the dead oak and took the cardboard box in which he and Allin had packed the money and stepped out of the car. There was not a sound in the dark night, yet he knew that somewhere not far away were the men who had his child.

He listened, suddenly swept again with the conviction he had had the night before, that she would cry out. She might even be this moment in the old mill. But there was not a sound. He stooped and put the box at the root of the tree.

And as he did this, he stumbled over a string raised from the ground about a foot. What was this? He followed it with his hands. It encircled the tree – a common piece of twine. Then it went under a stone, and under the stone was a piece of paper. He seized it, snapped on his cigarette lighter, and read the clumsy writing.

If everything turns out like we told you to do, go to your hired mans house at twelve tomorrow night for the kid. If you double-cross us you get it back dead.

He snapped off the light. He'd get her back dead! It all depended on what he did. And what he did, he would have to do alone. He would not go home to Allin until he had decided every step.

He drove steadily away. If he did not call the man in grey, Betsy might be at Peter's alive. If he called, and they did not find out, she might be alive anyway. But if the man fumbled and they did find out, she would be dead.

He knew what Allin would say: 'Just so we get her home, Kent, nothing else! People have to think for themselves, first.' Yes, she was right. He would keep quiet; anyway, he would give the kidnappers a chance. If she were safe and alive, that would be justification for anything. If she were dead . . .

Then he remembered that there was something courageous and reassuring about that little man. He alone had seemed to know what to do. And anyway, what about those parents who had tried to manage it all themselves? Their children had never come back either. No, he had better do what he knew he ought to do.

He tramped into the house. Allin was lying upstairs on her bed, her eyes closed.

'Darling,' he said gently. Instantly she opened her eyes and sat up. He handed her the paper and sat down on her bed. She lifted miserable eyes to him.

'Twenty-four more hours!' she whispered. 'I can't do it, Kent.'

'Yes, you can,' he said harshly. 'You'll do it because you damned well have to.' He thought. She can't break now, if I have to whip her! 'We've got to wait,' he went on. 'Is there anything else we can do? Tell Mike O'Brien? Let the newspapers get it and ruin everything?'

She shook her head. 'No.'

He got up. He longed to take her in his arms, but he did not dare. If this was ever over, he would tell her what he thought of her – how wonderful she was, how brave and game – but he could not now. It was better for them both to stay away from that edge of breaking.

'Get up,' he said. 'Let's have something to eat. I haven't really eaten all day.'

It would be good for her to get up and busy herself. She had not eaten either.

'All right, Kent,' she said. 'I'll wash my face in cold water and be down.'

'I'll be waiting,' he replied.

This gave him the moment he had made up his mind he would use – damned if he wouldn't use it! The scoundrels had his money now, and he would take the chance on that quiet little man. He called the number, and almost instantly he heard the fellow's drawl.

'Hello?' the man said.

'This is Kent Crothers,' he answered. 'I've had that invitation.'

'Yes?' The voice was alert.

'Twelve tomorrow.'

'Yes? Where? Midnight, of course. They always make it midnight.'

'My gardener's house.'

'Okay, Mr. Crothers. Go right ahead as if you hadn't told us.' The phone clicked.

Kent listened, but there was nothing more. Everything

seemed exactly the same, but nothing was the same. This very telephone wire was cut somewhere, by someone. Someone was listening to every word anyone spoke to and from his house. It was sinister and yet reassuring – sinister if you were the criminal.

He heard Allin's step on the stair and went out to meet her. 'I have a hunch.' he told her, smiling.

'What?' She tried to smile back.

He drew her towards the dining room. 'We're going to win,' he said.

Within himself he added, If she were still alive, that little heart of his life. Then he put the memory of Betsy's face away from him resolutely.

'I'm going to eat,' he declared, 'and so must you. We'll beat them tomorrow.'

But tomorrow very nearly beat them. Time stood still – there was no making it pass. They filled it full of a score of odd jobs about the house. Lucky for them it was Sunday; luckier that Kent's mother had a cold and telephoned that she and Kent's father would not be over for their usual weekly visit.

They stayed together, a little band of three. By mid-afternoon Kent had cleaned up everything – a year's odd jobs – and there were hours to go.

They played games with Bruce, and at last it was his supper-time and they put him to bed. Then they sat upstairs in their bedroom again, near the nursery, each with a book.

Sometime, after these hours were over, he would have to think about a lot of things again. But everything had to wait now, until this life ended at midnight. Beyond that no thought could reach.

At 11 he rose. 'I'm going now,' he said, and stooped to kiss her. She clung to him, and then in an instant they drew apart. In strong accord they knew it was not yet time to give way.

He ran the car as noiselessly as he could and left it at the end of the street, six blocks away. Then he walked past the few tumbledown bungalows, past two empty lots, to Peter's rickety gate. There was no light in the house. He went to the door and knocked softly. He heard Peter's mumble: 'Who's dat?'

'Let me in, Peter,' he called in a low voice. The door opened. 'It's I, Peter – Kent Crothers. Let me in. Peter, they're bringing the baby here.'

'To mah house? Lemme git de light on.'

'No, Peter, no light. I'll just sit down here in the darkness, like this. Only don't lock the door, see? I'll sit by the door. Where's a chair? That's it.' He was trembling so that he stumbled into the chair Peter pushed forward.

'Mist' Crothers, suh, will yo' have a drink? Ah got some corn likker.'

'Thanks, Peter.'

He heard Peter's footsteps shuffling away, and in a moment a tin cup was thrust into his hand. He drank the reeking stuff down. It burned him like indrawn flame, but he felt steadier for it.

'Ain't a thing Ah can do, Mist' Crothers? Peter's whisper came ghostly out of the darkness.

'Not a thing. Just wait.'

'Ah'll wait here, then. Mah ole 'ooman's asleep. Ah'll jest git thrashin' round if Ah go back to bed.'

'Yes, only we mustn't talk,' Kent whispered back.

'Nosuh.'

This was the supremest agony of waiting in all the long agony that this day had been. To sit perfectly still, straining to hear, knowing nothing, wondering . . .

Suppose something went wrong with the man in grey, and they fumbled, and frightened the man who brought Betsy back. Suppose he just sat here waiting and waiting until dawn came. And at home Allin was waiting.

The long day had been nothing to this. He sat reviewing all his life, pondering on the horror of this monstrous situation in which he and Allin now were. A free country, was it? No one was free when his lips were locked against crime, because he dared not speak lest his child be murdered. If Betsy were dead, if they didn't bring her back, he'd never tell Allin he had telephoned the man in grey. He was still glad he had done it. After all, were respectable men and women to be at the mercy of – but if Betsy were dead, he'd wish he had killed himself before he had anything to do with the fellow!

He sat, his hands interlocked so tightly he felt them grow cold and bloodless and stinging, but he could not move. Someone came down the street roaring out a song.

'Thass a drunk man,' Peter whispered.

Kent did not answer. The street grew still again.

And then in the darkness – hours after midnight, it seemed to him – he heard a car come up to the gate and stop. The gate creaked open and then shut, and the car drove away.

'Guide me down the steps,' he told Peter.

It was the blackest night he had ever seen. But the stars were shining when he stepped out. Peter pulled him along the path. Then, by the gate Peter stooped.

'She's here,' he said.

And Kent, wavering and dizzy, felt her in his arms again, limp and heavy. 'She's warm,' he muttered. 'That's something.'

He carried her into the house, and Peter lighted a candle and held it up. It was she – his little Betsy, her white dress filthy and a man's sweater drawn over her. She was breathing heavily.

'Look lak she done got a dose of sumpin,' Peter muttered.

'I must get her home,' Kent whispered frantically. 'Help me to the car, Peter.'

'Yassah,' Peter said, and blew out the candle.

They walked silently down the street, Peter's hand on Kent's arm. When he got Betsy home, he – he –

'Want I should drive you?' Peter was asking him.

'I – maybe you'd better,' he replied.

He climbed into the seat with her. She was so fearfully limp. Thank God he could hear her breathing! In a few minutes he would put Betsy into her mother's arms.

'Don't stay, Peter,' he said.

'Nosuh,' Peter answered.

Allin was at the door, waiting. She opened it and without a word reached for the child. He closed the door behind them.

Then he felt himself grow sick. 'I was going to tell you,' he gasped, 'I didn't know whether to tell you – ' He swayed and felt himself fall upon the floor.

Allin was a miracle; Allin was wonderful, a rock of a woman. This tender thing who had endured the torture of these days was at his bedside when he woke next day, smiling, and only a little pale.

'The doctor says you're not to go to work darling,' she told him.

'The doctor?' he repeated.

'I had him last night for both of you – you and Betsy. He won't tell anyone.'

'I've been crazy,' he said, dazed. 'Where is she? How – '

'She's going to be all right,' Allin said.

'No, but – you're not telling me!'

'Come in here and see,' she replied.

He got up, staggering a little. Funny how his legs had collapsed under him last night!

They went into the nursery. There in her bed she lay, his beloved child. She was more naturally asleep now, and her face bore no other mark than pallor.

'She won't even remember it,' Allin said. 'I'm glad it wasn't Bruce.'

He did not answer. He couldn't think – nothing had to be thought about now.

'Come back to bed, Kent,' Allin was saying. 'I'm going to bring your breakfast up. Bruce is having his downstairs.'

He climbed back into bed, shamefaced at his weakness. 'I'll be all right after a little coffee. I'll get up then, maybe.'

But his bed felt wonderfully good. He lay back, profoundly grateful to it – to everything. But as long as he lived he would wake up to sweat in the night with memory.

The telephone by his bed rang, and he picked it up. 'Hello?' he called.

'Hello, Mr. Crothers,' a voice answered. It was the voice of the man in grey. 'Say, was the little girl hurt?'

'No!' Kent cried. 'She's all right!'

'Fine. Well, I just wanted to tell you we caught the fellow last night.'

'You *did!'* Kent leaped up. 'No! Why, that's extraordinary.'

'We had a cordon around the place for blocks and got him.

You'll get your money back, too.'

'That – it doesn't seem to matter. Who was he?'

'Fellow named Harry Brown – a young chap in a drug store.'

'I never heard of him!'

'No, he says you don't know him – but his dad went to school with yours, and he's heard a lot of talk about you. His dad's a poor stick, I guess, and got jealous of yours. That's about it, probably. Fellow says he figured you sort of owed him something. Crazy, of course. Well, it was an easy case – he wasn't smart, and scared to death, besides. You were sensible about it. Most people ruin their chances with their own fuss. So long, Mr. Crothers. Mighty glad.'

The telephone clicked. That was all. Everything was incredible, impossible. Kent gazed around the familiar room. Had this all happened? It had happened, and it was over.

When he went downstairs he would give the servants their hundred dollars apiece. Mollie had had nothing to do with it, after all. The mystery had dissolved like a mist at morning.

Allin was at the door with his tray. Behind her came Bruce, ready for school. She said, so casually Kent could hardly catch the tremor underneath her voice, 'What would you say, darling, if we let Peter walk to school with Bruce today?'

Her eyes pleaded with him: 'No? Oughtn't we to? What shall we do?'

Then he thought of something else that indomitable man in grey had said, that man whose name he would never know, one among all those other men trying to keep the law for the nation.

'We're a lawless people,' the little man had said that afternoon in the car. 'If we made a law against paying ransoms, nobody would obey it any more than they did Prohibition. No, when the Americans don't like a law, they break it. And so we still have kidnappers. It's one of the prices you pay for a democracy.'

Yes, it was one of the prices. Everybody paid – he and Allin; the child they had so nearly lost? that boy locked up in prison.

'Bruce has to live in his own country,' he said. 'I guess you can go alone, can't you, son?'

'Course I can,' Bruce said sturdily.

IVAN BUNIN

The Gentleman from San Francisco

Translated by David Richards

The gentleman from San Francisco – no one remembered his name either in Naples or on Capri – was travelling to the Old World for two whole years, with his wife and daughter, purely for entertainment.

He was firmly convinced that he possessed a perfect right to rest, pleasures and an exclusively first-class tour. His justification for this was first that he was rich and secondly that he was only just beginning to live, in spite of his fifty-eight years. Until now he had not lived, but merely existed, true not at all badly, but still resting all his hopes on the future. He had worked tirelessly – the Chinese coolies whom he had enlisted in their thousands to labour for him knew only too well what that meant! – and at last he saw that he had achieved much, almost overhauling those whom he had accepted as models, and decided to take a break. People in the circle to which he belonged tended to start enjoying life with a voyage to Europe, India or Egypt. He too resolved to do the same. Of course he meant primarily to reward himself for his years of labour, but he was also happy for his wife and daughter. His wife had never been particularly sensitive, but all middle-aged American women are keen travellers. As for his daughter, a somewhat ailing girl of marriageable age, for her the journey was frankly essential – quite apart from the benefit to her health, didn't journeys sometimes provide opportunities for happy meetings? One can find oneself sitting at table or admiring frescoes next to a multi-millionaire.

The gentleman from San Francisco had worked out an extensive itinerary. In December and January he was hoping to enjoy the sun of Southern Italy, the monuments of antiquity, the tarantella, the serenades of wandering musicians and also – something to which men of his age are particularly susceptible – the love of young Neapolitan girls, even if it should not be given entirely disinterestedly; he planned spending carnival time in Nice and Monte Carlo, where at that season the most select company gathers to indulge in motor-car and yacht racing, in roulette, in what is commonly called flirtation, or in pigeon-shooting – against the background of a forget-me-not-blue sea, birds very prettily soar up into the air from cages on emerald lawns, immediately to thud down on to the ground like little white bundles; he intended devoting the beginning of March to Florence, and then towards Holy Week he was to travel to Rome to hear a *Miserere;* his plans also included Venice and Paris, a bull-fight in Seville, sea-bathing in the British Isles, then Athens, Constantinople, Palestine, Egypt, and even Japan – the last of course on the return journey. . . . And at first everything went splendidly.

It was the end of November, and until they reached Gibraltar they had to sail through an icy murk alternating with flurries of wet snow, but they sailed perfectly safely. The passengers were numerous, but the liner, the famous *Atlantis,* was like an enormous hotel with every luxury – an all-night bar, Turkish baths and its own newspaper – and life aboard followed a strictly measured routine. They would get up early to the sound of a bugle which echoed sharply down the passageways at that shadowy hour when the slow, bleak dawn broke over the grey-green watery waste swelling heavily in the mist; donning their flannel dressing-gowns, they drank coffee, chocolate or cocoa; then they took baths and did exercises to stimulate their appetities and a feeling of well-being; they washed, dressed and went to breakfast; it was the done thing until eleven to stroll briskly about the deck, inhaling the cold ocean freshness, or to play shuffleboard and other games to stimulate their appetites anew, and at eleven to fortify themselves with broth and sandwiches; once fortified, they would contentedly read the newspaper and placidly await lunch, which was still more nourishing and varied than breakfast; the next two hours were devoted to rest; for this all the decks were covered with long cane chairs on which the travellers lay, and the foaming ridges which appeared fleetingly at the side of the ship or lapsed into a sweet somnolence; between four and five, glowing and cheerful, they were regaled with strong perfumed tea and biscuits; at seven bugle calls would herald that which constituted the supreme aim and consummation of their existence. . . . And at this point the gentleman from San Francisco would hurry to his luxurious cabin to dress for dinner.

In the evenings the portholes on the many decks of the *Atlantis* stared into the darkness like countless fiery eyes, and a great multitude of servants worked in the kitchens, sculleries and wine-stores. The ocean running outside was awesome, but no one gave it a thought, firmly trusting to the power exercised over it by the captain, a red-haired man of monstrous height and weight who always seemed half-asleep; in his uniform with its heavy gold braid he looked like an enormous idol, and very rarely emerged from his mysterious quarters to show himself to the passengers. Every few minutes a siren on the forecastle would emit moans of infernal despair or yelp with frenzied malice, but very few of the diners heard that siren, muffled as it was by the sound of a fine string orchestra playing elegantly and tirelessly in the two-toned dining-room which was suffused with a festive light and packed with *décolleté* ladies, men in tails and dinner-jackets, slender waiters and polite *maîtres d'hôtel,* one of whom, the one who took orders only for wine, even paraded with a chain round his neck, like a lord mayor. The gentleman from San Francisco's dinner-jacket and starched linen made him look much younger. Dry, short, wrongly cut but firmly sewn, he sat in the pearly-gold radiance of that palatial dining-room behind a bottle of wine, a whole row of delicate glasses and a lush display of hyacinths. There was something Mongolian about his sallow face with its trimmed silvery moustache; his big teeth gleamed with gold fillings and his strong bald head glistened like old ivory. His wife, a large, solid, reserved woman, was attired expensively, but appropriately for her age; his daughter, tall and slender with magnificent, superbly coiffured hair, breath redolent of violet water and the tiniest of pink pimples by her lips and between her lightly powdered shoulder-blades, wore a dress which was elaborate but light, transparent and innocently revealing. Dinner lasted over an hour, and after dinner the ballroom offered dancing; during this the men, including of course the gentleman from San Francisco, put their feet up, smoked Havana cigars until their faces grew crimson and drank liqueurs from the bar manned by negroes in red waistcoats and with eyes like shelled hard-boiled eggs. The mountainous black ocean waves ran booming outside while the snowstorm whistled powerfully through the burdened rigging, and the whole liner would shudder as it strove against both storm and waves, like a plough turning over the ocean's heaving mass which incessantly seethed and soared up with lappets of foam; the siren, muffled by the mist, groaned in mortal anguish; the men on watch froze in the cold and felt their minds wandering from over-concentrated attention; the underwater depths of the liner, where gigantic furnaces voicelessly crackled and with their candescent gorges devoured the piles of coal clangorously shovelled into them by half-naked men who were bathed in acrid, dirty sweat and lurid from the flames, were like the torrid dark bowels of the last, ninth circle of the inferno; but in the bar the passengers jauntily put their feet up on the arms of chairs, decanted brandy and liqueurs and swam in waves of heady smoke; the ballroom sparkled and everything exuded light, warmth and joy; couples spun round in the waltz or bent in the tango, while the music in its sweetly brazen melancholy insistently implored ever one and the same thing . . . Among this resplendent throng was a certain great tycoon, clean-shaven and tall in his old-fashioned tails, there was a celebrated Spanish author, there was an international beauty, and there was an elegant couple very much in love whom everyone watched with curiosity and who made no attempt to conceal their happiness: he danced only with her and everything they did was so refined and charming that only the captain knew that they were paid by Lloyds to feign their love for high wages and had long been sailing on one ship after another.

In Gibraltar the sun suddenly cheered them; it was like early spring. A new passenger, the crown prince of some Asian state, travelling incognito, appeared on board the *Atlantis* and attracted universal interest; he was a small man, completely wooden, with broad cheeks and slit eyes; he wore gold spectacles and although there was something uninviting about the way the skin showed through the long hairs of his moustache, as on a corpse, he seemed on the whole pleasant, straightforward and modest. In the Mediterranean heavy waves were running, like many-hued peacocks' tails; in the bright sunshine and under a perfectly clear sky they were whipped up by the *tramontana* which blew towards them in its cheerful fury . . . Then on the second day the sky began to pale and the horizon grew misty: land was approaching. Ischia and Capri suddenly came into view, and through binoculars Naples was already visible, spread out like lumps of sugar at the foot of some blue-grey mass . . . Many of the ladies and gentlemen had already put on light fur-trimmed coats, and the meek Chinese cabin-boys who always spoke in whispers, bandy-legged youths with jet-black pigtails down to their heels and girlishly thick eyelashes, were unhurriedly dragging rugs, walking-sticks, suitcases and overnight bags towards the companion-ways . . . The gentleman from San Francisco's daughter was standing on the deck beside the prince, who by a happy concidence had been introduced to her the previous evening, and pretending to look attentively into the distance towards where he was pointing as he rapidly explained something to her in a low voice. With his short stature he looked like a boy among the other passengers; he was not at all handsome, indeed even a little odd with his spectacles, his bowler hat, his English coat, his sparse moustache just like horsehair, and the delicate dark, almost varnished skin which seemed to be tightly stretched over his flat face, but the girl listened to him and in her agitation took in nothing of what he said to her; her heart was beating with incomprehensible rapture: absolutely everything about him was different – his dry hands and his pure skin under which ancient royal blood flowed; even his perfectly simple, but somehow especially neat, European clothes held an inexplicable charm. The gentleman from San Francisco himself, wearing grey spats, kept eyeing the international beauty who was standing beside him, a tall blonde with an amazing figure and eyes made up in the latest Paris fashion who incessantly conversed with a tiny, cringing, hairless dog which she held on a silver chain. And his daughter, feeling vaguely embarrassed, tried not to look at him.

He had been fairly generous during the voyage and so fully accepted as genuine the solicitude shown by all who brought him food and drink, served him from dawn to dusk, anticipating his slightest desire, kept him clean and rested, carted his things, summoned porters for him and conveyed his trunks to hotels. So it had been everywhere, so it had been during the cruise, and so it was to be in Naples too. Naples was growing larger and coming closer; the band, their brass instruments gleaming, had already assembled on deck and suddenly they deafened everyone with the exultant roar of a march; the giant captain appeared on his bridge in his dress uniform and waved a hand in greeting to the passengers like a benevolent pagan god. When the *Atlantis* finally entered the harbour and brought its packed, many-storeyed bulk to a halt alongside the quay and the gangways clattered down, what a horde of porters and their assistants in gold-braided caps, what a horde of agents of various sorts, whistling urchins and sturdy tatterdemalions with sheafs of coloured postcards in their hands surged towards him offering their services! He smiled at the tatterdemalions as he made his way towards the car sent from the hotel where the prince too would probably be staying and calmly repeated under his breath, now in English, now in Italian:

'Go away! *Via!*'

Life in Naples immediately fell into its set routine. Early in the morning there was breakfast in the gloomy dining-room, an unpromising sky and a throng of guides at the entrance to the vestibule; then came the first smiles of a warm, pinkish sun and from their high overhanging balcony they enjoyed the view: Vesuvius, completely enveloped in a radiant morning haze, the pearly-silver ripples of the bay with the faint outline of Capri on the horizon, the little donkeys running along the quay below, pulling their two-wheelers, and detachments of tiny soldiers marching off somewhere to cheerfully defiant music; then they would step out to the car and take a slow drive through the crowded, narrow, wet, corridor-like streets, between the tall, many-windowed buildings, visit deadly clean museums, where the light was as even and pleasant but as boring as snow, or inspect cold churches smelling of wax, every one of which offered exactly the same – a magnificent entrance with a heavy leather awning, and then inside a huge empty silence, the faint little flames of a seven-branched candelabrum flickering red on a lace-covered altar at the far end, a solitary old woman among the dark wooden pews, slippery memorial plaques under the feet and someone's invariably famous *Descent from the Cross;* at one o'clock came lunch on San Martino, where a good few top-class people always congregated towards noon and where on one occasion the gentleman from San Francisco's daughter was almost taken ill, as she fancied she saw the prince sitting in the dining-room, even though she knew from the newspapers that he was in Rome; at five there was tea at the hotel, in the elegant salon, made warm by its carpets and blazing fires; and then again the preparations for dinner – again the strings of silk-clad, *décolleté* ladies reflected in the mirrors and rustling down the stairs, again the wide and hospitably open palatial dining-room with the red-jacketed musicians on the rostrum and the black throng of waiters around the *maître d'hôtel* who with extraordinary dexterity ladled a thick pink soup into rows of plates . . . Again the dinners were so lavish with main dishes and wines and mineral waters and puddings and fruit that by eleven o'clock chambermaids were going round all the bedrooms with rubber hot-water bottles to soothe the stomachs of those who had dined.

However, December turned out less than successful. Whenever the porters were asked about the weather they only shrugged their shoulders ruefully and muttered that no one could recall another year like it, though it wasn't the first time they had had to mutter this and cite the dreadful things happening everywhere else: unheard-of downpours and storms on the Riveria, snow in Athens, Etna also covered in snow and glowing at night, and tourists running away from Palermo to escape the frosts. . . . Every day the morning sun was deceptive in that after midday the sky would cloud over and the rain would come down harder and colder; then the palm trees outside the entrance to the hotel would gleam like wet tin, the town would seem especially dirty and crowded, the museums excessively dull, the cigar-butts of the fat cabmen in their wind-blown rubber capes insufferably foul, the energetic cracking of their whips over the heads of their scrawny horses obviously false, the footwear of the *signori* sweeping the tramlines ghastly, and the women splashing through the mud with their dark heads bare to the rain outrageously short-legged; the overwhelming dampness and the stink of putrid fish coming from the sea foaming along the quay were simply indescribable. The gentleman from San Francisco and his wife began to bicker in the mornings; their daughter would look pale and complain of headaches, or recover, go into raptures over everything and be sweet and beautiful; beautiful too were those tender, complex feelings which had been aroused in her by that encounter with the ugly man of special blood, for in the end it is perhaps not all that important what awakens a maiden's heart – money, fame, or illustrious ancestry . . . Everyone assured them that it was quite different in Sorrento and on Capri – warmer and sunnier, the lemon trees in blossom, manners more honest and the wine more pure. And so the family from San Francisco decided to set off with all their trunks for Capri to look it over, to tread on the stones at the sites of Tiberius's palaces, visit the fabulous caves of the Blue Grotto, and listen to the Abruzzian bagpipers who roam all over the island for a whole month before Christmas singing praises to the Virgin Mary; then they were to move to Sorrento.

On the day of departure – that memorable day for the family from San Francisco – there was no sun from earliest morning. A thick mist covered Vesuvius down to its foot and hung grey over the leaden ripples of the sea. Capri was completely invisible, just as if it had never existed. And the little steamer making her way towards the island rolled from side to side so heavily that the family from San Francisco lay immobile on divans in the passengers' saloon with rugs over their legs and their eyes shut from sea-sickness. The wife thought she was suffering the most; several times she was overcome and believed she was dying, but the stewardess, who kept running to her with a bowl and who for many years, summer and winter, had been tossed about daily by these waves and was still indefatigable, only laughed. The daughter was dreadfully pale and held a slice of lemon between her teeth. The gentleman himself, lying on his back in a full overcoat and a wide peaked cap, kept his teeth clenched the whole way; his face grew dark, his moustache turned white and he had a severe headache; during the previous few days the bad wather had led him to drink heavily in the evenings and feast his eyes on too many *tableaux vivants* in various nightclubs. And the rain beat against the shuddering glass panes and dripped onto the divans, the howling wind rushed against the masts and from time to time, with the help of a swooping wave, turned the little steamer almost onto her side, and every time she did so something rolled about down below with a clanging noise. It was slightly calmer at the two stopping-places, Castellammare and Sorrento, but there too the tossing was frightful, so that the shore, with all its ravines and gardens, pine trees, pink and white hotels and smoky, crisp-green mountains, appeared to rise and fall as if on a seesaw; boats banged against the sides of the steamer, the moist wind blew through the doorway and a guttural-voiced boy on a rocking barge with a pennant proclaiming *Hotel Royal* yelled ceaselessly, trying to entice travellers onto his boat. And the gentleman from San Francisco, feeling – as well he might – a thoroughly old man, was already thinking anguished and malicious thoughts about all those grasping and garlicky little people whom the world called Italians; opening his eyes during one of the stops and sitting up on the divan, he caught sight of a huddle of such wretched, mould-encrusted stone houses under a rocky slope, stuck together right at the water's edge among a clutter of boats, rags, tins and brown nets, that, remembering this was the real Italy which he had come to enjoy, he was seized with despair . . . At last, when it was already dusk, the dark mass of the island loomed up, seemingly pitted with red lights at its base; the wind grew softer, warmer and more fragrant, and golden snakes of light from the lamps on the jetty came shooting across the waves which were rippling like black oil. Then suddenly the anchor clattered and plopped heavily into the water, and the frenzied vying shouts of the boatmen echoed around. Relief was felt at once, the lights in the saloon seemed to shine more brightly and everyone wanted to eat, drink, smoke and move about. Ten minutes later the family from San Francisco stepped down into a big wooden barge, and in another five they climbed onto the stone quay and entered a brightly-coloured little cable car which with a humming noise glided up the hillside through fields of vine-stakes, dilapidated walls and gnarled, damp orange trees, protected here and there by straw canopies, which all slipped back downhill, with their gleaming fruit and thick, lustrous foliage, past the open windows of the little compartment . . . The earth of Italy smells sweet after rain, and each Italian island has its own peculiar aroma.

The island of Capri was wet and dark that evening. But it momentarily revived and brightened up in places. At the top of the mountain, on the funicular's arrival platform, a throng of those to whom it had fallen to offer a fitting welcome to the gentleman from San Francisco already stood in wait. There were other arrivals too, but none worthy of attention – a few Russians who had settled on Capri, slovenly, bearded and absent-minded men in glasses and with the collars of their worn overcoats turned up, and a band of long-legged, round-headed German youths in Tyrolean costumes, with knapsacks on their backs; they had no need of anyone's services and were decidedly unfree with their money. The gentleman from San Francisco, who calmly kept his distance from both these groups, was immediately marked. He and his ladies were quickly helped to alight, people ran ahead to show them the way, and once again he found himself surrounded by urchins and those sturdy Capriote peasant-women who carry the cases and trunks of respectable tourists on their heads. Their wooden soles clattered across the tiny, operative square, above which an electric globe swung in the moist wind, the horde of urchins whistled like birds and turned somersaults while the gentleman from San Francisco walked in their midst as though across a stage towards a medieval archway under a group of houses which seemed to merge into one another; beyond the archway the brightly lit entrance to the hotel was approached uphill by a tiny ringing street, with a fringe of palm trees visible above flat roofs to the left and the blue stars standing out against the black sky above and ahead. And it was as if everything in the wet little stone town on that rocky Mediterranean island had revived specifically in honour of the visitors from San Francisco, it seemed that it was they who had made the proprietor of the hotel so happy and welcoming and that it was only they who had been awaited by the Chinese gong which sent its summons to dinner booming through every floor just as they entered the vestibule.

The proprietor, an exquisitely elegant young man who gave a polite, refined bow as he greeted them, momentarily disconcerted the gentleman from San Francisco: he suddenly recalled that amidst all the turmoil that had filled his sleep the previous night he had dreamt of this very man, exactly as he stood there in that same morning-coat and with that same mirror-smooth hair. Astonished, he hesitated for a moment. But since his heart had long since ceased to harbour the smallest grain of any so-called mystical intuitions, his astonishment immediately faded. Jokingly, he told his wife and daughter about this strange coincidence of dream and reality as they walked through the hotel corridors. His daughter at that moment darted an alarmed glance at him: her heart had suddenly contracted in anguish, at a feeling of terrible loneliness on that alien, dark island. . .

A distinguished visitor to Capri, Prince Reuss XVII, had just left. And the visitors from San Francisco were installed in the very apartments which he had occupied. To them were assigned the prettiest and most expert chambermaid, a

Belgian girl with a slender, tightly corseted waist and a little starched cap like a small serrated crown, the most presentable footman, a coal-black, fiery-eyed Sicilian, and the most efficient boots, little fat Luigi who had held many similar posts in his time. A minute later the French *maître d'hôtel* tapped lightly on the door of the gentleman from San Francisco's room to ask whether the esteemed new visitors would be dining and to announce – in the event of an affirmative response which was of course not in doubt – that today there was lobster, beef, asparagus, pheasant, etc. The floor was still swaying under the gentleman from San Francisco, such a shaking-up had he been given by that wretched little Italian steamer, but carefully, though from unfamiliarity somewhat clumsily, he shut the window which had rattled as the *maître d'hôtel* entered and through which now wafted aromas from the distant kitchen and the wet flowers in the garden, and replied with slow precision that they would be dining, that a table should be reserved for them at the far end of the dining-room, away from the entrance, and that they would drink the local wine; and to each word the *maître d'hôtel* expressed his assent in a range of intonations all of which implied that there was not and could not possibly be any doubt about the appropriateness of the gentleman from San Francisco's wishes and that every one of them would be carried out to the letter. Finally he inclined his head and fastidiously inquired:

'Is that all, sir?'

Receiving in response a drawled 'Yes', he added that that evening there was to be a tarantella display in the vestibule, danced by Carmela and Giuseppe, who were famed throughout Italy and 'the entire tourist world'.

'I've seen picture-postcards of her,' said the gentleman from San Francisco in an expressionless voice. 'And this Giuseppe's her husband?'

'Her cousin, sir,' replied the *maître d'hôtel*.

Then, after a short pause during which he pondered but said nothing, the gentlman from San Francisco dismissed him with a nod.

Once again he began to get ready, as though preparing

himself for a wedding. He turned on every electric switch, filling the mirrors with brilliant light and the reflections of the furniture and open trunks, and started to wash, shave and repeatedly ring his bell, while other bells, from his wife and daughter's rooms, also echoed through the corridor, vying with his. And Luigi in his red apron, with the agility characteristic of many fat people and making grimaces of horror which reduced to tears the maids hurrying past with procelain jugs, rolled head over heels in the direction of the bell and, rapping on the door with his knuckles, inquired with feigned timidity and a deference bordering on imbecility:

'Ha sonato, signore?'

And from the other side of the door came a slow, grating, irritatingly polite voice:

'Yes, come in.'

What was the gentleman from San Francisco thinking and feeling on that significant evening? Like everyone who has endured a rolling ship, he was simply very hungry and was looking forward to his first spoonful of soup and his first mouthful of wine and was even completing the ordinary task of dressing in a state of mild excitement which left no room for feeling or speculation.

When he had shaved, washed and inserted one or two false teeth, he stood in front of the mirror, moistened the remaining strands of his pearly-grey hair and arranged them round his sallow skull with a pair of silver-backed brushes, drew cream silk underpants onto his firm elderly body with its overfed, spreading waist and slipped black silk socks and evening shoes over his dry, flat feet. Then with a quick bend of the knees he arranged his black trousers, pulled high with silk braces, and then his snow-white, billowing shirt, inserted cuff-links into the dazzling cuffs and embarked on a painful chase after the stud under the stiff collar. The floor still swayed under him and the tips of his fingers hurt as the stud kept digging into the flabby skin in the hollow under his Adam's apple, but he persisted and at last, with eyes shining from the exertion and face flushed from the tight collar which constricted his throat, succeeded in his efforts and sank exhausted in front of the pier-glass which threw back his full reflection, as did all the other mirrors.

'God, this is dreadful!' he muttered, dropping his strong bald head, but not trying to work out or even think about what exactly was so dreadful; then, as was his habit, he inspected his stubby fingers with their gout-stiffened joints and their big, bulging, almond-coloured nails and repeated with certainty: 'This is dreadful!'

At that moment, as if from a pagan temple, the second gong resounded throughout the building. Quickly getting to his feet, the gentleman from San Francisco straightened his tie and buttoned up his open waistcoat, squeezing both his neck and his stomach even more tightly, put on his dinner-jacket, adjusted his cuffs and again inspected himself in the mirror. 'That Carmela,' he found himself thinking, 'with her dark skin and provocative eyes like a mulatto woman and that bright orange dress – she must be a beautiful dancer.' He stepped briskly out of his room and along the carpet to the adjoining one, his wife's, to inquire in a loud voice whether the other two were nearly ready.

'Five minutes,' tinkled an already merry, girlish voice the other side of the door.

'Fine,' siad the gentleman from San Francisco.

And he set off slowly through thc corridors and down the red-carpeted stairway to look for the reading-room. Servants in his path pressed themselves against the wall, but he continued on his way as if unaware of them. Late for dinner, an old woman, bent and with milky-white hair, but *décolleté* in her grey silk dress, hurried along ahead of him as fast as she could with an absurd, hen-like gait, but he easily overtook her. By the glass doors of the dining-room, where everyone had already assembled and begun to eat, he paused in front of a table piled with boxes of cigars and Egyptian cigarettes, took a large Manila and tossed down three lire; on the winter veranda he shot a glance through an open window. A gentle breeze wafted over him out of the darkness, he fancied he could see the top of an old palm tree, spreading its seemingly gigantic fronds against the stars, and the distant, even roar of the sea reached his ears . . . In the quiet and comfortable reading-room, with lights only over the tables, stood a grey-haired German, rustling the newspapers; with his round silver spectacles and wild, surprised eyes he looked like Ibsen. Eyeing him coldly, the gentleman from San Francisco sat down in a deep leather armchair in the corner beside a lamp with a green shade, put on his pince-nez and, jerking his head away from his strangling collar, hid behind a newspaper. He had rapidly glanced over several headlines, read a few sentences about the interminable war in the Balkans and turned the page over with a practised flick of the wrist, when suddenly the lines flared up before him in a glassy shimmer, his neck went taut, his eyes bulged and his pince-nez flew off his nose . . . He lunged forward, trying to gulp in air, and gave out a savage wheeze; his jaw dropped, making his whole mouth light up with the gold of his fillings, his head rolled onto his shoulder and drooped there, the front of his shirt puffed out into a box-like shape and his whole body writhed as he dug the heels of his shoes into the carpet and slid to the floor in a desperate struggle with someone.

But for the German in the reading-room the hotel would have been able to hush up this dreadful incident. They would have seized the gentleman from San Francisco by head and feet and instantly hustled him out through the back corridors as far away as possible – and not a single visitor would have realized what he had done. But the German dashed out of the reading-room shouting; he roused the whole building, certainly the whole dining-room. Many of those dining leapt up, many of them, turning pale, ran to the reading-room and 'What, what's happened?' was heard in every language – and no one could give an intelligible answer, no one understood anything, because even today people still marvel above all else at death and refuse to accept it. The proprietor rushed from one visitor to another, trying to restrain those who were running and calm them with hasty assurances that it was nothing, just a fainting fit that had overcome a certain gentleman from San Francisco. But no one listened to him, many of them had seen the footmen and boots tearing off the gentleman's tie, waistcoat, crumpled dinner-jacket and even for some reason the evening shoes from those black silk feet with the flat soles. And he was still fighting. He was tenaciously struggling with death, by no means willing to give in to the enemy that had so unexpectedly and crudely fallen upon him. He shook his head, wheezed like a stuck pig and rolled his eyes as if drunk . . . He was hurriedly carried off and laid on the bed in room 43, the smallest, nastiest, dampest and coldest room in the hotel, at the end of the bottom corridor; his daughter rushed in with her hair loose and her half-bare bosom propped up by her corset, followed by his large wife, dressed up for dinner, her mouth round with horror . . . But by then he had already stopped shaking his head.

A quarter of an hour later the hotel had returned to some sort of order. But the evening had been irreparably spoilt. A certain number of people returned to the dining-room and finished their meal, but in silence and with injured expressions on their faces, while the proprietor went round them, shrugging his shoulders in impotent, decorous irritation, feeling baselessly guilty and assuring everyone that he perfectly understood 'how unpleasant it was' and promising to take 'all possible measures within his power' to remove the unpleasantness; the tarantella display had to be cancelled, all unnecessary lights were extinguished; most of the visitors went off to a bar in the town and the hotel grew so quiet that the clock could be heard ticking in the vestibule, where only a solitary parrot muttered woodenly as it fussed about its cage before going to sleep, contriving to doze off with one foot awkwardly raised onto the upper perch . . . The gentleman from San Francisco lay on a cheap iron bedstead under some coarse woollen blankets, onto which light fell from a single bulb in the ceiling. An ice-bag hung loosely on his wet, cold forehead. His grey, already lifeless face was gradually chilling, and the wheezing gurgle coming from his open mouth with the gleaming gold fillings grew fainter. It was not the gentleman from San Francisco wheezing – he was no more – but someone else. His wife, his daughter, a doctor and the staff stood watching him. Suddenly what they feared and expected occurred – the wheezing ceased. Then very slowly, before their eyes, a pallor spread across the dead man's face, while his features became sharper and more lucent . . .

The proprietor came in.

'Già è morto,' the doctor whispered to him.

The proprietor shrugged dispassionately. The wife, with tears rolling silently down her cheeks, went over to him and timidly suggested that the deceased should now be taken back to his room.

'Oh no, madame,' replied the proprietor quickly, correctly, but no longer with any civility, and in French rather than English: he no longer had any interest in the trifling sums the visitors from San Francisco might now leave in his till. 'That is quite impossible, madame,' he said and added in explanation that a high value was set on those particular rooms and that if he acceded to her request then all Capri would hear of it and tourists would shun them.

The daughter, who had been watching him the whole time with a strange expression on her face, sat down on a chair and began to sob, covering her mouth with a handkerchief. The wife's tears suddenly dried up and her face flared. She raised her voice and began to insist, speaking in her own language and still unable to believe that all respect for her husband had finally been forfeited. The proprietor cut her short with a dignified politeness: if madame did not like the hotel's procedures he would not dream of detaining her; he firmly declared that the body must be removed at first light, that the police had already been notified and that one of their representatives would shortly come and complete the necessary formalities . . . Madame asks whether perhaps a plain, ready-made coffin might be obtained on Capri? Unfortunately not, under no circumstances, nor could one be constructed in time. Other arrangements would have to be made. English soda water, for instance, was delivered in large, long crates . . . The partitions could be removed from one of these. . .

That night the whole hotel slept. Someone opened the window of room 43 – it looked out onto a corner of the garden where a puny banana tree grew against a high stone wall topped with broken glass – turned off the electric light, locked the door and went away. The dead man lay in darkness; the blue stars watched him from the sky, and a cricket on the wall began to chirrup with sad abandon . . . Out in the dimly lit corridor two chambermaids sat on a window-sill darning. Luigi entered in his slippers, with a pile of linen over one arm.

'Pronto?' he asked anxiously in a loud whisper, indicating with his eyes the awesome door at the end of the corridor. Then he made a circling movement with his free hand in the same direction.

'Partenza!' he shouted in a whisper; it was the word usually called out when the trains leave Italian stations and the maids collapsed with noiseless laughter, laying their heads on each other's shoulders.

Then he skipped lightly up to the door itself, pretended to knock and, cocking his head to one side, asked in the politest undertone:

'Ha sonato, signore?'

And constricting his throat and pushing out his lower jaw, he answered himself, in English, in a slow, grating, sad voice, which seemed to come from the other side of the door:

'Yes, come in . . .'

At dawn, as it grew light outside the window of room 43, and a moist wind rustled through the ragged leaves of the banana tree, as the blue morning sky rose and spread over the island of Capri and the pure clear summit of Monte Solaro turned to gold under the sun coming up from behind the distant azure mountains of Italy, and as the labourers who mended the tourist paths on the island set off for work, a long soda-water crate was carried into room 43. Soon it had become very heavy and was straining the knees of the junior porter who then quickly carted it in a single-horse cab along the white road winding over the Capriote hillsides, between the stone walls and the vineyards, down and down to the sea. The cabman, a sickly fellow with red eyes, wearing an old jacket with short sleeves and down-at-heel boots, had a hangover – he had been playing dice all night in the *trattoria* – and kept whipping his wiry little horse which was all decked out in Sicilian style: a variety of little bells jingled fussily on the bridle with its coloured woolly pompoms and on the points of the high brass saddle-strap pad, while a yard-long feather sticking out of the animal's trimmed fringe trembled as it trotted along. The cabman was silent, oppressed by his dissipation, his vices and the fact that the previous evening he had lost everything down to his last lira. But the morning was fresh; in that air, by the sea and under the morning sky a hangover soon evaporates and man soon feels trouble-free; moreover, the cabman was cheered by the unexpected bonus brought to him by some gentleman from San Francisco whose lifeless head was rocking in the crate at his back. The little steamer, lying like a water-beetle far below on the soft clear blue expanse which stretches the length and breadth of the Bay of Naples, was already giving its final hoots which echoed briskly through the whole island, each of whose contours, hilltops and stones stood out so clearly that there might have been no atmosphere at all. Beside the jetty the junior porter was overtaken by his senior, driving down in a car with the gentleman's wife and daughter, their faces white and their eyes hollow from tears and a sleepless night. Ten minutes later the little steamer set off once more for Sorrento and Castellammare, bearing away from Capri for ever the family from San Francisco. And peace and tranquility returned once more to the island.

On that island two thousand years ago there lived a man unspeakably loathsome in the pursuit of his lists and somehow possessing power over millions of people whom he subjected to immeasurable cruelties; mankind has remembered him for all time, and countless visitors from all quarters of the globe come to gaze at the ruins of the stone palace where he lived at the top of one of the island's steepest ascents. That superb morning all those who had travelled to Capri for this purpose were still asleep in their hotels, although at the hotel entrances drivers were already gathering their mousy little donkeys with the red saddles into which, once they had wakened and breakfasted, elderly Americans and Germans were due to clamber again that day and behind which old Capriote beggar-women were again due to run along the stone paths, always uphill, right to the summit of

Monte Tiberio, with sticks in their sinewy hands for goading the donkeys. Soothed by the knowledge that the dead gentleman from San Francisco (who had been planning to go with them, but who had instead only succeeded in frightening them by reminding them of death) had already been dispatched to Naples, the travellers were sleeping soundly, and the island was still quiet, with the shops in the town still silent. The only market open was the little one in the square selling fish and vegetbales, and only the common folk were there; among them, idle as always, stood Lorenzo, a tall elderly boatman, an irresponsible rake and a handsome figure who was renowned throughout Italy, having served numerous painters as a model. He had brought along and already sold for a song two lobsters which he had caught during the night and which were rustling in the apron of the cook from the very hotel where the family from San Francisco had spent the night, and now he could stand there the whole day if he chose, looking about him with a royal air and striking poses in his rags, with his clay pipe and with a red woollen beret pulled down over one ear. And through the ravines of Monte Solaro two Abruzzian highlanders were descending from Anacapri down the stone steps of the ancient Phoenician road cut through the rocks. Under his leather cloak one of them held a bagpipe, a large goatskin with two stems while the other had a sort of ancient wooden flute. They walked along and the whole countryside, joyous, beautiful and sunny, spread out beneath them; they could see the stony humps of the island lying almost in its entirety at their feet and the fabulous blue expanse on which it floated, and the radiant morning haze over the sea to the east under a brilliant sun which was already burning fiercely as it rose higher and higher, and the massive, misty blue silhouette of Italy still shimmering in the morning light, and her mountains both close and distant, whose beauty no human words can describe. Halfway down the descent their steps slowed: above the road, in a grotto hewn out of the rock-face of Monte Solaro, an image of the Holy Virgin stood radiant in the warm brilliance of the sun, in her snow-white plaster robes and rusty royal golden crown, gentle and benevolent and with eyes uplifted towards the eternally blissful mansions of her thrice-blessed son. The highlanders bared their heads, their naive, humble and joyous praises streamed forth to the sun, to the morning, to her, the immaculate Protectress of all who suffer in this wicked and beautiful world, and to the child born of her womb in that Bethlehem stable, refuge of lowly shepherds in the far Judaean land. . . .

The body of the dead gentleman from San Francisco, however, was returning home to the shores of the New World, to its grave. After many degradations and much human neglect, after a week or so of being shunted from one harbourside warehouse to another, it at last found itself again on that same famous ship in which so recently and with such esteem he had been borne to the Old World. But now he was hidden from the living: in a tarred coffin he had been lowered into a black hold. And again, once again, the ship set off on its long voyage. It was night when it sailed past the island of Capri, and to those who were looking out from that shore its lights seemed sad as they gradually faded into the dark sea. But on board in the bright, chandelier-lit state-rooms there was, as usual, a crowded ball that night.

A ball was held the following night and again on the next one – again amid a furious blizzard, racing over an ocean which droned like a funeral mass and arrayed its mountainous waves in a mourning garb of silver foam. Through the snow the ship's numerous fiery eyes were barely visible to the Devil who, from the rocks of Gibraltar, that stony gateway between two worlds, was watching the ship receding into the night and the blizzard. The Devil was huge, like a cliff, but huge too was the ship, many-tiered and many-funnelled, created by the arrogance of Modern Man with his ancient heart. The blizzard hurled itself against the rigging and the wide-mouthed funnels which had turned white in the snow, but the ship was steadfast, firm, majestic and terrible. Towering up into the blizzard, high above the top deck, were those lonely, comfortable, dimly-lit quarters where the weighty captain, immersed in a sensitive and uneasy somnolence, sat in state over the whole ship, like a pagan idol. He could hear the storm stifling the low howls and the furious yelps of the ship's siren, but he took heart from the proximity of what for him was ultimately the most incomprehensible thing on board – that seemingly armoured cabin next to his own which was constantly full of the mysterious hum, tremor and dry crackle of blue sparks which flared up and exploded around the pale-faced telegraphist with the metal half-hoop on his head. At the bottom of the ship in the underwater depths of the *Atlantis* the massive steel bulk of the boilers and other machines glistened in the gloom, husky with steam and running with boiling water and grease, like an oven heated from below by infernal fireboxes to produce the ship's propulsion. Awesomely concentrated energy bubbled up, to be transmitted into the ship's keel through the infinitely long dungeon of a round dimly-lit tunnel, in which in its oily bed a gigantic shaft slowly revolved with soul-searing inexorability, like a living monster snaking its way through that muzzle-like tunnel. And in the heart of the *Atlantis*, in the dining-room and the ball-rooms, there was light and joy, the humming conversation of an elegantly attired throng, the fragrance of fresh flowers and the lilt of the string orchestra. And again amid this throng, amid the glitter of lights, silks, diamonds and bare female shoulders, the refined and supple pair of hired lovers executed their tense contortions and occasional convulsive collisions – the sinfully modest girl with lowered eyelashes and innocent coiffure and the strapping young man, pale with powder, with his black, almost glued-on hair, his elegant patent-leather shoes and his narrow, long-tailed coat, an Adonis with the appearance of a huge leech. And nobody knew that this pair had long ago grown tired of feigning their tense bliss to the brazenly melancholy music, nor what was lying deep, deep beneath them, at the bottom of a dark hold next to the gloomy, torrid bowels of the ship as it resolutely strove against the gloom, the ocean and the blizzard . . .

October 1915

ALBERT CAMUS

The Guest

The schoolmaster was watching the two men climb towards him. One was on horseback, the other on foot. They had not yet tackled the abrupt rise leading to the schoolhouse built on the hillside. They were toiling onwards, making slow progress in the snow, among the stones, on the vast expanse of the high, deserted plateau. From time to time the horse stumbled. Without hearing anything yet, he could see the breath issuing from the horse's nostrils. One of the men, at least, knew the region. They were following the trail although it had disappeared days ago under a layer of dirty white snow. The schoolmaster calculated that it would take them half an hour to get on to the hill. It was cold; he went back into the school to get a sweater.

He crossed the empty, frigid classroom. On the blackboard the four rivers of France, drawn with four different coloured chalks, had been flowing towards their estuaries for the past three days. Snow had suddenly fallen in mid-October after eight months of drought without the transition of rain, and the twenty pupils, more or less, who lived in the villages scattered over the plateau had stopped coming. With fair weather they would return. Daru now heated only the single room that was his lodging, adjoining the classroom and giving also on to the plateau to the east. Like the class windows, his window looked to the south too. On that side the school was a few kilometres from the point where the plateau began to slope towards the south. In clear weather could be seen the purple mass of the mountain range where the gap opened on to the desert.

Somewhat warmed, Daru returned to the window from which he had first seen the two men. They were no longer visible. Hence they must have tackled the rise. The sky was not so dark, for the snow had stopped falling during the night. The morning had opened with a dirty light which had scarcely become brighter as the ceiling of clouds lifted. At two in the afternoon it seemed as if the day were merely beginning. But still this was better than those three days when the thick snow was falling amidst unbroken darkness with little gusts of wind that rattled the double door of the classroom. Then Daru had spent long hours in his room, leaving it only to go to the shed and feed the chickens or get some coal. Fortunately the delivery truck from Tadjid, the nearest village to the north, had brought his supplies two days before the blizzard. It would return in forty-eight hours.

Besides, he had enough to resist a siege, for the little room was cluttered with bags of wheat that the administration left as a stock to distribute to those of his pupils whose families had suffered from the drought. Actually they had all been victims because they were all poor. Every day Daru would distribute a ration to the children. They had missed it, he knew, during these bad days. Possibly one of the fathers or big brothers would come this afternoon and he could supply them with grain. It was just a matter of carrying them over to the next harvest. Now shiploads of wheat were arriving from France and the worst was over. But it would be hard to forget that poverty, that army of ragged ghosts wandering in the sunlight, the plateaux burned to a cinder month after month, the earth shrivelled up little by little, literally scorched, every stone bursting into dust under one's foot. The sheep had died then by thousands and even a few men, here and there, sometimes without anyone's knowing.

In contrast with such poverty, he who lived almost like a monk in his remote schoolhouse, none the less satisfied with the little he had and with the rough life, had felt like a lord with his whitewashed walls, his narrow couch, his unpainted shelves, his well, and his weekly provision of water and food. And suddenly this snow, without warning, without the foretaste of rain. This is the way the region was, cruel to live in, even without men – who didn't help matters either. But Daru had been born here. Everywhere else, he felt exiled.

He stepped out on to the terrace in front of the schoolhouse. The two men were now half-way up the slope. He recognized the horseman as Balducci, the old gendarme he had known for a long time. Balducci was holding on the end of a rope an Arab who was walking behind him with hands bound and head lowered. The gendarme waved a greeting to which Daru did not reply, lost as he was in contemplation of the Arab dressed in a faded blue jellaba, his feet in sandals but covered with socks of heavy raw wool, his head surmounted by a narrow, short *chèche*. They were approaching. Balducci was holding back his horse in order not to hurt the Arab, and the group was advancing slowly.

Within earshot, Balducci shouted: 'One hour to do the three kilometres from El Ameur!' Daru did not answer. Short and square in his thick sweater, he watched them climb. Not once had the Arab raised his head. 'Hello,' said Daru when they got up on to the terrace. 'Come in and warm up.' Balducci painfully got down from his horse without letting go the rope. From under his bristling moustache he smiled at the schoolmaster. His little dark eyes, deep-set under a tanned forehead, and his mouth surrounded with wrinkles made him look attentive and studious. Daru took the bridle, led the horse to the shed, and came back to the two men, who were now waiting for him in the school. He led them into his room. 'I am going to heat up the classroom,' he said. 'We'll be more comfortable there.' When he entered the room again, Balducci was on the couch. He had undone the rope tying him to the Arab, who had squatted near the stove. His hands still bound, the *chèche* pushed back on his head, he was looking towards the window. At first Daru noticed only his huge lips, fat, smooth, almost negroid; yet his nose was straight, his eyes were dark and full of fever. The *chèche* revealed an obstinate forehead and, under the weathered skin now rather discoloured by the cold, the whole face had a restless and rebellious look that struck Daru when the Arab, turning his face towards him, looked him straight in the eyes.

'Go into the other room,' said the schoolmaster, 'and I'll make you some mint tea.' 'Thanks,' Balducci said. 'What a nuisance! How I long for retirement.' And addressing his prisoner in Arabic: 'Come on, you.' The Arab got up and, slowly, holding his bound wrists in front of him, went into the classroom.

With the tea, Daru brought a chair. But Balducci was already enthroned on the nearest pupil's desk and the Arab had squatted against the teacher's platform facing the stove, which stood between the desk and the window. When he held out the glass of tea to the prisoner, Daru hesitated at the sight of his bound hands. 'He might perhaps be untied.' 'Certainly,' said Balducci. 'That was for the journey.' He started to get to his feet. But Daru, setting the glass on the floor, had knelt beside the Arab. Without saying anything, the Arab watched him with his feverish eyes. Once his hands were free, he rubbed his swollen wrists against each other, took the glass of tea, and sucked up the burning liquid in swift little sips.

'Good,' said Daru. 'And where are you headed for?'

Balducci withdrew his moustache from the tea. 'Here, my boy.'

'Odd pupils! And you're spending the night?'

'No. I'm going back to El Ameur. And you will deliver this fellow to Tinguit. He is expected at police headquarters.'

Balducci was looking at Daru with a friendly little smile.

'What's this story?' asked the schoolmaster. 'Are you pulling my leg?'

'No, my boy. Those are the orders.'

'The orders? I'm not . . .' Daru hesitated, not wanting to hurt the old Corsican. 'I mean, that's not my job.'

'What! What's the meaning of that? In wartime people do all kinds of jobs.'

'Then I'll wait for the declaration of war!'

Balducci nodded.

'OK. But the orders exist and they concern you too. Things are brewing, it appears. There is talk of a forthcoming revolt. We are mobilized, in a way.'

Daru still had his obstinate look.

'Listen, my boy,' Balducci said. 'I like you and you must understand. There's only a dozen of us at El Ameur to patrol throughout the whole territory of a small department and I must get back in a hurry. I was told to hand this man over to you and return without delay. He couldn't be kept there. His village was beginning to stir; they wanted to take him back. You must take him to Tinguit tomorrow before the day is over. Twenty kilometres shouldn't worry a husky fellow like you. After that, all will be over. You'll come back to your pupils and your comfortable life.'

Behind the wall the horse could be heard snorting and pawing the earth. Daru was looking out of the window. Decidedly, the weather was clearing and the light was increasing over the snowy plateau. When all the snow was melted, the sun would take over again and once more would burn the fields of stone. For days, still, the unchanging sky would shed its dry light on the solitary expanse where nothing had any connexion with man.

'After all,' he said, turning around towards Balducci, 'what did he do?' And, before the gendarme had opened his mouth, he asked: 'Does he speak French?'

'No, not a word. We had been looking for him for a month, but they were hiding him. He killed his cousin.'

'Is he against us?'

'I don't think so. But you can never be sure.'

'Why did he kill?'

'A family squabble, I think. One owed the other grain, it seems. It's not at all clear. In short, he killed his cousin with a billhook. You know, like a sheep, *kreezk*!'

Balducci made the gesture of drawing a blade across his throat and the Arab, his attention attracted, watched him with a sort of anxiety. Daru felt a sudden wrath against the man, against all men with their rotten spite, their tireless hates, their blood lust.

But the kettle was singing on the stove. He served Balducci more tea, hesitated, then served the Arab again, who, a second time, drank avidly. His raised arms made the jellaba fall open and the schoolmaster saw his thin, muscular chest.

'Thanks, my boy,' Balducci said. 'And now, I'm off.'

He got up and went towards the Arab, taking a small rope from his pocket.

'What are you doing?' Daru asked dryly.

Balducci, disconcerted, showed him the rope.

'Don't bother.'

The old gendarme hesitated. 'It's up to you. Of course, you are armed?'

'I have my shot-gun.'

'Where?'

'In the trunk.'

'You ought to have it near your bed.'

'Why? I have nothing to fear.'

'You're mad. If there's an uprising, no one is safe, we're all in the same boat.'

'I'll defend myself. I'll have time to see them coming.'

Balducci began to laugh, then suddenly the moustache covered the white teeth.

'You'll have time? OK. That's just what I was saying. You have always been a little cracked. That's why I like you, my son was like that.'

At the same time he took out his revolver and put in on the desk.

'Keep it; I don't need two weapons from here to El Ameur.'

The revolver shone against the black paint of the table. When the gendarme turned towards him, the schoolmaster caught the smell of leather and horseflesh.

'Listen, Balducci,' Daru said suddenly, 'every bit of this disgusts me, and most of all your fellow here. But I won't hand him over. Fight, yes, if I have to. But not that.'

The old gendarme stood in front of him and looked at him severely.

'You're being a fool,' he said slowly. 'I don't like it either. You don't get used to putting a rope on a man even after years of it, and you're even ashamed – yes, ashamed. But you can't let them have their way.'

'I won't hand him over,' Daru said again.

'It's an order, my boy, and I repeat it.'

'That's right. Repeat to them what I've said to you: I won't hand him over.'

Balducci made a visible effort to reflect. He looked at the Arab and at Daru. At last he decided.

'No, I won't tell them anything. If you want to drop us, go ahead; I'll not denounce you. I have an order to deliver the prisoner and I'm doing so. And now you'll just sign this paper for me.'

'There's no need. I'll not deny that you left him with me.'

'Don't be mean with me. I know you'll tell the truth. You're from hereabouts and you are a man. But you must sign, that's the rule.'

Daru opened his drawer, took out a little square bottle of purple ink, the red wooden penholder with the 'sergeant-major' pen he used for making models of penmanship, and signed. The gendarme carefully folded the paper and put it into his wallet. Then he moved towards the door.

'I'll see you off,' Daru said.

'No,' said Balducci. 'There's no use being polite. You insulted me.'

He looked at the Arab, motionless in the same spot, sniffed peevishly, and turned away towards the door. 'Good-bye, son,' he said. The door shut behind him. Balducci appeared suddenly outside the window and then disappeared. His footsteps were muffled by the snow. The horse stirred on the other side of the wall and several chickens fluttered in fright. A moment later Balducci reappeared outside the window leading the horse by the bridle. He walked towards the little rise without turning round and disappeared from sight with the horse following him. A big stone could be heard bounding down. Daru walked back towards the prisoner, who, without stirring, never took his eyes off him. 'Wait,' the schoolmaster said in Arabic and went towards the bedroom. As he was going through the door, he had a second thought, went to the desk, took the revolver, and stuck it in his pocket. Then, without looking back, he went into his room.

For some time he lay on his couch watching the sky gradually close over, listening to the silence. It was this silence that had seemed painful to him during the first days here, after the war. He had requested a post in the little town at the base of the foothills separating the upper plateaux from the desert. There, rocky walls, green and black to the north, pink and lavender to the south, marked the frontier of eternal summer. He had been named to a post farther north, on the plateau itself. In the beginning, the solitude and the silence had been hard for him on these wastelands peopled only by stones. Occasionally, furrows suggested cultivation, but they had been dug to uncover a certain kind of stone good for building. The only ploughing here was to harvest rocks. Elsewhere a thin layer of soil accumulated in the hollows would be scraped out to enrich paltry village gardens. This is the way it was: bare rock covered three-quarters of the region. Towns sprang up, flourished, then disappeared; men came by, loved one another or fought bitterly, then died. No one in this desert, neither he nor his guest, mattered. And yet, outside this desert neither of them, Daru knew, could have really lived.

When he got up, no noise came from the classroom. He was amazed at the unmixed joy he derived from the mere thought that the Arab might have fled and that he would be alone with no decision to make. But the prisoner was there. He had merely stretched out between the stove and the desk. With eyes open, he was staring at the ceiling. In that position, his thick lips were particularly noticeable, giving him a pouting look. 'Come,' said Daru. The Arab got up and followed him. In the bedroom, the schoolmaster pointed to a chair near the table under the window. The Arab sat down without taking his eyes off Daru.

'Are you hungry?'

'Yes,' the prisoner said.

Daru set the table for two. He took flour and oil, shaped a cake in a frying-pan, and lighted the little stove that functioned on bottled gas. While the cake was cooking, he went out to the shed to get cheese, eggs, dates, and condensed milk. When the cake was done he set it on the window-sill to cool, heated some condensed milk diluted with water, and beat up the eggs into an omelet. In one of his motions he knocked against the revolver stuck in his right pocket. He set the bowl down, went into the classroom, and put the revolver in his desk drawer. When he came back to the room, night was falling. He put on the light and served the Arab. 'Eat,' he said. The Arab took a piece of the cake, lifted it eagerly to his mouth, and stopped short.

'And you?' he asked.

'After you. I'll eat too.'

The thick lips opened slightly. The Arab hesitated, then bit into the cake determinedly.

The meal over, the Arab looked at the schoolmaster. 'Are you the judge?'

'No, I'm simply keeping you until tomorrow.'

'Why do you eat with me?'

'I'm hungry.'

The Arab fell silent. Daru got up and went out. He brought back a folding bed from the shed, set it up between the table and the stove, at right angles to his own bed. From a large suitcase which, upright in a corner, served as a shelf for papers, he took two blankets and arranged them on the camp-bed. Then he stopped, felt useless, and sat down on his bed. There was nothing more to do or to get ready. He had to look at this man. He looked at him, therefore, trying to imagine his face bursting with rage. He couldn't do so. He could see nothing but the dark yet shining eyes and the animal mouth.

'Why did you kill him?' he asked in a voice whose hostile tone surprised him.

The Arab looked away.

'He ran away. I ran after him.'

He raised his eyes to Daru again and they were full of a sort of woeful interrogation. 'Now what will they do to me?'

'Are you afraid?'

He stiffened, turning his eyes away.

'Are you sorry?'

The Arab stared at him open-mouthed. Obviously he did not understand. Daru's annoyance was growing. At the same time he felt awkward and self-conscious with his big body wedged between the two beds.

'Lie down there,' he said impatiently. 'That's your bed.'

The Arab didn't move. He called to Daru:

'Tell me!'

The schoolmaster looked at him.

'Is the gendarme coming back tomorrow?'

'I don't know.'

'Are you coming with us?''

'I don't know. Why?'

The prisoner got up and stretched out on top of the blankets, his feet towards the window. The light from the electric bulb shone straight into his eyes and he closed them at once.

'Why?' Daru repeated, standing beside the bed.

The Arab opened his eyes under the blinding light and looked at him, trying not to blink.

'Come with us,' he said.

In the middle of the night, Daru was still not asleep. He had gone to bed after undressing completely; he generally slept naked. But when he suddenly realized that he had nothing on, he hesitated. He felt vulnerable and the temptation came to him to put on his clothes again. Then he shrugged his shoulders; after all, he wasn't a child and, if need be, he could break his adversary in two. From his bed he could observe him, lying on his back, still motionless with his eyes closed under the harsh light. When Daru turned out the light, the darkness seemed to coagulate all of a sudden. Little by little, the night came back to life in the window where the starless sky was stirring gently. The schoolmaster soon made out the body lying at his feet. The Arab still did not move, but his eyes seemed open. A faint wind was prowling around the schoolhouse. Perhaps it would drive away the clouds and the sun would reappear.

During the night the wind increased. The hens fluttered a little and then were silent. The Arab turned over on his side with his back to Daru, who thought he heard him moan. Then he listened for his guest's breathing, become heavier and more regular. He listened to that breath so close to him and mused without being able to go to sleep. In this room where he had been sleeping alone for a year, this presence bothered him. But it bothered him also by imposing on him a sort of brotherhood he knew well but refused to accept in the present circumstances. Men who share the same rooms, soldiers or prisoners, develop a strange alliance as if, having cast off their armour with their clothing, they fraternized every evening, over and above their differences, in the ancient community of dream and fatigue. But Daru shook himself; he didn't like such musings, and it was essential to sleep.

A little later, however, when the Arab stirred slightly, the schoolmaster was still not asleep. When the prisoner made a second move, he stiffened, on the alert. The Arab was lifting himself slowly on his arms with almost the motion of a sleepwalker. Seated upright in bed, he waited motionless without turning his head towards Daru, as if he were listening attentively. Daru did not stir; it had just occurred to him that the revolver was still in the drawer of his desk. It was better to act at once. Yet he continued to observe the prisoner, who, with the same slithery motion, put his feet on the ground, waited again, then began to stand up slowly. Daru was about to call out to him when the Arab began to walk, in a quite natural but extraordinarily silent way. He was heading towards the door at the end of the room that opened into the shed. He lifted the latch with precaution and went out, pushing the door behind him but without shutting it. Daru had not stirred. 'He is running away,' he merely thought. 'Good riddance!' Yet he listened attentively. The hens were not fluttering, the guest must be on the plateau. A faint sound of water reached him, and he didn't know what it was until the Arab again stood framed in the doorway, closed the door carefully, and came back to bed without a sound. Then Daru turned his back on him and fell asleep. Still later he seemed, from the depths of his sleep, to hear furtive steps around the schoolhouse. 'I'm dreaming!' he repeated to himself. And he went on sleeping.

When he awoke, the sky was clear, the loose window let in a cold, pure air. The Arab was asleep, hunched up under the blankets now, his mouth open, utterly relaxed. But when Daru shook him, he started dreadfully, staring at Daru with wild eyes as if he had never seen him and such a frightened expression that the schoolmaster stepped back. 'Don't be afraid. It's me. You must eat.' The Arab nodded his head and said yes. Calm had returned to his face, but his expression was vacant and listless.

The coffee was ready. They drank it seated together on the folding bed as they munched their pieces of the cake. Then Daru led the Arab under the shed and showed him the tap where he washed. He went back into the room, folded the blankets and the bed, made his own bed and put the room in order. Then he went through the classroom and out on to the terrace. The sun was already rising in the blue sky; a soft, bright light was bathing the deserted plateau. On the ridge the snow was melting in spots. The stones were about to reappear. Crouched on the edge of the plateau, the schoolmaster looked at the deserted expanse. He thought of Balducci. He had hurt him, for he had sent him off in a way as if he didn't want to be associated with him. He could still hear the gendarme's farewell and, without knowing why, he felt strangely empty and vulnerable. At that moment, from the other side of the schoolhouse, the prisoner coughed. Daru listened to him almost despite himself and then, furious, threw a pebble that whistled through the air before sinking into the snow. That man's stupid crime revolted him, but to hand him over was contrary to honour. Merely thinking of it made him smart with humiliation. And he cursed at one and the same time his own people who had sent him this Arab and the Arab too who had dared to kill and not managed to get away. Daru got up, walked in a circle on the terrace, waited motionless, and then went back into the schoolhouse.

The Arab, leaning over the cement floor of the shed, was washing his teeth with two fingers. Daru looked at him and said: 'Come.' He went back into the room ahead of the prisoner. He slipped a hunting-jacket on over his sweater and put on walking-shoes. Standing, he waited until the Arab had put on his *chèche* and sandals. They went into the classroom and the schoolmaster pointed to the exit, saying: 'Go ahead.' The fellow didn't budge. 'I'm coming,' said Daru. The Arab went out. Daru went back into the room and made a package of pieces of rusk, dates, and sugar. In the classroom, before going out, he hesitated a second in front of his desk, then crossed the threshold and locked the door. 'That's the way,' he said. He started towards the east, followed by the prisoner. But, a short distance from the schoolhouse, he thought he heard a slight sound behind them. He retraced his steps and examined the surroundings of the house; there was no one there. The Arab watched him without seeming to understand. 'Come on,' said Daru.

They walked for an hour and rested beside a sharp peak of limestone. The snow was melting faster and faster and the sun was drinking up the puddles at once, rapidly cleaning the plateau, which gradually dried and vibrated like the air itself. When they resumed walking, the ground rang under their feet. From time to time a bird rent the space in front of them with a joyful cry. Daru breathed in deeply the fresh morning light. He felt a sort of rapture before the vast familiar expanse, now almost entirely yellow under its dome of blue sky. They walked an hour more, descending towards the south. They reached a level height made up of crumbly rocks. From there on, the plateau sloped down, eastward, towards a low plain where there were a few spindly trees and, to the south, towards outcroppings of rock that gave the landscape a chaotic look.

Daru surveyed the two directions. There was nothing but the sky on the horizon. Not a man could be seen. He turned towards the Arab, who was looking at him blankly. Daru held out the package to him. 'Take it,' he said. 'There are dates, bread, and sugar. You can hold out for two days. Here are a thousand francs too.' The Arab took the package and the money but kept his full hands at chest level as if he didn't know what to do with what was being given him. 'Now look,' the schoolmaster said as he pointed in the direction of the east, 'there's the way to Tinguit. You have a two-hour walk. At Tinguit you'll find the administration and the police. They are expecting you.' The Arab looked towards the east, still holding the package and the money against his chest. Daru took his elbow and turned him rather roughly towards the south. At the foot of the height on which they stood could be seen a faint path. 'That's the trail across the plateau. In a day's walk from here you'll find pasture lands and the first nomads. They'll take you in and shelter you according to their law.'

The Arab had now turned towards Daru and a sort of panic was visible in his expression. 'Listen,' he said. Daru shook his head: 'No, be quiet. Now I'm leaving you.' He turned his back on him, took two long steps in the direction of the school, looked hesitantly at the motionless Arab, and started off again. For a few minutes he heard nothing but his own step resounding on the cold ground and did not turn his head. A moment later, however, he turned around. The Arab was still there on the edge of the hill, his arms hanging now, and he was looking at the schoolmaster. Daru felt something rise in his throat. But he swore with impatience, waved vaguely, and started off again. He had already gone some distance when he again stopped and looked. There was no longer anyone on the hill.

Daru hesitated. The sun was now rather high in the sky and was beginning to beat down on his head. The schoolmaster retraced his steps, at first somewhat uncertainly, then with decision. When he reached the little hill, he was bathed in sweat. He climbed it as fast as he could and stopped, out of breath, at the top. The rock-fields to the south stood out sharply against the blue sky, but on the plain to the east a steamy heat was already rising. And in that slight haze, Daru, with heavy heart, made out the Arab walking slowly on the road to prison.

A little later, standing before the window of the classroom, the schoolmaster was watching the clear light bathing the whole surface of the plateau, but he hardly saw it. Behind him on the blackboard, among the winding French rivers, sprawled the clumsily chalked-up words he had just read: 'You handed over our brother. You will pay for this.' Daru looked at the sky, the plateau, and, beyond, the invisible lands stretching all the way to the sea. In this vast landscape he had loved so much, he was alone.

T. S. ELIOT

Macavity: The Mystery Cat

Macavity's a Mystery Cat: he's called the Hidden Paw –
For he's the master criminal who can defy the Law.
He's the bafflement of Scotland Yard, the Flying Squad's despair:
For when they reach the scene of crime – *Macavity's not there!*

Macavity, Macavity, there's no one like Macavity,
He's broken every human law, he breaks the law of gravity.
His powers of levitation would make a fakir stare,
And when you reach the scene of crime – *Macavity's not there!*
You may seek him in the basement, you may look up in the air –
But I tell you once and once again, *Macavity's not there!*

Macavity's a ginger cat, he's very tall and thin;
You would know him if you saw him, for his eyes are sunken in.
His brow is deeply lined with thought, his head is highly domed;
His coat is dusty from neglect, his whiskers are uncombed.
He sways his head from side to side, with movements like a snake;
And when you think he's half asleep, he's always wide awake.

Macavity, Macavity, there's no one like Macavity,
For he's a fiend in feline shape, a monster of depravity.
You may meet him in a by-street, you may see him in the square –
But when a crime's discovered, then *Macavity's not there!*

He's outwardly respectable. (They say he cheats at cards.)
And his footprints are not found in any file of Scotland Yard's.
And when the larder's looted, or the jewel-case is rifled,
Or when the milk is missing, or another Peke's been stifled,
Or the greenhouse glass is broken, and the trellis past repair –
Ay, there's the wonder of the thing! *Macavity's not there!*

And when the Foreign Office find a Treaty's gone astray,
Or the Admiralty lose some plans and drawings by the way,
There may be a scrap of paper in the hall or on the stair –
But it's useless to investigate – Macavity's not there!
And when the loss has been disclosed, the Secret Service say:
'It *must* have been Macavity!' – but he's a mile away.
You'll be sure to find him resting, or a-licking of his thumbs,
Or engaged in doing complicated long division sums.

Macavity, Macavity, there's no one like Macavity,
There never was a Cat of such deceitfulness and suavity.
He always has an alibi, and one or two to spare:
At whatever time the deed took place – *MACAVITY WASN'T THERE!*
And they say that all the Cats whose wicked deeds are widely known,
(I might mention Mungojerrie, I might mention Griddlebone)
Are nothing more than agents for the Cat who all the time
Just controls their operations: the Napoleon of Crime!

WILLIAM FAULKNER

Smoke

Anselm Holland came to Jefferson many years ago. Where from, no one knew. But he was young then and a man of parts, or of presence at least, because within three years he had married the only daughter of a man who owned two thousand acres of some of the best land in the county, and he went to live in his father-in-law's house, where two years later his wife bore him twin sons and where a few years later still the father-in-law died and left Holland in full possession of the property, which was now in his wife's name. But even before that event, we in Jefferson had already listened to him talking a trifle more than loudly of 'my land, my crops'; and those of us whose fathers and grandfathers had been bred here looked upon him a little coldly and a little askance for a ruthless man and (from tales told about him by both white and Negro tenants and by others with whom he had dealings) for a violent one. But out of consideration for his wife and respect for his father-in-law, we treated him with courtesy if not with regard. So when his wife, too, died while the twin sons were still children, we believed that he was responsible, that her life had been worn out by the crass violence of an underbred outlander. And when one day six months ago he was found dead, his foot fast in the stirrup of the saddled horse which he rode, and his body pretty badly broken where the horse had apparently dragged him through a rail fence (there still showed at the time on the horse's back and flanks the marks of the blows which he had dealt it in one of his fits of rage), there was none of us who was sorry, because a short time before that he had committed what to men of our town and time and thinking was the unpardonable outrage. On the day he died it was learned that he had been digging up the graves in the family cemetery where his wife's people rested, among them the grave in which his wife had lain for thirty years. So the crazed, hate-ridden old man was buried among the graves which he had attempted to violate, and in the proper time his will was offered for probate. And we learned the substance of the will without surprise. We were not surprised to learn that even from beyond the grave he had struck one final blow at those alone whom he could now injure or outrage: his remaining flesh and blood.

At the time of their father's death the twin sons were forty. The younger one, Anselm, Junior, was said to have been the mother's favourite – perhaps because he was the one who was most like his father. Anyway, from the time of her death, while the boys were still children almost, we would hear of trouble between Old Anse and Young Anse, with Virginius, the other twin, acting as mediator and being cursed for his pains by both father and brother; he was that sort, Virginius was. And Young Anse was his sort too; in his late teens he ran away from home and was gone ten years. When he returned he and his brother were of age, and Anselm made formal demand upon his father that the land which we now learned was held by Old Anse only in trust, be divided and he – Young Anse – be given his share. Old Anse refused violently. Doubtless the request had been as violently made, because the two of them, Old Anse and Young Anse, were so much alike. And we heard that, strange to say, Virginius had taken his father's side. We heard that, that is. Because the land remained intact, and we heard how, in the midst of a scene of unparalleled violence even for them – a scene of such violence that the Negro servants all fled the house and scattered for the night – Young Anse departed, taking with him the team of mules which he did own; and from that day until his father's death, even after Virginius also had been forced to leave home, Anselm never spoke to his father and brother again. He did not leave the county this time, however. He just moved back into the hills ('where he can watch what the old man and Virginius are doing,' some of us said and all of us thought); and for the next fifteen years he lived alone in a dirt-floored, two-room cabin, like a hermit, doing his own cooking, coming into town behind his two mules not four times a year. Some time earlier he had been arrested and tried for making whiskey. He made no defense, refusing to plead either way, was fined both on the charge and for contempt of court, and flew into a rage exactly like his father when his brother Virginius offered to pay the fine. He tried to assault Virginius in the courtroom and went to the penitentiary at his own demand and was pardoned eight months later for good behaviour and returned to his cabin – a dark, silent, aquiline-faced man whom both neighbours and strangers left severely alone.

The other twin, Virginius, stayed on, farming the land which his father had never done justice to even while he was alive. (They said of Old Anse, 'Wherever he came from and whatever he was bred to be, it was not a farmer.' And so we said among ourselves, taking it to be true, 'That's the trouble between him and Young Anse: watching his father mistreat the land which his mother aimed for him and Virginius to have.') But Virginius stayed on. It could not have been much fun for him, and we said later that Virginius should have known that such an arrangement could not last. And then later than that we said 'Maybe he did know.' Because that was Virginius. You didn't know what he was thinking at the time, any time. Old Anse and Young Anse were like water. Dark water, maybe; but men could see what they were about. But no man ever knew what Virginius was thinking or doing until afterward. We didn't even know what happened that time when Virginius, who had stuck it out alone for ten years while Young Anse was away, was driven away at last; he didn't tell it, not even to Granby Dodge, probably. But we knew Old Anse and we knew Virginius, and we could imagine it, about like this:

We watched Old Anse smouldering for about a year after Young Anse took his mules and went back into the hills. Then one day be broke out; maybe like this, 'You think that, now your brother is gone, you can just hang around and get it all, don't you?'

'I don't want it all,' Virginius said. 'I just want my share.'

'Ah,' Old Anse said. 'You'd like to have it parcelled out right now too, would you? Claim like him it should have been divided up when you and him came of age.'

'I'd rather take a little of it and farm it right than to see it all in the shape it's in now,' Virginius said, still just, still mild – no man in the county ever saw Virginius lose his temper or even get ruffled, not even when Anselm tried to fight him in the courtroom about that fine.

'You would, would you?' Old Anse said. 'And me that's kept it working at all, paying the taxes on it, while you and your brother have been putting money by every year, tax-free.'

'You know Anse never saved a nickel in his life,' Virginius said. 'Say what you want to about him, but don't accuse him of being forehanded.'

'Yes, by heaven! He was man enough to come out and claim what he thought was his and get out when he never got it. But you. You'll just hang around, waiting for me to go, with that damned meal mouth of yours. Pay me the taxes on your half back to the day your mother died, and take it.'

'No,' Virginius said. 'I won't do it.'

'No,' Old Anse said. 'No. Oh, no. Why spend your money for half of it when you can set down and get all of it some day without putting out a cent.' Then we imagined Old Anse (we thought of them as sitting down until now, talking like two civilized men) rising, with his shaggy head and his heavy eyebrows. 'Get out of my house!' he said. But Virginius didn't move, didn't get up, watching his father. Old Anse came toward him, his hand raised. 'Get. Get out of my house. By heaven, I'll . . .'

Virginius went, then. He didn't hurry, didn't run. He packed up his belongings (he would have more than Anse; quite a few little things) and went four or five miles to live with a cousin, the son of a remote kinsman of his mother. The cousin lived alone, on a good farm too, though now eaten up with mortgages, since the cousin was no farmer either, being half a stock-trader and half a lay preacher – a small, sandy, nondescript man whom you would not remember a minute after you looked at his face and then away – and probably no better at either of these than at farming. Without haste Virginius left, with none of his brother's foolish and violent finality; for which, strange to say, we thought none the less of Young Anse for showing, possessing. In fact, we always looked at Virginius a little askance too; he was a little too much master of himself. For it is human nature to trust quickest those who cannot depend on themselves. We called Virginius a deep one; we were not surprised when we learned how Old Anse had refused to pay the taxes on his land and how, two days before the place would have gone delinquent, the sheriff received anonymously in the mail cash to the exact penny of the Holland assessment. 'Trust Virginius,' we said, since we believed we knew that the money needed no name to it. The sheriff had notified Old Anse.

'Put it up for sale and be damned,' Old Anse said. 'If they think that all they have to do is sit there waiting, the whole brood and biling of them. . .'

The sheriff sent Young Anse word. 'It's not my land,' Young Anse sent back.

The sheriff notified Virginius. Virginius came to town and looked at the tax books himself. 'I got all I can carry myself, now,' he said. 'Of course, if he lets it go, I hope I can get it. But I don't know. A good farm like that won't last long or go cheap.' And that was all. No anger, no astonishment, no regret. But he was a deep one; we were not surprised when we learned how the sheriff had received that package of money, with the unsigned note: *Tax money for Anselm Holland farm. Send receipt to Anselm Holland Senior.* 'Trust Virginius,' we said. We thought about Virginius quite a lot during the next year, out there in a strange house, farming strange land, watching the farm and the house where he was born and that was rightfully his going to ruin. For the old man was letting it go completely now: year by year the good broad fields were going back to jungle and gully, though still each January the sheriff received that anonymous money in the mail and sent the receipt to Old Anse, because the old man had stopped coming to town altogether now, and the very house was falling down about his head, and nobody save Virginius ever stopped there. Five or six times a year he would ride up to the front porch, and the old man would come out and bellow at him in savage and violent vituperation, Virginius taking it quietly, talking to the few remaining Negroes once he had seen with his own eyes that his father was all right, then riding away again. But nobody else ever stopped there, though now and then from a distance someone would see the old man going about the mournful and shaggy fields on the old white horse which was to kill him.

Then last summer we learned that he was digging up the graves in the cedar grove where five generations of his wife's people rested. A Negro reported it, and the county health officer went out there and found the white horse tied in the grove, and the old man himself came out of the grove with a shotgun. The health officer returned, and two days later a deputy went out there and found the old man lying beside the horse, his foot fast in the stirrup, and on the horse's rump the savage marks of the stick – not a switch: a stick – where it had been struck again and again and again.

So they buried him, among the graves which he had violated. Virginius and the cousin came to the funeral. They were the funeral, in fact. For Anse, Junior, didn't come. Nor did he come near the place later, though Virginius stayed long enough to lock the house and pay the Negroes off. But he too went back to the cousin's and in due time Old Anse's will was offered for probate to Judge Dukinfield. The substance of the will was no secret; we all learned of it. Regular it was, and we were surprised neither at its regularity nor at its substance nor its wording: . . . *with the exception of these two bequests, I give and bequeath . . . my property to my elder son Virginius, provided it be proved to the satisfaction of the . . . Chancellor that it was the said Virginius who has been paying the taxes on my land, the . . . Chancellor to be the sole and unchallenged judge of the proof.*

The two other bequests were:

To my younger son Anselm, I give . . . two full sets of mule harness, with the condition that this . . . harness be used by . . . Anselm to make one visit to my grave. Otherwise this . . . harness to become and remain part . . . of my property as described above.

To my cousin-in-law Granby Dodge I give . . . one dollar in cash, to be used by him for the purchase of a hymn book or hymn books, as a token of my gratitude for his having fed and lodged my son Virginius since . . . Virginius quitted my roof.

That was the will. And we watched and listened to hear or see what young Anse would say or do. And we heard and saw nothing. And we watched to see what Virginius would do. And he did nothing. Or we didn't know what he was doing, what he was thinking. But that was Virginius. Because it was all finished then, anyway. All he had to do was to wait until Judge Dukinfield validated the will, then Virginius could give Anse his half – if he intended to do this. We were divided there. 'He and Anse never had any trouble.' some said. 'If you go by that token, he will have to divide that farm with the whole county.' 'But it was Virginius that tried to pay Anse's fine that time,' the first ones said. 'And it was Virginius that sided with his father when Young Anse wanted to divide the land, too,' the second ones said.

So we waited and we watched. We were watching Judge Dukinfield now; it was suddenly as if the whole thing had sifted into his hands; as though he sat godlike above the vindictive and jeering laughter of that old man who even underground would not die, and above these two irreconcilable brothers who for fifteen years had been the same as dead to each other. But we thought that in his last coup, Old Anse had overreached himself; that in choosing Judge Dukinfield, the old man's own fury had checkmated him; because in Judge Dukinfield we believed that Old Anse had chosen the one man among us with sufficient probity and honour and good sense – that sort of probity and honour which has never had time to become confused and self-doubting with too much learning in the law. The very fact that the validating of what was a simple enough document appeared to be taking him an overlong time, was to us but fresh proof that Judge Dukinfield was the one man among us who believed that justice is half legal knowledge and half unhaste and confidence in himself and in God.

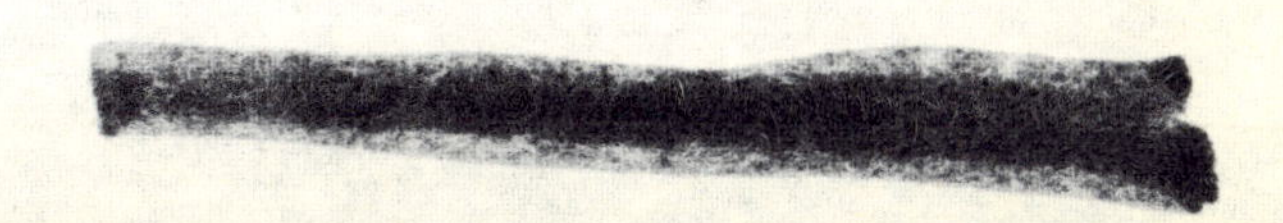

So as the expiration of the legal period drew near, we watched Judge Dukinfield as he went daily between his home and his office in the courthouse yard. Deliberate and unhurried he moved – a widower of sixty and more, portly, white-headed, with an erect and dignified carriage which the Negroes called 'rearbackted.' He had been appointed Chancellor seventeen years ago; he possessed little knowledge of the law and a great deal of hard common sense; and for thirteen years now no man had opposed him for re-election, and even those who would be most enraged by his air of bland and affable condescension voted for him on occasion with a kind of childlike confidence and trust. So we watched him without impatience, knowing that what he finally did would be right, not because he did it, but because he would not permit himself or anyone else to do anything until it was right. So each morning we would see him cross the square at exactly ten minutes past eight o'clock and go on to the courthouse, where the Negro janitor had preceded him by exactly ten minutes, with the clocklike precision with which the block signal presages the arrival of the train, to open the office for the day. The Judge would enter the office, and the Negro would take his position in a wire-mended splint chair in the flagged passage which separated the office from the courthouse proper, where he would sit all day long and doze, as he had done for seventeen years. Then at five in the afternoon the Negro would wake and enter the office and perhaps wake the Judge too, who had lived long enough to have learned that the onus of any business is usually in the hasty minds of those theoreticians who have no business of their own; and then we would watch them cross the square again in single file and go on up the street toward home, the two of them, eyes front and about fifteen feet apart, walking so erect that the two frock coats made by the same tailor and to the Judge's measure fell from the two pairs of shoulders in single boardlike planes, without intimation of waist or of hips.

Then one afternoon, a little after five o'clock, men began to run suddenly across the square, toward the courthouse. Other men saw them and ran too, their feet heavy on the

paving, among the wagons and the cars, their voices tense, urgent, 'What? What is it?' 'Judge Dukinfield,' the word went; and they ran on and entered the flagged passage between the courthouse and the office, where the old Negro in his cast-off frock coat stood beating his hands on the air. They passed him and ran into the office. Behind the table the judge sat, leaning a little back in his chair, quite comfortable. His eyes were open and he had been shot neatly once through the bridge of the nose, so that he appeared to have three eyes in a row. It was a bullet, yet no man about the square that day, or the old Negro who had sat all day long in the chair in the passage, had heard any sound.

It took Gavin Stevens a long time, that day – he and the little brass box. Because the Grand Jury could not tell at first what he was getting at – if any man in that room that day, the jury, the two brothers, the cousin, the old Negro, could tell. So at last the Foreman asked him point blank:

'Is it your contention, Gavin, that there is a connection between Mr. Holland's will and Judge Dukinfield's murder?'

'Yes,' the county attorney said. 'And I'm going to contend more than that.'

They watched him: the jury, the two brothers. The old Negro and the cousin alone were not looking at him. In the last week the Negro had apparently aged fifty years. He had assumed public office concurrently with the Judge; indeed, because of the fact, since he had served the Judge's family for longer than some of us could remember. He was older than the Judge though until that afternoon a week ago he had looked forty years younger – a wizened figure, shapeless in the voluminous frock coat, who reached the office ten minutes ahead of the Judge and opened it and swept it and dusted the table without disturbing an object upon it, all with a skillful slovenliness that was fruit of seventeen years of practice, and then repaired to the wire-bound chair in the passage to sleep. He seemed to sleep, that is. (The only other way to reach the office was by means of the narrow private stair which led down from the courtoom, used only by the presiding judge during court term, who even then had to cross the passage and pass within eight feet of the Negro's chair unless he followed the passage to where it made an L beneath the single window in the office, and climbed through that window.) For no man or woman had ever passed that chair without seeing the wrinkled eyelids of its occupant open instantaneously upon the brown, irisless eyes of extreme age. Now and then we would stop and talk to him, to hear his voice roll in rich mispronunciation of the orotund and meaningless legal phraseology which he had picked up unawares, as he might have disease germs, and which he reproduced with an ex-cathedra profundity that caused more than one of us to listen to the Judge himself with affectionate amusement. But for all that he was old; he forgot our names at times and confused us with one another; and, confusing our faces and our generations too, he waked sometimes from his light slumber to challenge callers who were not there, who had been dead for many years. But no one had ever been known to pass him unawares.

But the others in the room watched Stevens – the jury about the table, the two brothers sitting at opposite ends of the bench, with their dark, identical aquiline faces, their arms folded in identical attitudes. 'Are you contending that Judge Dukinfield's slayer is in this room?' the Foreman asked.

The county attorney looked at them, at the faces watching him. 'I'm going to contend more than that,' he said.

'Contend?' Anselm, the younger twin, said. He sat alone at his end of the bench, with the whole span of bench between him and the brother to whom he had not spoken in fifteen years, watching Stevens with a hard furious, unwinking glare.

'Yes.' Stevens said. He stood at the end of the table. He began to speak, looking at no one in particular, speaking in an easy, anecdotal tone, telling what we already knew, referring now and then to the other twin, Virginius, for corroboration. He told about Young Anse and his father. His tone was fair, pleasant. He seemed to be making a case for the living, telling about how Young Anse left home in anger, in natural anger at the manner in which his father was treating that land which had been his mother's and half of which was at the time rightfully his. His tone was quite just, specious, frank; if anything, a little partial to Anselm, Junior. That was it. Because of that seeming partiality, that seeming glozing, there began to emerge a picture of Young Anse that was damning him to something which we did not then know, damned him because of that very desire for justice and affection for his dead mother, warped by the violence which he had inherited from the very man who had wronged him. And the two brothers sitting there, with that space of friction-smooth plank between them, the younger watching Stevens with that leashed, violent glare, the elder as intently, but with a face unfathomable. Stevens now told how Young Anse left in anger, and how a year later Virginius, the quieter one, the calmer one, who had tried more than once to keep peace between them, was driven away in turn. And again he drew a specious, frank picture: of the brothers separated, not by the living father, but by what each had inherited from him; and drawn together, bred together, by that land which was not only rightfully theirs, but in which their mother's bones lay.

'So there they were, watching from a distance that good land going to ruin, the house in which they were born and their mother was born falling to pieces because of a crazed old man who attempted at the last, when he had driven them away and couldn't do anything else to them, to deprive them of it for good and all by letting it be sold for nonpayment of taxes. But somebody foiled him there, someone with foresight enough and self-control enough to keep his own counsel about what wasn't anybody else's business anyway so long as the taxes were paid. So then all they had to do was to wait until the old man died. He was old anyway and, even if he had been young, the waiting would not have been very hard for a self-controlled man, even if he did not know the contents of the old man's will. Though that waiting wouldn't have been so easy for a quick, violent man, especially if the violent man happened to know or suspect the substance of the will and was satisfied and, further, knew himself to have been irrevocably wronged; to have had citizenship and good name robbed through the agency of a man who had already despoiled him and had driven him out of the best years of his life among men, to live like a hermit in a hill cabin. A man like that would have neither the time nor the inclination to bother much with either waiting for something or not waiting for it.'

They stared at him, the two brothers. They might have been carved in stone, save for Anselm's eyes. Stevens talked quietly, not looking at anyone in particular. He had been county attorney for almost as long as Judge Dukinfield had been Chancellor. He was a Harvard graduate: a loose-jointed man with a mop of untidy iron-gray hair, who could discuss Einstein with college professors and who spent whole afternoons among the squatting men against the walls of country stores, talking to them in their idiom. He called these his vacations.

'Then in time the father died, as any man who possessed self-control and foresight would have known. And his will was submitted for probate; and even folks way back in the hills heard what was in it, heard how at last that mistreated land would belong to its rightful owner. Or owners, since Anse Holland knows as well as we do that Virge would no more take more than his rightful half, will or no will, now than he would have when his father gave him the chance. Anse knows that because he knows that he would do the same thing – give Virge his half – if he were Virge. Because they were both born to Anselm Holland, but they were born to Cornelia Mardis too. But even if Anse didn't know, believe, that, he would know that the land which had been his mother's and in which her bones now lie would now be treated right. So maybe that night when he heard that his father was dead, maybe for the first time since Anse was a child, since before his mother died maybe and she would come upstairs at night and look into the room where he was asleep and go away; maybe for the first time since then, Anse slept. Because it was all vindicated then, you see: the outrage, the injustice, the lost good name, and the penitentiary stain – all gone now like a dream. To be forgotten now, because it was all right. By that time, you see, he had got used to being a hermit, to being alone; he could not have changed after that long. He was happier where he was, alone back there. And now to know that it was all past like a bad dream, and that the land, his mother's land, her heritage and her mausoleum, was now in the hands of the one man whom he could and would trust, even though they did not speak to each other. Don't you see?'

We watched him as we sat about the table which had not been disturbed since the day Judge Dukinfield died, upon which lay still the objects which had been, next to the pistol muzzle, his last sight on earth, and with which we were all familiar for years – the papers, the foul inkwell, the stubby pen to which the Judge clung, the small brass box which had been his superfluous paper weight. At their opposite ends of the wooden bench, the twin brothers watched Stevens, motionless, intent.

'No, we don't see,' the Foreman said. 'What are you getting at? What is the connection between all this and Judge Dukinfield's murder?'

'Here it is,' Stevens said. 'Judge Dukinfield was validating that will when he was killed. It was a queer will; but we all expected that of Mr. Holland. But it was all regular, the beneficiaries are all satisfied; we all know that half of that land is Anse's the minute he wants it. So the will is all right. Its probation should have been just a formality. Yet Judge Dukinfield had had it in abeyance for over two weeks when he died. And so that man who thought that all he had to do was to wait – '

'What man?' the Foreman said.

'Wait,' Stevens said. 'All that man had to do was to wait. But it wasn't the waiting that worried him, who had already waited fifteen years. That wasn't it. It was something else, which he learned (or remembered) when it was too late, which he should not have forgotten; because he is a shrewd man, a man of self-control and foresight; self-control enough to wait fifteen years for his chance, and foresight enough to have prepared for all the incalculables except one: his own memory. And when it was too late, he remembered that there was another man who would also know what he had forgotten about. And that other man who would know it was Judge Dukinfield. And that thing which he would also know was that that horse could not have killed Mr. Holland.'

When his voice ceased there was no sound in the room. The jury sat quietly about the table, looking at Stevens. Anselm turned his leashed, furious face and looked once at his brother, then he looked at Stevens again, leaning a little forward now. Virginius had not moved; there was no change in his grave, intent expression. Between him and the wall the cousin sat. His hands lay on his lap and his head was bowed a little, as though he were in church. We knew of him only that he was some kind of an itinerant preacher, and that now and then he gathered up strings of scrubby horses and mules and took them somewhere and swapped or sold them. Because he was a man of infrequent speech who in his dealing with men betrayed such an excruciating shyness and lack of confidence that we pitied him, with that kind of pitying disgust you feel for a crippled worm, dreading even to put him to the agony of saying 'yes' or 'no' to a question. But we heard how on Sundays, in the pulpits of country churches, he became a different man, changed; his voice then timbrous and moving and assured out of all proportion to his nature and his size.

'Now, imagine the waiting,' Stevens said, 'with that man knowing what was going to happen before it had happened, knowing at last that the reason why nothing was happening, why that will had apparently gone into Judge Dukinfield's office and then dropped out of the world, out of the knowledge of man, was because he had forgotten something which he should not have forgotten. And that was that Judge Dukinfield also knew that Mr. Holland was not the man who beat that horse. He knew that Judge Dukinfield knew that the man who struck that horse with that stick so as to leave marks on its back was the man who killed Mr. Holland first and then hooked his foot in that stirrup and struck that horse with a stick to make it bolt. But the horse didn't bolt. The man knew beforehand that it would not; he had known for years that it would not, but he had forgotten that. Because while it was still a colt it had been beaten so severely once that ever since, even at the sight of a switch in the rider's hand, it would lie down on the ground, as Mr. Holland knew, and as all who were close to Mr. Holland's family knew. So it just lay down on top of Mr. Holland's body. But that was all right too, at first; that was just as well. That's what that man thought for the next week or so, lying in his bed at night and waiting, who had already waited fifteen years. Because even then, when it was too late and he realized that he had made a mistake, he had not even then remembered all that he should never have forgotten. Then he remembered that too, when it was too late, after the body had been found and the marks of the stick on the horse seen and remarked and it was too late to remove them. They were probably gone from the horse by then, anyway. But there was only one tool he could use to remove them from men's minds. Imagine him then, his terror, his outrage, his feeling of having been tricked by something beyond retaliation: that furious desire to turn time back for just one minute, to undo or to complete when it is too late. Because the last thing which he remembered when it was too late was that Mr. Holland had bought that horse from Judge Dukinfield, the man who was sitting here at this table, passing on the validity of a will giving away two thousand acres of some of the best land in the county. And he waited, since he had but one tool that would remove those stick marks, and nothing happened. And nothing happened, and he knew why. And he waited as long as he dared, until he believed that there was more at stake than a few roods and squares of earth. So what else could he do but what he did?'

His voice had hardly ceased before Anselm was speaking. His voice was harsh, abrupt. 'You're wrong,' he said.

As one, we looked at him where he sat forward on the bench, in his muddy boots and his worn overalls, glaring at Stevens; even Virginius turned and looked at him for an instant. The cousin and the old Negro alone had not moved. They did not seem to be listening. 'Where am I wrong?' Stevens said.

But Anselm did not answer. He glared at Stevens. 'Will Virginius get the place in spite of . . . of . . .'

'In spite of what?' Stevens said.

'Whether he . . . that . . .'

'You mean your father? Whether he died or was murdered?'

'Yes,' Anselm said.

'Yes. You and Virge get the land whether the will stands up or not, provided, of course, that Virge divides with you if it does. But the man that killed your father wasn't certain of that and he didn't dare to ask. Because he didn't want that will to stand.'

'You're wrong,' Anselm said, in that harsh, sudden tone. 'I killed him. But it wasn't because of that damned farm. Now bring on your sheriff.'

And now it was Stevens who, gazing steadily at Anselm's furious face, said quietly: 'And I say that you are wrong, Anse.'

For some time after that we who watched and listened dwelt in anticlimax, in a dreamlike state in which we seemed to know beforehand what was going to happen, aware at the same time that it didn't matter because we should soon wake. It was as though we were outside of time, watching events from outside; still outside of and beyond time since that first instant when we looked again at Anselm as though we had never seen him before. There was a sound, a slow, sighing sound, not loud; maybe of relief – something. Perhaps we were all thinking how Anse's nightmare must be really over at last; it was as though we too had rushed suddenly back to where he lay as a child in his bed and the mother who they said was partial to him, whose heritage had been lost to him, and even the very resting place of her tragic and long quiet dust outraged, coming in to look at him for a moment before going away again. Far back down time that was, straight though it be. And straight though that corridor was, the boy who had lain unawares in that bed had got lost in it, as we all do, must, ever shall; that boy was as dead as any other of his blood in that violated cedar grove, and the man at whom we looked, we looked at across the irrevocable chasm, with pity perhaps, but not with mercy. So it took the sense of Stevens' words about as long to penetrate to us as it did to Anse; he had to repeat himself, 'Now I say that you are wrong, Anse.'

'What?' Anse said. Then he moved. He did not get up, yet somehow he seemed to lunge suddenly, violenty, 'You're a liar. You – '

'You're wrong, Anse. You didn't kill your father. The man who killed your father was the man who could plan and conceive to kill that old man who sat here behind this table every day, day after day, until an old Negro would come in and wake him and tell him it was time to go home – a man who never did man, woman, or child aught but good as he believed that he and God saw it. It wasn't you that killed your father. You demanded of him what you believed was yours, and when he refused to give it, you left, went away, never spoke to him again. You heard how he was mistreating the place but you held your peace, because the land was just "that damned farm." You held your peace until you heard how a crazy man was digging up the graves where your mother's flesh and blood and your own was buried. Then, and then only, you came to him, to remonstrate. But you were never a man to remonstrate, and he was never a man to listen to it. So you found him there, in the grove, with the shotgun. I don't even expect you paid much attention to the shotgun. I reckon you just took it away from him and whipped him with your bare hands and left him there beside the horse; maybe you thought that he was dead. Then somebody happened to pass there after you were gone and found him; maybe that someone had been there all the time, watching. Somebody that wanted him dead too; not in anger and outrage, but by calculation. For profit, by a will, maybe. So he came there and he found what you had left and he finished it: hooked your father's foot in that stirrup and tried to beat that horse into bolting to make it look well, forgetting in his haste what he should not have forgot. But it wasn't you. Because you went back home, and when you heard what had been found, you said nothing. Because you thought something at the time which you did not even say to yourself. And when you heard what was in the will you believed that you knew. And you were glad then. Because you had lived alone until youth and wanting things were gone out of you; you just wanted to be quiet as you wanted your mother's dust to be quiet. And besides, what could land and position among men be to a man without citizenship, with a blemished name?'

We listened quietly while Stevens' voice died in that little room in which no air ever stirred, no draught ever blew because of its position, its natural lee beaneath the courthouse wall.

'It wasn't you that killed your father or Judge Dukinfield either, Anse. Because if that man who killed your father had remembered in time that Judge Dukinfield once owned that horse, Judge Dukinfield would be alive today.'

We breathed quietly, sitting about the table behind which Judge Dukinfield had been sitting when he looked up into the pistol. The table had not been disturbed. Upon it still lay the papers, the pens, the inkwell, the small curiously chased brass box which his daughter had fetched him from Europe twelve years ago – for what purpose neither she nor the Judge knew, since it would have been suitable only for bath salts or tobacco, neither of which the Judge used – and which he had kept for a paper weight, that, too, superfluous where no draft ever blew. But he kept it there on the table, and all of us knew it, had watched him toy with it while he talked, opening the spring lid and watching it snap viciously shut at the slightest touch.

When I look back on it now, I can see that the rest of it should not have taken as long as it did. It seems to me now that we must have known all the time; I still seem to feel that kind of disgust without mercy which after all does the office of pity, as when you watch a soft worm impaled on a pin, when you feel that retching revulsion – would even use your naked palm in place of nothing at all, thinking, 'Go on. Mash it. Smear it. Get it over with.' But that was not Stevens' plan. Because he had a plan, and we realized afterward that, since he could not convict the man, the man himself would have to. And it was unfair, the way he did it; later we told him so. ('Ah,' he said. 'But isn't justice always unfair? Isn't it always composed of injustice and luck and platitude in unequal parts?')

But anyway we could not see yet what he was getting at as he began to speak again in that tone – easy, anecdotal, his hand resting now on the brass box. But men are moved so much by preconceptions. It is not realities, circumstances, that astonish us; it is the concussion of what we should have known, if we had only not been so busy believing what we discovered later we had taken for the truth for no other reason than that we happened to be believing it at the moment. He was talking about smoking again, about how a man never really enjoys tobacco until he begins to believe that it is harmful to him, and how non-smokers miss one of the greatest pleasures in life for a man of sensibility: the knowledge that he is succumbing to a vice which can injure himself alone.

'Do you smoke, Anse?' he said.

'No,' Anse said.

'You don't either, do you, Virge?'

'No,' Virginius said. 'None of us ever did – father or Anse or me. We heired it, I reckon.'

'A family trait,' Stevens said. 'Is it in your mother's family too? Is it in your branch, Granby?'

The cousin looked at Stevens, for less than a moment. Without moving he appeared to writhe slowly within his neat, shoddy suit. 'No sir. I never used it.'

'Maybe because you are a preacher,' Stevens said. The cousin didn't answer. He looked at Stevens again with his mild, still, hopelessly abashed face. 'I've always smoked,' Stevens said. 'Ever since I finally recovered from being sick at it at the age of fourteen. That's a long time, long enough to have become finicky about tobacco. But most smokers are, despite the psychologists and the standardized tobacco. Or maybe it's just cigarettes that are standardized. Or maybe they are just standardized to laymen, non-smokers. Because I have noticed how non-smokers are apt to go off half cocked about tobacco, the same as the rest of us go off half cocked about what we do not ourselves use, are not familiar with, since man is led by his pre- (or mis-) conceptions. Because you take a man who sells tobacco even though he does not use it himself, who watches customer after customer tear open the pack and light the cigarette just across the counter from him. You ask him if all tobacco smells alike, if he cannot distinguish one kind from another by the smell. Or maybe it's the shape and colour of the package it comes in; because even the psychologists have not yet told us just where seeing stops and smelling begins, or hearing stops and seeing begins. Any lawyer can tell you that.'

Again the Foreman checked him. We had listened quietly enough, but I think we all felt that to keep the murderer confused was one thing, but that we, the jury, were another. 'You should have done all this investigating before you called us together,' the Foreman said. 'Even if this be evidence, what good will it do without the body of the murderer be apprehended? Conjecture is all well enough – '

'All right,' Stevens said. 'Let me conjecture a little more, and if I don't seem to progress any, you tell me so, and I'll stop my way and do yours. And I expect that at first you are going to call this taking a right smart of liberty even with conjecture. But we found Judge Dukinfield dead, shot between the eyes, in this chair behind this table. That's not conjecture. And Uncle Job was sitting all day long in that chair in the passage, where anyone who entered this room (unless he came down the private stair from the courtroom and climbed through the window) would have to pass within three feet of him. And no man that we know of has passed Uncle Job in that chair in seventeen years. That's not conjecture.'

'Then what is your conjecture?'

But Stevens was talking about tobacco again, about smoking. 'I stopped in West's drug store last week for some tobacco, and he told me about a man who was particular about his smoking also. While he was getting my tobacco from the case, he reached out a box of cigarettes and handed it to me. It was dusty, faded, like he had had it a long time, and he told me how a drummer had left two of them with him years ago. "Ever smoke them?" he said. "No," I said. "They must be city cigarettes." Then he told me how he had sold the other package just that day. He said he was behind the counter, with the newspaper spread on it, sort of half reading the paper and half keeping the store while the clerk was gone to dinner. And he said he never heard or saw the man at all until he looked up and the man was just across the counter, so close that it made him jump. A smallish man in city clothes, West said, wanting a kind of cigarette that West had never heard of. "I haven't got that kind," West said. "I don't carry them." "Why don't you carry them?" the man said. "I have no sale for them," West said. And he told about the man in his city clothes, with a face like a shaved wax doll, and eyes with a still way of looking and a voice with a still way of talking. Then West said he saw the man's eyes and he looked at his nostrils, and then he knew what was wrong. Because the man was full of dope right then. "I don't have any calls for them," West said. "What am I trying to do now?" the man said. "Trying to sell you flypaper?" Then the man bought the other package of cigarettes and went out. And West said that he was mad and he was sweating too, like he wanted to vomit, he said. He said to me, 'If I had some devilment I was scared to do myself, you know what I'd do? I'd give that fellow about ten dollars and I'd tell him where the devilment was and tell him not to never speak to me again. When he went out, I felt just exactly like that. Like I was going to be sick." '

Stevens looked about us; he paused for a moment. We watched him. 'He came here from somewhere in a car, a big roadster, that city man did. That city man that ran out of his own kind of tobacco.' He paused again, and then he turned his head slowly and he looked at Virginius Holland. It seemed like a full minute that we watched them looking steadily at one another. 'And a Negro told me that that big car was parked in Virginius Holland's barn the night before Judge Dukinfield was killed.' And for another time we watched the two of them looking steadily at each other, with no change of expression on either face. Stevens spoke in a tone quiet, speculative, almost musing. 'Someone tried to keep him from coming out here in that car, that big car that anyone who saw it once would remember and recognize. Maybe that someone wanted to forbid him to come in it, threaten him. Only the man that Doctor West sold those cigarettes to wouldn't have stood for very much threatening.'

'Meaning me, by "someone," ' Virginius said. He did not move or turn away his steady stare from Stevens' face. But

Anselm moved. He turned his head and he looked at his brother, once. It was quite quiet, yet when the cousin spoke we could not hear or understand him at once; he had spoken but one time since we entered the room and Stevens locked the door. His voice was faint; again and without moving he appeared to writhe faintly beneath his clothes. He spoke with that abashed faintness, that excruciating desire for effacement with which we were all familiar.

'That fellow you're speaking of, he come to see me,' Dodge said. 'Stopped to see me. He stopped at the house about dark that night and said he was hunting to buy up little-built horses to use for this – this game –'

'Polo?' Stevens said. The cousin had not looked at anyone while he spoke; it was as though he were speaking to his slowly moving hands upon his lap.

'Yes sir. Virginius was there. We talked about horses. Then the next morning he took his car and went on. I never had anything that suited him. I don't know where he come from nor where he went.'

'Or who else he came to see,' Stevens said. 'Or what else he came to do. You can't say that.'

Dodge didn't answer. It was not necessary, and again he had fled behind the shape of his effacement like a small and weak wild creature into a hole.

'That's my conjecture,' Stevens said.

And then we should have known. It was there to be seen, bald as a naked hand. We should have felt it – the somcone in that room who felt what Stevens had called that horror, that outrage, that furious desire to turn time back for a second, to unsay, to undo. But maybe that someone had not felt it yet, had not yet felt the blow, the impact, as for a second or two a man may be unaware that he has been shot. Because now it was Virge that spoke, abruptly, harshly, 'How are you going to prove that?'

'Prove what, Virge?' Stevens said. Again they looked at each other, quiet, hard, like two boxers. Not swordsmen, but boxers; or at least with pistols. 'Who it was who hired that gorilla, that thug, down here from Memphis? I don't have to prove that. He told that. On the way back to Memphis he ran down a child at Battenburg (he was still full of dope; likely he had taken another shot of it when he finished his job here), and they caught him and locked him up and when the dope began to wear off he told where he had been, whom he had been to see, sitting in the cell in the jail there, jerking and snarling, after they had taken the pistol with the silencer on it away from him.'

'Ah,'' Virginius said. 'That's nice. So all you've got to do is to prove that he was in this room that day. And how will you do that? Give that old Negro another dollar and let him remember again?'

But Stevens did not appear to be listening. He stood at the end of the table, between the two groups, and while he talked now he held the brass box in his hand, turning it, looking at it, talking in that easy, musing tone. 'You all know the peculiar attribute which this room has. How no draught ever blows in it. How when there has been smoking here on a Saturday, say, the smoke will still be here on Monday morning when Uncle Job opens the door, lying against the baseboard there like a dog asleep, kind of. You've all seen that.'

We were sitting a little forward now, like Anse, watching Stevens.

'Yes,' the Foreman said. 'We've seen that.'

'Yes,' Stevens said, still as though he were not listening, turning the closed box this way and that in his hand. 'You asked me for my conjecture. Here it is. But it will take a conjecturing man to do it – a man who could walk up to a merchant standing behind his counter, reading a newspaper with one eye and the other eye on the door for customers, before the merchant knew he was there. A city man, who insisted on city cigarettes. So this man left that store and crossed to the courthouse and entered and went on upstairs, as anyone might have done. Perhaps a dozen men saw him; perhaps twice that many did not look at him at all, since there are two places where a man does not look at faces: in the sanctuary of civil law, and in public lavatories. So he entered the courtroom and came down the private stair and into the passage, and saw Uncle Job asleep in his chair. So maybe he followed the passage and climbed through the window behind Judge Dukinfield's back. Or maybe he walked right past Uncle Job, coming up from behind, you see. And to pass within eight feet of a man asleep in a chair would not be very hard for a man who could walk up to a merchant leaning on the counter of his own store. Perhaps he even lighted the cigarette from the pack that West had sold him before even Judge Dukinfield knew that he was in the room. Or perhaps the Judge was asleep in his chair, as he sometimes was. So perhaps the man stood there and finished the cigarette and watched the smoke pour slowly across the table and bank up against the wall, thinking about the easy money, the easy hicks, before he even drew the pistol. And it made less noise than the striking of the match which lighted the cigarette, since he had guarded so against noise that he forgot about silence. And then he went back as he came, and the dozen men and the two dozen saw him and did not see him, and at five that afternoon Uncle Job came in to wake the Judge and tell him it was time to go home. Isn't that right, Uncle Job?'

The old Negro looked up. 'I looked after him, like I promised Mistis,' he said. 'And I worried with him, like I promised Mistis I would. And I come in here and I thought at first he was asleep, like he sometimes – '

'Wait,' Stevens said. 'You came in and you saw him in the chair, as always, and you noticed the smoke against the wall behind the table as you crossed the floor. Wasn't that what you told me?'

Sitting in his mended chair, the old Negro began to cry. He looked like an old monkey, weakly crying black tears, brushing at his face with the back of a gnarled hand that shook with age, with something. 'I come in here many's the time in the morning, to clean up. It would be laying there, that smoke, and him that never smoked a lick in his life coming in and sniffing with that high nose of hisn and saying, "Well, Job, we sholly smoked out that corpus juris coon last night." '

'No,' Stevens said. 'Tell about how the smoke was there behind that table that afternoon when you came to wake him to go home, when there hadn't anybody passed you all that day except Mr. Virge Holland yonder. And Mr. Virge don't smoke, and the Judge didn't smoke. But that smoke was there. Tell what you told me.'

'It was there. And I thought that he was asleep like always, and I went to wake him up – '

'And this little box was sitting on the edge of the table where he had been handling it while he talked to Mr. Virge, and when you reached your hand to wake him – '

'Yes sir. It jumped off the table and I thought he was asleep – '

'The box jumped off the table. And it made a noise and you wondered why that didn't wake the Judge, and you looked down at where the box was lying on the floor in the smoke, with the lid open, and you thought that it was broken. And so you reached your hand down to see, because the Judge liked it because Miss Emma had brought it back to him from across the water, even if he didn't need it for a paper weight in his offce. So you close the lid and set it on the table again. And then you found that the Judge was more than asleep.'

He ceased. We breathed quietly, hearing ourselves breathe. Stevens seemed to watch his hand as it turned the box slowly this way and that. He had turned a little from the table in talking with the old Negro, so that now he faced the bench rather than the jury, the table. 'Uncle Job calls this a gold box. Which is as good a name as any. Better than most. Because all metal is about the same; it just happens that some folks want one kind more than another. But it all has certain general attributes, likenesses. One of them is, that whatever is shut up in a metal box will stay in it unchanged for a longer time than in a wooden or paper box. You can shut up smoke, for instance, in a metal box with a tight lid like this one, and even a week later it will still be there. And not only that, a chemist or a smoker or tobacco seller like Doctor West can tell what made the smoke, what kind of tobacco, particularly if it happens to be a strange brand, a kind not sold in Jefferson, and of which he just happened to have two packs and remembered who he sold one of them to.'

We did not move. We just sat there and heard the man's urgent stumbling feet on the floor, then we saw him strike the box from Stevens' hand. But we were not particularly watching him, even then. Like him, we watched the box bounce into two pieces as the lid snapped off, and emit a fading vapour which dissolved sluggishly away. As one we leaned across the table and looked down upon the sandy and hopeless mediocrity of Granby Dodge's head as he knelt on the floor and flapped at the fading smoke with his hands.

'But I still don't . . .' Virginius said. We were outside now, in the courthouse yard, the five of us, blinking a little at one another as though we had just come out of a cave.

'You've got a will, haven't you?' Stevens said. Then Virginius stopped perfectly still, looking at Stevens.

'Oh,' he said at last.

'One of those natural mutual deed-of-trust wills that any two business partners might execute.' Stevens said. 'You and Granby each the other's beneficiary and executor, for mutual protection of mutual holdings. That's natural. Likely Granby was the one who suggested it first, by telling you how he had made you his heir. So you'd better tear it up, yours, your copy. Make Anse your heir, if you have to have a will.'

'He won't need to wait for that,' Virginius said. 'Half of that land is his.'

'You just treat it right, as he knows you will,' Stevens said. 'Anse don't need any land.'

'Yes,' Virginius said. He looked away. 'But I wish . . .'

'You just treat it right. He knows you'll do that.'

'Yes,' Virginius said. He looked at Stevens again. 'Well, I reckon I . . . we both owe you . . .'

'More than you think,' Stevens said. He spoke quite soberly. 'Or to that horse. A week after your father died, Granby bought enough rat poison to kill three elephants, West told me. But after he remembered what he had forgotten about that horse, he was afraid to kill his rats before that will was settled. Because he is a man both shrewd and ignorant at the same time: a dangerous combination. Ignorant enough to believe that the law is something like dynamite: the slave of whoever puts his hand to it first, and even then a dangerous slave; and just shrewd enough to believe that people avail themselves of it, resort to it, only for personal ends. I found that out when he sent a Negro to see me one day last summer, to find out if the way in which a man died could affect the probation of his will. And I knew who had sent the Negro to me, and I knew that whatever information the Negro took back to the man who sent him, that man had already made up his mind to disbelieve it, since I was a servant of the slave, the dynamite. So if that had been a normal horse, or Granby had remembered in time, you would be underground now. Granby might not be any better off than he is, but you would be dead.'

'Oh,' Virginius said, quietly, soberly, 'I reckon I'm obliged.'

'Yes,' Stevens said. 'You've incurred a right smart of obligation. You owe Granby something.' Virginius looked at him. 'You owe him for those taxes he has been paying every year now for fifteen years.'

'Oh,' Virginius said. 'Yes I thought that father . . . Every November, about, Granby would borrow money from me, not much, and not ever the same amount. To buy stock with, he said. He paid some of it back. But he still owes me . . . no. I owe him now.' He was quite grave, quite sober. 'When a man starts doing wrong, it's not what he does; it's what he leaves.'

'But it's what he does that people will have to hurt him for, the outsiders. Because the folks that'll be hurt by what he leaves won't hurt him. So it's a good thing for the rest of us that what he does takes him out of their hands. I have taken him out of your hands now. Virge, blood or no blood.

'I understand,' Virginius said. 'I wouldn't anyway . . .' Then suddenly he looked at Stevens. 'Gavin,' he said.

'What?' Stevens said.

Virginius watched him. 'You talked a right smart in yonder about chemistry and such, about that smoke. I reckon I believed some of it and I reckon I didn't believe some of it. And I reckon if I told you which I believed and didn't believe, you'd laugh at me,' His face was quite sober. Stevens' face was quite grave too. Yet there was something in Stevens' eyes, his glance; something quick and eager; not ridiculing, either. 'That was a week ago. If you had opened that box to see if that smoke was still in there, it would have got out. And if there hadn't been any smoke in that box, Granby wouldn't have given himself away. And that was a week ago. How did you know there was going to be any smoke in that box?'

'I didn't,' Stevens said. He said it quickly, brightly, cheerfully, almost happily, almost beaming. 'I didn't. I waited as long as I could before you all came into the room. I filled that box full of pipe smoke and shut it up. But I didn't know. I was a lot scareder than Granby Dodge. But it was all right. That smoke stayed in that box almost an hour.'

ANATOLE FRANCE

The Majesty of Justice

CHAPTER I

In every sentence pronounced by a judge in the name of the sovereign people dwells the whole majesty of justice. The august character of that justice was brought home to Jérôme Crainquebille, costermonger, when accused of having insulted a policeman, he appeared in the police court. Having taken his place in the dock, he beheld in the imposing sombre hall magistrates, clerks, lawyers in their robes, the usher wearing his chains, *gendarmes,* and, behind a rail, the bare heads of the silent spectators. He, himself, occupied a raised seat, as if some sinister honour were conferred on the accused by his appearance before the magistrate. At the end of the hall, between two assessors, sat President Bourriche. The palm-leaves of an officer of the Academy decorated his breast. Over the tribune were a bust representing the Republic and a crucifix, as if to indicate that all laws divine and human were suspended over Crainquebille's head. Such symbols naturally inspired him with terror. Not being gifted with a philosophic mind, he did not inquire the meaning of the bust and the crucifix; he did not ask how far Jesus and the symbolical bust harmonized in the Law Courts. Neverheless, here was matter for reflection; for after all, pontifical teaching and canon law are in many points opposed to the constitution of the Republic and to the civil code. So far as we know the Decretals have not been abolished. Today, as formerly, the Church of Christ teaches that only those powers are lawful to which it has given its sanction. Now the French Republic claims to be independent of pontifical power. Crainquebille might reasonably say:

'Gentlemen and magistrates, in so much as President Loubet has not been anointed, the Christ, whose image is suspended over your heads, repudiates you through the voice of councils and of Popes. Either he is here to remind you of the rights of the Church, which invalidate yours, or His presence has no rational signification.'

Whereupon President Bourriche might reply:

'Prisoner Crainquebille, the kings of France have always quarrelled with the Pope. Guillaume de Nogaret was excommunicated, but for so trifling a reason he did not resign his office. The Christ of the tribune is not the Christ of Gregory VII or of Boniface VIII. He is, if you will, the Christ of the Gospels, who knew not one word of canon law, and had never heard of the holy Decretals.'

Then Crainquebille might not without reason have answered:

'The Christ of the Gospels was an agitator. Moreover, he was the victim of a sentence, which for nineteen hundred years all Christian peoples have regarded as a grave judicial error. I defy you, Monsieur le Président, to condemn me in His name to so much as forty-eight hours' imprisonment.'

But Crainquebille did not indulge in any considerations either historical, political or social. He was wrapped in amazement. All the ceremonial, with which he was surrounded, impressed him with a very lofty idea of justice. Filled with reverence, overcome with terror, he was ready to submit to his judges in the matter of his guilt. In his own conscience he was convinced of his innocence; but he felt how insignificant is the conscience of the costermonger in the face of the panoply of the law, and the ministers of public prosecution. Already his lawyer had half persuaded him that he was not innocent.

A summary and hasty examination had brought out the charges under which he laboured.

CHAPTER II

Crainquebille's Misadventure

Up and down the town went Jérôme Crainquebille, costermonger, pushing his barrow before him and crying: 'Cabbages! Turnips! Carrots!' When he had leeks he cried: 'Asparagus!' For leeks are the asparagus of the poor. Now it happened that on October 20, at noon, as he was going down the Rue Montmartre, there came out of her shop the shoemaker's wife, Madame Bayard. She went up to Crainquebille's barrow and scornfully taking up a bundle of leeks, she said:

'I don't think much of your leeks. What do you want a bundle?'

'Sevenpence halfpenny, mum, and the best in the market!'

'Sevenpence halfpenny for three wretched leeks?'

And disdainfully she cast the leeks back into the barrow.

Then it was that Constable 64 came and said to Crainquebille:

'Move on.'

Moving on was what Crainquebille had been doing from morning till evening for fifty years. Such an order seemed right to him, and perfectly in accordance with the nature of things. Quite prepared to obey, he urged his customer to take what she wanted.

'You must give me time to choose,' she retorted sharply.

Then she felt all the bundles of leeks over again. Finally, she selected the one she thought the best, and held it clasped to her bosom as saints in church pictures hold the palm of victory.

'I will give you sevenpence. That's quite enough; and I'll have to fetch it from the shop, for I haven't anything on me.'

Still embracing the leeks, she went back into the shop, whither she had been preceded by a customer, carrying a child.

Just at this moment Constable 64 said to Crainquebille for the second time:

'Move on.'

'I'm waiting for my money,' replied Crainquebille.

'And I'm not telling you to wait for your money; I'm telling you to move on,' retorted the constable grimly.

Meanwhile, the shoemaker's wife in her shop was fitting blue slippers on to a child of eighteen months, whose mother was in a hurry. And the green heads of the leeks were lying on the counter.

For the half century that he had been pushing his barrow through the streets, Crainquebille had been learning respect of authority. But now his position was a peculiar one: he was torn asunder between what was his due and what was his duty. His was not a judicial mind. He failed to understand that the possession of an individual's right in no way exonerated him from the performance of a social duty. He attached too great importance to his claim to receive sevenpence, and too little to the duty of pushing his barrow and moving on, for ever moving on. He stood still.

For the third time Constable 64 quietly and calmly ordered him to move on. Unlike Inspector Mantauciel, whose habit it is to threaten constantly but never to take proceedings, Constable 64 is slow to threaten and quick to act. Such is his character. Though somewhat sly he is an excellent servant and loyal soldier. He is as brave as a lion and as gentle as a child. He knows naught save his official instructions.

'Don't you understand when I tell you to move on?'

To Crainquebille's mind his reason for standing still was too weighty for him not to consider it sufficient. Wherefore, artlessly and simply he explained it:

'Good Lord! Don't I tell you that I am waiting for my money.'

Constable 64 merely replied:

'Do you want me to summons you? If you do you have only to say so.'

At these words Crainquebille slowly shrugged his shoulders looked sadly at the constable, and then raised his eyes to heaven, as if he would say:

'I call God to Witness! Am I a lawbreaker? Am I one to make light of the by-laws and ordinances which regulate my ambulatory calling? At five o'clock in the morning I was at the market. Since seven, pushing my barrow and wearing my hands to the bones, I have been crying: ''Cabbages! Turnips! Carrots'' I am turned sixty. I am worn out. And you ask me whether I have raised the black flag of rebellion. You are mocking me and your joking is cruel.'

Either because he failed to notice the expression on Crainquebille's face, or because he considered it no excuse for disobedience, the constable inquired curtly and roughly whether he had been understood.

Now, just at that moment the block of traffic in the Rue Montemartre was at its worst. Carriages, drays, carts, omnibuses, trucks, jammed one against the other, seemed indissolubly welded together. From their quivering immobility proceeded shouts and oaths. Cabmen and butchers' boys grandiloquent and drawling insulted one another from a distance, and omnibus conductors, regarding Crainquebille as the cause of the block, called him 'a dirty leek.'

Meanwhile, on the pavement the curious were crowding round to listen to the dispute. Then the constable, finding himself the centre of attention, began to think it time to display his authority:

'Very well,' he said, taking a stumpy pencil and a greasy notebook from his pocket.

Crainquebille persisted in his idea, obedient to a force within. Besides, it was now impossible for him either to move on or to draw back. The wheel of his barrow was unfortunately caught in that of a milkman's cart.

Tearing his hair beneath his cap he cried:

'But don't I tell you I'm waiting for my money! Here's a fix! *Misere de misere! Bon sang de bon sang!*'

By these words, expressive rather of despair than of rebellion, Constable 64 considered he had been insulted. And, because to his mind all insults must necessarily take the consecrated, regular, traditional, liturgical, ritual form so to speak of *Mort aux vaches*, thus the offender's words were heard and understood by the constable.

'Ah! You said: *Mort aux vaches.* Very good. Come along.'

Stupefied with amazement and distress, Crainquebille

opened his great rheumy eyes and gazed at Constable 64. With a broken voice proceeding now from the top of his head and now from the heels of his boots, he cried, with his arms folded over his blue blouse:

'I said *'Mort aux vaches'?* I? . . . Oh!'

The tradesmen and errand boys hailed the arrest with laughter. It gratified the taste of all crowds for violent and ignoble spectacles. But there was one serious person who was pushing his way through the throng; he was a sad-looking old man, dressed in black, wearing a high hat; he went up to the constable and said to him in a low voice very gently and firmly:

'You are mistaken. This man did not insult you.'

'Mind your own business,' replied the policeman, but without threatening, for he was speaking to a man who was well dressed.

The old man insisted calmly and tenaciously. And the policeman ordered him to make his declaration to the Police Commissioner.

Meanwhile Crainquebille was explaining:

'Then I did say *"Mort aux vaches!"* Oh! . . .'

As he was thus giving vent to his astonishment, Madame Bayard, the shoemaker's wife, came to him with sevenpence in her hand. But Constable 64 already had him by the collar; so Madame Bayard, thinking that no debt could be due to a man who was being taken to the police-station, put her sevenpence into her apron pocket.

Then, suddenly beholding his barrow confiscated, his liberty lost, a gulf opening beneath him and the sky overcast, Crainquebille murmured:

'It can't be helped!'

Before the Commissioner, the old gentleman declared that he had been hindered on his way by the block in the traffic, and so had witnessed the incident. He maintained that the policeman had not been insulted, and that he was labouring under a delusion. He gave his name and profession: Dr. David Matthieu, chief physician at the Ambroise-Paré Hospital, officer of the Legion of Honour. At another time such evidence would have been sufficient for the Commissioner.

But just then men of science were regarded with suspicion in France.

Crainquebille continued under arrest. He passed the night in the lock-up. In the morning he was taken to the Police Court in the prison van.

He did not find prison either sad or humiliating. It seemed to him necessary. What struck him as he entered was the cleanliness of the walls and of the brick floor.

'Well, for a clean place, yes, it is a clean place. You might eat off the floor.'

When he was left alone, he wanted to draw out his stool; but he perceived that it was fastened to the wall. He expressed his surprise aloud:

'That's a queer idea! Now there's a thing I should never have thought of, I'm sure.'

Having sat down, he twiddled his thumbs and remained wrapped in amazement. The silence and the solitude overwhelmed him. The time seemed long. Anxiously he thought of his barrow, which had been confiscated with its load of cabbages, carrots, celery, dandelion and corn-salad. And he wondered asking himself with alarm:

'What have they done with my barrow?'

On the third day he received a visit from his lawyer, Maître Lemerle, one of the youngest members of the Paris Bar, President of a section of La Ligue de la Patrie Française.

Crainquebille endeavoured to tell him his story; but it was not easy, for he was not accustomed to conversation. With a little help he might perhaps have succeeded. But his lawyer shook his head doubtfully at everything he said; and turning over his papers, muttered:

'Hm! Hm! I don't find anything about all this in my brief.'

Then, in a bored tone, twirling his fair moustache he said:

'In your own interest it would be advisable, perhaps, for you to confess. Your persistence in absolute denial seems to me extremely unwise.'

And from that moment Crainquebille would have made confession if he had known what to confess.

CHAPTER III

Crainquebille before the Magistrates

President Bourriche devoted six whole minutes to the examination of Crainquebille. The examination would have been more enlightening if the accused had replied to the questions asked him. But Crainquebille was unaccustomed to discussion; and in such a company his lips were sealed by reverence and fear. So he was silent: and the President answered his own questions; his replies were staggering. He concluded: 'Finally, you admit having said, *''Mort aux vaches''.*'

'I said, *''Mort aux vaches!''* because the policeman said, *''Mort aux vaches!''* So then I said *''Mort aux vaches!''* '

He meant that, being overwhelmed by the most unexpected of accusations, he had in his amazement merely repeated the curious words falsely attributed to him, and which he had certainly never pronounced. He had said, *'Mort aux vaches!'* as he might have said, 'I capable of insulting anyone! How could you believe it?'

President Bourriche put a different interpretation on the incident.

'Do you maintain,' he said, 'that the policeman was, himself, the first to utter the exclamation?'

Crainquebille gave up trying to explain. It was too difficult.

'You do not persist in your statement. You are quite right,' said the President.

And he had the witness called.

Constable 64, by name Bastien Matra, swore he spoke the truth and nothing but the truth. Then he gave evidence in the following terms:

'I was on my beat on October 20, at noon, when I noticed in the Rue Montmartre a person who appeared to be a hawker, unduly blocking the traffic with his barrow opposite No. 328. Three times I intimated to him the order to move on, but he refused to comply. And when I gave him warning that I was about to charge him, he retorted by crying: *''Mort aux vaches!''* Which I took as an insult.'

This evidence delivered in a firm and moderate manner,

the magistrates received with obvious approbation. The witnesses for the defence were Madame Bayard, shoemaker's wife, and Dr. David Matthieu, chief physician to the Hospital Ambroise-Paré, officer of the Legion of Honour. Madame Bayard had seen nothing and heard nothing. Dr. Matthieu was in the crowd which had gathered round the policeman, who was ordering the costermonger to move on. His evidence led to a new episode in the trial.

'I witnessed the incident,' he said, 'I observed that the constable had made a mistake; he had not been insulted. I went up to him and called his attention to the fact. The officer insisted on arresting the costermonger, and told me to follow him to the Commissioner of Police. This I did. Before the Commissioner, I repeated my declaration.'

'You may sit down,' said the President. 'Usher, recall witness Matra.'

'Matra, when you proceeded to arrest the accused, did not Dr. Matthieu point out to you that you were mistaken?'

'That is to say, Monsieur le Président, that he insulted me.'

'What did he say?

'He said, *"Mort aux vaches!"* '

Uproarious laughter arose from the audience.

'You may withdraw,' said the President hurriedly.

And he warned the public that if such unseemly demonstrations occurred again he would clear the court. Meanwhile, Counsel for the defence was haughtily fluttering the sleeves of his gown, and for the moment it was thought that Crainquebille would be acquitted.

Order having been restored, Maître Lemerle rose. He opened his pleading with a eulogy of policement: 'those unassuming servants of society who, in return for a trifling salary, endure fatigue and brave incessant danger with daily herosim. They were soldiers once, and soldiers they remain; soldiers, that word expresses everything . . .'

From this consideration Maître Lemerle went on to descant eloquently on the military virtues. He was one of those, he said, who would not allow a finger to be laid on the army, on that national army, to which he was so proud to belong.

The President bowed. Maître Lemerle happened to be

lieutenant in the Reserves. He was also nationalist candidate for Les Vielles Haudriettes. He continued:

'No, indeed, I do not esteem lightly the invaluable services unassumingly rendered, which the valiant people of Paris receive daily from the guardians of the peace. And had I beheld in Crainquebille, gentlemen, one who had insulted an ex-soldier, I should never have consented to represent him before you. My client is accused of having said: *"Mort aux vaches!"* The meaning of such an expression is clear. If you consult *Le Dictionnaire de la Langue* (slang) you will find: *"Vachard,* a sluggard, an idler, one who stretches himself out lazily like a cow instead of working. *Vache,* one who sells himself to the police; spy." *Mort aux vaches!* is an expression employed by certain people. But the question resolves itself into this: how did Crainquebille say it? And, further, did he say it at all. Permit me to doubt it, gentlemen.

'I do not suspect Constable Matra of any evil intention. But, as we have said, his calling is arduous. He is sometimes harassed, fatigued, overdone. In such conditions he may have suffered from an aural hallucination. And, when he comes and tells you, gentlemen, that Dr. David Matthieu, officer of the Legion of Honour, chief physician at the Ambroise-Paré Hospital, a gentleman and a prince of science, cried: *"Mort aux vaches!"* then we are forced to believe that Matra is obsessed, and if the term be not too strong, suffering from the mania of persecution.

'And even if Crainquebille did cry, *"Mort aux vaches!"* it remains to be proved whether such words on his lips can be regarded as an offense. Crainquebille is the natural child of a costermonger, depraved by years of drinking and other evil courses. Crainquebille was born alcoholic. You behold him brutalized by sixty years of poverty. Gentlemen, you must conclude that he is irresponsible.'

Maître Lemerle sat down. Then President Bourriche muttered a sentence condemning Jérôme Crainquebille to pay fifty francs fine and to go to prison for a fortnight. The magistrates convicted him on the strength of the evidence given by Constable Matra.

As he was being taken down the long dark passage of the

Palais, Crainquebille felt an intense desire for sympathy. He turned to the municipal guard who was his escort and called him three times:

' 'Cipal! . . . 'cipal . . . Eh! 'cipal!' And he sighed:

'If anyone had told me only a fortnight ago that this would happen!'

Then he reflected:

'They speak too quickly, these gentlemen. They speak well, but they speak too quickly. You can't make them understand you . . . 'cipal, don't you think they speak too quickly?'

But the soldier marched straight on without replying or turning his head.

Crainquebille asked him:

'Why don't you answer me?'

The soldier was silent. And Crainquebille said bitterly:

'You would speak to a dog. Why not to me? Do you never open your mouth? Is it because your breath is foul?'

CHAPTER IV

An apology for President Bourriche

After the sentence had been pronounced, several members of the audience and two or three lawyers left the hall. The clerk was already calling another case. Those who went out did not reflect on the Crainquebille affair, which had not greatly interested them; and they thought no more about it. Monsieur Jean Lermite, an etcher, who happened to be at the Palais, was the only one who meditated on what he had just seen and heard. Putting his arm on the shoulder of Maître Joseph Aubarée, he said:

'President Bourriche must be congratulated on having kept his mind free from idle curiosity, and from the intellectual pride which is determined to know everything. If he had weighed one against the other the contradictory evidence of Constable Matra and Dr. David Matthieu, the magistrate would have adopted a course leading to nothing but doubt and uncertainty. The method of examining facts in a critical spirit would be fatal to the administration of justice. If the judge were so imprudent as to follow that method, his sentences would depend on his personal sagacity, of which he has generally no very great store, and on human infirmity which is universal. Where can he find a criterion? It cannot be denied that the historical method is absolutely incapable of providing him with the certainty he needs. In this connexion you may recall a story told of Sir Walter Raleigh.

' "One day, when Raleigh, a prisoner in the Tower of London, was working, as was his wont, at the second part of his "History of the World," there was a scuffle under his window. He went and looked at the brawlers; and when he returned to his work, he thought he had observed them very carefully. But on the morrow, having related the incident to one of his friends who had witnessed the affair and had even taken part in it, he was contradicted by his friend on every point. Reflecting, therefore, that if he were mistaken as to events which passed beneath his very eyes, how much greater must be the difficulty of ascertaining the truth concerning events far distant, he threw the manuscript of his history into the fire."

'If the judges had the same scruples as Sir Walter Raleigh, they would throw all their notes into the fire. But they have no right to do so. They would thus be flouting justice; they would be committing a crime. We may despair of knowing, we must not despair of judging. Those who demand that sentences pronounced in Law Courts should be founded upon a methodical examination of facts, are dangerous sophists, and perfidious enemies of justice both civil and military. President Bourriche has too judicial a mind to permit his sentences to depend on reason and knowledge, the conclusions of which are eternally open to question. He founds them on dogma and moulds them by tradition, so that the authority of his sentences is equal to that of the Church's commandments. His sentences are indeed canonical. I mean that he derives them from a certain number of sacred canons. See, for example, how he classifies evidence, not according to the uncertain and deceptive qualities of appearances and of human veracity, but according to intrinsic, permanent and manifest qualities. He weighs them in the scale, using weapons of war for weights. Can anything be at once simpler and wise? Irrefutable for him is the evidence of a guardian of the peace, once his humanity be abstracted, and be conceived as a registered number, and according to the categories of an ideal police. Not that Matra (Bastien), born at Cinto-Monte in Corsica, appears to him incapable of error. He never thought that Bastien Matra was gifted with any great faculty of observation, nor that he applied any secret and vigorous method to the examination of facts. In truth it is not Bastien Matra he is considering, but Constable 64. A man is fallible, he thinks. Peter and Paul may be mistaken. Descartes and Gassendi, Leibnitz and Newton, Bichat and Claude Bernard were capable of error. We may all err and at any moment. The causes of error are innumerable. The perceptions of our senses and the judgment of our minds are sources of illusion and causes of uncertainty. We dare not rely on the evidence of a single man: *Testis unus, testis nullus.* But we may have faith in a number. Bastien Matra, of Cinto-Monte, is fallible. But Constable 64, when abstraction has been made of his humanity, cannot err. He is an entity. An entity has nothing in common with a man, it is free from all that confuses, corrupts and deceives men. It is pure unchangeable and unalloyed. Wherefore the magistrates did not hesitate to reject the evidence of the mere man, Dr. David Matthieu, and to admit that of Constable 64, who is the pure idea, an emanation from divinity come down to the judgment bar.

'By following such a line of argument, President Bourriche attains to a kind of infallibility, the only kind to which a magistrate may aspire. When the man who bears witness is armed with a sword, it is the sword's evidence that must be listened to, not the man's. The man is contemptible and may be wrong. The sword is not contemptible and is always right. President Bourriche has seen deeply into the spirit of laws. Society rests on force; force must be respected as the august foundation of society. Justice is the administration of force. President Bourriche knows that Constable 64 is an integral part of the Government. The Government is immanent in each one of its officers. To slight the authority of Constable

64 is to weaken the State. To eat the leaves of an artichoke is to eat the artichoke, as Bossuct puts it in his sublime language. *(Politique tirée de l'Ecriture sainte, passim).*

'All the swords of the State are turned in the same direction. To oppose one to the other is to overthrow the Republic. For that reason, Crainquebille, the accused, is justly condemned to a fortnight in prison and a fine of fifty francs, on the evidence of Constable 64. I seem to hear President Bourriche, himself, explaining the high and noble considerations which inspired his sentence. I seem to hear him saying:

' "I judged this person according to the evidence of Constable 64, because Constable 64 is the emanation of public force. And if you wish to prove my wisdom, imagine the consequences had I adopted the opposite course. You will see at once that it would have been absurd. For if my judgments were in opposition to force, they would never be executed. Notice, gentlemen, that judges are only obeyed when force is on their side. A judge without policemen would be but an idle dreamer. I should be doing myself an injury if I admitted a policeman to be in the wrong. Moreover, the very spirit of laws is in opposition to my doing so. To disarm the strong and to arm the weak would be to subvert that social order which it is my duty to preserve. Justice is the sanction of established injustice. Was justice ever seen to oppose conquerors and usurpers? When an unlawful power arises, justice has only to recognize it and it becomes lawful. Form is everything; and between crime and innocence there is but the thickness of a piece of stamped paper. It was for you, Crainquebille, to be the strongest. If, after having cried: "*Mort aux vaches!*" you had declared yourself emperor, dictator, President of the Republic or even town councillor, I assure you you would not have been sentenced to pass a fortnight in prison, and to pay a fine of fifty francs. I should have acquitted you. You may be sure of that."

'Such would have doubtless been the words of President Bourriche; for he has a judicial mind, and he knows what a magistrate owes to society. With order and regularity he defends social principles. Justice is social. Only wrong-headed persons would make justice out to be human and reasonable. Justice is administered upon fixed rules, not in obedience to physical emotions and flashes of intelligence. Above all things do not ask justice to be just, it has no need to be just since it is justice, and I might even say that the idea of just justice can have only arisen in the brains of an anarchist. True, President Magnaud pronounces just sentences; but if they are reversed, that is still justice.

'The true judge weighs his evidence with weights that are weapons. So it was in the Crainquebille affair, and in other more famous cases.'

Thus said Monsieur Jean Lermite as he paced up and down the Salle des Pas Perdus.

Scratching the tip of his nose, Maître Joseph Aubarré, who knows the Palais well, replied:

'If you want to hear what I think, I don't believe that President Bourriche rose to so lofty a metaphysical plane. In my opinion, when he received as true the evidence of Constable 64, he merely acted according to precedent. Imitation lies at the root of most human actions. A respectable person is one who conforms to custom. Poeple are called good when they do as others do.'

CHAPTER V

Crainquebille submits to the Laws of the Republic

Having been taken back to his prison, Crainquebille sat down on his chained stool, filled with astonishment and admiration. He, himself, was not quite sure whether the magistrates were mistaken. The tribunal had concealed its essential weakness beneath the majesty of form. He could not believe that he was in the right, as against magistrates whose reasons he had not understood: it was impossible for him to conceive that anything could go wrong in so elaborate a ceremony. For, unaccustomed to attending Mass or frequenting the Elysée, he had never in his life witnessed anything so grand as a police court trial. He was perfectly aware that he had never cried *'Mort aux vaches!'* That for having said it he should have been sentenced to a fortnight's imprisonment seemed to him an august mystery, one of those articles of faith to which believers adhere without understanding them, an obscure, striking, adorable and terrible revelation.

This poor old man believed himself guilty of having mystically offended Constable 64, just as the little boy learning his first Cathechism believes himself guilty of Eve's sin. His sentence had taught him that he had cried *'Mort aux vaches!'* He must, therefore, have cried *'Mort aux vaches!'* in some mysterious manner, unknown to himself. He was transported into a supernatural world. His trial was his apocalypse.

If he had no very clear idea of the offence, his idea of the penalty was still less clear. His sentence appeared to him a solemn and superior ritual, somewhat dazzling and incomprehensible, which is not to be discussed, and for which one is neither to be praised nor pitied. If at that moment he had seen President Bourriche, with white wings and a halo round his forehead, coming down through a hole in the ceiling, he would not have been surprised at this new manifestation of judicial glory. He would have said: 'This is my trial continuing!'

On the next day his lawyer visited him:

'Well, my good fellow, things aren't so bad after all! Don't be discouraged. A fortnight is soon over. We have not much to complain of.'

'As for that, I must say the gentlemen were very kind, very polite: not a single rude word. I shouldn't have believed it. And the *cipal* was wearing white gloves. Did you notice?'

'Everything considered, we did well to confess.'

'Perhaps.'

'Crainquebille, I have a piece of good news for you. A charitable person, whose interest I have elicited on your behalf, gave me fifty francs for you. The sum will be used to pay your fine.'

'When will you give me the money?'

'It will be paid into the clerk's office. You need not trouble about it.'

'It does not matter. All the same I am very grateful to this person.' And Crainquebille murmured meditatively: 'It's something out of the common that's happening to me.'

'Don't exaggerate, Crainquebille. Your case is by no means rare, far from it.

'You couldn't tell me where they've put by barrow?'

CHAPTER VI

Crainquebille in the light of public opinion

After his discharge from prison Crainquebille trundled his barrow along the Rue Montemarte, crying: 'Cabbages, turnips, carrots!' He was neither ashamed nor proud of his adventure. The memory of it was not painful. He classed it in his mind with dreams, travels and plays. But, above all things, he was glad to be walking in the mud, along the paved streets, and to see overhead the rainy sky of the town. At every corner he stopped to have a drink; then, gay and unconstrained, spitting in his hands in order to moisten his horny palms, he would seize the shafts and push on his barrow. Meanwhile a flight of sparrows, as poor and as early as he, seeking their livelihood in the road, flew off at the sound of his familiar cry: 'Cabbages, turnips, carrots!' An old housewife, who had come up, said to him as she felt his celery:

'What's happened to you, Pére Crainquebille? We haven't seen you for three weeks. Have you been ill? You look rather pale.'

'I'll tell you, M'ame Mailloche, I've been doing the gentleman.'

Nothing in life changed, except that he went oftener to the pub, because he had an idea it was a holiday and that he had made the acquaintance of charitable folk. He returned to his garret rather gay. Stretched on his mattress he drew over him the sacks borrowed from the chestnut-seller at the corner which served him as blankets, and he pondered: 'Well, prison is not so bad; one has everything one wants there. But all the same one is better at home.'

His contentment did not last long. He soon perceived that his customers looked at him askance.

'Fine celery, M'ame Cointreau!

'I don't want anything.'

'What! nothing! do you live on air, then?'

And M'ame Cointreau without deigning to reply returned to the large bakery of which she was the mistress. The shopkeepers and caretakers, who had once flocked round his barrow all green and blooming, now turned away from him. Having reached the shoe-maker's, at the sign of l'Ange Gardien, the place where his adventures with justice had begun, he called:

'M'ame Bayard, M'ame Bayard, you owe me sevenpence halfpenny from last time.'

But M'ame Bayard, who was sitting at her counter, did not deign to turn her head.

The whole of the Rue Montmartre was aware that Pére Crainquebille had been in prison, and the whole of the Rue Montemartre gave up his acquaintance. The rumour of his conviction had reached the Faubourg and the noisy corner of the Rue Richer. There, about noon, he perceived Madame Laure, a kind and faithful customer, leaning over the barrow of another costermonger, young Martin. She was feeling a large cabbage. Her hair shone in the sunlight like masses of golden threads loosely twisted. And young Martin, a nobody, a good-for-nothing, was protesting with his hand on his heart that there were no finer vegetables than his. At this sight Crainquebille's heart was rent. He pushed his barrow up to young Martin's, and in a plaintive broken voice said to Madame Laure: 'It's not fair of you to forsake me.'

As Madame Laure herself admitted, she was no duchess. It was not in society that she had acquired her ideas of the prison van and the police-station. But can one not be honest in every station of life? Everyone has his self respect; and one does not like to deal with a man who has just come out of prison. So the only notice she took of Crainquebille was to give him a look of disgust. And the old costermonger resenting the affront shouted:

'Dirty wench go along with you.'

Madame Laure let fall her cabbage and cried:

'Eh! Be off with you, you bad penny. You come out of

prison and then insult folk!'

If Crainquebille had had any self-control he would never have reproached Madame Laure with her calling. He knew only too well that one is not master of one's fate, that one cannot always choose one's occupation, and that good people may be found everywhere. He was accustomed discreetly to ignore her customers' business with her; and he despised no one. But he was beside himself. Three times he called Madame Laure drunkard, wench, harridan. A group of idlers gathered round Madame Laure and Crainquebille. They exchanged a few more insults as serious as the first; and they would soon have exhausted their vocabulary, if a policeman had not suddenly appeared, and at once, by his silence and immobility, rendered them as silent and motionless as himself. They separated. But this scene put the finishing touch to the discrediting of Crainquebille in the eyes of the Faubourg Montemartre and the Rue Richer.

CHAPTER VII

Results

The old man went along mumbling:

'For certain she's a hussy, and none more of a hussy than she.'

But at the bottom of his heart that was not the reproach he brought against her. He did not scorn her for being what she was. Rather he esteemed her for it, knowing her to be frugal and orderly. Once they had liked to talk together. She used to tell him of her parents who lived in the country. And they had both resolved to have a little garden and keep poultry. She was a good customer. And then to see her buying cabbages from young Martin, a dirty, good-for-nothing wretch; it cut him to the heart; and when she pretended to despise him, that put his back up, and then . . .

But she, alas; was not the only one who shunned him as if he had the plague. Every one avoided him. Just like Madame Laure, Madam Cointreau the baker, Madame Bayard of l'Ange Gardien scorned and repulsed him. Why! the whole of society refused to have anything to do with him.

So because one had been put away for a fortnight one was not good enough even to sell leeks! Was it just? Was it reasonable to make a decent chap die of starvation because he had got into difficulties with a copper? If he was not to be allowed to sell vegetables then it was all over with him. Like a badly doctored wine he turned sour. After having had words with everyone. For a mere nothing he would tell his customers what he thought of them and in no ambiguous terms, I assure you. If they felt his wares too long he would call them to their faces chatterer, soft head. Like-wise at the wine-shop he bawled at his comrades. His friend, the chestnut-seller, no longer recognized him; old Pére Crainquebille, he said, had turned into a regular porcupine. It cannot be denied: he was becoming rude, disagreeable, evil-mouthed, loquacious. The truth of the matter was that he was discovering the imperfections of society; but he had not the facilities of a Professor of Moral and Political Science for the expression of his ideas concerning the vices of the system and the reforms necessary; and his thoughts evolved devoid of order and moderation.

Misfortune was rendering him unjust. He was taking revenge on those who did not wish him ill and sometimes on those who were weaker than he. One day he boxed Alphonse, the wine-seller's little boy, on the ear, because he had asked him what it was like to be sent away. Crainquebille struck him and said:

'Dirty brat! It's your father who ought to be sent away instead of growing rich by selling poison.'

A deed and a speech which did him no honour; for, as the chestnut-seller justly remarked, one ought not to strike a child, neither should one reproach him with a father whom he has not chosen.

Crainquebille began to drink. The less money he earned the more brandy he drank. Formerly frugal and sober, he himself marvelled at the change.

'I never used to be a waster,' he said. 'I suppose one doesn't improve as one grows old.'

Sometimes he severely blamed himself for his misconduct

and his laziness:

'Crainquebille, old chap, you ain't good for anything but liftin' your glass.'

Sometimes he deceived himself and made out that he needed the drink.

'I must have it now and then; I must have a drop to strengthen me and cheer me up. It seems as if I had a fire in my inside; and there's nothing like the drink for quenching it.'

It often happened that he missed the auction in the morning and so had to provide himself with damaged fruit and vegetables on credit. One day, feeling tired and discouraged, he left his barrow in its shed, and spent the livelong day hanging round the stall of Madame Rose, the tripe-seller, or lounging in and out of the wine-shops near the market. In the evening, sitting on a basket, he meditated and became conscious of his deterioration. He recalled the strength of his early years: the achievements of former days, the arduous labours and the glad evenings: those days quickly passing, all alike and fully occupied; the pacing in the darkness up and down the market pavement, waiting for the early auction; the vegetables carried in armfuls and artistically arranged in the barrow; the piping hot black coffee of Mère Théodore swallowed standing, and at one gulp; the shafts grasped vigorously; and then the loud cry, piercing as cock crow, rending the morning air as he passed through the crowded streets. All that innocent rough life of the human pack-horse came before him. For half a century on his travelling stall, he had borne to townsfolk worn with care and vigil the fresh harvest of kitchen gardens. Shaking his head he sighed:

'No! I'm not what I was. I'm done for. The pitcher goes so often to the well that at last it comes home broken. And then I've never been the same since my affair with the magistrates. No, I'm not the man I was.'

In short he was demoralized. And when a man reaches that condition he might as well be on the ground and unable to rise. All the passers-by tread him under foot.

CHAPTER VIII

The final result

Poverty came, black poverty. The old costermonger who used to come back from the Faubourg Montemarte with a bag full of five-franc pieces, had not a single coin now. Winter came. Driven out of his garret, he slept under the carts in a shed. It had been raining for days; the gutters were overflowing, and the shed was flooded.

Crouching in his barrow, over the pestilent water, in the company of spiders, rats and half-starved cats, he was meditating in the gloom. Having eaten nothing all day and no longer having the chestnut-seller's sacks for a covering, he recalled the fortnight when the Government had provided him with food and clothing. He envied the prisoners' fate. They suffer neither cold nor hunger, and an idea occurred to him:

'Since I know the trick why don't I use it?'

He rose and went out into the street. It was a little past eleven. The night was dark and chill. A drizzling mist was falling, colder and more penetrating than rain. The few passers-by crept along under cover of the houses.

Crainquebille went past the Church of Saint-Eustache and turned into the Rue Montemartre. It was deserted. A guardian of the peace stood on the pavement, by the apse of the church. He was under a gas-lamp, and all around fell a fine rain looking reddish in the gaslight. It fell on to the policeman's hood. He looked chilled to the bone; but, either because he preferred to be in the light or because he was tired of walking he stayed under the lamp, and perhaps it seemed to him a friend, a companion. In the loneliness of the night the flickering flame was his only entertainment. In his immobility he appeared hardly human. The reflection of his boots on the wet pavement, which looked like a lake, prolonged him downwards and gave him from a distance the air of some amphibious monster half out of water. Observed more closely he had at once a monkish and a military appearance. The coarse feature of his countenance, magnified under the shadow of his hood, were sad and placid. He wore a thick moustache, short and grey. He was an old copper, a man of some two-score years. Crainquebille went up to him softly, and in a weak hesitating voice, said: *'Mort aux vaches!'*

Then he awaited the result of those sacred words. But nothing came of them. The constable remained motionless and silent, with his arms folded under his short cloak. His eyes were wide open; they glistened in the darkness and regarded Crainquebille with sadness, vigilance and scorn.

Crainquebille, astonished, but still resolute, muttered:

'*Mort aux vaches!* I tell you.'

There was a long silence in the chill darkness and the falling of the fine penetrating rain. At last the constable spoke:

'Such things are not said . . . For sure and for certain they are not said. At your age you ought to know better. Pass on.'

'Why don't you arrest me?' asked Crainquebille.

The constable shook his head beneath his dripping hood:

'If we were to take up all the addlepates who say what they oughtn't to, we should have our work cut out! . . . And what would be the use of it?'

Overcome by such magnanimous disdain. Crainquebille remained for some time stolid and silent, with his feet in the gutter. Before going, he tried to explain:

'I didn't mean to say: *Mort aux vaches!* to you. It was not for you more than for another. It was only an idea.'

The constable replied sternly but kindly:

'Whether an idea or anything else it ought not to be said, because when a man does his duty and endures much, he ought not to be insulted with idle words . . . I tell you again to pass on.'

Crainquebille, with head bent and arms hanging limp, plunged into the rain and darkness.

JOHN GALSWORTHY

Blackmail

I

The affectionate if rather mocking friend who had said of Charles Granter: '*Ce n'est pas un homme, c'est un bâtiment,*' seemed justified, to the thin dark man following him down Oakley Street, Chelsea, that early October afternoon. From the square foundations of his feet to his square fair beard and the top of his head under a square black bowler, he looked very big, solid as granite, indestructible – steel-clad, too, for his grey clothes increase his bulk in the mild sunlight; too big to be taken by the board – only fit to be submarined. And the man, dodging in his wake right down to the Embankment, ran up once or twice under his counter and fell behind again, as if appalled by the vessel's size and unconsciousness. Considering the heat of the past summer, the plane-trees were still very green, and few of their twittering leaves had dropped or turned yellow – just enough to confirm the glamorous melancholy of early Fall. Granter, though he lived with his wife in some mansions close by, went out of his way to pass under those trees and look at the river. This seeming disclosure of sensibility, perhaps, determined the shadowy man to dodge up again and become stationary close behind. Ravaged and streaked, as if he had lived submerged, he stood carefully noting with his darting dark eyes that they two were quite alone; then, swallowing violently so that the strings of his lean neck writhed, he moved stealthily up beside Granter, and said in a hurried, hoarse voice: 'Beg pardon, Mister – ten pound, and I'll say nothin'.'

The face which Granter turned towards that surprising utterance was a good illustration of the saying, 'And things are not what they seem.' Above that big building of a body it quivered, ridiculously alive, and complex, as of a man full of nerves, humours, sarcasms; and a deep continuous chinking sound arose – of Charles Granter jungling coins in his trouser pocket. The quiver settled into raised eyebrows, into crows' feet running out on to the broad cheekbones, into a sarcastic smile drooping the corners of the lips between moustache and beard. He said in his rather high voice:

'What's the matter with you, my friend?'

'There's a lot the matter with me, Mister. Down and out I am. I know where you live, I know your lady; but – ten pound and I'll say nothin'.'

'About what?'

'About your visitin' that gell, where you've just come from. Ten pound. It's cheap – I'm a man of me word.'

With lips still sarcastically drooped, Granter made a little derisive sound.

Blackmail, by George!

'Come on, Guv'nor – I'm desperate;. I mean to have that ten pound. You give it me here at six o'clock this evenin', if you'aven't got it on you.' His eyes flared suddenly in his hungry face. 'But no tricks! I aint killed Huns for nothin'.'

Granter surveyed him for a moment, then turned his back and looked at the water.

'Well, you've got two hours to get it in – six o'clock, Mister; and no tricks – I warn you.'

The hoarse voice ceased, the sound of footsteps died away; Granter was alone. The smile still clung to his lips, but he was not amused; he was annoyed, with the measured indignation of a big man highly civilised and innocent. Where had this ruffian sprung from? To be spied on, without knowing it, like this! His ears grew red. The damned scoundrel!

The thing was too absurd to pay attention to. And, instantly, his highly-sophisticated consciousness began to pay attention. How many visits had he made to this distressed flower-girl? Three? And all because he didn't like handing over the case to that Society which always found out the worst. They said private charity was dangerous. Apparently it was! Blackmail! A consideration came perching like a crow on the branches of his mind: why hadn't he mentioned the flower-girl to his wife, and made *her* do the visiting? Why! Because Olga would have said the girl was a fraud. And perhaps she was! A put-up job! Would the scoundrel have ventured on this threat at all if the girl were not behind him? She might support him with lies! His wife might believe them – She – she had such a vein of cynicism! How sordid, how domestically unpleasant!

Granter felt quite sick. Every decent human value seemed suddenly in question. And a second crow came croaking. Could one leave a scoundrel like this to play his tricks with impunity? Oughtn't one to go to the police? He stood extraordinarily still – a dappled leaf dropped from a plane-tree and lodged on his bowler hat; at the other end of him a little dog mistook him for a lamp-post. This was no joke! For a man with a reputation for humanity, integrity and commonsense – no joke at all! A Police Court meant the prosecution of a fellow-creature; getting him perhaps a year's imprisonment, when one had always felt that punishment practically never fitted crime! Staring at the river, he seemed to see cruelty hovering over himself, his wife, Society, the flower-girl, even over that scoundrel – naked cruelty, waiting to pounce on one or all. Whichever way one turned, the thing was dirty, cruel. No wonder blackmail was accounted such a heinous crime. No other human act was so cold-blooded, spider-like, and slimy; none plunged so deadly a dagger into the bowels of compassion so eviscerated humanity, so murdered faith! And it would have been worse, if his conscience had not been clear. But was it so extremely clear? Would he have taken the trouble to go to that flower-girl's dwelling, not once, but three times, unless she had been attractive, unless her dark brown eyes had been pretty, and her common voice so soft? Would he have visited the blowsy old flower-woman at that other corner, in circumstances, no doubt, just as strenuous? His honesty answered: No. But his sense of justice added that, if he did like a pretty face, he was not vicious – he was fastidious and detested subterfuge. But then Olga was so cynical; she would certainly ask him why he hadn't visited the old flower-woman as well, and the lame man who sold matches, and all the other stray unfortunates of the neighbourhood. Well, there it was; and a bold course always the best! But what was the bold course? To go to the police? To his wife? To that girl, and find out if she were in this ramp? To wait till six o'clock, meet the ruffian, and shake the teeth out of him? Granter could not decide. All seemed equally bold – would do equally well. And a fifth course presented itself which seemed even bolder: Ignore the thing!

The tide had just turned, and the full waters below him were in suspense, of a sunlit soft grey colour. This stillness of the river restored to Charles Granter something of the impersonal mood in which he had crossed the Embankment to look at it. Here, by the mother stream of this great town, was he, tall, strong, well-fed, and, if not rich, quite comfortable; and here, too, were hundreds of thousands like that needy flower-girl and this shadowy scoundrel, skating on the edge of destitution. And here this water was – to him a source of aesthetic enjoyment – to them a possible last refuge. The girl had talked of it – beggar's patter, perhaps, like the blackmailer's words: 'I'm desperate – I'm down and out.'

One wanted to be just! If he had known all about them – but there it was, he knew nothing!

'I can't believe she's such an ungrateful little wretch!' he thought. 'I'll go back and see her again.' . . .

He retraced his way up Oakley Street to the Mews which she inhabited, and, ascending a stairway scented with petrol, knocked on a half-open door, whence he could see her baby, of doubtful authorship, seated in an empty flower-basket – a yellow baby, who stared up at him with the placidity of one recently fed. That stare seemed to Granter to be saying: 'You look out that you're not taken for my author. Have you got an alibi, old man?' And almost unconsciously he began to calculate where he had been about fourteen or fifteen months ago. Not in London – thank goodness! In Brittany with his wife – all that July, August, and September. Jingling his money, he contemplated the baby. It seemed more, but it *might* be only four months old! The baby opened its mouth in a toothless smile. 'Ga!' it said, and stretched out a tiny hand. Granter ceased to jingle the coins and gazed round the room. The first time he came, a month ago, to test her street-corner story, its condition had been deplorable. His theory that people were never better than their environments had prompted the second visit, and that of this afternoon. He had, he told himself, wanted to know that he was not throwing away his money. And there certainly was some appearance of comfort now in a room so small that he and the baby and a bed almost filled it. But the longer he contemplated them, the greater fool he felt for ever having come there even with those best intentions which were the devil. And, turning to go, he saw the girl herself coming up the stairs, with a paper bag in her hand and evident bull's-eye in her mouth, for a scent of peppermint preceded her. Surely her cheekbones were higher than he had thought, her eyebrows more oblique – a gipsy look! Her eyes, dark and lustrous as a hound puppy's, smiled at him, and he said in his rather high voice:

'I came back to ask you something.'

'Yes, sir.'

'Do you know a dark man with a thin face and a slight squint, who's been in the Army?'

'What's his name, sir?'

'I don't know; but he followed me from here, and tried to blackmail me on the Embankment. You know what blackmail is?'

'No sir.'

Feline, swift, furtive, she had passed him and taken up her baby, slanting her dark glance at him from behind it. Granter's eyes were very round just then, the corners of his mouth very drawn down. He was experiencing a most queer sensation. Really it was as if – though he disliked poetic emphasis – as if he had suddenly seen something pre-civilised, pre-human, snake-like, cat-like, monkey-like too, in those dark sliding eyes and that yellow baby. Sure, as he stood there, she was in it; or, if not in it, she knew of it!

'A dangerous game, that,' he said. 'Tell him – for his own good – he had better drop it.'

And, while he went, very square, downstairs, he thought: 'This is one of the finest opportunities you ever had for getting to the bottom of human nature, and you're running away from it.' So strongly did this thought obsess him that he halted, in two minds, outside. A chauffeur, who was cleaning his car, looked at him curiously. Charles Granter moved away.

II

When he reached the little drawing-room of their flat, his wife was making tea. She was rather short, with a good figure, and brown eyes in a flattish face, powdered and by no means unattractive. She had Slav blood in her – Polish; and Granter never now confided to her the finer shades of his thoughts and conduct because she had long made him feel he was her superior in moral sensibility. He had no wish to feel superior – it was often very awkward; but he could not help it. In view of this attempt at blackmail, it was more than awkward. For it is extraordinarily unpleasant to fall from a pedestal on which you do not wish to be.

He sat down, very large, in a lacquered chair with black cushions, spoke of the leaves turning, saw her look at him and smile, and felt that she knew he was disturbed.

'Do you ever wonder,' he said, tinkling his teaspoon, 'about the lives that other people live?'

'What sort of people, Charles?'

'Oh – not our sort; matchsellers, don't you know, flower-sellers, people down and out?'

'No, I don't think I do.'

If only he could tell her of this monstrous incident without slipping from his pedestal!

'It interests me enormously; there are such queer depths to reach, don't you know.'

Her smile seemed to answer: 'You don't reach the depths in me.' And it was true. She was very Slav, with the warm gleam in her eyes and the opaque powdered skin of her flat comely face. An enigma – flatly an enigma! There were deep waters below the pedestal, like – like Phylæ, with columns still standing in the middle of the Nile Dam. Absurd!

'I've often wondered,' he said, 'how I should feel if I were down and out.'

'You? You're too large, Charles, and too dignified, my dear; you'd be on the Civil List before you could turn round.' Granter rose from the lacquered chair, jingling his coins. The most vivid pictures at that moment were like a film, unrolled before his mind – of the grey sunlit river, and that accosting blackguard with his twisted murky face, and lips uttering hoarse sounds; of the yellow baby, and the girl's gipsy-dark glance from behind it; of a Police Court, and himself standing there and letting the whole cart-load of the Law fall on them. And he said suddenly:

'I was blackmailed this afternoon, on the Embankment.'

She did not answer, and, turning with irritation, he saw that her fingers were in her ears.

'I do wish you wouldn't jingle your money so!' she said.

Confound it! She had not heard him.

'I've had an adventure,' he began again. 'You know the flower-girl who stands at that corner in Tite Street?'

'Yes; a gipsy baggage.'

'H'm! Well, I bought a flower from her one day, and she told me such a pathetic story that I went to her den to see if it was true. It seemed all right, so I gave her some money, don't you know. Then I thought I'd better see how she was spending it, so I went to see her again, don't you know.'

A faint 'Oh! Charles!' caused him to hurry on.

'And – what d'you think – a blackguard followed me today and tried to blackmail me for ten pounds on the Embankment.'

A sound brought his face round to attention. His wife was lying back on the cushions of her chair in paroxysms of soft laughter.

It was clear to Granter, then, that what he had really been afraid of was just this. His wife would laugh at him – laugh at him slipping from the pedestal! Yes! it was that he had dreaded – not any disbelief in his fidelity. Somehow he felt too large to be laughed at. He *was* too large! Nature had set a size beyond which husbands – !

'I don't see what there is to laugh at!' he said frigidly; 'there's no more odious crime than blackmail.'

His wife was silent; two tears were trickling down her cheeks.

'Did you give it him?' she said in an extinguished voice.

'Of course not.'

'What was he threatening?'

'To tell you.'

'But what?'

'His beastly interpretation of my harmless visits.'

The tears had made runlets in her powder, and he added viciously: 'He doesn't know you, of course.'

His wife dabbed her eyes, and a scent of geranium arose.

'It seems to me,' said Granter, 'that you'd be even more amused if there were something in it!'

'Oh! no, Charles, but – perhaps there is.'

Granter looked at her fixedly.

'I'm sorry to disappoint you, there is not.'

He saw her cover her lips with that rag of handkerchief, and abruptly left the room.

He went into his study and sat down before the fire. So it was funny to be a faithful husband? And suddenly he thought: 'If my wife can treat this as a joke, what – what about herself?' A nasty thought! An unconscionable thought! Really, it was as though that blackmailing scoundrel had dirtied human nature, till it seemed to function only from low motives. A church clock chimed. Six already! The ruffian would be back there on the Embankment, waiting for his ten pounds. Granter rose. His duty was to go out and hand him over to the police.

'No!' he thought viciously, 'let him come here! I'd very much like him to come here. I'd teach him!'

But a sort of shame beset him. Like most very big men, he was quite unaccustomed to violence – had never struck a blow in his life, not even in his schooldays – had never had occasion to. He went across to the window. From there he could just see the Embankment parapet though the trees, in the failing light, and presently – sure enough – made out the fellow's figure slinking up and down like a hungry dog. And he stood, watching, jingling his money – nervous, sarcastic, angry, very interested. What would the rascal do now? Would he beard this great block of flats? And was the girl down there too – the girl, with her yellow baby? He saw the slinking figure cross from the far side and vanish under the loom of the mansions. In that interesting moment Granter burst through the bottom of one of his trousers pockets: several coins jingled on to the floor and rolled away. He was still looking for the last when he heard the door-bell ring – he had never really believed the ruffian would come up! Straightening himself abruptly, he went out into the hall. Service was performed by the mansions staff, so there was no one in the flat but himself and his wife. The bell rang again, and she, too, appeared.

'This is my Embankment friend who amuses you so much. I should like you to see him,' he said grimly. He noted a quizzical apology on her face and opened the hall door.

Yes! there stood the man! By electric light, in upholstered surroundings, more 'down and out' than ever. A bad lot, but a miserable poor wretch, with his broken boots, his thin, twisted, twitching face, his pinched shabby figure – only his hungry eyes looked dangerous.

'Come in,' said Granter. 'You want to see my wife, I think.'

The man recoiled.

'I don't want to see 'er,' he muttered, 'unless you force me to. Give us *five* pound, Guv'nor, and I won't worry you again. I don't want to cause trouble between man and wife.'

'Come in,' repeated Granter; 'she's expecting you.'

The man stood, silently passing a pale tongue over a pale upper lip, as though conjuring some new resolution from his embarrassment.

'Now, see 'ere, Mister,' he said suddenly, 'you'll regret it if I come in – you will, straight.'

'I shall regret it if you don't. You're a very interesting fellow, and an awful scoundrel.'

'Well, who made me one?' the man burst out; 'you answer me that.'

'Are you coming in?'

'Yes, I am.'

He came, and Granter shut the door behind him. It was like inviting a snake or a mad dog into one's parlour; but the memory of having been laughed at was so fresh within him that he rather welcomed the sensation.

'Now,' he said, 'have the kindness!' and opened the drawing-room door.

The man slunk in, blinking in the stronger light.

Granter went towards his wife, who was standing before the fire.

'This gentleman has an important communication to make to you, it seems.'

The expression of her face struck him as peculiar – surely she was not frightened! And he experienced a kind of pleasure in seeing them both look so exquisitely uncomfortable.

'Well,' he said ironically, 'perhaps you'd like me not to listen.' And, going back to the door, he stood leaning aginst it with his hands up to his ears. He saw the fellow give him a furtive look and go nearer to her; his lips moved rapidly, hers answered, and he thought: 'What on earth am I covering my ears for?' As he took his hands away, the man turned round and said:

'I'm goin' now, Mister; a little mistake – sorry to 'ave troubled you.'

His wife had turned to the fire again; and with a puzzled feeling Granter opened the door. As the fellow passed, he took him by the arm, twisted him round into the study locking the door, put the key into his pocket.

'Now, then,' he said, 'you precious scoundrel!'

The man shifted on his broken boots. 'Don't you hit me, Guv'nor. I got a knife here.'

'I'm not going to hit you. I'm going to hand you over to the police.'

The man's eyes roved, looking for a way of escape, then rested, as if fascinated, on the glowing hearth.

'What's ten pound?' he said suddenly. 'You'd never ha' missed it.'

Granter smiled.

'You don't seem to realise, my friend, that blackmail is the most devilish crime a man can commit.' And he crossed over to the telephone.

The man's eyes, dark, restless, violent, and yet hungry, began to shift up and down the building of a man before him.

'No,' he said suddenly, with a sort of pathos, 'don't do that, Guv'nor!'

Something – the look of his eyes or the tone of his voice – affected Granter.

'But if I don't,' he said slowly, 'you'll be blackmailing the next person you meet. You're as dangerous as a viper.'

The man's lips quivered; he covered them with his hand, and said from behind it:

'I'm a man like yourself. I'm down and out – that's all. Look at me!'

Granter's glance dwelt on the trembling hand. 'Yes, but you fellows destroy all belief in human nature,' he said vehemently.

'See 'ere, Guv'nor; you try livin' like me – you try it! My Gawd! You try my life these last six months – cadgin' and crawlin' for a job!' He made a deep sound. 'A man 'oo's done 'is bit, too. Wot life is it? A stinkin' life, not fit for a dawg, let alone a 'uman bein'. An' when I see a great big chap like you, beggin' your pardon, Mister – well fed, with everything to 'is 'and – it was regular askin' for it. It come over me, it did.'

'No, no,' said Granter grimly; 'that won't do. It couldn't have been sudden. You calculated – you concocted this. Blackmail is sheer filthy cold-blooded blackguardism. You don't care two straws whom you hurt, whose lives you wreck, what faiths you destroy.' And he put his hand on the receiver.

The man squirmed.

'Steady on, Guv'nor! I've gotta find food. I've gotta find clothes. I can't live on air. I can't go naked.'

Granter stood motionless, while the man's voice continued to travel to him across the cosy room.

'Give us a chawnce, Guv'nor! Ah! give us a chawnce! You can't understand my temptations. Don't 'ave the police to me. I won't do this again – give you me word – so 'elp me! I've got it in the neck. Let me go, Guv'nor!'

In Granter, motionless as the flats he lived in, a really heavy struggle was in progress – not between duty and pity, but between revengeful anger and a sort of horror at using the strength of prosperity against so broken a wretch.

'Let me go, Mister!' came the hoarse voice again. 'Be a sport!'

Granter dropped the receiver, and unlocked the door.

'All right; you can go.'

The man crossed swiftly.

'Christ!' he said; 'good luck! And as to the lady – I take it back. I never see 'er. It's all me eye.'

He was across the hall and gone before Granter could say a word; the scurrying shuffle of his footsteps down the stairs died away. 'And as to the lady – I take it back – I never see her. It's all me eye!' Good God! The scoundrel, having failed with him, had been trying to blackmail his wife – his wife, who had laughed at his fidelity! – his wife who had looked – frightened! 'All me eye!' Her face started up before Granter – *scared* under its powder, with a mask drawn over it. And he had let that scoundrel go! Scared! That was the meaning! . . . Blackmail – of all poisonous human action ? . . . His wife ! . . . But . . . what now . . . !

1921

NADINE GORDIMER

The Moment Before the Gun Went Off

Marais Van der Vyver shot one of his farm labourers, dead. An accident, there are accidents with guns every day of the week – children playing a fatal game with a father's revolver in the cities where guns are domestic objects, nowadays, hunting mishaps like this one, in the country – but these won't be reported all over the world. Van der Vyver knows his will be. He knows that the story of the Afrikaner farmer – regional Party leader and Commandant of the local security commando – shooting a black man who worked for him will fit exactly ***their*** version of South Africa, it's made for them. They'll be able to use it in their boycott and divestment campaigns, it'll be another piece of evidence in their truth about the country. The papers at home will quote the story as it has appeared in the overseas press, and in the back-and-forth he and the black man will become those crudely-drawn figures on anti-apartheid banners, units in statistics of white brutality against the blacks quoted at the United Nations – he, whom they will gleefully be able to call 'a leading member' of the ruling Party.

People in the farming community understand how he must feel. Bad enough to have killed a man, without helping the Party's, the government's, the country's enemies, as well. They see the truth of that. They know, reading the Sunday papers, that when Van der Vyver is quoted saying he is 'terribly shocked', he will 'look after the wife and children', none of those American and English, and none of those people at home who want to destroy the white man's power will believe him. And how they will sneer when he even says of the farm boy (according to one paper, if you can trust any of those reporters), 'He was my friend, I always took him hunting with me.' Those city and overseas people don't know it's true: farmers usually have one particular black boy they like to take along with them in the lands; you could call it a kind of friend, yes, friends are not only your own white people, like yourself, you take into your house, pray with in church and work with on the Party committee. But how can those others know that? They don't want to know it. They think all blacks are like the big-mouth agitators in town. And Van der Vyver's face, in the photographs, strangely opened by distress – everyone in the district remembers Marais Van der Vyver as a little boy who would go away and hide himself if he caught you smiling at him, and everyone knows him now as a man who hides any change of expression round his mouth behind a thick, soft moustache, and in his eyes by always looking at some object in hand, leaf of a crop fingered, pen or stone picked up, while concentrating on what he is saying, or while listening to you. It just goes to show what shock can do; when you look at the newspaper photographs you feel like apologizing, as if you had stared in on some room where you should not be.

There will be an inquiry; there had better be, to stop the assumption of yet another case of brutality against farm workers, although there's nothing in doubt – an accident, and all the facts fully admitted by Van der Vyver. He made a statement when he arrived at the police station with the dead man in his bakkie. Captain Beetge knows him well, of course; he gave him brandy. He was shaking, this big, calm, clever son of Willem Van der Vyver, who inherited the old man's best farm. The black was stone dead, nothing to be done for him. Beetge will not tell anyone that after the brandy Van der Vyver wept. He sobbed, snot running onto his hands, like a dirty kid. The Captain was ashamed, for him, and walked out to give him a chance to recover himself.

Marais Van der Vyver left his house at three in the afternoon to cull a buck from the family of kudu he protects in the bush areas of his farm. He is interested in wildlife and sees it as the farmers' sacred duty to raise game as well as cattle. As usual, he called at his shed workshop to pick up Lucas, a twenty-year-old farmhand who had shown mechanical aptitude and whom Van der Vyver himself had taught to maintain tractors and other farm machinery. He hooted, and Lucas followed the familiar routine, jumping onto the back of the truck. He liked to travel standing up there, spotting game before his employer did. He would lean forward, braced against the cab below him.

Van der Vyver had a rifle and .300 ammunition beside him in the cab. The rifle was one of his father's, because his own was at the gunsmith's in town. Since his father died (Beetge's sergeant wrote 'passed on') no one had used the rifle and so when he took it from a cupboard he was sure it was not loaded. His father had never allowed a loaded gun in the house; he himself had been taught since childhood never to ride with a loaded weapon in a vehicle. But this gun was loaded. On a dirt track, Lucas thumped his fist on the cab roof three times to signal: look left. Having seen the white-ripple-marked flank of a kudu, and its fine horns raking through disguising bush, Van der Vyver drove rather fast over a pot-hole. The jolt fired the rifle. Upright, it was pointing straight through the cab roof at the head of Lucas. The bullet pierced the roof and entered Lucas's brain by way of his throat.

That is the statement of what happened. Although a man of such standing in the district, Van der Vyver had to go through the ritual of swearing that it was the truth. It has gone on record, and will be there in the archive of the local police station as long as Van der Vyver lives, and beyond that, through the lives of his children, Magnus, Helena and Karel – unless things in the country get worse,the example of black mobs in the towns spreads to the rural areas and the place is burned down as many urban police stations have been. Because nothing the government can do will appease the agitators and the whites who encourage them. Nothing satisfies them, in the cities: blacks can sit and drink in white hotels, now, the Immorality Act has gone, blacks can sleep with whites . . . It's not even a crime any more.

Van der Vyver has a high barbed security fence round his farmhouse and garden which his wife, Alida, thinks spoils completely the effect of her artificial stream with its tree-ferns beneath the jacarandas. There is an aerial soaring like a flag-pole in the back yard. All his vehicles, including the truck in which the black man died, have aerials that swing their whips when the driver hits a pot-hole: they are part of the security system the farmers in the district maintain, each farm in touch with every other by radio, twenty-four hours out of twenty-four. It has already happened that infiltrators from over the border have mined remote farm roads, killing white farmers and their families out on their own property for a Sunday picnic. The pot-hole could have set off a land-mine, and Van der Vyver might have died with his farm boy. When neighbours use the communications system to call up and say they are sorry about 'that business' with one of Van der Vyver's boys, there goes unsaid: it could have been worse.

It is obvious from the quality and fittings of the coffin that the farmer has provided money for the funeral. And an elaborate funeral means a great deal to blacks; look how they will deprive themselves of the little they have, in their lifetime, keeping up payments to a burial society so they won't go in boxwood to an unmarked grave. The young wife is pregnant (of course) and another little one, wearing red shoes several sizes too large, leans under her jutting belly. He is too young to understand what has happened, what he is witnessing that day, but neither whines nor plays about; he is solemn without knowing why. Blacks expose small children to everything, they don't protect them from the sight of fear and pain the way whites do theirs. It is the young wife who rolls her head and cries like a child, sobbing on the breast of this relative and that.

All present work for Van der Vyver or are the families of those who work; and in the weeding and harvest seasons, the women and children work for him, too, carried – wrapped in their blankets, on a truck, singing – at sunrise to the fields. The dead man's mother is a woman who can't be more than in her late thirties (they start bearing children at puberty) but she is heavily mature in a black dress between her own parents, who were already working for old Van der Vyver when Marais, like their daughter, was a child. The parents hold her as if she were a prisoner or a crazy woman to be restrained. But she says nothing, does nothing. She does not look up; she does not look at Van der Vyver, whose gun went off in the truck, she stares at the grave. Nothing will make her look up; there need be no fear that she will look up; at him. His wife, Alida, is beside him. To show the proper respect, as for any white funeral, she is wearing the navy-blue-and-cream hat she wears to church this summer. She is always supportive, although he doesn't seem to notice it; this coldness and reserve – his mother says he didn't mix well as a child – she accepts for herself but regrets that it has prevented him from being nominated, as he should be, to stand as the Party's parliamentary candidate for the district. He does not let her clothing or that of anyone else gathered closely make contact with him. He, too, stares at the grave. The dead man's mother and he stare at the grave in communication like that between the black man outside and the white man inside the cab the moment before the gun went off.

The moment before the gun went off was a moment of high excitement shared through the roof of the cab, as the bullet was to pass, between the young black man outside and the white farmer inside the vehicle. There were such moments, without explanation, between them, although often around the farm the farmer would pass the young man without returning a greeting, as if he did not recognize him. When the bullet went off what Van der Vyver saw was the kudu stumble in fright at the report and gallop away. Then he heard the thud behind him, and past the window saw the young man fall out of the vehicle. He was sure he had leapt up and toppled – in fright, like the buck. The farmer was almost laughing with relief, ready to tease, as he opened his door, it did not seem possible that a bullet passing through the roof could have done harm.

The young man did not laugh with him at his own fright. The farmer carried him in his arms, to the truck. He was sure,

sure he could not be dead. But the young black man's blood was all over the farmer's clothes, soaking against his flesh as he drove.

How will they ever know, when they file newspaper clippings, evidence, proof, when they look at the photographs and see his face – guilty! guilty! they are right! – how will they know, when the police stations burn with all the evidence of what has happened now, and what the law made a crime in the past. How could they know that they do not know. Anything. The young black callously shot through the negligence of the white man was not the farmer's boy; he was his son.

ERNEST HEMINGWAY

The Killers

The door of Henry's lunchroom opened and two men came in. They sat down at the counter.

'What's yours?' George asked them.

'I don't know,' one of the men said. 'What do you want to eat, Al?'

'I don't know,' said Al. 'I don't know what I want to eat.'

Outside it was getting dark. The street light came on outside the window. The two men at the counter read the menu. From the other end of the counter Nick Adams watched them. He had been talking to George when they came in.

'I'll have a roast pork tenderloin with apple sauce and mashed potatoes,' the first man said.

'It isn't ready yet.'

'What the hell do you put it on the card for?'

'That's the dinner,' George explained. 'You can get that at six o'clock.'

George looked at the clock on the wall behind the counter.

'It's five o'clock.'

'The clock says twenty minutes past five,' the second man said.

'It's twenty minutes fast.'

'Oh, to hell with the clock,' the first man said. 'What have you got to eat?'

'I can give you any kind of sandwiches,' George said. 'You can have ham and eggs, bacon and eggs, liver and bacon, or a steak.'

'Give me chicken croquettes with green peas and cream sauce and mashed potatoes.'

'That's the dinner.'

'Everything we want's the dinner, eh? That's the way you work it.'

'I can give you ham and eggs, bacon and eggs, liver – '

'I'll take ham and eggs,' the man called Al said. He wore a derby hat and a black overcoat buttoned across the chest. His face was small and white and he had tight lips. He wore a silk muffler and gloves.

'Give me bacon and eggs,' said the other man. He was about the same size as Al. Their faces were different, but they were dressed like twins. Both wore overcoats too tight for them. They sat leaning forward, their elbows on the counter.

'Got anything to drink?' Al asked.

'Silver beer, bevo, ginger-ale,' George said.

'I mean you got anything to *drink?*'

'Just those I said.'

'This is a hot town,' said the other. 'What do they call it?'

'Summit.'

'Ever hear of it?' Al asked his friend.

'No,' said the friend.

'What do you do here nights?' Al asked.

'They eat the dinner,' his friend said. 'They all come here and eat the big dinner.'

'That's right,' George said.

'So you think that's right?' Al asked George.

'Sure,'

'You're a pretty bright boy, aren't you?'

'Sure,' said George.

'Well, you're not,' said the other little man. 'Is he, Al?'

'He's dumb,' said Al. he turned to Nick. 'What's your name?'

'Adams.'

'Another bright boy,' Al said. 'Ain't he a bright boy, Max?'

'The town's full of bright boys,' Max said.

George put the two platters, one of ham and eggs, the other of bacon and eggs on the counter. He set down two side dishes of fried potatoes and closed the wicket into the kitchen.

'Which is yours?' he asked Al.

'Don't you remember?

'Ham and eggs.'

'Just a bright boy,' Max said. He leaned forward and took the ham and eggs. Both men ate with their gloves on. George watched them eat.

'What are *you* looking at?' Max looked at George.

'Nothing.'

'The hell you were. You were looking at me.'

'Maybe the boy meant it for a joke, Max,' Al said.

George laughed.

'*You* don't have to laugh,' Max said to him. '*You* don't have to laugh at all, see?'

'All right,' said George.

'So he thinks it's all right.' Max turned to Al. 'He thinks it's all right. That's a good one.'

'Oh, he's a thinker.' Al said. They went on eating.

'What's the bright boy's name down the counter?' Al asked Max.

'Hey, bright boy,' Max said to Nick. 'You go around on the other side of the counter with your boy friend.'

'What's the idea?' Nick asked.

'There isn't any idea.'

'You better go around, bright boy,' Al said. Nick went around behind the counter.

'What's the idea?' George asked.

'None of your damn business,' Al said. 'Who's out in the kitchen?'

'The nigger.'

'What do you mean the nigger?'

'The nigger that cooks.'

'Tell him to come in.'

'What's the idea?'

'Tell him to come in.'

'Where do you think you are?'

'We know damn well where we are,' the man called Max said. 'Do we look silly?'

'You talk silly,' Al said to him. 'What the hell do you argue with this kid for? Listen,' he said to George, 'tell the nigger to come out here.'

'What are you going to do him?'

'Nothing. Use your head, bright boy. What would we do to a nigger?'

George opened the slit that opened back into the kitchen. 'Sam,' he called. 'Come in here a minute.'

The door to the kitchen opened and the nigger came in. 'What was it?' he asked. The two men at the counter took a look at him.

'All right, nigger. You stand right there,' Al said.

Sam, the nigger, standing in his apron, looked at the two men sitting at the counter. 'Yes, sir,' he said. Al got down from his stool.

'I'm going back to the kitchen with the nigger and bright boy,' he said. 'Go on back to the kitchen, nigger. You go with him, bright boy.' The little man walked after Nick and Sam, the cook, back into the kitchen. The door shut after them. The man called Max sat at the counter opposite George. He didn't look at George but looked in the mirror that ran along back of the counter. Henry's had been made over from a saloon into a lunch counter.

'Well, bright boy,' Max said, looking into the mirror, 'why don't you say something?'

'What's it all about?'

'Hey, Al,' Max called, 'bright boy wants to know what it's all about.'

'Why don't you tell him?' Al's voice came from the kitchen.

'What do you think it's all about?

'I don't know.'

'What do you think?'

Max looked into the mirror all the time he was talking.

'I wouldn't say.'

'Hey, Al, bright boy says he wouldn't say what he thinks it's all about.'

'I can hear you, all right,' Al said from the kitchen. He had propped open the slit that dishes passed through into the kitchen with a catsup bottle. 'Listen, bright boy,' he said from the kitchen to George. 'Stand a little further along the bar.

You move a little to the left, Max.' He was like a photographer arranging for a group picture.

'Talk to me, bright boy,' Max said. 'What do you think's going to happen?'

George did not say anything.

'I'll tell you,' Max said. 'We're going to kill a Swede. Do you know a big Swede named Ole Andreson?'

'Yes.'

'He comes here to eat every night, don't he?'

'Sometimes he comes here. He comes here at six o'clock, don't he?'

'If he comes.'

'We know all that, bright boy,' Max said. 'Talk about something else. Ever go to the movies?'

'Once in a while.'

'You ought to go to the movies more. The movies are fine for a bright boy like you.'

'What are you going to kill Ole Andreson for? What did he ever do to you?'

'He never had a chance to do anything to us. He never even seen us.'

'And he's only going to see us once,' Al said from the kitchen.

'What are you going to kill him for, then?' George asked.

'We're killing him for a friend. Just to oblige a friend, bright boy.'

'Shut up,' said Al from the kitchen. 'You talk too goddam much.'

'Well, I got to keep bright boy amused. Don't I, bright boy?'

'You talk too damn much,' Al said. 'The nigger and my bright boy are amused by themselves. I got them tied up like a couple of girl friends in the convent.'

'I suppose you were in a convent.'

'You never know.'

'You were in a kosher convent. That's where you were.'

George looked up at the clock.

'If anybody comes in you tell them the cook is off, and if they keep after it, you tell them you'll go back and cook yourself. Do you get that, bright boy?'

'All right,' George said. 'What you going to do with us afterwards?'

'That'll depend,' Max said. 'That's one of those things you never know at the time.'

George looked up at the clock. It was a quarter past six. The door from the street opened. A street-car motorman came in.

'Hello, George, he said 'Can I get supper?'

'Sam's gone out,' George said. 'He'll be back in about half an hour.'

'I'd better go up the street, the motorman said. George looked at the clock. It was twenty minutes past six.

'That was nice, bright boy,' Max said. 'You're a regular little gentleman.'

'He knew I'd blow his head off,' Al said from the kitchen.

'No,' said Max. 'It ain't that. Bright boy is nice. He'a a nice boy. I like him.'

At six-fifty-five George said: 'He's not coming.'

Two other people had been in the lunchroom. Once George had gone out to the kitchen and made a ham-and-egg sandwich 'to go' that a man wanted to take with him. Inside the kitchen he saw Al, his derby hat tipped back, sitting on a stool beside the wicket with the muzzle of a sawed-off shotgun resting on the ledge. Nick and the cook were back to back in the corner, a towel tied in each of their mouths. George had cooked the sandwich, wrapped it up in oiled paper, put it in a bag, brought it in, and the man had paid for it and gone out.

'Bright boy can do everything,' Max said. 'He can cook and everything. You'd make some girl a nice wife, bright boy.'

'Yes?' George said. 'Your friend, Ole Andreson, isn't going to come.'

'We'll give him ten minutes.' Max said.

Max watched the mirror and the clock. The hands of the clock marked seven o'clock, and then five minutes past seven.

'Come on, Al, said Max. 'We better go. He's not coming.'

'Better give him five minutes,' Al said from the kitchen.

In the five minutes a man came in, and George explained that the cook was sick.

'Why the hell don't you get another cook?' the man asked. 'Aren't you running a lunch counter?' He went out.

'Come on, Al,' Max said.

'What about the two bright boys and the nigger?'

'They're all right.'

'You think so?'

'Sure. We're through with it.'

'I don't like it,' said Al. 'It's sloppy. You talk too much.'

'Oh, what the hell,' said Max. 'We got to keep amused, haven't we?'

'You talk too much, all the same,' Al said. He came out from the kitchen. The cut-off barrels of the shotgun made a slight bulge under the waist of his too-tight-fitting overcoat. He straightened his coat with his gloved hands.

'So long, bright boy,' he said to George. 'You got a lot of luck.'

'That's the truth,' Max said. 'You ought to play the races, bright boy.'

The two of them went out the door. George watched them, through the window, pass under the arc light and across the street. In their tight overcoats and derby hats they looked like a vaudeville team. George went back through the swinging door into the kitchen and untied Nick and the cook.

'I don't want any more of that,' said Sam, the cook. 'I don't want any more of that.'

Nick stood up. He had never had a towel in his mouth before.

'Say,' he said. 'What the hell?' He was trying to swagger it off.

'They were going to kill Ole Andreson, George said. 'They were going to shoot him when he came in to eat.'

'Ole Andreson?'

'Sure.'

The cook felt the corners of his mouth with his thumbs.

'They all gone?' he asked.

'Yeah,' said George. 'They're gone now.'

'I don't like it,' said the cook. 'I don't like any of it at all.'

'Listen,' George said to Nick. 'You better go see Ole Andreson.'

'All right.'

'You better not have anything to do with it at all,' Sam, the cook, said. 'You better stay way out of it.'

'Don't go if you don't want to.' George said.

'Mixing up in this ain't going to get you anywhere,' the cook said. 'You stay out of it.'

'I'll go see him,' Nick said to George. 'Where does he live?' The cook turned away.

'Little boys always know what they want to do,' he said.

'He lives up at Hirsch's rooming house,' George said to Nick.

'I'll go up there.'

Outside the arc light shone through the bare branches of a tree. Nick walked up the street beside the car tracks and turned at the next arc light down a side street. Three houses up the street was Hirsch's rooming house. Nick walked up the two steps and pushed the bell. A woman came to the door.

'Is Ole Andreson here?'

'Do you want to see him?'

'Yes, if he's in.'

Nick followed the woman up a flight of stairs and back to the end of a corridor. She knocked on the door.

'Who is it?'

'It's somebody to see you, Mr. Andreson,' the woman said.

'It's Nick Adams.'

'Come in.'

Nick opened the door and went into the room. Ole Andreson was lying on the bed with all his clothes on. He had been a heavyweight prizefighter and he was too long for the bed. He lay with his head on two pillows. He did not look at Nick.

'What was it? he asked.

'I was up at Henry's, Nick said, 'and two fellows came in and tied up me and the cook, and they said they were going to kill you.'

It sounded silly when he said it. Ole Andreson said nothing.

'They put us out in the kitchen.' Nick went on. 'They were

going to shoot you when you came in to supper.'

Ole Andreson looked at the wall and did not say anything.

'George thought I better come and tell you about it.'

'There isn't anything I can do about it.' Ole Andreson said.

'I'll tell you what they were like.'

'I don't want to know what they were like,' Ole Anderson said. He looked at the wall. 'Thanks for coming to tell me about it.'

'That's all right.'

Nick looked at the big man lying on the bed.

'Don't you want me to go and see the police?'

'No, Ole Andreson said. 'That wouldn't do any good.'

'Isn't there something I could do.'

'Maybe it was just a bluff.'

'No. It ain't just a bluff.'

Ole Andreson rolled over towards the wall.

'The only thing is.' he said, talking towards the wall, 'I just can't make up my mind to go out. I been in here all day.'

'Couldn't you get out of town?'

'No, Ole Andreson said. 'I'm through with all that running around.'

He looked at the wall.

'There ain't anything to do now.'

'Couldn't you fix it up some way?'

'No, I got in wrong.' He talked in the same flat voice. 'There ain't anything to do. After a while I'll make up my mind to go out.'

'I better go back and see George,' Nick said.

'So long,' said Ole Andreson. He did not look toward Nick. 'Thanks for coming around.'

Nick went out. As he shut the door he saw Ole Andreson with all his clothes on, lying on the bed looking at the wall.

'He's been in his room all day,' the landlady said downstairs.

'I guess he don't feel well. I said to him: "Mr. Andreson, you ought to go out and take a walk on a nice fall day like this," but he didn't feel like it.'

'He doesn't want to go out.'

'I'm sorry he don't feel well,' the woman said. 'He's an

awfully nice man. He was in the ring, you know.'

'I know it.'

'You never know it except from the way his face is.' the woman said. They stood talking just inside the street door. 'He's just as gentle.'

'Well, good night, Mrs. Hirsch,' Nick said.

'I'm not Mrs. Hirsch,' the woman said. 'She owns the place. I just look after it for her. I'm Mrs. Bell.'

'Well, good night, Mrs. Bell,' Nick said.

'Good night,' the woman said.

Nick walked up the dark street to the corner under the arc light, and then along the car tracks to Henry's eating house. George was inside, back of the counter. 'Did you see Ole?'

'Yes,' said Nick. 'He's in his room and he won't go out.'

The cook opened the door from the kitchen when he heard Nick's voice.

'I don't even listen to it,' he said and shut the door.

'Did you tell him about it?' George asked.

'Sure. I told him but he knows what it's all about.'

'What's he going to do?'

'Nothing.'

'They'll kill him.'

'I guess they will.'

'He must have got mixed up in something in Chicago.'

'I guess so,' said Nick.

'It's a hell of a thing.'

'It's an awful thing,' Nick said.

They did not say anything. George reached down for a towel and wiped the counter.

'I wonder what he did?' Nick said.

'Double-crossed somebody. That's what they kill them for.'

'I'm going to get out of this town,' Nick said.

'Yes,' said George. 'That's a good thing to do.'

'I can't stand to think about him waiting in the room and knowing he's going to get it. It's too damned awful. '

'Well,' said George, 'you better not think about it.'

RUDYARD KIPLING

The Return of Imray

Imray achieved the impossible. Without warning, for no conceivable motive, in his youth, at the threshold of his career he chose to disappear from the world – which is to say, the little Indian station where he lived.

Upon a day he was alive, well, happy, and in great evidence among the billiard tables at his Club. Upon a morning, he was not, and no manner of search could make sure where he might be. He had stepped out of his place; he had not appeared at his office at the proper time, and his dogcart was not upon the public roads. For these reasons, and because he was hampering, in a microscopical degree, the administration of the Indian Empire, that Empire paused for one microscopical moment to make inquiry into the fate of Imray. Ponds were dragged, wells were plumbed, telegrams were despatched down the lines of railways and to the nearest seaport town – 1200 miles away; but Imray was not at the end of the dragropes nor the telegraph wires. He was gone, and his place knew him no more. Then the work of the great Indian Empire swept forward, because it could not be delayed, and Imray from being a man became a mystery – such a thing as men talk over at their tables in the Club for a month, and then forget utterly. His guns, horses, and carts were sold to the highest bidder. His superior officer wrote an altogether absurd letter to his mother, saying that Imray had unaccountably disappeared, and his bungalow stood empty.

After three or four months of the scorching hot weather had gone by, my friend Strickland, of the Police, saw fit to rent the bungalow from the native landlord. This was before he was engaged to Miss Youghal – an affair which has been described in another place – and while he was pursuing his investigations into native life. His own life was sufficiently peculiar, and men complained of his manners and customs. There was always food in his house, but there were no regular times for meals. He ate, standing up and walking about, whatever he might find at the sideboard, and this is not good for human beings. His domestic equipment was limited to six rifles, three shotguns, five saddles, and a collection of stiff-jointed mahseer rods, bigger and stronger than the largest salmon rods. These occupied one-half of his bungalow, and the other half was given up to Strickland and his dog Tietjens – an enormous Rampur slut who devoured daily the rations of two men. She spoke to Strickland in a language of her own; and whenever, walking abroad, she saw things calculated to destroy the peace of Her Majesty the Queen-Empress, she returned to her master and laid information. Strickland would take steps at once, and at the end of his labours was trouble and fine and imprisonment for other people. The natives believed that Tietjens was a familiar spirit, and treated her with the great reverence that is born of hate and fear. One room in the bungalow was set apart for her special use. She owned a bedstead, a blanket, and a drinking trough, and if anyone came into Strickland's room at night her custom was to knock down the invader and give tongue till someone came with a light. Strickland owed his life to her, when he was on the Frontier, in search of a local murderer, who came in the grey dawn to send Strickland much farther than the Andaman Islands. Tietjens caught the man as he was crawling into Strickland's tent with a dagger between his teeth; and after his record of iniquity was established in the eyes of the law he was hanged. From that date Tietjens wore a collar of rough silver, and employed a monogram on her night blanket, and the blanket was of double woven Kashmir cloth, for she was a delicate dog.

Under no circumstances would she be separated from Strickland; and once, when he was ill with fever, made great trouble for the doctors, because she did not know how to help her master and would not allow another creature to attempt aid. Macarnaght, of the Indian Medical Service, beat her over her head with a gun-butt before she could understand that she must give room for those who could give quinine.

A short time after Strickland had taken Imray's bungalow, my business took me through that Station, and naturally, the Club quarters being full, I quartered myself upon Strickland. It was a desirable bungalow, eight-roomed and heavily thatched against any chance of leakage from rain. Under the pitch of the roof ran a ceiling-cloth which looked just as neat as a whitewashed ceiling. Unless you knew how Indian bungalows were built you would never have suspected that above the cloth lay the dark three-cornered cavern of the roof, where the beams and the underside of the thatch harboured all manner of rats, bats, ants, and foul things.

Tietjens met me in the verandah with a bay like the boom of the bell of St. Paul's, putting her paws on my shoulder to show she was glad to see me. Strickland had contrived to claw together a sort of meal which he called lunch, and immediately after it was finished went out about his business. I was left alone with Tietjens and my own affairs. The heat of the summer had broken up and turned to the warm damp of the rains. There was no motion in the heated air, but the rain fell like ramrods on the earth, and flung up a blue mist when it splashed back. The bamboos, and the custard-apples, the poinsettias, and the mango trees in the garden stood still while the warm water lashed through them, and the frogs began to sing among the aloe hedges.

A little before the light failed, and when the rain was at its worst, I sat in the back verandah and heard the water roar from the eaves, and scratched myself because I was covered with the thing called prickly-heat. Tietjens came out with me and put her head in my lap and was very sorrowful; so I gave her biscuits when tea was ready, and I took tea in the back verandah on account of the little coolness found there. The rooms of the house were dark behind me. I could smell Strickland's saddlery and the oil on his guns, and I had no desire to sit among these things. My own servant came to me in the twilight, the muslin of his clothes clinging tightly to his drenched body, and told me that a gentleman had called and wished to see someone. Very much against my will, but only because of the darkness of the rooms, I went into the naked drawing-room, telling my man to bring the lights. There might or might not have been a caller waiting – it seemed to me that I saw a figure by one of the windows – but when the lights came there was nothing save the spikes of the rain without, and the smell of the drinking earth in my nostrils. I explained to my servant that he was no wiser than he ought to be, and went back to the verandah to talk to Tietjens. She had gone out into the wet, and I could hardly coax her back to me; even with biscuits with sugar tops. Strickland came home, dripping wet, just before dinner, and the first thing he said was,

'Has anyone called?'

I explained, with apologies, that my servant had summoned me into the drawing-room on a false alarm; or that some loafer had tried to call on Strickland, and thinking better of it had fled after giving his name. Strickland ordered dinner, without comment, and since it was a real dinner with a white tablecloth attached, we sat down.

At 9 o'clock Strickland wanted to go to bed, and I was tired too. Tietjens, who had been lying underneath the table, rose up, and swung into least exposed verandah as soon as her master moved to his own room, which was next to the stately chamber set apart for Tietjens. If a mere wife had wished to sleep out of doors in that pelting rain it would not have mattered; but Tietjens was a dog, and therefore the better animal. I looked at Strickland, expecting to see him flay her with a whip. He smiled queerly, as a man would smile after telling some unpleasant domestic tragedy. 'She has done this ever since I moved in here,' said he. 'Let her go.'

The dog was Strickland's dog, so I said nothing, but I felt all that Strickland felt in being thus made light of. Tietjens encamped outside my bedroom window, and storm after storm came up, thundered on the thatch, and died away. The lightning spattered the sky as a thrown egg spatters a barn door, but the light was pale blue, not yellow, and looking through my split bamboo blinds, I could see the great dog standing, not sleeping, in the verandah, the hackles alift on her back and her feet anchored as tensely as the drawn wire-rope of a suspension bridge. In the very short pauses of the thunder I tried to sleep, but it seemed that someone wanted me very urgently. He, whoever he was, was trying to call me by name, but his voice was no more than a husky whisper. The thunder ceased and Tietjens went into the garden and howled at the low moon. Somebody tried to open my door, walked about and about through the house and stood breathing heavily in the verandahs, and just when I was falling asleep I fancied that I heard a wild hammering and clamouring above my head or on the door.

I ran into Strickland's room and asked him whether he was ill, and had been calling for me. He was lying on his bed half dressed, a pipe in his mouth. 'I thought you'd come.' he said. 'Have I been walking round the house recently?'

I explained that he had been trampling in the dining-room and the smoking-room and two or three other places, and he laughed and told me to go back to bed. I went back to bed and slept till the morning, but through all my mixed dreams I was sure I was doing someone an injustice in not attending to his wants. What those wants were I could not tell; but a fluttering, whispering, bolt-fumbling, lurking, loitering Someone was reproaching me for my slackness, and, half awake, I heard the howling of Tietjens in the garden and the threshing of the rain.

I lived in that house for two days. Strickland went to his office daily, leaving me alone for eight or ten hours with Tietjens for my only companion. As long as the full light lasted I was comfortable, and so was Tietjens; but in the twilight she and I moved into the back verandah and cuddled each other for company. We were alone in the house, but none the less it was much too fully occupied by a tenant with whom I did not wish to interfere. I never saw him, but I could see the curtains between the rooms quivering where he had just passed through; I could hear the chairs creaking as the bamboos sprung under a weight that had just quitted them; and I could feel when I went to get a book from the dining-room that somebody was waiting in the shadows of the front verandah till I should have gone away. Tietjens made the twilight more interesting by glaring into the darkened rooms with every hair erect, and following the motions of something that I could not see. She never entered the rooms, but her eyes moved interestedly: that was quite sufficient. Only when my servant came to trim the lamps and make all light and habitable she would come in with me and spend her time sitting on her haunches, watching an invisible extra man as he moved about behind my shoulder. Dogs are cheerful companions.

I explained to Strickland, gently as might be, that I would go over to the Club and find quarters there. I admired his hospitality, was pleased with his guns and rods, but I did not much care for his house and its atmosphere. He heard me out to the end, and then smiled very wearily, but without contempt, for he is a man who understands things. 'Stay on,' he said, 'and see what this thing means. All you have talked about I have known since I took the bungalow. Stay on and wait. Tietjens has left me. Are you going too?'

I had seen him through one little affair, connected with a heathen idol, that had brought me to the doors of a lunatic asylum, and I had no desire to help him through further experiences. He was a man to whom unpleasantnesses arrived as do dinners to ordinary people.

Therefore I explained more clearly than ever that I liked him immensely, and would be happy to see him in the daytime; but that I did not care to sleep under his roof. This was after dinner, when Tietjens had gone out to lie in the verandah.

'Pon my soul, I don't wonder,' said Strickland, with his eyes on the ceiling-cloth. 'Look at that!'

The tails of two brown snakes were hanging between the cloth and the cornice of the wall. They threw long shadows in the lamplight.

'If you are afraid of snakes of course – ' said Strickland.

I hate and fear snakes, because if you look into the eyes of any snake you will see that it knows all and more of the mystery of man's fall, and that it feels all the contempt that the Devil felt when Adam was evicted from Eden. Besides which its bite is generally fatal, and it twists up trouser legs.

'You ought to get your thatch overhauled,' I said 'Give me a mahseer rod, and we'll poke 'em down.'

'They'll hide among the roof beams,' said Strickland. 'I can't stand snakes overhead. I'm going up into the roof. If I shake 'em down, stand by with a cleaning rod and break their backs.'

I was not anxious to assist Strickland in his work, but I took the cleaning rod and waited in the dinning-room, while Strickland brought a gardener's ladder from the verandah, and set it against the side of the room. The snake-tails drew themselves up and disappeared. We could hear the dry rushing scuttle of long bodies running over the baggy ceiling-cloth. Strickland took a lamp with him, while I tried to make clear to him the danger of hunting snakes between a ceiling-cloth and a thatch, apart from the deterioration of property caused by ripping out ceiling-cloths.

'Nonsense!' said Strickland. 'They're sure to hide near the walls by the cloth. The bricks are too cold for 'em, and the heat of the room is just what they like.' He put his hand to the corner of the stuff and ripped it from the cornice. It gave with a great sound of tearing, and Strickland put his head through the opening into the dark of the angle of the roof beams. I set my teeth and lifted the rod, for I had not the least knowledge of what might descend.

'H'm!' said Strickland, and his voice rolled and rumbled in the roof. 'There's room for another set of rooms up here, and, by Jove, some one is occupying 'em!'

'No. It's a buffalo. Hand me up the two last joints of a mahseer rod, and I'll prod it. It's lying on the main roof beam.'

I handed up the rod.

'What a nest for owls and serpents! No wonder the snakes live here,' said Strickland, climbing farther into the roof. I could see his elbow thrusting with the rod. 'Come out of that, whoever you are! Heads below there! It's falling.'

I saw the ceiling-cloth nearly in the centre of the room bag with a shape that was pressing it downwards towards the lighted lamp on the table. I snatched the lamp out of danger and stood back. Then the cloth ripped out from the walls, tore, split, swayed, and shot down upon the table something that I dared not look at, till Strickland had slid down the ladder and was standing by my side.

He did not say much, being a man of few words; but he picked up the loose end of the tablecloth and threw it over the remnants on the table.

'It strikes me,' said he, putting down the lamp, 'our friend Imray has come back. Oh! you would, would you?'

There was a movement under the cloth, and a little snake wriggled out, to be back-broken by the butt of the mahseer rod. I was sufficiently sick to make no remarks worth recording.

Strickland meditated, and helped himself to drinks. The arrangement under the cloth made no more signs of life.

'Is it Imray?' I said.

Strickland turned back the cloth for a moment, and looked.

'It is Imray,' he said; 'and his throat is cut from ear to ear.'

Then we spoke, but together and to ourselves: 'That's why he whispered about the house.'

Tietjens, in the garden, began to bay furiously. a little later her great nose heaved open the dining-room door.

She sniffed and was still. The tattered ceiling-cloth hung down almost to the level of the table, and there was hardly room to move away from the discovery.

Tietjens came in and sat down; her teeth bared under her lip and her forepaws planted. She looked at Strickland.

'It's a bad business, old lady,' said he. 'Men don't climb up into the roofs of their bungalows to die, and they don't fasten up the ceiling cloth behind 'em. Let's think it out.'

'Let's think it out somewhere else,' I said.

'Excellent idea! Turn the lamps out. We'll get into my room.'

I did not turn the lamps out. I went into Strickland's room first, and allowed him to make the darkness. Then he followed me, and we lit tobacco and thought. Strickland thought. I smoked furiously because I was afraid.

'Imray is back,' said Strickland. 'The question is – who

killed Imray? Don't talk, I've a notion of my own. When I took this bungalow I took over most of Imray's servants. Imray was guileless and inoffensive, wasn't he?'

I agreed; though the heap under the cloth had looked neither one thing nor the other.

'If I call in all the servants they will stand fast in a crowd and lie like Aryans. What do you suggest?'

'Call 'em in one by one,' I said.

'They'll run away and give the news to all their fellows,' said Strickland. 'We must segregate 'em. Do you suppose your servant knows anything about it?'

'He may, for all I know; but I don't think it's likely. He has only been here two or three days,' I answered. 'What's your notion?'

'I can't quite tell. How the dickens did the man get the wrong side of the ceiling-cloth?'

There was a heavy coughing outside Strickland's bedroom door. This showed that Bahadur Khan, his body-servant, had wakened from sleep and wished to put Strickland to bed.

'Come in,' said Strickland. 'It's a very warm night, isn't it?'

Bahadur Khan, a great, green-turbanned, six-foot Mohammedan, said that it was a very warm night; but that there was more rain pending, which, by his Honour's favour, would bring relief to the country.

'It will be so, if God pleases,' said Strickland, tugging off his boots. 'It is in my mind, Bahadur Khan, that I have worked thee remorselessly for many days – ever since that time when thou first camest into my service. What time was that?'

'Has the Heaven-born forgotten? It was when Imray Sahib went secretly to Europe without warning given; and I – even I – came into the honoured service of the protector of the poor.'

'And Imray Sahib went to Europe?'

'It is so said among those who were his servants.'

'And thou wilt take service with him when he returns?'

'Assuredly, Sahib. He was a good master, and cherished his dependents.'

'That is true. I am very tired, but I go buck shooting tomorrow. Give me the little sharp rifle that I use for black buck; it is in the case yonder.'

The man stooped over the case, handed barrels, stock, and fore-end to Strickland, who fitted all together, yawning dolefully. Then he reached down to the gun case, took a solid-drawn cartridge, and slipped it into the breech of the .360 Express.

'And Imray Sahib has gone to Europe secretly! That is very strange, Bahadur Khan, is it not?'

'What do I know of the ways of the white man, Heaven-born?'

'Very little, truly. But thou shalt know more anon. It has reached me that Imray Sahib has returned from his so long journeyings, and that even now he lies in the next room.'

'Sahib!'

The lamplight slid along the barrels of the rifle as they levelled themselves at Bahadur Khan's broad breast.

'Go and look! said Strickland. 'Take a lamp. Thy master is tired, and he waits thee. Go!'

The man picked up a lamp, and went into the dining-room, Strickland following, and almost pushing him with the muzzle of the rifle. He looked for a moment at the black depths behind the ceiling-cloth; at the writhing snake under foot; and last, a grey glaze settling on his face, at the thing under the cloth.

'Hast thou seen?' said Strickland.

'I have seen. I am clay in the white man's hands. What does the Presence do?'

'Hang thee within the month. What else?'

'For killing him? Nay Sahib, consider. Walking among us, his servants, he cast his eyes upon my child, who was four years old. Him he bewitched, and in ten days he died of the fever – my child!'

'What said Imray Sahib?'

'He said he was a handsome child, and patted him on the head; wherefore my child died. Wherefore I killed Imray Sahib in the twilight, when he had come back from the office, and was sleeping. Wherefore I dragged him up into the roof beams and made all fast behind him. The Heaven-born knows all things. I am the servant of the Heaven born;'

Strickland looked at me.

'Thou art witness to this saying? He has killed.'

Bahadur Khan stood ashen grey in the light of the one lamp. The need for justification came upon him very swiftly. 'I am trapped,' he said, 'but the offence was that man's. He cast an evil eye upon my child, and I killed and hid him. Only such as are served by devils,' he glared at Tietjens, crouched stolidly before him, 'only such could know what I did.'

'It was clever. But thou shouldst have lashed him to the beam with a rope. Now, thou thyself wilt hang by a rope. Orderly!'

A drowsy policeman answered Strickland's call. He was followed by another. Tietjens sat wondrous still.

'Take him to the police station,' said Strickland.

'Do I hang then?' said Bahadur Khan, making no attempt to escape, and keeping his eyes on the ground.

'If the sun shines or the water runs – yes!' said Strickland.

Bahadur Khan stepped back one long pace, quivered, and stood still.

'Go!' said Strickland.

'Nay; but I go very swiftly,' said Bahadur Khan. 'Look! I am even now a dead man.'

He lifted his foot, and to the little toe there clung the head of the half-killed snake, firm fixed in the agony of death.

'I come of land-holding stock,' said Bahadur Khan, rocking where he stood. 'It were a disgrace to me to go to the public scaffold: therefore I take this way. Be it remembered that the Sahib's shirts are correctly enumerated, and that there is an extra piece of soap in his washbasin. My child was bewitched, and I slew the wizard. Why should you seek to slay me with the rope? My honour is saved, and – and – I die.'

At the end of an hour he died, as they die who are bitten by the little brown *karait*, and the policemen bore him and the thing under the cloth to their appointed places.

'This,' said Strickland, very calmly, as he climbed into bed, 'is called the Nineteenth Century. Did you hear what the man said?'

'I heard,' I answered. 'Imray made a mistake.'

'Simply and solely through not knowing the nature of the

Oriental, and the concidence of a little seasonal fever. Bahadur Khan had been with him for four years.'

I shuddered. My own servant had been with me for exactly that length of time. When I went over to my own room I found my man waiting, impassive as the copper head on a penny.

'What has befallen Bahadur Khan?' said I.

'He was bitten by a snake and died. The rest the Sahib knows.'

'And how much of this matter hast thou known?'

'As much as might be gathered from One coming in the twilight to seek satisfaction. Gently, Sahib. Let me pull off those boots.'

I had just settled to the sleep of exhaustion when I heard Strickland shouting from his side of the house –

'Tietjens has come back to her place!'

And so she had. The great deerhound was couched stately on her own bedstead on her own blanket, while, in the next room, the idle, empty ceiling-cloth waggled as it trailed on the table.

SINCLAIR LEWIS

The Post-Mortem Murder

I went to Kennuit to be quiet through the summer vacation. I was tired after my first year as associate professor, and I had to finish my *Life of Ben Johnson.* Certainly the last thing I desired was that dying man in the hot room and the pile of scrawled booklets.

I boarded with Mrs. Nickerson in a cottage of silver-grey shingles under silver-grey poplars, heard only the harsh fiddling of locusts and the distant rage of the surf, looked out on a yard of bright wild grass and a jolly windmill weather vane, and made notes about Ben Johnson. I was as secluded and happy as old Thoreau raising beans and feeling superior to Walden.

My fiancée – Quinta Gates, sister of Professor Gates and lovelier than ever in the delicate culture she had attained at thirty-seven – Quinta urged me to join them at Fleet Harbour. It is agreeable to be with Quinta. While I cannot say that we are stirred to such absurd manifestations as kissing and hand-holding – why any sensible person should care to hold a damp female hand is beyond me – we do find each other inspiriting. But Fleet Harbour would be full of 'summerites', dreadful young people in white flannels, singing their jazz ballads.

No, at thought of my spacious, leafy freedom I wriggled with luxury and settled down to an absorbed period when night and day glided into one ecstasy of dreaming study. Naturally, then, I was angry when I heard a puckery voice outside in the tiny hall-way:

'Well, if he's a professor, I got to see him.'

A knock. I affected to ignore it. It was irritatingly repeated until I roared, 'Well, well, well?' I am normally, I trust, a gentle person, but I desired to give them the impression of annoyance.

Mrs. Nickerson billowed in, squeaking:

'Mis' White from Lobster Pot Neck wants to see you.'

Past her wriggled a pinch-faced, humourless-looking woman. She glared at Mrs. Nickerson, thrust her out, and shut the door. I could hear Mrs. Nickerson protesting, 'Well, upon my word!'

I believe I rose and did the usual civilities. I remember this woman Miss or Mrs. White, immediately asking me, with extraordinary earnestness:

'Are you a professor?'

'I teach English.'

'You write books?'

I pointed to a box of manuscript.

'Then, please, you got to help us. Byron Sanders is dying. He says he's got to see a learned man to give him some important papers.' Doubtless I betrayed hesitation, for I can remember her voice rising in creepy ululation: 'Please! He's dying – that good old man that never hurt nobody!'

I fluttered about the room to find my cap. I fretted that her silly phrase of 'important papers' sounded like a melodrama, with maps of buried treasure, or with long-lost proofs that the chore boy is really the kidnapped son of royalty. But these unconscious defences against the compulsion expressed in her face, with its taut and terrified oval of open mouth, were in vain. She mooned at me, she impatiently waited. I dabbled at my collar and lapels with my fingers, instead of decently brushing off the stains of smoking and scribbling. I came stumbling and breathless after her.

She walked rapidly, unspeaking, intense, and I followed six inches behind, bespelled by her red-and-black gingham waist and her chip of a brown hat. We slipped among the grey houses of the town, stumped into country scilly and shimmering with late afternoon. By a trail among long salty grasses we passed an inlet where sandpipers sprinted and horsehoe crabs bobbed on the crisping ripples. We crossed a moorland to a glorious point of blowing grasses and sharp salt odour, with the waves of the harbour flickering beyond. In that resolute place my embarrassed awe was diluted, and I almost laughed as I wondered:

'What is this story-book errand? Ho, for the buried treasure! I'll fit up a fleet, out of the six hundred dollars I have in the savings bank, and find the pirates' skellingtons. 'Important papers!' I'll comfort the poor dying gentleman, and be back in time for another page before supper. The harbour is enchanting. I really must have a sail this summer or go swimming.'

My liveliness, uneasy at best in the presence of that frightened, fleeing woman, wavered when we dipped down through a cranberry bog and entered a still, hot wood of dying pines. They were dying, I tell you, as that old man in there way dying. The leaves were of a dry colour of brick dust; they had falled in heaps that crunched beneath my feet; the trunks were lean and black, with an irritation of branches; and all the dim alleys were choking with dusty odour of decay. It was hot and hushed, and my throat tickled, my limbs dragged in a hopeless languor.

Through ugly trunks and red needles we came to a restrained dooryard and an ancient, irregular house, a dark house, very sullen. No one had laughed there these many years. The windows were draped. The low porch between the main structure and a sagging ell was drifted with the pine needles. My companion's tread was startling and indecent on the flapping planks. She held open the door. I hesitated. I was not annoyed now; I was afraid, and I knew not of what I was afraid.

Prickly with unknown disquietude, I entered. We traversed a hall choked with relics of the old shipping days of Kennuit: a whale's vertebra, a cribbage board carved in a walrus-tusk, a Chinese screen of washed-out gold pagodas on faded, weary black. We climbed a narrow stair over which jutted, like a secret trap door, the corner of a mysterious chamber above. My companion opened a door on the upper hall and croaked, 'In there.'

I went in slowly. I am not sure now, after two years, but I think I planned to run out again, to flee downstairs, to defend myself with that ivory tusk if I should be attacked by – whatever was lurking in that shadowy, silent place. As I edged in, about me crept an odour of stale air and vile medicines and ancient linen. The shutters were fast; the light was grudging. I was actually relieved when I saw in the four-poster bed a pitiful, vellum-faced old man, and the worst monster I had to face was normal illness.

I have learned that Byron Sanders was only seventy-one then, but he seemed ninety. He was enormous. He must have been hard to care for. His shoulders, in the mended linen nightgown thrust up above the patchwork comforter, were bulky; his neck was thick; his head a shiny dome – an Olympian, majestic even in dissolution.

The room had been lived in too long. It was a whirl of useless things: staggering chairs, clothes in piles, greasy medicine bottles, and a vast writing desk pouring out papers, and dingy books with bindings of speckled brown. Amid the litter, so still that she seemed part of it, I was startled to discern another woman. Who she may have been I have never learned.

The man was ponderously turning in bed, peering at me through the shaky light.

'You are a professor?' he wheezed.

'That depends upon what you mean, sir. I teach English. I am not – '

'You understand poetry, essays, literary history?'

'I am supposed to.'

'I'm kind of a colleague of yours. Byron – ' He stopped, choked frightfully. The repressed woman beside the bed, moving with stingy patience, wiped his lips. 'My name is Byron Sanders. For forty years, till a year ago, I edited the *Kennuit Beacon.*'

The nauseating vanity of man! In that reverent hour, listening to the entreaties of a dying man, I was yet piqued at having my stripped athletic scholarship compared to editing the *Beacon,* with its patent-medicine advertisements, its two straggly columns of news about John Brown's cow and Jim

White's dory.

His eyes trusting me, Byron Sanders went on:

'Can't last long. It's come quicker – no time to plan. I want you to take the literary remains of my father. He was not a good man, but he was a genius. I have his poetry here, and the letters. I haven't read them for years, and – too late – give them to world. You must – '

He was desperately choking. The still woman crept up, thrust into my hands a box of papers and a pile of notebooks which had been lying on the bed.

'You must go,' she muttered. 'Say, "Yes," and go. He can't stand any more.'

'Will you?' the broken giant wailed to me, a stranger!

'Yes, yes, indeed; I'll give them to the world.' I mumbled, while the woman pushed me toward the door.

I fled down the stairs, through the coppery pine woods, up to the blithe headland that was swept by the sea breeze.

I knew of course, what the 'poetry' of that poor 'genius' his father would be – Christmas doggerel and ditties about 'love' and 'dove', 'heart' and 'must part'. I was, to be honest, irritated. I wanted to take this debris back to Mr. Sanders, and that was the one thing I could not do. For once I was sensible: I took it home and tried to forget it.

In the next week's *Kennuit Beacon*, discovered on Mrs. Nickerson's parlour table, crowning a plush album, I read that Byron Sanders 'the founder and for many years the highly esteemed editor of this paper.' had died.

I sought relatives to whom I could turn over his father's oddments. There was no one; he was a widower and childless. For months the bothersome papers were lost in my desk back at the university. On the opening day of the Christmas vacation I remembered that I had not read a word of them. I was to go to Quinta Gates's for tea at a quarter to five, and to her serene companionship I looked forward as, in a tired, after-term desultoriness, I sat down to glance at Jason Sanders's caterwaulings. That was at four. It was after nine when the flabby sensation of hunger brought me back to my room and the dead fire.

In those five hours I had discovered a genius. The poetry

at which I had so abominably sneered was minted glory.

I stood up, and in that deserted dormitory I shouted, and listened to the tremor of the lone sound and defiantly shouted again. That I was 'excited' is too pallid a word. My life of Jonson could go hang! I was selfish about it: it meant fame for me. But I think something higher than selfishness had already come into my devotion to Jason Sanders; something of the creator's passion and the father's pride.

I was hungry enough, but I walked the room contemptuous of it. I felt unreal. 1918 was fantastically unreal. I had for hours been veritably back in 1850. It was all there; manuscripts which had not been touched since 1850, which still held in their wrinkles the very air of seventy years ago: a diary; daguerreotypes; and letters, preserved like new in the darkness, from Poe, Emerson, Thoreau, Hawthorne, and the young Tennyson!

The diary had been intermittently kept for fifteen years. It was outline enough for me to reconstruct the story of Jason Sanders, born at Kennuit in 1825, probably died in Greece in 1853.

Between Cape Cod and the ocean is a war sinister and incessant. Here and there the ocean has gulped a farm, or a lighthouse reared on a cliff, but at Kennuit the land has been the victor. Today there are sandy flats and tepid channels where a hundred years ago was an open harbour brilliant with a hundred sails, crackling with tidings from the Banks, proud of whalers back from years of cruising off Siberia and of West Indiamen pompous with rum and sugar and the pest.

Captain Bethuel Sanders, master and owner of the *Sally S.*, was on a voyage out of Kennuit to Pernambuco when his only child, Jason Sanders, was born. He never came back. In every Cape Cod burying-ground, beside the meeting-house, there are a score of headstones with 'Lost at sea'. There is one, I know now, at Kennuit for Bethuel Sanders.

His widow, daughter of a man of God who for many years had been pastor at Truro, was a tight, tidy, capable woman. Bethuel left her a competence. She devoted herself to keeping house and to keeping her son from going to sea. He was not to die as his father had, perhaps alone, last man on a wave-smashed brig. Theirs was a neat, unkindly cottage with no windows on the harbour side. The sailors' womenfolk did not greatly esteem the view to sea, for thither went the strong sons who would never return. In a cottage with a low wall blank toward the harbour lived Mrs. Sanders, ardently loving her son, bitterly restraining him. Jason was obsessed by her. She was mother, father, sweetheart, teacher, tyrant. He stroked her cheeks, and he feared her eye, which was a frozen coal when she caught him lying.

In the first pages of Jason's diary, when he was only thirteen, he raged that while his schoolmates were already off to the Banks or beholding, as cabin boys, the shining Azores, he was kept at his lessons, unmanned, in apron strings. Resources of books he had from his parson grandsire: Milton, Jeremy Taylor, Pope. If the returned adventurers sneered at him, he dusted their jackets. He must have been hardy and reasonably vicious. He curtly records that he beat Peter Williams, son of the Reverend Abner Williams, 'till he could scarce move'. and that for this ferocity he was read out of meeting. He became a hermit, the village 'bad boy'.

He was at once scorned as a 'softy' by his mates because he did not go to sea, dreaded by their kin because he was a marking fighter, bombarded by his Uncle Ira because he would not become a grocer, and chided by his mother because he had no calling to the ministry. Nobody, apparently, took the trouble to understand him. The combination of reading and solitude led him inevitably to scribbling. On new-washed Cape Cod afternoons, when grasses rustled on the cream-shadowed dunes, he sat looking out to sea, chin in hand, staring at ardent little waves and lovely sails that bloomed and vanished as the schooners tacked; and through evenings rhythmic with the surf he sought with words which should make him enviable to justify himself and his mocked courage.

At twenty he ran off to sea on a fishing schooner.

Twenty he was and strong, but when he returned his mother larruped him. Apparently he submitted; his comment in the famous diary is: 'Mother kissed me in welcome, then, being a woman of whimsies somewhat distasteful to a man of my sober nature, she stripped off my jacket and lashed me with a strip of whalebone long and surprisingly fanged. I shall never go a-whaling if so very little of a whale can be so very unamiable.'

This process neatly finished, Mrs. Sanders – she was a swift and diligent woman – immediately married the young bandit off to a neighbour woman four years his senior, a comely woman, pious, and gifted with dullness. Within the year was born a son, the Byron Sanders whom I saw dying as a corpulent elder.

That was in 1847, and Jason was twenty-two.

He went to work – dreaming and the painful carving of beautiful words not being work – in the Mammoth Store and Seamen's Outfitters. He was discharged for, *imprimis*, being drunk and abusive; further, stealing a knife of the value of two shillings. For five or six years he toiled in a sail-loft. I fancy that between stitchings of thick canvas he read poetry, a small book hidden in the folds of a topsail, and with a four-inch needle he scratched on shingles a plan of Troy. He was discharged now and then for roistering, and now and then was grudgingly hired again.

I hope that nothing I have said implies that I consider Jason a young man of virtue. I do not. He drank Jamaica rum, he stole strawberries, his ways with the village girls were neither commendable nor in the least commended, and his temper was such that he occasionally helped himself to a fight with sailors, and regularly, with or without purpose, thrashed the unfortunate Peter Williams, son of the Reverend Abner.

Once he betrayed a vice far meaner. A certain Boston matron, consort of a highly esteemed merchant, came summering to Kennuit, first of the tennis-yelping hordes who now infest the Cape and interrupt the meditations of associate professors. This worthy lady was literary, and doubtless musical and artistic. She discovered that Jason was a poet. She tried to patronize him; in a highfalutin way she commanded him to appear next Sunday, to read aloud and divert her cousins from Boston. For this she would give him a shilling and what was left of the baked chicken. He gravely notes: 'I told her to go to the devil. She seemed put out.' The joke is that three weeks later he approached the good matron with a petition to be permitted to do what he had scorned. She rightly, he records without comment, 'showed me the door.'

No, he was not virtuous save in bellicose courage, and he was altogether casual about deserting his wife and child when, the year after his mother died, he ran away to the Crimean War. But I think one understands that better in examining, as I have examined with microscope and aching eye, the daguerreotypes of Jason and his wife and boy.

Straight-nosed and strong-lipped was Jason at twenty-six or seven. Over his right temple hung an impatient lock. He wore the high, but open and flaring, collar of the day, the space in front filled with the soft folds of a stock. A fluff of side-whiskers along the jaws set off his resoluteness of chin and brow. His coat was long-skirted and heavy, with great collar and wide lapels, a cumbrous garment, yet on him as graceful as a cloak. But his wife! Her eyes stared, and her lips, though for misery and passionate prayer they had dark power, seem in the mirrory old picture to have had no trace of smiles. Their son was dumpy. As I saw him dying there in the pine woods, Byron Sanders appeared a godly man and intelligent; but at six or seven he was pudding-faced, probably with a trick of howling. In any case, with or without reason, Jason foully deserted them.

In 1853, at the begining of the struggle between Russia and Turkey that was to develop into the Crimean War, Greece planned to invade Turkey. Later, to prevent alliance between Greece and Russia, the French and English forces held Piraeus; but for a time Greece seemed liberated.

Jason's diary closes with a note:

> Tomorrow I leave this place of sand and sandy brains; make by friend Bearse's porgy boat for Long Island, thence to New York and ship for Piraeus, for the glory of Greece and the memory of Byron. How better can a man die? And perhaps some person of intelligence there will comprehend me. Thank fortune my amiable spouse knows naught. If ever she finds this, may she grant forgiveness, as I grant it to her!

That is all – save a clipping from the *Lynmouth News Letter* of seven years later announcing that as no word of Mr. Jason Sanders had come since his evanishment, his widow was petitioning the court to declare him legally dead.

This is the pinchbeck life of Jason Sanders. He lived not in life, but in his writing, and that is tinct with genius. Five years before Whitman was known he was composing what today we call 'free verse'. There are in it impressions astoundingly like Amy Lowell. The beauty of a bitter tide-scourged garden and of a bitter sea-scourged woman who walks daily in that sterile daintiness is one of his themes, and the poem is as radiant and as hard as ice.

Then the letters.

Jason had sent his manuscripts to the great men of the day. From most of them he had noncommittal acknowledgments. His only encouragement came from Edgar Allan Poe, who in 1849, out of the depths of his own last discouragement, wrote with sympathy:

> I pledge you my heart that you have talent. You will go far if you can endure hatred and disgust, forgetfulness and bitter bread, blame for your most valorous and for your weakness and meekness, the praise of matrons and the ladylike.

That letter was the last thing I read before dawn on Christmas day.

On the first train after Christmas I hastened down to the winter-clutched Cape.

As Jason had died sixty five years before, none but persons of eighty or more would remember him. One woman of eighty-six I found, but beyond, 'Heh? Whas sat?' she confided only:'Jassy Sanders was a terror to snakes. Run away from his family, that's what he done! Poetry? Him write poetry? Why, he was a sailmaker!'

I heard then of Abiathar Gould, eighty-seven years old, and already become a myth streaked with blood and the rust of copper bottoms. He had been a wrecker, suspected of luring ships ashore with false lights in order that he might plunder them with his roaring mates. He had had courage enough, plunging in his whale-boat through the long swells after a storm, but mercy he had not known. He was not in Kennuit itself; he lived down by the Judas Shoals, on a lean spit of sand running seven miles below Lobster Pot Neck.

How could one reach him? I asked Mrs. Nickerson.

Oh, that was easy enough: one could walk! Yes, and one did walk, five miles against a blast whirling with snow, grinding with teeth of sand. I cursed with surprising bitterness, and planned to give up cigarettes and to do patent chest exercises. I wore Mr. Aaron Bloomer's coonskin coat, Mrs. Nickerson's grey flannel muffler, David Dill's fishing-boots, and Mrs. Antonia Sparrow's red flannel mittens; but, by the gods, the spectacles were my own, and mine the puffing, the cramped calves, and the breath that froze white on that itchy collar! Past an inlet with grasses caught in the snow-drifted ice; along the frozen beach, which stung my feet at every pounding step; among sand dunes, which for a moment gave blessed shelter; out again into the sweep of foam-slavering wind, the bellow of the surf, I went.

I sank all winded on the icy step of Captain Abiather Gould's bachelor shack.

He was not deaf and he was not dull at eighty-seven. He came to the door, looked down on me studiously, and grunted:

'What do you want? D'yuh bring me any hootch?'

I hadn't. There was much conversation bearing on that point while I broiled and discovered new muscles by his stove. He had only one bunk, a swirl of coiled blankets and comforters and strips of gunny-sacking. I did not care to spend the night; Captain Gould cared even less. I had to be back. I opened:

'Cap'n you knew Jason Sanders?'

'Sanders? I knew Byron Sanders, and Gideon Sanders of Wellfleet and Cephas Sanders of Falmouth and Bessie Sanders, but I never knew no Jason – oh wa'n't he Byron's pa? Sure I remember him. Eight or nine years older'n I was.

Died in foreign parts. I was a boy on the *Dancing Jig* when he went fishing. Only time he ever went. Wa'n't much of a fisherman.'

'Yes, but what do you remember – '

'Don't remember nothing. Jassy never went with us fellows; had his nose in a book. Some said he was a good fighter; I dunno.'

'But didn't you – how did he talk, for instance?'

'Talk? Talked like other folks, I suppose. But he wa'n't a fisherman, like the rest of us. Oh, one time he tanned my hide for tearing up some papers with writin' on 'em that I swiped for gun-wadding.'

'What did he say then?'

'He said – '

On second thought it may not be discreet to report what Jason said.

Beyond that Captain Gould testified only:

'Guess I kind of get him mixed up with the other fellows; good many years ago. But' – he brightened – 'I recollect he wa'n't handy round a schooner. No, he wa'n't much of a fisherman.'

When I got back Kennuit my nose was frozen.

No newspapers had been published in Kennuit before 1877, and I unearthed nothing more. Yet this very blankness made Jason Sanders my own province. I knew incomparably more about him than any other living soul. He was at once my work, my spiritual ancestor, and my beloved son. I had a sense of the importance and nobility of all human life such as – I acknowledge sadly – I had never acquired in dealing with cubbish undergraduates. I wondered how many Jasons might be lost in the routine of my own classes. I forgot my studies of Ben Jonson. I was obsessed by Jason. I was, I fancy, like a jitney pilot turned racing driver.

Quinta Gates – I don't know – when I met her at the president's reception in February, she said I had been neglecting her. At the time I supposed that she was merely teasing; but I wonder now. She was – oh, too cool; she hadn't quite the frankness I had come to depend on in her. I don't care. Striding the dunes with Jason, I couldn't return to Quinta and the discussion of sonatas in a lavender twilight over thin teacups.

I gave Jason Sanders to the world in a thumping article in *The Weekly Gonfalon.*

Much of it was reprinted in the *New York Courier's* Sunday literary section, with Jason's picture, and – I note it modestly – with mine, the rather interesting picture of me in knickers sitting beside Quinta's tennis court. Then the *New York Gem* took him up. It did not mention me or my article. It took Jason under its own saffron wing and crowed, at the head of a full-page Sunday article:

VICIOUS EUROPEAN CONSPIRACY HIDES DEATH OF GREATEST AMERICAN BARD

I was piqued by their theft, but I was also amused to see the creation of a new mythical national hero. The *Gem* had Jason sailing nine of the seven seas, and leading his crew to rescue a most unfortunate Christian maiden who had been kidnapped by the Turks – at Tangier! About the little matter of deserting his wife and son the *Gem* was absent-minded. According to them, Jason's weeping helpmate bade him, 'Go where duty calls you', whereupon he kissed her, left her an agreeable fortune, and departed with banners and bands. But the *Gem's* masterpiece was the interview with Captain Abiathar Gould, whose conversational graces I have portrayed. In the *Gem* Captain Gould rhapsodizes:

> We boys was a wild lot, sailing on them reckless ships. But Captain Jason Sanders was, well, sir, he was like a god to us. Not one of the crew would have dared, like he done, to spring overboard in a wintry blast to rescue the poor devils capsized in a dory, and yet he was so quiet and scholarly, always a-reading at his poetry books between watches. Oh, them was wonderful days on the barkantine *Dancing Jig!*

The *Gem* reporter must have taken down to Abiathar some of the 'hootch' I failed to bring.

I was – to be honest, I was unacademically peeved. My hero was going out of my hands, and I wanted him back. I got him back. No one knew what had happened to Jason after he went to Greece, but I found out. With a friend in the European history department I searched all available records of Greek history in 1853-54. I had faith that the wild youngster would tear his way through the driest pages of reports.

We discovered that in '54, when the French and English occupied Piraeus, a mysterious Lieutenant Jasmin Sandec appeared as a popular hero in Athens. Do you see the resemblance? Jasmin Sandec – Jason Sanders. The romantic boy had coloured his drab Yankee name. Nobody quite knew who Lieutenant Sandec was. He was not Greek. The French said he was English, the English said he was French. He led a foray of rollicking young Athenians against the French lines; he was captured and incontinently shot. After his death an American sea captain identified Lieutenant Sandec as a cousin of his! He testified that Sandec was not his name, though what his name was the skipper did not declare. He ended his statement:

'My cousin comes from the town of Kennebunkport, and has by many been thought to be insane.'

Need I point out how easily the Greek scribe confused Kennebunkport with Kennuit? As easily as the miserable cousinly captain confused insanity with genius.

Do you see the picture of Jason's death? Was it not an end more fitting than moulding away in a sail-loft, or becoming a grocer, a parson, an associate professor? The Grecian afternoon sun glaring on whitewashed wall, the wine-dark sea, the marble-studded hills of Sappho, and a youth, perhaps in a crazy uniform, French shako and crimson British coat, Cape Cod breeches and Grecian boots, lounging dreamily, not quite understanding; a line of soldiers with long muskets; a volley, and that fiery flesh united to kindred dust from the bright body of Helen and the thews of Ajax.

The report of these facts about Jason's fate I gave in my second article in the *Gonfalon*. By this time people were everywhere discussing Jason. It was time for my book.

Briefly, it was a year's work. It contained all his writing and the lives of three genertions of Sanderses. It had a reasonable success, and it made of Jason's notoriety a solid fame. So, in 1919, sixty-five years after his death, he began to live.

An enterprising company published his picture in a large carbon print which appeared on schoolroom walls beside portraits of Longfellow, Lowell, and Washington. So veritably was he living that I saw him! In New York, at a pageant representing the great men of America, he was enacted by a clever young man made up to the life, and shown as talking to Poe. That, of course, was inaccurate. Then he appeared as a character in a novel; he was condescendingly mentioned by a celebrated visiting English poet; his death was made the subject of a painting; a motion-picture person inquired as to the possibilities of 'filming' him, and he was, in that surging tide of new living, suddenly murdered!

The poison which killed Jason the second time was in a letter to the *Gonfalon* from Whitney A. Edgerton, Ph.D., adjunct professor of English literature in Melanchthon College.

Though I had never met Edgerton, we were old combatants. The dislike had started with my stern, but just, review of his edition of Herrick. Edgerton had been the only man who had dared to sneer at Jason. In a previous letter in the *Gonfalon* he had hinted that Jason had stolen his imagery from Chinese lyrics, a pretty notion, since Jason probably never knew that the Chinese had any literature save laundry checks. But now I quote his letter:

> I have seen reproductions of a very bad painting called 'The Death of Jason Sanders', portraying that admirable young person as being shot in Greece. It happens that Mr Sanders was not shot in Greece. He deserved to be, but he wasn't. Jason Sanders was not Jasmin Sandec. The changing of his own honest name to such sugar-candy was the sort of thing he would have done. But he didn't do it. What kept Jason from heroically dying in Greece in 1854 was the misfortune that from December '53, to April, '58, he was doing time in the Delaware State Penitentiary for the proved crimes of

arson and assault with intent to kill. His poetic cell in Delaware was the nearest he ever, in his entire life, came to Greece. Yours, etc.,

Whitney Edgeton

The editor of the *Gonfalon* telegraphed me the contents of the letter just too late for me to prevent its printing, and one hour later I was bound for Delaware, forgetting, I am afraid, that Quinta had invited me to dinner. I knew that I would 'show up', as my students say, this Edgerton.

The warden of the penitentiary was interested. He helped me. He brought out old registers. We were thorough. We were too thorough. We read that Jason Sanders of Kennuit, Massachusetts, married, profession sailmaker, was committed to the penitentiary in December, 1853, for arson and murderous assault, and that he was incarcerated for over four years.

In the Wilmington library, in the files of a newspaper long defunct, I found an item dated November, 1853:

> What appears to have been a piece of wretched scoundrelism was perpetrated at the house of Mr. Palatinus, a highly esteemed farmer residing near Christiansburg, last Thursday. Mr. Palatinus gave food and shelter to a tramp calling himself Sanders, in return for some slight labour. The second evening the fellow found some spirits concealed in the barn, became intoxicated, demanded money from Mr. Palatinus, struck him, cast the lamp upon the floor and set fire to the dwelling. He has been arrested and is held for trial. He is believed to have been a sailor on Cape Cod. Where are our officers of the peace that such dangerous criminals should roam unapprehended?

I did not make any especial haste to communicate my discoveries.

It was a *New York Gem* correspondent who did that. His account was copied rather widely.

The pictures of Jason were taken down from schoolroom walls.

I returned to the university. I was sustained only by Quinta's faith. As she sat by the fire, chin resting against fragile fingers, she asserted, 'Perhaps there has been some mistake.' That inspired me. I left her, too hastily, it may be, but she is ever one to understand and forgive. I fled to my rooms, stopping only to telephone to my friend of the history department. He assured me that there was a common Greek family name, Palatainos. You will note its resemblance to Palatinus! At this I jiggled in the drugstore telephone booth and joyfully beat on the resounding walls, and looked out to see one of my own students, purchasing a bar of chocolate, indecently grinning at me. I sought to stalk out, but I could not quiet my rejoicing feet.

I began my new letter to the *Gonfalon* at ten in the evening. I finished it at five of a cold morning. I remember myself as prowling through the room with no dignity, balancing myself ridiculously on the brass bar at the foot of my bed, beating my desk with my fists, lighting and hurling down cigarettes.

In my letter I pointed out – I virtually proved – that the Delaware farmer's name was not Palatinus, but Palatainos. He was a Greek. He could not have sheltered Jason 'in return for some slight labour', because this was December, when farm work was slackest. No, this Palatainos was an agent of the Greek revolutionists. Jason was sent from New York to see him. Can you not visualize it?

The ardent youngster arrives, is willing to take from Palatainos any orders, however desperate. And he finds that Palatainos is a traitor, is in the pay of the Turks! Sitting in the kitchen, by a fireplace of whitewashed bricks, Palatainos leers upon the horrified Yankee lad with the poisonous sophistication of an international spy. He bids Jason spy upon the Greeks in America. Staggered, Jason goes feebly up to bed. All next day he resists the traitor's beguilement. Palatainos plies him with brandy. The poet sits brooding; suddenly he springs up, righteously attacks Palatainos, the lamp is upset the house partly burned, and Jason, a stranger and friendless, is arrested by the besotted country constable. He was, in prison, as truly a martyr to freedom as if he had veritably been shot in a tender-coloured Grecian afternoon!

My reconstruction of the history was – though now I was so distressed that I could take but little pride in it – much quoted from the *Gonfalon* not only in America, but abroad. The *Mercure de France* mentioned it, inexcusably misspelling my name. I turned to the tracing of Jason's history after his release from the penitentiary, since now I did not know when and where he actually had died. I was making plans when there appeared another letter from Whitney Edgerton, the secret assassin of Jason. He snarled that Palatinus's name was not Palatainos. It was Palatinus. He was not a Greek: he was a Swede.

I wrote to Edgerton, demanded his proofs, his sources for all this information. He did not answer. He answered none of my half-dozen letters.

The *Gonfalon* announced that it had been deceived in regard to Jason, that it would publish nothing more about him. So for the third time Jason Sanders was killed, and this time he seemed likely to remain dead.

Shaky, impoverished by my exploration on Cape Cod and in Delaware, warned by the dean that I should do well to stick to my teaching and cease 'these unfortunate attempts to gain notoriety', I slunk into quiet classwork, seemingly defeated. Yet all the while I longed to know when and where Jason really had died. Might he not have served valorously in the American Civil War? But how was I to know? Then came my most extraordinary adventure in the service of Jason Sanders.

I went to Quinta's for tea. I have wondered sometimes if Quinta may not have become a bit weary of my speculations about Jason. I did not mean to bore her; I tried not to: but I could think of nothing else, and she alone was patient with me.

'How – how – how can I force Edgerton to tell all he knows?' I said with a sigh.

'Go see him!' Quinta was impatient.

'Why, you know I can't afford to, with all my savings gone, and Edgerton way out in Nebraska.'

She shocked me by quitting the room. She came back holding out a cheque – for three hundred dollars! The

Gateses are wealthy, but naturally I could not take this. I shook my head.

'Please!' she said sharply. 'Let's get it over.'

I was suddenly hopeful.

'Then you do believe in Jason? I'd thought you were almost indifferent to him.'

'I – ' It flared out, that sound. She went on compactly: 'Let's not talk about it, please. Now tell me, didn't you think they made a mistake at the symphony – '

I had a not at all pleasant conference with the dean before I took my train for Melanchthon, Nebraska.

I had a plan. This was towards the end of the academic year 1919-20. I would pretend to be a chap who, after working in offices, that sort of thing, desired to begin graduate work in English, but had first to make up for the courses he had forgotten since college. I wanted the celebrated Dr. Whitney Edgerton to tutor me. I would lure him into boarding me at his house; a young professor like Edgerton would be able to use the money. Once dwelling there, it would be easy enough to search his study, to find what histories or letters had furnished his secret knowlege of Jason.

I adopted as *nom de guerre* the name Smith. That was, perhaps, rather ingenious, since it is a common name, and therefore unlikely to arouse attention. It was all reasonable, and should have been easy.

But when in Melanchthon, I was directed to Edgerton's house, I perceived that, instead of being a poor devil, he was uncomfortably rich. His was a monstrous Georgian house, all white columns and dormers and iron window-railings and brick terrace and formal gardens. Reluctantly, I gained entrance, and addressed myself to Edgerton.

He was a square-built, pompous, rimless-eyeglassed, youngish man. His study was luxurious, with velvet curtains at the windows, with a vast desk, with built-in cases containing books I yearned to possess; a vast apartment, all white and tender blue, against which my two patchy rooms in Hendrik Hall seemed beggarly. I had expected to have to conceal hatred, but instead I was embarrassed. Yet by the gods it was I, the shabby scholar, who had created Jason, and this silken, sulky dilettante who without reason had stabbed him!

While I peeped about, I was telling Edgerton, perhaps less deftly than I had planned, of my desire to be tutored.

He answered:

'You're very complimentary, I'm sure, but I'm afraid it's impossible. I'll recommend you to someone – By the way, what was your college?'

Heaven knows how it popped into my head, but I recalled an obscure and provincial school, Titus College, of which I knew nothing.

He lightened.

'Oh, really? Did you know I had my first instructorship in Titus? Haven't had any news from there for years. How is President Dolson, and Mrs. Siebel? Oh, and how is dear old Cassaworthy?'

May the trustees of Titus College forgive me! I had President Dolson sick of a fever, and Cassaworthy – professor, janitor, village undertaker, or whatever he was – taking to golf. As for Mrs. Siebel, she'd given me a cup of tea only a few months ago. Edgerton seemed astonished. I have often wondered whether Mrs Siebel would actually be most likely to serve tea, gin, or vitriol.

Edgerton got rid of me. He amiably kicked me out. He smiled, gave me the name of a 'suitable tutor', mesmerized me toward the door, and did not invite me to return. I sat on a bench in the Malanchthon station. Apparently I had come from the Atlantic seaboard to Nebraska to sit on this broken bench and watch an undesirable citizen spit at a box of sawdust.

I spent the night at a not agreeable tavern or hotel, and next day I again called on Edgerton. I had surmised that he would be bored by the sight of me. He was. I begged him to permit me to look over his library. Impatiently, he left me alone, hinting, 'When you go out, be sure and close the front door.'

With the chance of someone entering, it wold not have been safe to scurry through his desk and his ingenious cabinets in search of data regarding Jason. But while I stood apparently reading, with a penknife I so loosened the screws in a window-catch that the window could be thrust up from outside.

I was going to burglarize the study.

That night, somewhat after twelve, I left my room in the hotel, yawned about the office, pretended to glance at the ragged magazines, sighed to the drowsy night clerk, 'I think I'll have some fresh air before I retire,' and sauntered out. In my inner pocket were a screwdriver and a small electric torch which I had that afternoon purchased at a hardware shop. I knew from the fiction into which I had sometimes dipped that burglars find these torches and screwdrivers, or 'jimmies', of value in their work.

I endeavoured, as I stole about the streets, to assume an expression of ferocity, to intimidate whoever might endeavour to interrupt me. For this purpose I placed my spectacles in my pocket and disarrayed my bow tie.

I was perhaps, thrown off my normal balance. For the good name of Jason Sanders, I would risk all of serene repute that had been precious to me. So I, who had been a lecturer to respectful students, edged beneath the cottonwoods, slipped across a lawn, crawled over a wire fence, and stood in the garden of Whitney Edgerton. It was fenced and walled on all sides save towards the street. That way, then, I should have to run in case of eruption – out into the illumination of a street lamp. I might be very prettily trapped. Suddenly I was a-tremble, utterly incredulous that I should be here.

I couldn't do it.

I was menaced from every side. Wasn't that someone peering from an upper window of the house? Didn't a curtain move in the study? What was that creak behind me? I, who had never in my life spoken to a policeman save to ask a direction had thrust myself in here, an intruder, to be treated like a common vagrant, to be shamed and roughly handled. As I grudgingly swayed towards the study windows I was uneasy before imaginary eyes. I do not remember a fear of being shot. It was something vaguer and more enfeebling: it was the staring disapproval of all my civilization, schools, churches, banks, the courts, and Quinta. But I came to the central window of the study, the window whose catch I had loosened.

I couldn't do it.

It had seemed so easy in fiction; but crawl in there? Into the darkness? Face the unknown? Shin over the sill like a freshman? Sneak and pilfer like a mucker?

I touched the window; I think I tried to push it up. It was beyond my strength.

Disgust galvanized me. I to thieve from the thief who had slain Jason Sanders? Never! I had a right to know his information; I had a right. By heavens! I'd shake it out of him; I'd face, beat, kill that snobbish hound. I remember running about the corner of the house, jabbing the button of the bell, bumping the door panels with sore palms.

A light, and Edgerton's voice: 'What is it? What is it?'

'Quick! A man hurt! Motor accident!' I bellowed.

He opened the door. I was on him, pushing him back into the hall, demanding.

'I want everything you have about Jason Sanders!' I noticed then that had a revolver. I am afriad I hurt his wrist. Somewhat after, when I had placed him in a chair in the study, I said: 'Where did you get your data? And where did Sanders die?'

'You must be this idiot that's been responsible for the Sanders folderol,' he was gasping.

'Will you be so good as to listen? I am going to kill you unless you give me what I wish, and immediately.'

'Wh – what! See here!'

I don't remember. It's curious; my head aches when I try to recall that part. I think I must have struck him, yet that seems strange, for certainly he was larger than I and better fed. But I can hear him piping:

'This is an outrage! You're insane! But if you insist, I had all my facts about Sanders from Peter Williams, a clergyman out in Yancey, Colorado.'

'Let me see your letters from him.'

'Is that necessary?'

'Do you think I'd trust you?'

'Well, I have only one letter here. The others are in my safe-deposit vault. Williams first wrote to me when he read my letter criticizing your articles. He has given me a good many details. He apparently has some reason to hate the memory of Sanders. Here's his latest epistle, some more facts about Sanders's delightful poetic career.'

One glance showed me that this was indeed the case. The sheet which Edgerton handed me had inartistically printed at the top, 'Rev. Peter F. Williams, Renewalist Brotherhood Congregation, Yancey, Colo.,' and one sentence was, 'Before this, Sanders's treatment of women in Kennuit was disgraceful – can't be too strongly condem'd.'

I had the serpent of whose venom Edgerton was but the bearer!

I backed out, left Edgerton. He said a silly thing, which shows that he was at least as flustered as I was:

'Good-bye, Lieutenant Sandec!'

I was certain that he would have me apprehended if I returned to my hotel, even for so long as would be needed to gather my effects. Instantly, I decided to abandon my luggage, hasten out of town. Fortunately, I had with me neither my other suit nor the fitted bag which Quinta had given me. Traversing only side streets, I sped out of town by the railway track. Then I was glad of the pocket flashlight which, outside the study window, had seemed absurd. I sat on the railway embankment. I can still feel the grittiness of sharp-cornered cinders and cracked rock, still see the soggy pile of rotting logs beside the embankment upon which my flashlight cast a milky beam as I switched it on in order that I might study Peter Williams's letter.

Already I had a clue.

Peter Williams was also the name of that son of the Reverend Abner Williams of Kennuit whom Jason had often trounced. I wished that he had trounced him oftener and more roundly. The Reverend Abner had hurled Jason out of his church. All this would naturally institute a feud between Jason and the Williamses. There might have been additional causes, perchance rivalry for a girl.

Well! The Reverend Peter Williams's letter to Edgerton was typewritten. That modernity would indicate, in a village parson, a man not over forty years old. Was it not logical to guess that Peter Williams of Colorado was the grandson of Peter Williams of Kennuit, and that he had utilized information long possessed by the whole tribe of the Williamses to destroy his grandsire's enemy, Jason?

By dawn I was on a way train; in the afternoon of the next day I was in Yancey, Colorado.

I found the Renewalist parsonage, residence of the Reverend Peter Williams, to be a small, dun-coloured cottage on a hill crest. I strode thither, vigorous with rage. I knocked. I faced a blank Teutonic maid. I demanded to see Mr Williams.

I was admitted to his rustic study. I saw a man not of forty, as his letter had suggested, but astoundingly old, an ancient dominie, as sturdy as a bison, with a bursting immensity of white beard. He was sitting in a hollowed rocker by the stove.

'Well?' said he.

'Is this the Reverend Peter Williams?'

'It be.'

'May I sit down?''

'You can.'

I sat calmly in a small, mean chair. My rage was sated by perceiving that I had to deal not with any grandson of Jason's foe, but with the actual original Peter Williams himself! I was beholding one who had been honoured by the fists of Jason Sanders. He was too precious a serpent not to draw him with cunning. Filially, I pursued:

'I was told – I once spent a summer on Cape Cod – '

'Who are you, young man?'

'Smith, William Smith. I am a – travelling salesman.'

'Well, well, let's have it.'

'I was told you came from the Cape – from Kennuit.'

'Who told ye?'

'Really, I can't seem for the moment to remember.'

'Well, what of it?'

'I just wondered if you weren't the son of the Reverend Abner Williams who used to be pastor in Kennuit way back about 1840.'

'I be. I am the son in the spirit of that man of holiness.'

Cautiously, oh, so cautiously, simulating veneration, I

hinted:

'Then you must have known this fellow I've been reading about; this Jason – what was it? – Sandwich?'

'Jason Sanders. Yes, sir, I knew him well, too well. A viler wretch never lived. A wine-bibber, a man of wrath, blind to the inner grace, he was all that I seek to destroy.' Williams's voice loomed like a cathedral service. I hated him, yet I was impressed. I ventured:

'One thing I've often wondered. They say this Sanders fellow didn't really die in Greece. I wonder when and where he did die.'

The old man was laughing; he was wrinkling his eyes at me; he was shaking.

'You're daft, but you have grit. I know who you be. Edgerton telegraphed me you were coming. So you like Jason, eh?'

'I do.'

'I tell you he was a thief, a drunkard – '

'And I tell you he was a genius!'

'You tell me! Huh!'

'See here, what reason has there been for your dogging Jason? It wasn't just your boyish fighting and – how did you find out what became of him after he left Kennuit?'

The old man looked at me as though I were a bug. He answered slowly, with a drawl maddening to my impatience – impatience so whelming now that my spine was cold, my abdomen constricted.

'I know it because in his prison – ' he stopped, yawned, rubbed his jaw – 'in his cell I wrestled with the evil spirit in him.'

'You won?'

'I did.'

'But after that – when did he die?' I asked.

'He didn't.'

'You mean Jason is alive now, sixty years after – '

'He's ninety-five years old. You see, I'm – I was till I rechristened myself Williams – I'm Jason Sanders,' he replied.

Then for two thousand miles, by village street and way

train and limited, sitting unmoving in berths and silent in smoking rooms, I fled to the cool solace of Quinta Gates.

GABRIEL GARCIA MARQUEZ

The Woman Who Came At Six O'Clock

The swinging door opened. At that hour there was nobody in José's restaurant. It had just struck six and the man knew that the regular customers wouldn't begin to arrive until six-thirty. His clientele was so conservative and regular that the clock hadn't finished striking six when a woman entered, as on every day at that hour, and sat down on the stool without saying anything. She had an unlighted cigarette tight between her lips.

'Hello, queen,' José said when he saw her sit down. Then he went to the other end of the counter, wiping the streaked surface with a dry rag. Whenever anyone came into the restaurant José did the same thing. Even with the woman, with whom he'd almost come to acquire a degree of intimacy, the fat and ruddy restaurant owner put on his daily comedy of a hard-working man. He spoke from the other end of the counter.

'What do you want today?' he said.

'First of all I want to teach you how to be a gentleman,' the woman said. She was sitting at the end of the stools, her elbows on the counter, the extinguished cigarette between her lips. When she spoke, she tightened her mouth so that José would notice the unlighted cigarette.

'I didn't notice,' José said.

'You still haven't learned to notice anything,' said the woman.

The man left the cloth on the counter, walked to the dark cupboards which smelt of tar and dusty wood, and came back immediately with the matches. The woman leaned over to get the light that was burning in the man's rustic, hairy hands. José saw the woman's lush hair, all greased with cheap, thick Vaseline. He saw her uncovered shoulder above the flowered brassiere. He saw the beginning of her twilight breast when the woman raised her head, the lighted butt between her lips now.

'You're beautiful tonight, queen,' José said.

'Stop your nonsense,' the woman said. 'Don't think that's going to help me pay you.'

'That's not what I meant, queen,' José said. 'I'll bet your lunch didn't agree with you today.'

The woman sucked in the first drag of thick smoke, crossed her arms, her elbows still on the counter, and remained looking at the street through the wide restaurant window. She had a melancholy expression. A bored and vulgar melancholy.

'I'll fix you a good steak,' José said.

'I still haven't got any money,' the woman said.

'You haven't had any money for three months and I always fix you something good,' José said.

'Today's different,' said the woman sombrely, still looking out at the street.

'Every day's the same,' José said. 'Every day the clock says six, then you come in and say you're hungry as a dog and then I fix you something good. The only difference is this: today you didn't say you were as hungry as a dog but that today is different.'

'And it's true,' the woman said. She turned to look at the man, who was at the other end of the counter checking the refrigerator. She examined him for two or three seconds. Then she looked at the clock over the cupboard. It was three minutes after six. 'It's true, José. Today is different,' she said. She let the smoke out and kept on talking with crisp, impassioned words. 'I didn't come at six today, that's why it's different, José.'

The man looked at the clock.

'I'll cut off my arm if that clock is one minute slow,' he said.

'That's not it, José. I didn't come at six o'clock today,' the woman said.

'It just struck six, queen,' José said. 'When you came in it was just finishing.'

'I've got a quarter of an hour that says I've been here,' the woman said.

José went over to where she was. He put his great puffy face up to the woman while he tugged one of his eyelids with his index finger.

'Blow on me here,' he said.

The woman threw her head back. She was serious, annoyed, softened, beautified by a cloud of sadness and fatigue.

'Stop your foolishness, José. You know I haven't had a drink for six months.'

'Tell it to somebody else,' he said, 'not to me. I'll bet you've had a pint or two at least.'

'I had a couple of drinks with a friend,' she said.

'Oh, now I understand,' José said.

'There's nothing to understand,' the woman said. 'I've been here for a quarter of an hour.'

The man shrugged his shoulders.

'Well, if that's the way you want it, you've got a quarter of an hour that says you've been here,' he said. 'After all, what difference does it make, ten minutes this way, ten minutes that way?'

'It makes a difference, José,' the woman said. And she stretched her arms over the glass counter with an air of careless abandon. She said: 'And it isn't that I wanted it that way; it's just that I've been here for a quarter of an hour.' She looked at the clock again and corrected herself: 'What am I saying – it's been twenty minutes.'

'OK, queen,' the man said. 'I'd give you a whole day and the night that goes with it just to see you happy.'

During all this time José had been moving about behind the counter, changing things, taking something from one place and putting it in another. He was playing his role.

'I want to see you happy,' he repeated. He stopped suddenly, turning to where the woman was. 'Do you know that I love you very much?'

The woman looked at him coldly.

'Ye-e-es . . . ? What a discovery, José. Do you think I'd go with you even for a million pesos?'

'I didn't mean that, queen,' José said. 'I repeat, I bet your lunch didn't agree with you.'

'That's not why I said it,' the woman said. And her voice became less indolent. 'No woman could stand a weight like yours, even for a million pesos.'

José blushed. he turned his back to the woman and began to dust the bottles on the shelves. He spoke without turning his head.

'You're unbearable today, queen. I think the best thing is for you to eat your steak and go home to bed.'

'I'm not hungry,' the woman said. She stayed looking out at the street again, watching the passers-by of the dusking city. For an instant there was a murky silence in the restaurant. A peacefulness broken only by José fiddling about in the cupboard. Suddenly the woman stopped looking out into the street and spoke with a tender, soft, different voice.

'Do you really love me, Pepillo?'

'I do,' José said dryly, not looking at her.

'In spite of what I've said to you?' the woman asked.

'What did you say to me?' José asked, still without any inflection in his voice, still without looking at her.

'That business about a million pesos,' the woman said.

'I'd already forgotten,' José said.

'So do you love me?' the woman asked.

'Yes,' said José.

There was a pause. José kept moving about, his face turned towards the cabinets, still not looking at the woman. She blew out another mouthful of smoke, rested her bust on the counter, and then, cautiously and roguishly, biting her tonguc before saying it, as if speaking on tiptoe:

'Even if you didn't go to bed with me?' she asked.

And only then did José turn to look at her.

'I love you so much that I wouldn't go to bed with you,' he said. Then he walked over to where she was. He stood looking into her face, his powerful arms leaning on the counter in front of her, looking into her eyes. He said: 'I love you so much that every night I'd kill the man who goes with you.'

At the first instant the woman seemed perplexed. Then she looked at the man attentively, with a wavering expression of compassion and mockery. Then she had a moment of brief disconcerted silence. And then she laughed noisily.

'You're jealous, José. That's wild, you're jealous!'

José blushed again with frank, almost shameful timidity, as might have happened to a child who'd revealed all his secrets all of a sudden. He said:

'This afternoon you don't seem to understand anything, queen.' And he wiped himself with the rag. He said:

'This bad life is brutalizing you.'

But now the woman had changed her expression.

'So, then,' she said. And she looked into his eyes again, with a strange glow in her look, confused and challenging at the same time.

'So you're not jealous.'

'In a way I am,' José said. 'But it's not the way you think.'

He loosened his collar and continued wiping himself, drying his throat with the cloth.

'So?' the woman asked.

'The fact is I love you so much that I don't like your doing it,' José said.

'What?' the woman asked.

'This business of going with a different man every day,' José said.

'Would you really kill him to stop him from going with me?' the woman asked.

'Not to stop him from going with you, no,' José said. 'I'd kill him because he *went* with you.'

'It's the same thing,' the woman said.

The conversation had reached an exciting destiny. The woman was speaking in a soft, low, fascinated voice. Her face was almost stuck up against the man's healthy, peaceful face, as he stood motionless, as if bewitched by the vapour of the words.

'That's true,' José said.

'So,' the woman said, and reached out her hand to stroke

the man's rough arm. With the other she tossed away her butt. 'So you're capable of killing a man?'

'For what I told you, yes,' José said. And his voice took on an almost dramatic stress.

The woman broke into convulsive laughter, with an obvious mocking intent.

'How awful, José. How awful,' she said, still laughing. 'José killing a man. Who would have known that behind the fat and sanctimonious man who never makes me pay, who cooks me a steak every day and has fun talking to me until I find a man, there lurks a murderer. How awful, José! You scare me!'

José was confused. Maybe he felt a little indignation. Maybe, when the woman started laughing, he felt defrauded.

'You're drunk, silly,' he said. 'Go get some sleep. You don't even feel like eating anything.'

But the woman had stopped laughing now and was serious again, pensive, leaning on the counter. She watched the man go away. She saw him open the refrigerator and close it again without taking anything out. Then she saw him move to the other end of the counter. She watched him polish the shining glass, the same as in the beginning. Then the woman spoke again with the tender and soft tone of when she said: 'Do you really love me, Pepillo?'

'José,' she said.

The man didn't look at her.

'José!'

'Go home and sleep,' José said. 'And take a bath before you go to bed so you can sleep it off.'

'Seriously, José,' the woman said. 'I'm not drunk.'

'Then you've turned stupid.' José said.

'Come here, I've got to talk to you,' the woman said.

The man came over stumbling, halfway between pleasure and mistrust.

'Come closer!'

He stood in front of the woman again. She leaned forward, grabbed him by the hair, but with a gesture of obvious tenderness.

'Tell me again what you said at the start,' she said.

'What do you mean?' José asked. He was trying to look at

her with his head turned away, held by the hair.

'That you'd kill a man who went to bed with me,' the woman said.

'I'd kill a man who went to bed with you, queen. That's right,' José said.

The woman let him go.

'In that case you'd defend me if I killed him, right?' she asked affirmatively, pushing José's enormous pig head with a movement of brutal coquettishness. The man didn't answer anything. He smiled.

'Answer me, José,' the woman said. 'Would you defend me if I killed him?'

'That depends,' José said. 'You know it's not as easy as you say.'

'The police wouldn't believe anyone more than you,' the woman said.

José smiled, honoured, satisfied. The woman leaned over towards him again, over the counter.

'It's true, José. I'm willing to bet that you've never told a lie in your life,' she said.

'You won't get anywhere this way,' José said.

'Just the same,' the woman said. 'The police know you and they'll believe anything without asking you twice.'

José began pounding the counter opposite her, not knowing what to say. The woman looked out at the street again. Then she looked at the clock and modified the tone of her voice, as if she were interested in finishing the conversation before the first customers arrived.

'Would you tell a lie for me, José?' she asked. 'Seriously.'

And then José looked at her again, sharply, deeply, as if a tremendous idea had come pounding up in his head. An idea that had entered through one ear, spun about for a moment, vague, confused and gone out through the other, leaving behind only a warm vestige of terror.

'What have you got yourself into, queen?' José asked. He leaned forward, his arms folded over the counter again. The woman caught the strong and ammonia-smelling vapour of his breath, which had become difficult because of the pressure that the counter was exercising on the man's stomach.

'This is really serious, queen. What have you got yourself into?' he asked.

The woman made her head spin in the opposite direction.

'Nothing,' she said. 'I was just talking to amuse myself.'

Then she looked at him again.

'Do you know you may not have to kill anybody?'

'I never thought about killing anybody,' José said, distressed.

'No, man,' the woman said. 'I mean nobody goes to bed with me.'

'Oh!' José said. 'Now you're talking straight out. I always thought you had no need to prowl around. I'll make a bet that if you drop all this I'll give you the biggest steak I've got every day, free.'

'Thank you, José,' the woman said. 'But that's not why. It's because I *can't* go to bed with anyone any more.'

'You're getting things all confused again,' José said. He was becoming impatient.

'I'm not getting anything confused,' the woman said. She stretched out on the seat and José saw her flat, sad breasts underneath her brassiere.

'Tomorrow I'm going away and I promise you I won't come back and bother you ever again. I promise you I'll never go to bed with anyone.'

'Where'd you pick up that fever?' José asked.

'I decided just a minute ago,' the woman said. 'Just a minute ago I realized it's a dirty business.'

José grabbed the cloth again and started to clean the glass in front of her. He spoke without looking at her.

He said:

'Of course, the way you do it it's a dirty business. You should have known that a long time ago.'

'I was getting to know it a long time ago,' the woman said, 'but I was only convinced of it just a little while ago. Men disgust me.'

José smiled. He raised his head to look at her, still smiling, but he saw her concentrated, perplexed, talking with her shoulders raised, twirling on the stool with a taciturn expression, her face gilded by premature autumnal grain.

'Don't you think they ought to lay off a woman who kills a man because after she's been with him she feels disgust with him and everyone who's been with her?'

'There's no reason to go that far,' José said, moved, a thread of pity in his voice.

'What if the woman tells the man he disgusts her while she watches him get dressed because she remembers that she's been rolling around with him all afternoon and feels that neither soap nor sponge can get his smell off her?'

'That all goes away, queen,' José said, a little indifferent now, polishing the counter. 'There's no reason to kill him. Just let him go.'

But the woman kept on talking, and her voice was a uniform, flowing, passionate current.

'But what if the woman tells him he disgusts her and the man stops getting dressed and runs over to her again, kisses her again, does . . .?'

'No decent man would ever do that,' José says.

'What if he does?' the woman asks, with exasperating anxiety. 'What if the man isn't decent and does it and then the woman feels that he disgusts her so much that she could die, and she knows that the only way to end it all is to stick a knife in under him?'

'That's terrible,' José said. 'Luckily there's no man who would do what you say.'

'Well,' the woman said, completely exasperated now. 'What if he did? Suppose he did.'

'In any case it's not that bad,' José said. He kept on cleaning the counter without changing position, less intent on the conversation now.

The woman pounded the counter with her knuckles. She became affirmative, emphatic.

'You're a savage, José,' she said. 'You don't understand anything.' She grabbed him firmly by the sleeve. 'Come on, tell me that the woman should kill him.'

'OK,' José said with a conciliatory bias. 'It's all probably just the way you say it is.'

'Isn't that self-defence?' the woman asked, grabbing him by

the sleeve.

Then José gave her a lukewarm and pleasant look.

'Almost, almost,' he said. And he winked at her, with an expression that was at the same time a cordial comprehension and fearful compromise of complicity. But the woman was serious. She let go of him.

'Would you tell a lie to defend a woman who does that?' she asked.

'That depends,' said José.

'Depends on what?' the woman asked.

'Depends on the woman,' said José.

'Suppose it's a woman you love a lot,' the woman said. 'Not to be with her, but like you say, you love her a lot.'

'OK, anything you say, queen,' José said, relaxed, bored.

He'd gone off again. He'd looked at the clock. He'd seen that it was going on half-past six. He'd thought that in a few minutes the restaurant would be filling up with people and maybe that was why he began to polish the glass with greater effort, looking at the street through the window. The woman stayed on her stool, silent, concentrating, watching the man's movements with an air of declining sadness. Watching him as a lamp about to go out might have looked at a man. Suddenly, without reacting, she spoke again with the unctuous voice of servitude.

'José!'

The man looked at her with a thick, sad tenderness, like a maternal ox. He didn't look at her to hear her, just to look at her, to know that she was there, waiting for a look that had no reason to be one of protection or solidarity. Just the look of a plaything.

'I told you I was leaving tomorrow and you didn't say anything,' the woman said.

'Yes,' José said. 'You didn't tell me where.'

'Out there,' the woman said. 'Where there aren't any men who want to sleep with somebody.'

José smiled again.

'Are you really going away?' he asked, as if becoming aware of life, quickly changing the expression on his face.

'That depends on you,' the woman said. 'If you know

enough to say what time I got here, I'll go away tomorrow and I'll never get mixed up in this again. Would you like that?'

José gave an affirmative nod, smiling and concrete. The woman leaned over to where he was.

'If I come back here some day I'll get jealous when I find another woman talking to you, at this time and on this same stool.'

'If you come back here you'll have to bring me something,' José said.

'I promise you that I'll look everywhere for the tame bear, bring him to you,' the woman said.

José smiled and waved the cloth through the air that separated him from the woman, as if he were cleaning an invisible pane of glass. The woman smiled too, with an expression of cordiality and coquetry now. Then the man went away, polishing the glass to the other end of the counter.

'What, then?' José said without looking at her.

'Will you really tell anyone who asks you that I got here at a quarter to six?' the woman said.

'What for?' José said, still without looking at her now, as if he had barely heard her.

'That doesn't matter,' the woman said. 'The thing is that you do it.'

José then saw the first customer come in through the swinging door and walk over to a corner table. He looked at the clock. It was six-thirty on the dot.

'OK, queen,' he said distractedly. 'Anything you say. I always do whatever you want.'

'Well,' the woman said. 'Start cooking my steak then.'

The man went to the refrigerator, took out a plate with a piece of meat on it, and left it on the table. Then he lighted the stove.

'I'm going to cook you a good farewell steak, queen,' he said.

'Thank you, Pepillo,' the woman said.

She remained thoughtful as if suddenly she had become sunken in a strange subworld peopled with muddy, unknown forms. Across the counter she couldn't hear the noise that the raw meat made when it fell into the burning grease. Afterwards she didn't hear the dry and bubbling crackle as José turned the flank over in the frying pan and the succulent smell of the marinated meat by measured moments saturated the air of the restaurant. She remained like that, concentrated, reconcentrated, until she raised her head again, blinking as if she were coming back out of a momentary death. Then she saw the man beside the stove, lighted up by the happy, rising fire.

'Pepillo.'

'What!'

'What are you thinking about?' the woman asked.

'I was wondering whether you could find the little wind-up bear someplace,' José said.

'Of course I can,' the woman said. 'But what I want is for you to give me everything I asked for as a going-away present.'

José looked at her from the stove.

'How often have I got to tell you?' he said. 'Do you want something besides the best steak I've got?'

'Yes,' the woman said.

'What is it?' José asked.

'I want another quarter of an hour.'

José drew back and looked at the clock. Then he looked at the customer, who was still silent, waiting in the corner, and finally at the meat roasting in the pan. Only then did he speak.

'I really don't understand, queen,' he said.

'Don't be foolish, José,' the woman said. 'Just remember that I've been here since five-thirty.'

LUIGI PIRANDELLO

All Passion Spent

A squalid ground-floor room in a tenement house. The body of an old man is lying on a rickety, shabbily-covered bed. The body lies stiffly, but it has not yet been composed in the traditional way that the dead are laid out. The balls of the eyes are staring in dismay at the world – they seem almost transparent under the delicately thin eyelids, thin as onion-skins: the beard is the unkempt beard of a sick man. The dead man's arms are outside the bedclothes, and his hands are clasped across his breast. The head of the bed is against the wall, and there is a Crucifix attached to the headboard. Beside the bed is a night-table on which are several medicine glasses, a bottle, and an iron candlestick. Centre back is a small door; it is half-open. Beyond it there is an old-fashioned and well-worn chest of drawers, from which the veneer is flaking; on top of it are some crude household articles. Kneeling on the floor by the right-hand side of the bed is the dead man's wife, an old woman. Her body from the waist up and her head have tumbled across the bed and are buried in the bed-clothes; her arms are flung full-length across the bed. She is dressed in black, and is wearing a violet-coloured kerchief on her head. She shows no sign of life. Standing by the half-open door is a little girl, about eight or nine years old. She is the daughter of one of the neighbours. She is standing there, with her eyes wide and staring, and with one finger in her mouth, looking at the body in utter dismay and bewilderment. In the shadow-filled passage, which you can see through the half-open door, you catch a glimpse of men and women who live thereabouts; they're peeping in, but don't dare to venture inside the door. In the wall right there is a window which looks out onto a courtyard. And when you look at the window, you see that there are faces there too. You get glimpses of them as they peer curiously in through the windowpanes, trying to see what's going on. Against the wall left is a decrepit double wardrobe of stained wood. There are a little table and some padded chairs.

Lora's voice is heard out in the passage, 'Let me get by! Mind out of the way!'

She comes in. She is only just over twenty. There is something equivocal about her. Her manner is abrupt, brusque.

She is carrying a paper package, containing a large wax candle and, loose in her hand, some brightly coloured fruit – oranges and apples.

As soon as she's in the room she says to the girl, 'Oh, so they've let you come in, have they, dear? So as you'll remember, when you're a big girl, the first time you ever saw a dead man. Would you like to touch him as well – Just with your finger . . . No? In that case run along! Off you go!'

She takes hold of her and pushes her through the door, saying at the same time to the people standing in the passage, 'There's a lovely funeral up at the top of the road. I saw it as I came by. There was a coach and four horses. Coachman in full rig-out, flunkeys in white wigs. it was really smart! Go on, run along and have a look! Go on! You're like a lot of flies, aren't you? You love a good muck-heap!'

And she draws the door to. She moves over towards the middle of the room and, shrugging her shoulders, exclaims, 'Yes! Yes! It's like the hippopotamus. That time you saw the hippopotamus at the Zoo. And you realized that God created the hippopotamus too! So what was there left for you to be surprised at? The hippopotamus is a fact. Just like the man who gets hold of little girls and then kills them. He's a fact too. And then there's the whore. She's a fact too. It's her job in life to be a whore. And there's the man who throws you out on to the streets. And then there's the flies. *Flies!*'

She sets the candle and the fruit down on the chest of drawers. Then her eyes wander across the room till they settle on the other group of people that's looking in through the window to see what she's doing. Irritated, she runs over to the window.

'God, look! They're even over here, with their noses glued to the windowpane!'

The moment she opens the window they make their escape. She sticks her head out through the window and shouts after them:

'Yes, it's me! It's me all right! Yes, it's me! I know. I'm a slut, aren't I? I'll corrupt everybody, won't I? But can you tell me why you're so much better than me, eh? I suppose it's because you stay at home and sell the stuff wholesale! Sell it by the length! While I hawk the stuff round the streets and sell it by the yard! What do you expect! You can still have a good time, seeing how you like the feel of the stuff. That's it – thumb and finger – feel it! I don't feel anything at all now. As far as I'm concerned it's all bankrupt. Just bankrupt stock! Go on, get up those stairs! Go on, up you go! You never know – you might be the next one to slide down . . . down . . . down . . . Cheer up, love! We came in here this morning, arm in arm. Together, death and dishonour! Yes, dears! *Dis – hon – our!* My! My! Just look at her face! Coo! Dear, dear! Wait a minute, love! I'll throw you an apple!'

She takes a red apple from off the chest of drawers and draws her arm back, in readiness to throw the apple to the girl whom, a short while before, she had pushed out of the room.

'Running away? Don't you want it? Oh, in that case I'll eat it myself.'

She sinks her teeth in the apple and closes the window. Immediately she has done so she puts her fingers to her nose and pinches it.

'Pooh! Pooh! This place stinks to high heaven of soap and water! It's like a wash-house!'

She looks at her father's body stretched out on the bed.

'Yes, I'm having something to eat! Yes, I'm having something to eat! And you hope it chokes me! I haven't had a bite to eat since yesterday morning! Those hands of yours

– look at them now! They won't do any moving now, will they? They've given me some hard knocks in their time, haven't they? And you even spat in my face! And grabbed me by the hair! And kicked me all around the room, you were so flaming mad! Even as a young girl I knew there was more to life than holy pictures! And now those hands of yours are like this. Crossed on your chest. And as cold ice.'

She goes over and shakes her mother by the shoulder. 'Get up, Mamma! You haven't had anything to eat since yesterday morning either! You must eat something!'

Suddenly the doubt assails her that they've diddled her in giving her her change. She starts working out what she's spent.

'Four and eight. Twelve. And five. That makes seventeen. Wait a minute! What else did I buy? Oh, yes. There's the fruit I got from that old fool! He was selling little birds in bunches. All tied together by string threaded through holes in their beaks. He just flung the fruit at me, the swine. Didn't even notice I was carrying a candle.'

She gives a little jump as she remembers.

'Oh, yes! The candle!'

She goes and fetches it from off the chest of drawers and unwraps it.

'Just so as people can't say we didn't light one for you.'

She takes the iron candlestick from off the night-table.

'Let's hope it'll stand up in this thing.'

She fixes the candle into the holder.

'Coo! Look, might have been made to measure!'

There is a box of matches on the night-table. She lights the candle and sets it down on the table.

'Just burn away. And drip, drip, drip. Lovely life! Like virgins. They just burn away and drip!

'Can you see the candle? No, you can't. And the wooden saints stuck up on the altar can't see them either. But we can see them. All lit up. And down on our knees we go. It all comes to faith – the whole business of candle-making depends on the faithful being faithful! And now we're all busy believing that you're busy enjoying it all up there! But you can't let us see you are, can you? Poor devil! Get up, Mum!

Oh! We'd better get him dressed before he starts going stiff on us! Yes! Go on, cry away! Cry your eyes out! You look as though you're dead yourself, sprawled out there like that! Now we'd better get on with this quick! It was lucky for us they waited until he was dead. They want to have everything out of here before it starts getting dark. And at four o'clock they'll be coming from the Chapel of Mercy. That won't even leave time for the candle to burn right down.'

She looks at the lighted candle, then raises her eyes to the Crucifix hanging on the wall.

'Oh! Better put him with his hands round the Crucifix!'

She goes over to the other side of the bed, pulls a chair up, gets onto it and takes down the Crucifix. She holds it in her hands for a moment or so.

'Oh, Christ! And the poor make haste to come unto You . . . You did it on purpose! Which of us would have the nerve to come complaining to You about how life's treating us? Come moaning to You about how everybody's doing this to him and doing that to him? You, who, though You were without sin, suffered them to nail You upon the Cross. With Your arms flung wide open. You, the Christ! You, the hope that we enjoy when we get to Heaven! Yes! You. The flame that burns from this tuppenny candle.'

She leaps off the chair and puts the Crucifix between the fingers of the dead man, saying to her mother, 'Now look! You'd better get moving! His fingers are quite stiff already. You won't be able to dress him now. You'll have to slit his jacket down the back and slip it on both arms separately. Do it in two bits. Aren't you going to budge? Don't you want to? Are you going to stick there until they come and grab you by the arm and sling you out of the door? Oh, well! All right! Now you watch me!'

She grabs hold of the chair and sits down on it.

'I'm going to settle down and wait too! I'll stick here till the dustman comes with his broom and shovel and chucks me on the dustcart. Blessed are they who have given up all thought of moving. Happy lot. No longer even to have to move across the room. Not even to have to lift the food to one's mouth. In the end you're right, when you no longer have the will to do anything, things just get done by themselves. They come in; they grab hold of you by the arm and shove you up on to your feet. You start toppling over. . . . Oh, don't worry, though! If they don't want you for anything, they don't give you time to topple over and bang youself. They give you a kick up the backside. Or else they give you a hefty shove. And out into the street you go – *sprawling.* All your old rags, the bed, body and all. The chest of drawers. All out in the middle of the street. Roll up! Roll up! Come along and take anything you fancy! And there you are sprawling in the gutter. You. Looking just like you're looking now sprawling on that bed. And everybody standing around gawking at you. Up comes a policeman, "Move along there! No sleeping in the street!" "Then where can I sleep?" "Come on, get moving! Move along there!" You stay where you are. You don't move along. You're not afraid. Then, if you're really stubborn about it – someone will see that you do move. You've still got the right – since you haven't got a home – to have some place whereon to lay your head. Yes – you can rest it on the ground. On the kerbstone. Just like a puppet that's been stuck there – so! On one of the steps leading up to the church; on a park bench. Up rush the little boys and girls! Yes, it's Granny! "What did you say, darling? I don't know what you mean, dear. Oh, you want to sit up here next to me. Granny doesn't want to play now. You'd better go and look at the fish in the pond. Yes, they're goldfish. . . ." Uh – huh! Praise be to God! Then you settle down. Hold out your hand like this, and a passer-by throws you a ha'penny and a crust of bread. But, not for me! Oh, no! Nothing like that for me! Pooh!' She spits. 'That's what I think of that for a notion! If it was me, I wouldn't stick out my hand and beg. . . . Oh, no! I'd stick it out so as I could scratch! And steal! And kill! And then – Oh, yes! Then I'd end up in gaol. Board and lodging free!'

Enraged, she gets up and goes over and says to her father, 'I'm taking this opportunity of getting my own back on you for all the wallops you gave me! You can't hear me now, so I can really let you have it! You didn't even try to understand, did you? You never even so much as tried to understand how – without knowing you've done so, and when you least think you're likely to be; how it happens that you're taken by a man. Even while you're crying your eyes out in utter despair. . . . Because your body – Suddenly he's touched you – there wasn't any special meaning in that touch – but your body suddenly feels an all-pervading sweet tenderness and you're tingling with life, even in the very midst of all your despair and desperation. With a rush you find yourself blazing into a living torch of joy. Everything around you is consumed. You no longer see anything at all. You're in a blind, intoxicated, desperate frenzy! You're lost in a world of delight such as you'd never dreamt was possible! That's how it happened. That's how it happened. Here – in this room. You left me here with him. Your nephew. His wife had been having an affair with another man. He was sitting here; on the very bed you're lying on now, crying his heart out. I took his head, like this, so as to try and comfort him. He started to rave about how – Oh, dear! Then he buried his head between my breasts. I didn't make myself a woman, it's not my doing that I feel pleasure when a man does that. The blood started to race faster in our veins. Passion seized us both. And then, afterwards. . . . Just like you, he lay stretched out there on the bed, like a dead man. Filled with terror and dismay at having taken my body. And then the miserable bastard went back home to his wife – all nice and consoled! And do you know what he said? He said that he'd learnt from what I'd done that there's no such thing as a chaste and virtuous woman! They're all the same, he said. In fact, they're no better than men. They're all made of the same flesh and blood, all lusting after the flesh. And so, said he, there's no reason why – if men are allowed to do it as often as they like – there's no reason why we should write a woman off as a dead loss if she does it once. "After all, you had your fun too, didn't you?" Miserable bastard! And what about the baby? But it's a bit different for me. . . . Oh yes, Dad! You're dead now and I forgive you. But if I'm damned like I am, it's all your fault! You all gang up together, you men, to condemn a woman! You're all the same! You cease to be the woman's father, or her brothers. No, as a matter of fact, instead of pleading for her, you're the most ferocious against her! And the most ferocious of them all was you! You flung me out into the street like a bitch. But listen! I wiped the tears away from my eyes. I wiped the spit off my face. And I offered myself to the first man that came along! The *street* . . . ! And all the rage I felt! The passionate longing I felt to throw in your face the shame that you hadn't wanted to keep hidden from the world! But then there was the baby . . . The baby. It's not true what they say! It's true afterwards – after it's – but not before. It's absolutely terrifying, feeling it inside you! And then, when he's born . . . Yes, it's true after he's born. This tiny little creature, nuzzling his way in, trying to find you. I came here and left him with you when he was eight months old. One night, I came and left him here, behind the door, in the box with all his baby clothes. They ought still to be here, those things of his. Or have you sold them? Thank you, God, for taking him to Yourself when he was so tiny! Come on! Come on! Let's get him dressed!'.

She goes over and opens the wardrobe. She takes out a brown suit that's hanging on a clothes-hanger, and turns to her mother and says, 'He used to sing him to sleep, didn't he? Every night he used to sing him to sleep, with that song – how did it go . . . ? The one you used to sing to me when I was a little girl. Somebody came and told me – It was one night when it was raining – came and told me how he'd heard him from the courtyard, singing to the baby. And the . . . Then he wanted to – to – Do you understand? After telling me *that*!'

She looks at her father's suit, which she's still holding. She examines it carefully.

'Oh, this suit's still in good condition! You might almost . . . Yes . . . In any case, if he's already appeared before God up in Heaven . . . why should he worry about the people that are coming to collect him in a few minutes? Why should he worry about what sort of suit he's got on to meet *them*? And you, sprawled out there like that! You'll be pretty hard up. There's some other stuff here; you might try and get something for it from the old-clothes man! Are you listening? We'd better make it up into a bundle! There's probably some stuff in the chest of drawers . . .'

She goes over to the chest of drawers, opens the top drawer and rummages inside – nothing but rags. She opens the next drawer – nothing at all. She opens the third drawer – inside are all the baby's clothes.

'Oh, this is where they are!'

She looks at them. She sinks down onto the ground. She takes out one of the garments. A rolled-up swaddling band, a little vest, a baby's bib. Then, last of all, she takes out a baby's bonnet. She clenches her fist and puts it into the hood of the bonnet, and just as if she were cradling a baby in her arms, she begins to hum, in a faraway kind of voice, the old song that her mother used to sing. And while she sings, gradually the room gets darker and darker until, with all other lights completely extinguished, nothing is to be seen but the flame of the candle.

Silence.

BERTRAND RUSSELL

The Corsican Ordeal of Miss X

I

I had occasion recently to visit my good friend, Professor N, whose paper on pre-Celtic Decorative Art in Denmark raised some points that I felt needed discussing. I found him in his study, but his usually benign and yet slightly intelligent expression was marred by some strange bewilderment. The books which should have been on the arm of the chair, and which he supposed himself to be reading, were scattered in confusion on the floor. The spectacles which he imagined to be on his nose lay idle on his desk. The pipe which was usually in his mouth lay smoking in his tobacco bowl, though he seemed completely unaware of its not occupying its usual place. His mild and somewhat silly philanthropy and his usual placid gaze had somehow dropped off him. A harassed, distracted, bewildered, and horrified expression was stamped upon his features.

'Good God! ' I said, 'what has happened?'

'Ah,' said he, 'it is my secretary, Miss X. Hitherto, I have found her level-headed, efficient cool, and destitute of those emotions which are only too apt to distract youth. But in an ill-advised moment I allowed her to take a fornight's holiday from her labours on decorative art, and she, in a still more ill-advised moment, chose to spend the fortnight in Corsica. When she returned I saw at once that something had happened. 'What *did* you do in Corsica?' I asked. 'Ah! What indeed!' she replied.'

II

The secretary was not in the room at the moment, and I hoped that Professor N might enlarge a little upon the misfortune that had befallen him. But in this I was disappointed. Not another word, so at least he assured me, had he been able to extract from Miss X. Horror piled upon horror glared from her eyes at the mere recollection, but nothing more specific could he discover.

I felt it my duty to the poor girl, who, so I had been given to understand, had hitherto been hard-working and conscientious, to see whether anything could be done to relieve her of the dreadful weight which depressed her spirits. I bethought me of Mrs. Menhennet, a middle-aged lady of considerable bulk, who, so I was informed by her grandchildren, had once had some pretences to beauty. Mrs. Menhennet, I knew, was the granddaughter of a Corsican bandit; in one of those unguarded moments, too frequent, alas, in that rough island, the bandit had assaulted a thoroughly respectable young lady, with the result that she had given birth, after a due interval, to the redoubtable Mr. Gorman.

Mr. Gorman, though his work took him into the City, pursued there the same kind of activities as had led to his existence. Eminent financiers trembled at his approach. Well-established bankers of unblemished reputation had ghastly visions of prison. Merchants who imported the wealth of the gorgeous East turned pale at the thought of the Customs House officers at the dead of night. All of which misfortunes, it was well understood, were set in motion by the machinations of the predacious Mr. Gorman.

His daughter, Mrs. Menhennet, would have heard of any strange and unwonted disturbance in the home of her paternal grandfather. I therefore asked for an interview, which was graciously accorded. At four o'clock on a dark afternoon in November I presented myself at her tea-table.

'And what,' she said, 'brings you here? Do not pretend that it is my charms. The day for such pretence is past. For ten years it would have been true; for another ten I should have believed it. Now it is neither true nor do I believe it. Some other motive brings you here, and I palpitate to know what it may be.'

This approach was somewhat too direct for my taste. I find a pleasure in a helicoidal approach to my subject. I like to begin at a point remote from that at which I am aiming, or on occasion, if I begin at a point near my ultimate destination, I like to approach the actual point by a boomerang course, taking me at first away from the final mark and thereby, I hope, deceiving my auditor. But Mrs. Menhennet would permit no such finesse. Honest, downright, and straightforward, she believed in the direct approach, a characteristic which she seemed to have inherited from her Corsican grandfather. I therefore abandoned all attempt at circumlocution and came straight to the core of my curiosity.

'Mrs. Menhennet,' I said, 'it has come to my knowledge that there have been in recent weeks strange doings in Corsica, doings which, as I can testify from ocular demonstration, have turned brown hairs grey and young springy steps leaden with the weariness of age. These doings, I am convinced, owing to certain rumours which have reached me, are of transcendent international importance. Whether some new Napoleon is marching to the conquest of Moscow, or some younger Columbus to the discovery of a still unknown Continent, I cannot guess. But something of this sort, I am convinced, is taking place in those wild mountains, something of the sort is being plotted secretly, darkly, dangerously, something of the sort is being concealed tortuously, ferociously, and criminally from those who rashly seek to pierce the veil. You, dear lady, I am convinced, in spite of the correctness of your tea-table and the elegance of your china and fragrance of your Lapsang Souchong, have not lost touch with the activities of your revered father. At his death, I know, you made yourself the guardian of those interests for which he stood. His father, who had ever been to him a shining light on the road towards swift success, inspired every moment of his life. Since his death, although perhaps some of your less perspicacious friends may not have pierced your very efficient disguise, you, I know, have worn his mantle. You, if anyone in this cold and dismal city, can tell me what is happening in that land of sunshine, and what plots, so dark as to cause eclipse even in the blaze of noon, are being hatched in the minds of those noble descendants of ancient greatness. Tell me, I pray you, what you know. The life of Professor N, or if not his life at least his reason, is trembling in the balance. He is, as you are well aware, a benevolent man, not fierce like you and me, but full of gentle loving-kindness. Owing to this trait in his character he cannot divest himself of responsibility for the welfare of his worthy secretary, Miss X, who returned yesterday from Corsica transformed completely from the sunny carefree girl that once she was to a lined, harassed, and weary woman weighed down by all the burdens of the world. What it was that happened to her she refuses to reveal, but if it cannot be discovered it is much to be feared that that great genius, which has already all but solved the many and intricate problems besetting the interpretation of pre-Celtic decorative art, will totter and disintegrate and fall a heap of rubble, like the old Campanile in Venice. You cannot, I am sure, be otherwise than horrified at such a prospect, and I therefore beseech you to unfold, so far as lies in your power, the dreadful secrets of your ancestral home.'

Mrs. Menhennet listened to my words in silence, and when I ceased to speak she still for a while abstained from all reply. At a certain point in my discourse the colour faded from her cheeks and she gave a great gasp. With an effort she composed herself, folded her hands, and compelled her breathing to become quiet.

'You put before me,' she said, 'a dreadful dilemma. If I remain silent, Professor N, not to mention Miss X, must be deprived of reason. But if I speak . . .' Here she shuddered, and no further word emerged.

At this point, when I had been at a loss to imagine what the next development would be, the parlour-maid appeared and mentioned that the chimney-sweep, in full professional attire, was waiting at the door, as he had been engaged to sweep the chimney of the drawing-room that very afternoon.

'Good heavens!' she exclaimed. 'While you and I have been

engaged in small talk and trivial badinage this proud man with his great duties to perform has been kept waiting at my doorstep. This will never do. For now this interview must be at an end. One last word, however. I advise you, if you are in earnest, but only if you are, to pay a visit to General Prz.'[1]

III

General Prz, as everybody remembers, greatly distinguished himself in the First World War by his exploits in defence of his native Poland. Poland, however, in recent years had shown herself ungrateful, and he had been compelled to take refuge in some less unsettled country. A long life of adventure had made the old man, in spite of his grey hairs, unwilling to sink into a quiet life. Although admirers offered him a villa at Worthing, a bijou residence at Cheltenham, or a bungalow in the mountains of Ceylon, none of these took his fancy. Mrs. Menhennet gave him an introduction to some of the more unruly of her relatives in Corsica, and among them he found once more something of the *élan,* the fire, and the wild energy which had inspired the exploits of his earlier years.

But although Corsica remained his spiritual home, and his physical home during the greater part of the year, he would allow himself on rare occasions to visit such of the capitals of Europe as were still west of the Iron Curtain. In these capitals he would converse with the elder statesmen, who would anxiously ask his opinion on all the major trends of recent policy. Whatever he deigned to say in reply they listened to with the respect justly owing to his years and valour. And he would carry back to his mountain fastness the knowledge of the part that Corsica – yes, even Corsica – could play in the great events to come.

As the friend of Mrs. Mehennet, he was at once admitted to the innermost circle of those who, within or without the law, kept alive the traditions of ancient liberty which their Ghibelline ancestors had brought from the still vigorous republics of Northern Italy. In the deep recesses of the hills,

[1] Pronounced 'Pish'.

hidden from the view of the casual tourist, who saw nothing but rocks and shepherds' huts and a few stunted trees, he was allowed to visit old palaces full of medieval splendour, the armour of ancient Gonfalonieri, and the jewelled swords of world-famous Condottieri. In their magnificent halls these proud descendants of ancient chieftains assembled and feasted, not perhaps always wisely but always too well. Even in converse with the General their lips were sealed as to some of the great secrets of their order, except indeed, in those moments of exuberant conviviality, when the long story of traditional hospitality overcame the scruples which at other times led to a prudent silence.

It was in these convivial moments that the General learned of the world-shaking design that these men cherished, a design that inspired all their waking actions and dominated the dreams in which their feasts too often terminated. Nothing loath, he threw himself into their schemes with all the ardour and all the traditional recklessness of the ancient Polish nobility. He thanked God that at a period of life when to most men nothing remains but reminiscence he had been granted the opportunity to share in great deeds of high adventure. On moonlight nights he would gallop over the mountains on his great charger, whose sire and dam alike had helped him to shed immortal glory upon the stricken fields of his native land. Inspired by the rapid motion of the night wind, his thoughts flowed through a mingled dream of ancient valour and future triumph, in which past and future blended in the alembic of his passion.

At the time when Mrs. Menhennet uttered her mysterious suggestion it happened that the General was engaged in one of his periodic rounds of visits to the elder statesmen of the Western world. He had in the past entertained a somewhat anachronistic prejudice against the Western hemisphere, but since he had learned from his island friends that Columbus was a Corsican he had endeavoured to think better than before of the consequences of that adverturer's somewhat rash activities. He could not quite bring himself actually to imitate Columbus, since he felt that there would be a slight taint of trade about any such journey, but he would call after due notice on the American Ambassador to the Court of St. James's, who always took pains to have a personal message from the President in readiness for his distinguished guest. He would, of course, visit Mr. Winston Churchill, but he never demeaned himself so far as to recognize the existence of Socialist ministers.

It was after he had been dining with Mr. Churchill that I had the good fortune to find him at leisure in the ancient club of which he was an honorary member. He honoured me with a glass of his pre-1914 Tokay, which was part of the *spolia opima* of his encounter with the eminent Hungarian general whom he left dead upon the field of honour with a suitable eulogy for his bravery. After due acknowledgment of the great mark of favour which he was bestowing upon me – a notable mark, for after all not even Hungarian generals go into battle with more than a few bottles of Tokay bound to their saddles – I led the conversation gradually towards Corsica.

'I have heard,' I said, 'that that island is not what it was. Education, they tell me, has turned brigands into bank clerks, and stilettos into stylographic pens. No longer, so they tell me, do ancient vendettas keep alive through the generations. I have even heard dreadful tales of intermarriage between families which had had a feud lasting eight hundred years, and yet the marriage was not accompanied by bloodshed. If all this is indeed true, I am forced to weep. I had always hoped, if fortune should favour my industry, to exchange the sanitary villa which I inhabit in Balham for some stormy peak in the home of ancient romance. But if romance even there is dead, what remains to me as a hope for old age? Perhaps you can reassure me; perhaps something yet lingers there. Perhaps amid thunder and lighting the ghost of Farinata degli Uberti is still to be seen looking around with great disdain. I have come to you tonight in the hope that you can give me such reassurance, since without it I shall not know how to support the burden of the humdrum years.'

As I was speaking his eyes gleamed. I saw him clench his fists and close his jaws fiercely. Scarcely could he wait for the end of my periods. And as soon as I was silent he burst forth.

'Young man,' he said, 'were you not a friend of Mrs.

Menhennet I should grudge you that noble nectar which I have allowed your unworthy lips to consume. I am compelled to think that you have been associating with the ignoble. Some few there may be among the riff-raff of the ports, and the ignoble gentry who concern themselves with the base business of bureaucracy – some few there may be, I repeat, of whom the dreadful things at which you have been hinting may be true. But they are not true Corsicans. They are but bastard Frenchmen, or gesticulating Italians, or toad-eating Catalans. The true Corsican breed is what it always was. It lives the free life, and emissaries of governments who seek to interfere die the death. No, my friend, all is yet well in that happy home of heroism.'

I leapt to my feet and took his right hand in both of mine.

'O happy day,' said I, 'when my faith is restored, and my doubts are quenched! Would that I might see with my own eyes the noble breed of men whom you have brought so forcibly before my imagination. Could you permit me to know even one of them I should live a happier life, and the banalities of Balham would become more bearable.'

'My young friend,' said he, 'your generous enthusiasm does you credit. Great though the favour may be, I am willing, in view of your enthusiasm, to grant the boon you ask. You shall know one of these splendid survivors of the golden age of man. I know that one of them, indeed one of my closest friends among them – I speak of the Count of Aspramonte – will be compelled to descend from the hills to pick up in Ajaccio a consignment of new saddles for his stallions. These saddles, you will of course understand, are made specially for him by the man who has charge of the racing stables of the Duke of Ashby-de-la-Zouche. The Duke is an old friend of mine, and as a great favour allows me occasionally to purchase from him a few saddles for the use of such of my friends as I deem worthy of so priceless a gift. If you care to be in Ajaccio next week, I can give you a letter to the Count of Aspramonte, who would be more accessible there than in his mountain fastness.'

With tears in my eyes I thanked him for his great kindness. I bowed low and kissed his hand. As I left his presence, my heart was filled with sorrow at the thought of the nobility that is perishing from our ignoble earth.

IV

Following the advice of General Prz, I flew the following week to Ajaccio, and inquired at the principal hotels for the Count of Aspramonte. At the third place of inquiry I was informed that he was at the moment occupying the imperial suite, but he was a busy man with little time for unauthorized visitors. From the demeanour of the hotel servants I inferred that he had earned their most profound respect. In an interview with the proprietor I handed over the letter of introduction from General Prz with the request that it should be put as soon as possible into the hands of the Count of Aspramonte, who, I learned, was at the moment engaged in business in the town.

The hotel was filled with a chattering throng of tourists of the usual description, all of them, so far as I could observe, trivial and transitory. Coming fresh from the dreams of General Prz I felt the atmosphere a strange one, by no means such as I could have wished. It was not in this setting that I could imagine the realization of the Polish nobleman's dreams. I had, however, no other clue, and was compelled to make the best of it.

After an ample dinner, totally indistinguishable from those provided in the best hotels of London, New York, Calcutta, and Johannesburg, I was sitting somewhat disconsolate in the lounge, when I saw approaching me a brisk gentleman of young middle age whom I took at first to be a successful American executive. He had the square jaw, the firm step, and the measured speech which I have learned to associate with that powerful section of society. But to my surprise, when he addressed me it was in English English with a continental accent. To my greater surprise he mentioned that he was the Count of Aspramonte.

'Come,' he said, 'to the sitting-room of my suite, where we can talk more undisturbed than in this mêlée.'

His suite, when we reached it, turned out to be ornate and

palatial in a somewhat garish style. He gave me a stiff whisky and soda and a large cigar.

'You are, I see,' so he began the conversation, 'a friend of that dear old gentleman, General Prz. I hope you have never been tempted to laugh at him. For us who live in the modern world the temptation undoubtedly exists, but out of respect for his grey hairs I resist it.

'You and I, my dear Sir,' he continued, 'live in the modern world and have no use for memories and hopes that are out of place in an age dominated by dollars. I for my part, although I live in a somewhat out of the way part of the world, and although I might, if I let myself be dominated by tradition, be as lost in misty dreams as the worthy General, have decided to adapt myself to our time. The main purpose of my life is the acquisition of dollars, not only for myself but for my island. "How," you may ask, "does your manner of life conduce to this end?" In view of your friendship with the General I feel that I owe you an answer to this not unnatural query.

'The mountains in which I have my home afford an ideal ground for the breeding and exercising of race-horses. The Arab stallions and mares which my father collected in the course of his wide travels gave rise to a breed of unexampled strength and swiftness. The Duke of Ashby-de-la-Zouche, as you of course are aware, has one great ambition. It is to own three successive Derby winners, and it is through me that he hopes to realize this ambition. His vast wealth is devoted mainly to this end. On the ground that the Derby offers an attraction to American tourists he is allowed to deduct the expenses of his stud from his income in his tax returns. He is thus able to retain that wealth which too many of his peers have lost. The Duke is not alone among my customers. Some of my best horses have gone to Virginia, others to Australia. There is no part of the world in which the royal sport is known where my horses are not famous. It is owing to them that I am able to keep up my palace and to preserve intact the sturdy human stock of our Corsican mountains.

'My life, as you will see, unlike that of General Prz, is lived on the plane of reality. I think more frequently of the dollar exchange than of Ghibelline ancestry, and I pay more attention to horse dealers than to even the most picturesque aristocratic relics. Nevertheless, when I am at home, the need to preserve the respect of the surrounding population compels me to conform to tradition. It is just possible that if you visit me in my castle you will be able to pick up some clue to the enigma which, as I see from the General's letter, is the cause of your visit to me. I shall be returning to my castle on horseback the day after tomorrow. It is a long journey, and an early start will be necessary, but if you care to present yourself at six o'clock in the morning I shall be happy to provide you with a horse on which you can accompany me to my home.'

Having by this time finished the whisky and the cigar, I thanked him somewhat effusively for his courtesy, and accepted his invitation.

V

It was still pitch dark when on the next day but one I presented myself at the door of the Count's hotel. It was a raw and gusty morning and bitterly cold, with a hint of snow in the air. But the Count seemed impervious to meteorological conditions when he appeared upon his magnificent steed. Another, almost equally magnificent, was led to the door by his servant, and I was bidden to mount him. We set off, soon leaving the streets of the town and then, by small roads which only long experience could have enabled a man to find, we wound up and up to ever greater heights, at first through woodlands and then through open country, grass, and rocks.

The Count, it appeared, was incapable of fatigue, or hunger, or thirst. Throughout a long day, with only a few moments' intermission during which we munched dry bread, ate some dates, and drank icy water from a stream, he conversed intelligently and informatively about this and that, showing a wide knowledge of the world of affairs and an acquaintance with innumerable rich men who found leisure for an interest in horses. But not one word did he utter throughout the whole of that long day on the matter which had brought me to Corsica. Gradually, in spite of the beauty of the scenery and the interest of his multi-lingual anecdotes, impatience mastered me.

'My dear Count,' I said, I cannot express to you how grateful I am for this chance to visit your ancestral home. But I must venture to remind you that I have come upon an errand of mercy, to save the life, or at least the reason, of a worthy friend of mine for whom I have the highest regard. You are leaving me in doubt as to whether I am serving this purpose by accompanying you on this long ride.'

'I understand your impatience,' he said, 'but you must realize that, however I adapt myself to the modern world, I cannot in these uplands accelerate the tempo which is immemorially customary. You shall, I promise you, be brought nearer to your goal before the evening ends. More than that I cannot say, for the matter does not rest with me.'

With these enigmatic words I had to be content.

We reached his castle as the sun was setting. It was built upon a steep eminence, and to every lover of architecture it was obvious that every part of it down to the minutest detail, dated from the thirteenth century. Crossing the drawbridge we entered by a Gothic gateway into a large courtyard. Our horses were taken by a groom, and the Count led me into a vast hall, out of which, by a narrow doorway, he conducted me into the chamber that I was to occupy for the night. A huge canopied bed and heavy carved furniture of ancient design filled much of the space. Out of window a vast prospect down innumerable winding valleys enticed the eye to a distant glimpse of sea.

'I hope,' he said, 'that you will succeed in being not too uncomfortable in this somewhat antiquated domicile.'

'I do not think that will be difficult,' said I, glancing at the blazing fire of enormous logs that spread a flickering light from the vast hearth. He informed me that dinner would be ready in an hour, and that after dinner, if all went well, something should be done to further my inquiries.

After a sumptuous dinner, he led me back to my room, and said:

'I will now introduce you to an ancient servant of this

house, who, from the long years of his service here, has become a repository of all its secrets. He, I have no doubt, will be able to help you towards the solution of your problem.'

He rang the bell, and when it was answered, requested the manservant to ask the senechal to join in our conversation. After a short interval the senechal approached. I saw before me an old man, bent double with rheumatism, with white locks, and the grave air of one who has lived through much.

'This man,' said my host, 'will give you as much enlightenment as this place can afford.'

With that he withdrew.

'Old man,' said I, 'I do not know whether at your great age I may hope that your wits are what they were. I am surprised, I must confess, that the Count should refer me to you. I had fondly imagined myself worthy to deal with equals, and not only with serving men in their dotage.'

As I uttered these words a strange transformation occurred. The old man, as I had supposed him to be, suddenly lost his rheumatic appearance, drew himself up to his full height of six-foot three, tore from his head the white wig which concealed his ample coal-black hair, threw off the ancient cloak which he had been wearing, and revealed beneath it the complete costume of a Florentine noble of the period when the castle was built. Laying his hand upon his sword, he turned upon me with flashing eyes, and said:

'Young man, were you not brought here by the Count, in whose sagacity I have much confidence, I should here and now order you to be cast into the dungeons, as an impertinent upstart, unable to perceive noble blood through the disguise of a seedy cloak.'

'Sir,' I said, with all due humility, 'I must humbly beg your pardon for an error which I cannot but think was designed both by you and by the Count. If you will accept my humble excuses, I shall be happy to learn who it is in whose presence I have the honour to be.'

'Sir,' said he, 'I will accept your speech as in some degree making amends for your previous impertinence, and you shall know who I am and what I stand for. I, Sir, am the Duke of Ermocolle. The Count is my right-hand man, and obeys me in all things. But in these sad times there is need of the wisdom of the serpent. You have seem him as a business man, adapting himself to the practices of our age, blaspheming for a purpose against the noble creed by which he and I alike are inspired. I decided to present myself to you in disguise in order to form some estimate of your character and outlook. You passed the test, and I will now tell you the little that I have a right to reveal concerning the trouble which has come into the life of your unworthy professorial friend.''

In reply to these words I spoke long and eloquently about the professor and his labours, about Miss X and her youthful innocence, and about the obligation which I felt that friendship had placed upon my inadequate shoulders. He listened to me in grave silence. At the end he said:

'There is only one thing that I can do for you, and that I will do.'

He thereupon took in his hand an enormous quill pen, and on a large sheet of parchment he wrote these words: 'To Miss X. You are hereby released from a part of the oath you swore. Tell all to the bearer of this note and to Professor N. Then ACT.' To this he appended his signature in full magnificence.

'That, my friend, is all that I can do for you.'

I thanked him and bade him a ceremonial good night.

I slept little. The wind howled, the snow fell, the fire died down. I tossed and turned upon my pillow. When at last a few moments of uneasy slumber came to me, strange dreams wearied me even more than wakefulness. When dawn broke, a leaden oppression weighed me down. I sought the Count and acquainted him with what had passed.

'You will understand,' I said, 'that in view of the message which I bear, it is my duty to return to England with all speed.'

Thanking him once more for his hospitality I mounted the same steed upon which I had come and, accompanied by a groom whom he sent with me to help me in finding the road, I slowly picked my way through snow and sleet and tempest until I reached the shelter of Ajaccio. From there next day I returned to England.

VI

On the morning after my return I presented myself at the house of Professor N. I found him sunk in gloom, decorative art forgotten, and Miss X absent.

'Old friend,' I said, 'it is painful to see you in this sad state. I have been active on your behalf, and returned but last night from Corsica. I was not wholly successful, but I was also not wholly unsuccessful. I bear a message, not to you, but to Miss X. Whether this message will bring relief or the opposite I cannot tell. But it is my plain duty to deliver it into her hands. Can you arrange that I may see her here in your presence, for it is in your presence that the message must be delivered.'

'It shall be done,' said he.

He called to him his aged housekeeper, who with sorrowful countenance approached to know his wishes.

'I wish you,' said he, 'to find Miss X, and request her presence urgently, imperatively, and at no matter what inconvenience.'

The housekeeper departed, and he and I sat in gloomy silence. After an interval of some two hours she returned and replied that Miss X had fallen into a lethargy which had caused her to keep to her bed, but on receipt of Professor N's message some spark of doleful animation had returned to her and she had promised to be with him within a very short time. Scarcely had the housekeeper uttered this message when Miss X herself appeared, pale, distraught, with wild eyes and almost lifeless movements.

'Miss X,' I said, 'it is my duty, whether painful or not I do not yet know, to deliver to you this message from one who I believe is known to you.'

I handed over the piece of parchment. She suddenly came to life, and seized it eagerly. Her eyes ran over its few lines in a moment.

'Alas!' she said. 'This is not the reprieve for which I had hoped. It will not remove the cause of sorrow, but it does enable me to lift the veil of mystery. The story is a long one, and when I have finished it you will wish it had been longer. For when it is ended, it can be succeeded only by horror.'

Then Professor, seeing that she was on the verge of collapse, administered a strong dose of brandy. He then seated us round a table and in a calm voice said:

'Proceed, Miss X.'

VII

'When I went to Corsica,' she began, 'and how long ago that seems, as though it had been in another existence. I was happy and carefree, thinking only of pleasure, of the light enjoyments which are considered suitable to my age, and of the delight of sunshine and new scenes. Corsica from the first moment enchanted me. I acquired the practice of long rambles in the hills, and each day I extended my rambles a little further. In the golden October sunshine, the leaves of the forest shone in their many bright colours. At last I found a path that led me beyond the forest on to the bare hills.

'In all-day rambles I caught a glimpse, to my immense surprise, of a great castle on a hill-top. My curiosity was aroused. Ah! would that it had been otherwise. It was too late that day to approach any nearer to this astonishing edifice. But next day, having supplied myself with some simple sustenance, I set out early in the morning, determined, if it were possible, to discover the secret of this stately pile. Higher and higher I climbed through the sparkling autumn air. I met no human soul, and as I approached the castle it might have belonged to the Sleeping Beauty for all the signs of life that I saw about it.

'Curiosity, that fatal passion which misled our first mother, lured me on. I wandered round the battlements, seeking for a mode of ingress. For a long time my search was vain. Ah! would that it had remained so! But a malign fate willed otherwise. I found at last a little postern gate which yielded to my touch. I entered a dark abandoned out-house. When I had grown accustomed to the gloom, I saw at the far end a door standing ajar. I tip-toed to the door and glanced through. What met my gaze caused me to gasp, and I nearly emitted a cry of amazement.

'I saw before me a vast hall, in the very centre of which, at a long wooden table, were seated a number of grave men, some old, some young, some middle-aged, but all bearing upon their countenances the stamp of resolution, and the look of men born to do great deeds. "Who may these be?" I wondered. You will not be surprised to learn that I could not bring myself to withdraw, and that standing behind that little door I listened to their words. This was my first sin on that day on which I was to sink to unimaginable depths of wickedness.

'At first I could not distinguish their words, though I could see that some portentous matter was being debated. But gradually, as my ears became attuned to their speech, I learned to follow what they were saying, and with every word my amazement grew.

' "Are we all agreed as to the day?" said the President.

' "We are," many voices replied.

' "So be it," said he. "I decree that Thursday, the 15th of November, is to be the day. And are we all agreed as to our respective tasks?" he asked.

' "We are," replied the same voices.

' "Then," he said, "I will repeat the conclusions at which we have arrived, and when I have done so, I will formally put them to the meeting and you will vote. All of us here are agreed that the human race is suffering from an appalling malady, and that the name of this malady is GOVERNMENT. We are agreed that if man is to recover the happiness that he enjoyed in the Homeric Age and which we, in this fortunate island, have in some measure retained, abolition of government is the first necessity. We are agreed also that there is only one way in which government can be abolished, and that is by abolishing governors. Twenty-one of us are here present, and we have agreed that there are twenty-one important states in the world. Each one of us on Thursday, the 15th November, will assassinate the head of one of these twenty-one states. I, as your President, have the privilege of assigning to myself the most difficult and dangerous of these twenty-one enterprises. I allude, of course, to... but it is needless for me to pronounce the name. Our work, however, will not be quite complete when these twenty-one have suffered the fate that they so richly deserve. There is one other person, so ignoble, so sunk in error, so diligent in the propagation of falsehood, that he almost must die. But as he is not of so exalted a status as these other twenty-one victims, I appoint my squire to effect his demise. You will all realize that I speak of Professor N, who has had the temerity to maintain in many learned journals and in a vast work which, as our secret service has informed us, is nearing completion, that it was from Lithuania, and not, as all of us know, from Corsica, that pre-Celtic decorative art spread over Europe. He also shall die.''

'At this point,' Miss X continued, amid sobs, 'I could contain myself no longer. The thought that my benevolent employer was to die so soon afflicted me profoundly, and I gave an involuntary cry. All heads looked towards the door. The henchman to whom the extermination of Professor N had been assigned was ordered to investigate. Before I could escape he seized me and led me before the twenty-one. The President bent stern eyes upon me and frowned heavily.

' ''Who are you,'' said he, ''that has so rashly, so impiously, intruded upon our secret councils? What has led you to eavesdrop upon the most momentous decision that any body of men has ever arrived at? Can you offer any reason whatever why you should not, here and now, die the death which your temerity has so richly merited?'' '

At this point hesitation overcame Miss X, and she was scarcely able to continue her account of the momentous interview in the castle. At length she pulled herself together and resumed the narrative.

'I come now,' she said, 'to the most painful part of my story. It is a merciful dispensation of Providence that the future is concealed from our gaze. Little did my mother think, as she lay exhausted, listening to my first cry, that it was to this that her new-born daughter was destined. Little did I think as I entered the Secretarial College that it was to lead to this. Little did I dream that Pitman's was but the gateway to the gallows. But I must not waste time in vain repining. What is done is done, and it is my duty to relate the plain unvarnished tale without the trimmings of futile remorse.

'As the President spoke to me of swift death, I glimpsed the pleasant sunshine without. I thought of the carefree years of my youth. I thought of the promise of happiness which but that very morning had accompanied me as I climbed the lonely hills. Visions of summer rain and winter firesides, of spring in meadows and autumn in the beech woods haunted my imagination. I thought of the golden years of innocent childhood, fled never to return. And I thought fleetingly and shyly of one in whose eyes I fancied that I had seen the light of love. All this in a moment passed through my mind. "Life," I thought, "is sweet. I am but young, and the best of life is still before me. Am I to be cut off thus, before I have known the joys, and the sorrows too, which make the warp and woof of human life? No," I thought, "this is too much. If there yet remains a means by which I may prolong my life I will seize it, even though it be at the price of dishonour." When Satan had led me to this dreadful resolve I answered with such calmness as I could command: "Oh, reverend Sir, I have been but an unwitting and unintentional offender. No thought of evil was in my mind as I strayed through that fatal door. If you will but spare my life I will do your will, whatever it may be. Have mercy, I pray you. You cannot wish that one so young and fair should perish prematurely. Let me but know your will and I will obey." Although he still looked down upon me with no friendly eye, I fancied I saw some slight sign of relenting. He turned to the other twenty, and said: "What is your will? Shall we execute justice, or shall we submit her to the ordeal? I will put it to the vote." Ten voted for justice, ten for the ordeal.

'Then turning again on me, he continued: "You may live, but on certain terms. What these terms are I will now explain to you. First of all you must swear a great oath – never to reveal by word or deed, by any hint or by any turn of demeanour, what you have learned in this hall. The oath which you must fulfil I will now tell you, and you must repeat the words after me: *I swear by Zoroaster and the beard of the Prophet, by Uriens, Paymon, Egyn, and Amaymon, by Marbuel,*

Aciel, Barbiel, Mephistophiel, and Apadiel, by Dirachiel, Amnodiel, Amudiel, Tagriel, Geliel, and Requiel, and by all the foul spirits of Hell, that I will never reveal or in any manner cause to be known any slightest hint of what I have seen and heard in this hall.'' When I had solemnly repeated this oath, he explained to me that this was but the first part of the ordeal, and that perhaps I might not have grasped its full immensity. Each of the infernal names that I had invoked possessed its own separate power of torture. By the magician's power invested in himself he was able to control the actions of these demons. If I infringed the oath, each separate one would, through all eternity, inflict upon me the separate torture of which he was master. But that, he said, was but the smallest part of my punishment.

' "I come now," said he, "to graver matters."

'Turning to the henchman, he said: "The goblet, please."

'The henchman, who knew the ritual, presented the goblet to the President.

' "This", he said, turning again to me, "is a goblet of bull's blood. You must drink every drop, without taking breath while you drink. If you fail to do so, you will instantly become a cow, and be pursued forever by the ghost of the bull whose blood you will have failed to drink in due manner." I took the goblet from him, drew a long breath, closed my eyes, and swallowed the noxious draught.

' "Two-thirds of the ordeal," he said "are now fulfilled. The last part is slightly more inconvenient. We have decreed, as you are unfortunately aware, that on the 15th prox., twenty-one heads of state shall die. We decided also that the glory of our nation demands the death of Professor N. But we felt that there would be a lack of symmetry if one of us were to undertake this just execution. Before we discovered your presence, we delegated this task to my henchman. But your arrival, while in many ways inopportune, has in one respect provided us with an opportunity for neatness which it would be unwise and inartistic to neglect. You, and not my henchman, shall carry out this execution. And this to do you shall swear by the same oath by which you swore secrecy."

' "Oh Sir!" I said, "do not put upon me this terrible

burden. You know much, But I doubt whether you know that it has been both my duty and my pleasure to assist Professor N in his researches. I have had nothing but kindness from him. It may be that his views on decorative art are not all that you could wish. Can you not permit me to continue serving him as before, and gradually I could wean him from his errors. I am not without influence upon the course of his thoughts. Several years of close association have shown me ways of guiding his inclinations in this direction or that, and I am persuaded that if you will but grant me time I can bring him round to your opinions on the function of Corsica in pre-Celtic decorative art. To slay this good old man, whom I have regarded as a friend and who has hitherto, and not unjustly, regarded me in not unlike manner, would be almost as terrible as the pursuit of the many fiends whom you have caused me to invoke. Indeed, I doubt whether life is worth purchasing at such a price."

' "Nay, my good maiden," said he, "I fear you are still indulging in illusions. The oath you have already taken was a sinful and blasphemous oath, and has put you forever in the power of the fiends, unless I, by my magic art, choose to restrain them. You cannot escape now. You must do my will or suffer." I wept, I implored him, I knelt and clasped his knees. "Have mercy," I said, "have mercy." But he remained unmoved. "I have spoken," he said. "If you do not wish to suffer forever the fifteen separate kinds of torment that will be inflicted by each of the fifteen fiends you have invoked, you must repeat after me, using the same dread names, the oath that on the 15th prox. you will cause the death of Professor N."

'Alas! dear Professor. It is impossible that you should pardon me, but in my weakness I swore this second oath. The 15th, no longer prox. but inst., is rapidly approaching, and I see not how I am to escape, when that day comes, the dread consequences of my frightful oath. As soon as I got away from that dreadful castle, remorse seized me and has gnawed at my vitals ever since. Gladly would I suffer the fifteen diverse torments of the fifteen fiends, could I but persuade myself that in doing so I should be fulfilling the behests of duty. But

I have sworn, and honour demands that I should fulfil my oath. Which is the greater sin, to murder the good man whom I revere, or to be false to the dictates of honour? I know not. But you, dear Professor, you who are so wise, you, I am sure, can resolve my doubts, and show me the clear path of duty.'

VIII

The Professor, as her narrative advanced towards its climax, somewhat surprisingly recovered cheerfulness and calm. With a kindly smile, with folded hands and a completely peaceful demeanour, he replied to her query.

'My dear young lady,' he said, 'nothing, nothing on earth, should be allowed to override the dictates of honour. If it lies in your power you must fulfil your oath. My work is completed, and my remaining years, if any, could have little importance. I should therefore tell you in the most emphatic manner that it is your duty to fulfil your oath if it is in any way possible. I should regret, however, I might even say I should regret deeply, that as a consequence of your sense of honour you should end your life upon the gallows. There is one thing, and one thing only, which can absolve you from your oath, and that is physical impossibility. You cannot kill a dead man.'

'So saying, he put his thumb and forefinger into his waistcoat pocket and with a lightning gesture conveyed them to his mouth. In an instant he was dead.

'Oh, my dear master,' cried Miss X, throwing herself upon his lifeless corpse, 'how can I bear the light of day now that you have sacrificed your life for mine? How can I endure the shame that every hour of sunshine and every moment of seeming happiness will gvenerate in my soul? Nay, not another moment can I endure this agony.'

With these words, she found the same pocket, imitated his gesture, and expired.

'I have not lived in vain,' said I, 'for I have witnessed two noble deaths,' But then I remembered that my task was not done, since the world's unworthy rulers must, I supposed, be saved from extinction. Reluctantly I bent my footsteps towards Scotland Yard.

ISAAC BASHEVIS SINGER

Under the Knife

I

Leib opened his one good eye, but it was dark in the cellar. He couldn't tell whether it was day or still night. He fumbled for the matches and pack of cigarettes he had left on a stool near the iron cot. Every time he waked in the windowless room in which he'd been living lately, the same doubt assailed him: what if his other eye had gone blind too? He struck a match and watched the flame glow. Lighting his cigarette, he inhaled deeply, and with the little blue fire that remained on the match lit a small kerosene lamp which had lost its glass chimney. Its trembling light fell on the peeling walls, on the floor that was completely rotted away. But if you don't have to pay rent, even a living grave is a bargain. Thank God, he still had some vodka left over from yesterday. The bottle stood on an egg crate, stopped up with paper. Thoughtfully, Leib lowered his bare feet, took a few steps towards the crate. Well, I'll just rinse my mouth, he joked to himself.

He put the bottle to his lips, drank it to the bottom, and then threw it aside. He sat for a while feeling the fumes rise from his stomach into his brain. All right, so I'm a fallen man, he muttered. Usually there were mice rustling around the room, but now the cold had driven them away. The place smelled of mould and subterranean odors. The air was damp. A fungus grew on the remains of the woodwork.

Leib leaned back against the wall, surrendering himself to the alcohol. When he drank, he stopped reasoning. His thoughts ran on by themselves, without his head so to speak.

He had lost everything: his left eye, his job, his wife, Rooshke. He, Leib, who at one time had been the second warden in the Society of Loving Friends was now a drunkard, a bum. I'll kill her, I'll kill her, Leib muttered to himself. She's done for. I'll kill her and then take my own life. Every day she survives is a gift to her. In a week she'll be in her grave, that whore, packed up to travel . . . if there is a God, he'll deal with her in the next world . . .

Leib had long since planned everything. He went over it again, only he thought he would postpone the end for a little while. The knife he was going to stick in tough Rooshke's belly was hidden in the straw mattress. He had sharpened it recently until it could cut a hair. He would thrust it in her belly and twist it twice to slash her guts. Then he would stamp his foot on Rooshke's breast and while she was in her death throes shout at her: Well, Rooshke, are you still tough? Eh? And he would spit in her face. After that he would go to the cemetery and, near Chaye's grave, slash his wrists.

Growing tired of sitting up, Leib stretched out on the cot again, covered himself with the black blanket scarred with cigarette burns, and blew out the lamp. The right moment would come. He had been waiting for it for a long time. First he had sold all his possessions; then he had borrowed from his friends. Now it took miracles to survive at all. He ate in soup kitchens. His old friends gave him a few pennies, a worn shirt, shorts, a pair of discarded boots. He was living like an animal, like one of the cats, dogs, rats which swarmed through the neighborhood. In the dark, Leib returned to his cherished vision: Rooshke, deathly pale, lay there, dress up, legs stretched out, the yellow-blonde hair in disorder, the knife in her stomach with only the metal handle sticking out. She began to scream in an agonized voice, pleading, gurgling, opening her blue eyes wide. He, Leib, holding his boot firmly on her chest, asked: Well, are you still tough, eh?

II

Leib awoke. During the last few days he had drowsed like a man in a fever. He no longer knew whether it was night or day, Tuesday or Thursday. It might even be Saturday already. There was no more vodka and he had smoked his last cigarette. He had been having a long dream, all about Rooshke, a strange one for he had been slitting her throat and at the same time making love to her, as if there were two Rooshkes. Remembering the senseless dream for a moment, he tried to interpret it, but soon let it go.Am I sick? he wondered. Perhaps I'll die in this hole and Rooshke will attend my funeral. But even in death I'll come and strangle her . . .

Some time later he shuddered and woke again. He touched his forehead, but it felt cool. His tiredness had evaporated; his strength had returned; he felt a need to dress and go out to the street. Enough of this rotting alive! Leib said to himself. He wanted to light the lamp but he couldn't find any matches. So I'll dress in the dark, he thought. His clothes were damp and stiff. Blindly he pulled on his trousers, put on his padded jacket, boots, his cap with the wide peak. Judging by the cold indoors Leib guessed it must be snowing outside. He went up the flight of stairs to the yard and saw that it was night. It wasn't raining or snowing, but the cobblestones were wet. Some of the windows were lit up so it couldn't be after midnight as he had at first thought. Well, I skipped a few days, Leib said to himself. Walking with shaky steps, as though after an attack of typhus, he went through the gates and outside. The stores were all closed, boarded up with shutters. Above the metal roofs the sky was heavy, reddish with cold, saturated with snow. As Leib stood there hesitating, the janitor closed the gates behind him. I wonder what Rooshke is doing now? Leib asked himself. He knew what she was doing. She would be sitting with Lemkin the barber eating a second supper of fresh rolls that crackled under the teeth, of cold cuts with mustard washed down with tea and preserves. The stove would be lit, the phonograph playing, the telephone ringing. Her friends would be gathering there: Leizer Tsitrin the apothecary, Kalman from the non-kosher butcher shop, Berele Bontz the fisherman, Shmuel Zeinvel the musician from the orchestra in the Vienna Wedding Hall. Rooshke would smile at everyone with her generous mouth, show her dimples, push up her skirt so that they could see her round knees, her red garters, the lace on her panties. She wouldn't give one thought to him, Leib. Such a thief, such a whore . . . one death was not enough for her . . .

Leib felt something in his boot top and reached down. I took the knife with me, he thought, surprised. But to have it with him made him feel more at ease. He had bought a leather sheath for it. The knife was his only friend now; with it he would pay off all his accounts. Leib pushed the knife deeper into his boot top so it would not bump against his ankle. Maybe I ought to pay her that visit now, he told himself. But he was just toying with the idea. He had to find her alone. The best time to go would be in the morning after Lemkin had gone to the barbershop and when the maid Tsipeh had gone out to shop in the market. Rooshke would still be in bed, dozing, or listening to her canaries singing. She loved to sleep in the nude. He would open the apartment door with the passkey he had had duplicated, enter her room quietly, pull the blanket off her and ask: Well, Rooshke, are you still tough? Eh?

Leib stopped, overpowered by the idea of revenge. Enough waiting, his inner voice commanded. This voice usually ordered him about like a superior officer – left, right, attention, forward march! And Leib never did anything until the voice commanded it. Now he knew why he had slept so much the past week. The invisible power directing him had been preparing him for action. While he slept the decision had been hatching inside him like a disease drawing to its crisis. A chill spread over his spine. Yes, he had delayed long enough. The time had come . . . He was not afraid but his ribs felt icy. His mind was amazingly clear, but he realized that he must think everything out to the last detail. He hadn't a penny, no vodka, no cigarettes. All the gates were closed now and there was nowhere he could go. Thinking about Rooshke's second supper had made him hungry. He too would like to swallow a few fresh rolls with salami or hot sausages. He felt a rumbling and gnawing in his intestines. For the first time in years Leib was seized with self-pity. Suddenly he recalled the words to a song he had sung as a child while acting in the Purim play. His friend Berish, wearing a tricornered hat shaped like a Purim cake and the black-mustached mask of the villain, had come at him, wanting to kill him, swinging a cardboard sword covered with silver paper. He, Leib, masquerading as a merchant with a red beard, had sung:

> *Take away my one piece of bread,*
> *But give me an hour before I'm dead;*
> *Take my bit of challah beside,*
> *But give me an hour with my bride.*

Berish was long since dead – he had been kicked by horse. It was he, Leib, who was going to be the murderer, and who hadn't even a piece of bread to redeem one hour from death . . .

Leib walked slowly, taking short steps. He put his trust in the power commanding him. He would have to have help. Without a drink, without cigarettes, without food in his stomach, he could not carry out the murder. With his one eye he stared into the semi-darkness surrounding him. Several people walked by but he did not really see them. Everything in him was listening; everything hung in the balance; something would happen. If nothing happens, thought Leib, I'll go home – deciding this, he felt as if he were flinging a challenge to the power that had ruled him for so many years and was about to lead him to the final step. He screwed up his eyes. Fiery straws seemed to radiate from the dim gaslights. A few raindrops hit his head. He felt drowsy. Simultaneously he felt that he had lived through this same experience before. At that moment Leib heard a voice which startled him even though he had expected it.

'Are you cold, Leibele? Come in and warm up . . .'

Leib looked around. A whore was standing near the gate of Number 6. Leib did not know her, but apparently she knew him. Under the light of the gas lamp, he saw that she was small, thin, had sunken cheeks smeared with rouge, eyes smudged with mascara. Her red hair was half-covered by a shawl and she was wearing a red dress and red boots that were wet and caked with mud. Leib stopped.

'You know me?'

'Yes I know you.'

'Can I really warm up with you? You're an old hag already,' Leib said, knowing it wasn't so.

'My enemies should die so young . . .'

'Maybe I can spend the night in your place?'

'For money you can do anything.'

Leib was silent for a moment.

'I don't have any money.'

'The only thing you get for nothing is death,' the woman answered.

Leib thought it over.

'Maybe you'll take something on account?'

'What on account? A gold watch?'

Leib knew it was foolish, but he put his hand into his boot top and took out the knife in its leather sheath.

'What's that – a knife?'

'Yes, a knife.'

'Why should I need a knife? I don't want to stab anyone.'

'It's worth three rubles. Take a look at the handle . . .'

Leib stepped under the gaslight and pulled the blade from the sheath. It shone like a flame and the girl moved back a step.

'With the sheath it's worth four rubles.'

'I don't need it.'

'Well then . . . forget it.'

But Leib did not move. He waited as if he expected the girl to change her mind. She wrapped herself deeper in her shawl.

'Why do you carry a knife with you? Do you want to kill someone?'

'Maybe.'

'Who? Tough Rooshke?'

Leib froze.

'What makes you say that?'

'People talk. They know all about you.'

'What do they say?'

'That Rooshke jilted you, that because of her you became a drunkard.'

Something tugged at Leib's heart. People knew about him, talked about him. And he thought the street had forgotten him as though he were dead. His eyes filled with tears.

'Let me come with you. I'll pay you tomorrow.'

The girl lifted her head. She looked at him searchingly, with a reserved smile as though all this talk were just a game and a test. She seemed to belong to his life as if she were a relative of his who waited for him, ready to help him in his need.

'You're lucky the madame isn't here. If she finds out, she'll eat me alive . . .'

III

Her room was in the basement. The passageway to it was so narrow that only one person could pass at a time. The girl walked ahead and Leib followed. On both sides brick walls hemmed them in; the ground was uneven; and Leib had to bend down in order not to hit his head. He felt as if he were already dead, wandering somewhere in subterranean caves amid devils from the nether world. A lamp glimmered in her room and the walls were painted pink. In the stove the coals glowed; on top a teakettle bubbled. A cat sat on a footstool squinting its green eyes. The bed had only a straw mattress with a dirty sheet, no other bedding. But that was for the guests. A pillow and a blanket were set on a chair in the corner. On the table lay half a loaf of bread. Leib saw himself reflected in the mirror: a large man with a pockmarked face, a long nose, a sunken mouth, a hole and a slit in place of a left eye. In the greenish glass, cracked, covered with dust, his image was refracted as if the glass were a murky pool. He hadn't shaved in over a week and a straw-colored beard covered his chin. The girl took off her shawl and for the first time Leib could really see her. She was small, flat-chested, with scrawny arms and bony shoulders. Her neck, too long, had a white spot on it. She had yellow eyebrows, yellow eyes, a crooked nose, a pointed chin. Her face was still youthful, but around her mouth there were two deep wrinkles, as though the mouth had aged all by itself. From her accent, she camc from the country. Leib stared, vaguely recognizing her.

'Are you the only one here?' he asked.

'The other one is in the hospital.'

'Where's the madame?'

'Her brother died. She's sitting *shiva.*'

'You could steal everything.'

'There's nothing to steal.'

Leib sat down on the edge of the bed. He no longer looked at the girl, but at the bread. Though he was not hungry, he could not take his eyes off the loaf. The girl took off her boots but left on her red stockings.

'I wouldn't let a dog stay out in such weather,' she said.

'Are you going back out in front of the gate tonight?' Leib asked.

'No, I'll stay here.'

'Then we can talk.'

'What is there to talk about with me? I've ruined my life. My father was an honorable man. Do you really want to stab Rooshke?'

'She doesn't deserve anything better.'

'If I wanted to stab everyone who'd hurt me, I'd have to go around with six knives in each hand.'

'Women are different.'

'Yes? One should wait and let God judge. Half of my enemies are already rotting in their graves and the other half will end badly too. Why spill blood? God waits a long time but he punishes well.'

'He doesn't punish Rooshke.'

'Just wait. Nothing lasts forever. She'll get hers sooner than you think.'

'Sooner than *you* think,' he answered with a laugh like a bark. Then he said: 'As long as I'm here, give me something to chew on.'

The girl blinked.

'Here. Have some bread. Pull up a chair to the table.'

Leib sat down. She brought him a glass of watery tea and with her bony fingers dug out two cubes of sugar from a tin box. She busied herself about him like a wife. Leib took the knife from his boot top and cut off a piece of bread. The girl, watching him, laughed, showing her sparse teeth that were rusty and crooked. In her yellow eyes shone something sisterly and cunning as if she were an accomplice of his.

'The knife is not for bread,' she observed.

'What is it for then, eh? Flesh?

She brought him a piece of salami from a cupboard and he sliced it in half with his knife. The cat jumped off her footstool and began to rub against his leg, meowing.

'Don't give her any. Let her eat the mice.'

'Are there enough mice?'

'Enough for ten cats.'

Leib cut his piece of salami in two and threw a slice to the cat. The girl looked at him crookedly, half-curiously, half-mockingly as though his whole visit were nothing but a joke. For a long while both of them were silent. Then Leib opened his mouth and asked without thinking:

'Would you like to get married?'

The girl laughed.

'I'll marry the Angel of Death.'

'I'm not joking.'

'As long as a woman breathes she wants to get married.'

'Would you marry me?'

'Even you – '

'Well then, let's get married.'

The girl was pouring water into the teakettle.

'Do you mean in bed or at the rabbi's?'

'First in bed, then at the rabbi's.'

'Whatever you want. I don't believe anybody any more, but what do I care if they pull my leg? If you say so, it's so. If you back out, nothing is lost. What's a word? Every third guest wants to marry me. Afterwards. they don't even want to pay the twenty kopecks.'

'I'll marry you. I've got nothing left to lose.'

'And what have I got to lose? Only my life.'

'Don't you have any money?'

The girl smiled familiarly, grimacing slightly as though she had expected Leib to ask this. Her whole face became aged, knowing, good-naturedly wrinkled like that of an old crone. She hesitated, glanced about, looked up at the small window covered with a black curtain. Her face seemed to laugh and at the same time to ponder something sorrowful and ancient. Then she nodded.

'My whole fortune is here in my stocking.'

She pointed with her finger to her knee.

IV

Next morning Leib waited until the janitor opened the gates. Then he walked outside. Everything had gone smoothly. It was still dark but on this side of the Vistula, in the east a piece of sky showed pale blue with red spots. Smoke was rising from chimneys. Peasant carts with meat, fruit, vegetables came by, the horses plodding along still half asleep. Leib breathed deeply. His throat felt dry. His guts were knotted up. Where could be get food and drink at this hour? He remembered Chaim Smetene's restaurant, which opened up when God was still asleep. Leib, shaking his head like a horse, set off in that direction. Well, it's all destined: I'm fulfilling my fate, he thought. Chaime Smetene's restaurant, smelling of tripe, beer, and goose gravy, was already open, its gaslights lit. Men who had been awake all night were sitting there eating but whether a meat breakfast or the remains of last night's supper was hard to know. Leib sat down at an empty table and ordered a bottle of vodka, onions with chicken fat, and an omelette. He drank three shots straight off on his empty stomach. Well, it's my last meal, he muttered to himself. Tomorrow by this time I'll be a martyr . . . ! The waiters were suspicious of him, thought maybe he was trying to get a free meal. The owner Chaim Smetene himself came over and asked:

'Leib, have you any money?'

Leib wanted to swing the bottle and hit him in his fat stomach which was draped with a chain of silver rubles.

'I'm no beggar.'

And Leib took a packet of banknotes tied with a red string from his pocket.

'Well, don't get mad.'

'Drop dead!'

'Leib wanted to forget the insult. He tossed off one shot after another, became so engrossed in his drinking that he even forgot about the omelette. He took out a paper bill, gave it to the waiter for a tip, and ordered another bottle of vodka, not forty or sixty proof this time but ninety proof. The place was filling up with customers, growing thick with haze, noisy with voices. Someone threw sawdust over the stone floor. Near Lieb men were talking, but though he heard the separate words, he could not grasp the connections between them. His ears felt as if filled with water. He leaned his head on the chair, snored, but at the same time kept his hand on the bottle to make sure it was not taken away. He was not asleep, but neither was he awake. He dreamed but the dream itself seemed far away. Someone was making a long speech to him, without interruption, like a preacher's sermon, but who was speaking and what he was saying, Leib could not understand. He opened his one eye, then closed it again.

After a while he sat up. It was bright day and the gaslights were out. The clock on the wall showed a quarter to nine. The room was full of people, but although he knew everyone on the street, he didn't recognize anyone. There was still some vodka in the bottle and he drank it. He tasted the cold omelette, grimaced, and began to bang his spoon on the plate for the waiter. Finally he left, walking out with unsteady legs. In front of his one eye hung a fog with something in the middle of it tossing about like jelly. I'm going completely blind, Leib said to himself. He went into Yanosh's bazaar, looking for Tsipeh, Rooshke's maid, who he knew came there every morning to shop. The bazaar was already packed with customers. Market women shouted their wares; fishmongers bent over tubs filled with fish; three slaughterers were killing fowl over a marble sink that glowed from the light of a kerosene lamp, handing them to pluckers who plucked and packed them, still alive, into baskets. Whoever has a knife uses it, Leib thought. God doesn't mind. Going towards the exit he spotted Tsipeh. She had just arrived with an empty basket. Well, now's the time!

He walked out of the bazaar and turned towards Rooshke's

yard. He was not afraid of being seen. He entered the gate, climbed up the stairs to the second floor where an engraved plaque said, 'Lemkin – Master Barber.' What will I do if the key doesn't fit? Leib asked himself. I'll break down the door, he answered. He could feel his strength; he was like Samson now. Taking the key from his breast pocket as if he were the owner of the flat, he put it into the keyhole and opened the door. The first thing he saw was a gas meter. A top hat was hanging on a hat-rack and he tapped it playfully. Through the half-open kitchen door he saw a coffee grinder, a brass mortar and pestle. Smells of coffee grounds and fried onions came from there. Well, Rooshke, your time is up! He stepped quietly along the carpet in the corridor, moving, head forward, as adroitly and carefully as a dogcatcher trying to catch a dog. Something like laughter seized him as he drew out the knife leaving the sheath in his boot top. Leib threw open the bedroom door. There was Rooshke, asleep under a red blanket, her bleached blonde hair spread out on a white pillow, her face yellowish, flabby, smeared with cream. Eyeballs protruded against her closed lids and a double chin covered her wrinkled throat. Leib stood gaping. He almost didn't recognize her. In the few months since he had last seen her, she had grown fat and bloated, had lost her girlish looks, become a matron. Grey hair was visible near the scalp. On a night table a set of false teeth stood in a glass of water. So that's it, Leib muttered. She was right. She really has become an old hag. He recalled her words before they parted: 'I've been used enough. I'm not getting any younger, only older . . .'

He couldn't go on standing there. Any minute someone would knock at the door. But neither could he leave. What must be must be, Leib said to himself. Approaching the bed, he pulled off the blanket. Rooshke was not sleeping naked, but in an unbuttoned nightgown which exposed a pair of flabby breasts like pieces of dough, a protruding stomach, thick, unusually wide hips. Leib would never have imagined Rooshke could have such a fat belly, that her skin could have become so yellowish, withered, and scarred. Leib expected her to scream, but she opened her eyes slowly as if, until now, she had been only pretending she was asleep. Her eyes stared at him seriously, sadly, as if she were saying: Woe unto you, what has become of you? Leib trembled. He wanted to say the words he had rehearsed so often, but he had forgotten them. They hung on the tip of his tongue. Rooshke herself had apparently lost her voice. She examined him with a strange calmness.

Suddenly she let out a scream. Leib raised the knife.

V

Well, it's really very easy, Leib muttered to himself. He closed the door and walked down the stairs slowly, banging his heels, as if he were looking for a witness, but he met no one either on the stairs or in the yard. Leaving, he stood for a while at the gates. The sky, which at sunrise had started out so blue, had turned dark and rainy. A porter passed by carrying a sack full of coal on his back. A hunchback shouted out, peddling pickled herring. At the dairy they were unloading milk cans. At the grocery a delivery man was piling loaves on his arm. The two horses in harness had put their heads together as if sharing a secret. Yes, it's the same street, nothing has changed, Leib thought. He yawned, shook himself. Then he remembered the words he had forgotten: Well, Rooshke, are you still tough eh? He felt no fear, only an emptiness. It is morning but it looks like dusk, he mused. He felt in his pocket for cigarettes but had lost them somewhere. He passed the stationery shop. At the butcher's he looked in. Standing at his block, Leizer the butcher was cutting a side of beef with a wide cleaver. A throng of pushing, shoving women were bargaining and stretching out their hands for marrowbones. He'll cut off some woman's finger yet, Leib muttered. Suddenly he found himself in front of Lemkin's barber shop and he looked in through the glass door. The assistant hadn't arrived yet.

Lemkin was alone, a small man, fat and pink, with a naked skull, short legs, and a pointed stomach. He was wearing striped pants, shoes with spats, a collar and bowtie, but no jacket, and his suspenders were short like those of a child.

Standing there, he was thumbing through a Polish newspaper. He doesn't even know yet that he is a widower, Leib said to himself. He watched him, baffled. It was hard to believe that he, Leib, had brooded about this swinish little man for so long and had hated him so terribly. Leib pushed open the door and Lemkin looked at him sideways, startled, even frightened. I'll fix him too, Leib decided. He bent down to draw the knife from his boot top, but some force held him back. An invisible power seemed to have grabbed his wrist. Well he's destined to live, Leib decided. He spoke:

'Give me a shave.'

'What? Sure, sure . . . sit down.'

Cheerfully, Lemkin put on his smock which lay ready on a chair, wrapped Leib in a fresh sheet, and poured warm water into a bowl. Soaping Leib, he half patted, half tickled his throat. Leib leaned his head back, closed the lid on his one eye, relaxed in the darkness. I think I'll take a nap, he decided. I'll tell him to cut my hair too. Leib felt a little dizzy and belched. A chill breeze ran through the barber shop and he sneezed. Lemkin wished him *Geshundheit.* The chair was too high and Lemkin lowered it. Taking a razor from its sheath, he stropped it on a leather strap and then began to scrape. Tenderly, as if they were relatives, he pinched Leib's cheek between his thick fingertips. Leib could feel the barber's breath as Lemkin said confidentially:

'You're a friend of Rooshke's . . . I know, I know . . . she told me everything.'

Lemkin waited for a reply from Leib. He even stopped scraping with his razor. After a while he began again.

'Poor Rooshke is sick.'

Leib was silent for a time.

'What's wrong with her?'

'Gallstones. The doctors say she should have an operation. She's been in the hospital two weeks now. But you don't go under the knife so easily.

Leib lifted his head.

'In the hospital? Where?'

'In Chista. I go there every day. '

'Who's at home then?'

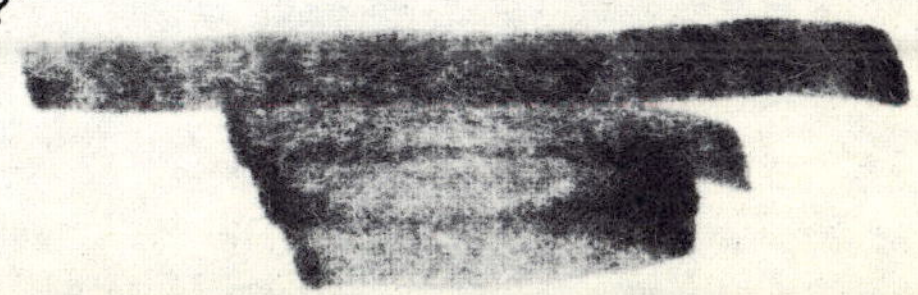

'A sister from Praga.An older one, eh?'

'A grandmother already.'

Leib lowered his head. Lemkin lifted it up again.

'Believe me, Rooshke's not your enemy,' he whispered in Leib's ear. 'She talks about you all the time. After all, what happened happened. We would like to do something for you, but you keep yourself a stranger . . . .'

Lemkin was bending so near Leib as almost to touch him with his forehead. He smelled of mouth rinse and a brotherly warmth. Leib wanted to say something, but outside there was a scream and people began to run.

Lemkin straightened up.

'I'll see what all the excitement's about.'

He walked outside, still in his smock, with the razor in his right hand and the left smeared with soap and beard. He lingered a minute or two, questioning someone. He came back in cheerfully.

'A whore's dead. Ripped open with a knife. The little redhead at Number 6.'

JOHN STEINBECK

The Murder

This happened a number of years ago in Monterey County, in central California. The Cañon del Castillo is one of those valleys in the Santa Lucia range which lie between its many spurs and ridges. From the main Cânon del Castillo a number of little arroyos cut back into the mountains, oak-wooded canyons, heavily brushed with poison oak and sage. At the head of the canyon there stands a tremendous stone castle, buttressed and towered like those strongholds the Crusaders put up in the path of their conquests. Only a close visit to the castle shows it to be a strange accident of time and water and erosion working on soft, stratified sandstone. In the distance the ruined battlements, the gates, the towers, even the arrow slits require little imagination to make out.

Below the castle, on the nearly level floor of the canyon, stand an old ranch house, a weathered and mossy barn and a warped feeding shed for cattle. The house is empty and deserted; the doors, swinging on rusted hinges, squeal and bang on nights when the wind courses down from the castle. Not many people visit the house. Sometimes a crowd of boys tramp through the rooms, peering into empty closets and loudly defying the ghosts they deny.

Jim Moore, who owns the land, does not like to have people about the house. He rides up from his new house, farther down the valley and chases the boys away. He has put 'No Trespassing' signs on his fences to keep curious and morbid people out. Sometimes he thinks of burning the old house down, but then a strange and powerful relation with the swinging doors, the blind and desolate windows forbids the destruction. If he should burn the house he would destroy a great and important piece of his life. He knows that when he goes to town with his plump and still pretty wife, people turn and look at his retreating back with awe and some admiration.

Jim Moore was born in the old house and grew up in it. He knew every grained and weathered board of the barn, every smooth, worn manger rack. His mother and father were both dead when he was thirty. He celebrated his majority by raising a beard. He sold the pigs and decided never to have any more. At last be bought a fine Guernsey bull to improve his stock, and he began to go to Monterey on Saturday nights, to get drunk and to talk with the noisy girls of the Three Star.

Within a year Jim Moore married Jelka Sepić, a Jugoslav girl, daughter of a heavy and patient farmer of Pine Canyon. Jim was not proud of her foreign family, of her many brothers and sisters and cousins, but he delighted in her beauty. Jelka had eyes as large and questioning as a doe's eyes. Her nose was thin and sharply faceted, and her lips were deep and soft. Jelka's skin always startled Jim, for between night and night he forgot how beautiful it was. She was so smooth and quiet and gentle, such a good housekeeper, that Jim often thought with disgust of her father's advice on the wedding day. The old man bleary and bloated with festival beer, elbowed Jim in the ribs and grinned suggestively, so that his little dark eyes almost disappeared behind puffed and wrinkled lids.

'Don't be big fool now,' he said. 'Jelka is Slav girl. He's not like American girl. If he is bad, beat him. If he's good too long, beat him too. I beat his mama. Papa beat my mama. Slave girl! He's not like a man that don't beat hell out of him.'

'I wouldn't beat Jelka,' Jim said.

The father giggled and nudged him again with his elbow. 'Don't be big fool,' he warned. 'Sometime you see.' He rolled back to the beer barrel.

Jim found soon enough that Jelka was not like American girls. She was very quiet. She never spoke first, but only answered his questions, and then with soft short replies. She learned her husband as she learned passages of Scripture. After they had been married a while, Jim never wanted for any habitual thing in the house but Jelka had it ready for him before he could ask. She was a fine wife, but there was no companionship in her. She never talked. Her great eyes followed him, and when he smiled, sometimes she smiled too, a distant and covered smile. Her knitting and mending and sewing were interminable. There she sat, watching her wise hands, and she seemed to regard with wonder and pride the little white hands that could do such nice and useful things. She was so much like an animal that sometimes Jim patted her head and neck under the same impulse that made him stroke a horse.

In the house Jelka was remarkable. No matter what time Jim came in from the hot dry range or from the bottom farm land, his dinner was exactly, steamingly ready for him. She watched while he ate, and pushed the dishes close when he needed them, and filled his cup when it was empty.

Early in the marriage he told her things that happened on the farm, but she smiled at him as a foreigner does who wishes to be agreeable even though he doesn't understand.

'The stallion cut himself on the barbed wire.' he said.

And she replied, 'Yes', with a downward inflection that held neither question nor interest.

He realized before long that he could not get in touch with her in any way. If she had a life apart, it was so remote as to be beyond his reach. The barrier in her eyes was not one that could be removed, for it was neither hostile nor intentional.

At night he stroked her straight black hair and her unbelievably smooth golden shoulders, and she whimpered a little with pleasure. Only in the climax of his embrace did she seem to have a life apart and fierce and passionate. And then immediately she lapsed into the alert and painfully dutiful wife.

'Why don't you ever talk to me?' he demanded. 'Don't you want to talk to me?'

'Yes,' she said. 'What do you want me to say?' She spoke the language of his race out of a mind that was foreign to his race.

When a year had passed, Jim began to crave the company of women, the chattery exchange of small talk, the shrill pleasant insults, the shame-sharpened vulgarity. He began to go again to town, to drink and to play with the noisy girls of the Three Star. They liked him there for his firm, controlled face and for his readiness to laugh.

'Where's your wife?' they demanded.

'Home in the barn,' he responded. It was a never failing joke.

Saturday afternoons he saddled a horse and put a rifle in the scabbard in case he should see a deer. Always he asked, 'You don't mind staying alone?'

'No. I don't mind.'

And once he asked, 'Suppose someone should come!'

Her eyes sharpened for a moment, and then she smiled. 'I would send them away,' she said.

'I'll be back about noon tomorrow. It's too far to ride in the night.' He felt that she knew where he was going, but she never protested nor gave any sign of disapproval. 'You should have a baby,' he said.

Her face lighted up. 'Sometime God will be good,' she said eagerly.

He was sorry for her loneliness. If only she visited with the other women of the canyon she would be less lonely, but she had no gift for visiting. Once every month or so she put horses to the buckboard and went to spend an afternoon with her mother, and with the brood of brothers and sisters and cousins who lived in her father's house.

'A fine time you'll have,' Jim said to her. 'You'll gabble your crazy language like ducks for a whole afternoon. You'll giggle with that big grown cousin of yours with the embarrassed face. If I could find any fault with you, I'd call you a damn foreigner.' He remembered how she blessed the bread with the sign of the cross before she put it in the oven, How she knelt at the bedside every night, how she had a holy picture tacked to the wall in the closet.

On Saturday of a hot dusty June, Jim mowed the farm flat. The day was long. It was after six o'clock when the mower tumbled the last band of oats. He drove the clanking machine up into the barnyard and backed it into the implement shed, and there he unhitched the horses and turned them out to graze on the hills over Sunday. When he entered the kitchen Jelka was just putting his dinner on the table. He washed his hands and face, and sat down to eat.

'I'm tired,' he said, 'but I think I'll go to Monterey anyway. There'll be a full moon.'

Her soft eyes smiled.

'I'll tell you what I'll do,' he said. 'If you would like to go, I'll hitch up a rig and take you with me.'

She smiled again and shook her head. 'No, the stores would be closed. I would rather stay here.'

'Well all right, I'll saddle a horse then. I didn't think I was going. The stock's all turned out. Maybe I can catch a horse easy. Sure you don't want to go?'

'If it was early, and I could go to the stores – but it will be ten o'clock when you get there.'

'Oh, no – well, anyway, on horseback I'll make it a little after nine.'

Her mouth smiled to itself, but her eyes watched him for the development of a wish. Perhaps because he was tired from the long day's work, he demanded, 'What are you thinking about?'

'Thinking about? I remember, you used to ask that nearly every day when we were first married.'

'But what are you?' he insisted irritably.

'Oh – I'm thinking about the eggs under the black hen.' She got up and went to the big calendar on the wall. 'They will hatch tomorrow or maybe Monday.'

It was almost dusk when he had finished shaving and putting on his blue serge suit and his new boots. Jelka had the dishes washed and put away. As Jim went through the kitchen he saw that she had taken the lamp to the table near the window, and that she sat beside it knitting a brown wool sock.

'Why do you sit there tonight?' he asked. 'You always sit over here. You do funny things sometimes.'

Her eyes arose slowly from her flying hands. 'The moon,'

she said quietly. 'You said it would be full tonight. I want to see the moon rise.'

'But you're silly. You can't see it from that window. I thought you knew direction better than that.'

She smiled remotely. 'I will look out of the bedroom window then.'

Jim put on his black hat and went out. Walking through the dark empty barn, he took a halter from the rack. On the grassy sidehill he whistled high and shrill. The horses stopped feeding and moved slowly in towards him, and stopped twenty feet away. Carefully he approached his bay gelding and moved his hand from its rump along its side and up and over its neck. The halterstrap clicked in its buckle. Jim turned and led the horse back to the barn. He threw his saddle on and cinched it tight, put his silver-bound bridle over the stiff ears, buckled the throat latch, knotted the tie-rope about the gelding's neck and fastened the neat coil-end to the saddle string. Then he slipped the halter and led the horse to the house. A radiant crown of soft red light lay over the eastern hills. The full moon would rise before the valley had completely lost the daylight.

In the kitchen Jelka still knitted by the window. Jim strode to the corner of the room and took up his 30-30 carbine. As he rammed shells into the magazine, he said, 'The moon glow is on the hills. If you are going to see it rise, you better go outside now. It's going to be a good red one at rising.'

'In a moment,' she replied, 'when I come to the end here.' He went to her and patted her sleek head.

'Good night. I'll probably be back by noon tomorrow.' Her dusty black eyes followed him out of the door.

Jim thrust the rifle into his saddle-scabbard, and mounted and swung his horse down the canyon. On his right, from behind the blackening hills, the great red moon slid rapidly up. The double light of the day's last afterglow and the rising moon thickened the outlines of the trees and gave a mysterious new perspective to the hills. The dusty oaks shimmered and glowed, and the shade under them was black as velvet. A huge, long-legged shadow of a horse and half a man rode to the left and slightly ahead of Jim. From the ranches near and distant came the sound of dogs tuning up for a night of song. And the roosters crowed, thinking a new dawn had come too quickly. Jim lifted the gelding to a trot. The spattering hoofsteps echoed back from the castle behind him. He thought of blonde May at the Three Star in Monterey. 'I'll be late. Maybe some one else'll have her,' he thought. The moon was clear of the hills now.

Jim had gone a mile when he heard the hoofbeats of a horse coming toward him. A horseman cantered up and pulled to a stop. 'That you, Jim?'

'Yes. Oh, hello George.'

'I was just riding up to your place. I want to tell you – you know the springhead at the upper end of my land?'

'Yes. I know.'

'Well, I was up there this afternoon. I found a dead camp fire and a calf's head and feet. The skin was in the fire, half burned, but I pulled it out and it had your brand.'

'The hell,' said Jim. 'How old was the fire?'

'The ground was still warm in the ashes. Last night, I guess. Look, Jim, I can't go up with you. I've got to go to town, but I thought I'd tell you, so you could take a look around.'

Jim asked quietly, 'Any idea how many men?'

'No. I didn't look close.'

'Well, I guess I better go up and look. I was going to town too. But if there are thieves working, I don't want to lose any more stock. I'll cut up through your land if you don't mind George.'

'I'd go with you, but I've got to go to town. You got a gun with you?'

'Oh yes, sure. Here under my leg. Thanks for telling me.'

'That's all right. Cut through any place you want. Good night.' The neighbour turned his horse and cantered back in the direction from which he had come.

For a few moments Jim sat in the moonlight, looking down at his stilted shadow. He pulled his rifle from its scabbard, levered a shell into the chamber, and held the gun across the pommel of his saddle. He turned left from the road, went up the little ridge, through the oak grove, over the grassy hog-back and down the other side into the next canyon.

In half an hour he had found the deserted camp. He turned over the heavy, leathery calf's head and felt its dusty tongue to judge by the dryness how long it had been dead. He lighted a match and looked at his brand on the half-burned hide. At last he mounted his horse again, rode over the bald grassy hills and crossed into his own land.

A warm summer wind was blowing on the hilltops. The moon, as it quartered up the sky, lost its redness and turned the colour of strong tea. Among the hills the coyotes were singing, and the dogs at the ranch houses below joined them with broken-hearted howling. The dark green oaks below and the yellow summer grass showed their colours in the moonlight.

Jim followed the sound of the cowbells to his herd, and found them eating quietly, and a few deer feeding with them. He listened long for the sound of hoofbeats or the voices of men on the wind.

It was after eleven when he turned his horse towards home. He rounded the west tower of the sandstone castle, rode through the shadow and out into the moonlight again. Below, the roofs of his barn and house shone dully. The bedroom window cast back a streak of reflection.

The feeding horses lifted their heads as Jim came down through the pasture. Their eyes glinted redly when they turned their heads. Jim had almost reached the corral fence – he heard a horse stamping in the barn. His hand jerked the gelding down. He listened. It came again, the stamping from the barn. Jim lifted his rifle and dismounted silently. He turned his horse loose and crept towards the barn.

In the blackness he could hear the grinding of the horse's teeth as it chewed hay. He moved along the barn until he came to the occupied stall. After a moment of listening he scratched a match on the butt of his rifle. A saddled and bridled horse was tied in the stall. The bit was slipped under the chin and the cinch loosened. The horse stopped eating and turned its head towards the light.

Jim blew out the match and walked quickly out of the barn. He sat on the edge of the horse trough and looked into the water. His thoughts came so slowly that he put them into words and said them under his breath.

'Shall I look through the window? No. My head would throw a shadow in the room.'

He regarded the rifle in his hand. Where it had been rubbed and handled, the black gun-finish had worn off, leaving the metal silvery.

At last he stood up with decision and moved towards the house. At the steps, an extended foot tried each board tenderly before he put his weight on it. The three ranch dogs came out from under the house and shook themselves, stretched and sniffed, wagged their tails and went back to bed.

The kithen was dark, but Jim knew where every piece of furniture was. He put out his hand and touched the corner of the table, a chair-back, the towel hanger, as he went along. He crossed the room so silently that even he could hear only his breath and the whisper of his trousers legs together, and the beating of his watch in his pocket. The bedroom door stood open and spilled a patch of moonlight on the kitchen floor. Jim reached the door at last and peered through.

The moonlight lay on the white bed. Jim saw Jelka lying on her back, one soft bare arm flung across her forehead and eyes. He could not see who the man was, for his head was turned away. Jim watched, holding his breath. Then Jelka twitched in her sleep and the man rolled his head and sighed – Jelka's cousin, her grown, embarassed cousin.

Jim turned and quickly stole back across the kitchen and down the back steps. He walked up the yard to the water trough again, and sat down on the edge of it. The moon was white as chalk, and it swam in the water, and lighted the straws and barley dropped by the horses' mouths. Jim could see the mosquito wigglers, tumbling up and down, end over end, in the water, and he could see a newt lying in the sun moss in the bottom of the trough.

He cried a few, dry, hard, smothered sobs, and wondered why, for his thought was of the grassed hilltops and of the lonely summer wind whisking along.

His thought turned to the way his mother used to hold a bucket to catch the throat blood when his father killed a pig.

She stood as far away as possible and held the bucket at arm's length to keep her clothes from getting spattered.

Jim dipped his hand into the trough and stirred the moon to broken, swirling streams of light. He wetted his forehead with his damp hands and stood up. This time he did not move so quietly, but he crossed the kitchen on tiptoe and stood in the bedroom door. Jelka moved her arm and opened her eyes a little. Then the eyes sprang wide, then they glistened with moisture. Jim looked into her eyes; his face was blank of expression. A little drop ran out of Jelka's nose and lodged in the hollow of her upper lip. She stared back at him.

Jim cocked the rifle. The steel click sounded through the house. The man on the bed stirred uneasily in his sleep. Jim's hands were quivering. He raised the gun to his shoulder and held it tightly to keep from shaking. Over the sights he saw the little white square between the man's brows and hair. The front sight wavered a moment and them came to rest.

The gun crash tore the air. Jim, still looking down the barrel, saw the whole bed jolt under the blow. A small, black, bloodless hole was in the man's forehead. But behind, the hollow-point bullet took brain and bone and splashed them on the pillow.

Jelka's cousin gurgled in his throat. His hands came crawling out from under the covers like big white spiders, and they walked for a moment, then shuddered and fell quiet.

Jim looked slowly back at Jelka. Her nose was running. Her eyes had moved from him to the end of the rifle. She whined softly, like a cold puppy.

Jim turned in panic. His boot-heels beat on the kitchen floor, but outside he moved slowly towards the watering trough again. There was a taste of salt in his throat, and his heart heaved painfully. He pulled his hat off and dipped his head into the water, then he leaned over and vomited on the ground. In the house he could hear Jelka moving about. She whimpered like a puppy. Jim straightened up, weak and dizzy.

He walked tiredly through the corral and into the pasture. His saddled horse came at his whistle. Automatically he tightened the cinch, mounted and rode away, down the road to the valley. The squat black shadow travelled under him. The moon sailed high and white. The uneasy dogs barked monotonously.

At daybreak a buckboard and pair trotted up to the ranch yard, scattering the chickens. A deputy sheriff and a coroner sat in the seat. Jim Moore half reclined against his saddle in the wagon-box. His tired gelding followed behind. The deputy sheriff set the brake and wrapped the lines around it. The men dismounted.

Jim asked, 'Do I have to go in? I'm too tired and wrought up to see it now.'

The coroner pulled his lip and studied. 'Oh, I guess not. We'll tend to things and look around.'

Jim sauntered away towards the watering trough. 'Say,' he called, 'kind of clean up a little, will you? You know.'

The men went on into the house.

In a few minutes they emerged, carrying the stiffened body between them. It was wrapped up in a comforter. They eased it up into the wagon-box. Jim walked back towards them. 'Do I have to go in with you now?'

'Where's your wife, Mr. Moore?' the deputy sheriff demanded.

'I don't know,' he said wearily. 'She's somewhere around.'

'You're sure you didn't kill her too?'

'No. I didn't touch her. I'll find her and bring her in this afternoon. That is, if you don't want me to go in with you now.'

'We've got your statement,' the coroner said. 'And by God, we've got eyes, haven't we, Will? Of course there's a technical charge of murder against you, but it'll be dismissed. Always is in this part of the country. Go kind of light on your wife, Mr. Moore.'

'I won't hurt her,' said Jim.

He stood and watched the buckboard jolt away. He kicked his feet reluctantly in the dust. The hot June sun showed its face over the hills and flashed viciously on the bedroom window.

Jim went slowly into the house, and brought out a nine-foot, loaded bull whip. He crossed the yard and walked into the barn. And as he climbed the ladder to the hayloft, he heard the high, puppy whimpering start.

When Jim came out of the barn again, he carried Jelka over his shoulder. By the watering trough he set her tenderly on the ground. Her hair was littered with bits of hay. The back of her shirtwaist was streaked with blood.

Jim wetted his bandana at the pipe and washed her bitten lips, and washed her face and brushed back her hair. Her dusty black eyes followed every move he made.

'You hurt me, she said. 'You hurt me bad.'

He nodded gravely. 'Bad as I could without killing you.'

The sun shone hotly on the ground. A few blowflies buzzed about, looking for the blood.

Jelka's thickened lips tried to smile. 'Did you have any breakfast at all?'

'No,' he said. 'None at all.'

'Well, then I'll fry you up some eggs.' She struggled painfully to her feet.

'Let me help you,' he said. 'I'll help you get your waist off. It's drying stuck to your back. It'll hurt.'

'No. I'll do it myself.' Her voice had a peculiar resonance in it. Her dark eyes dwelt warmly on him for a moment, and then she turned and limped into the house.

Jim waited, sitting on the edge of the watering trough. He saw the smoke start up out of the chimney and sail straight up into the air. In a very few moments Jelka called him from the kitchen door.

'Come, Jim. Your breakfast.'

Four fried eggs and four thick slices of bacon lay on a warmed plate for him. 'The coffee will be ready in a minute,' she said.

'Won't you eat?'

'No. Not now. My mouth's too sore.'

He ate his eggs hungrily and then looked up at her. Her black hair was combed smooth. She had on a fresh white shirtwaist. 'We're going to town this afternoon,' he said. 'I'm going to order lumber. We'll build a new house farther down the canyon.'

Her eyes darted to the closed bedroom door and then back to him. 'Yes' she said. 'That will be good.' And then, after a moment, 'Will you whip me any more – for this?'

'No, not any more, for this.'

Her eyes smiled. She sat down on a chair beside him, and Jim put out his hand and stroked her hair, and the back of her neck.